D0934963

COMPUESTA POR

MIGUÈL DE CERVANTES SAAVEDRA.

Con muy bellas Eſtampas, gravadas ſobre los Dibujos de Coypel, primer Pintor de el Rey de Françia.

EN QUATRO TOMOS.

TOMO PRIMERO.

EN HAIA,

Por P. GOSSE y A. MOETJENS.

M. DCC. XLIV.

MARCEL PROUST

A LA RECHERCHE

DU TEMPS PERDU

TOME I

DU CÔTÉ
DE CHEZ SWANN

DIX-NEUVIÈME ÉDITION

* *

PARIS

ÉDITIONS DE LA

NOUVELLE REVUE FRANÇAISE

35 ET 37, RUE MADAME

The Delighted States

THE DELIGHTED STATES

*A Book of Novels, Romances, & Their Unknown
Translators, Containing Ten Languages, Set on Four
Continents, & Accompanied by Maps, Portraits, Squiggles,
Illustrations, & a Variety of Helpful Indexes*

ADAM THIRLWELL

FARRAR, STRAUS AND GIROUX
NEW YORK

Farrar, Straus and Giroux
18 West 18th Street, New York 10011

Printed in the United States of America
Originally published in 2007 by Jonathan Cape, Great Britain, as *Miss Herbert*
Published in the United States by Farrar, Straus and Giroux
First American edition, 2008

Owing to limitations of space, acknowledgements for permission to reprint
previously published and unpublished material can be found on pages 469–70.

Grateful acknowledgement is made for permission to reprint Paul Klee's
Line, Circumscribing Itself, © DACS 2008.

Library of Congress Cataloging-in-Publication Data
Thirlwell, Adam, 1978–
    The delighted states : a book of novels, romances, & their unknown
translators, containing ten languages, set on four continents, & accompanied
by maps, portraits, squiggles, illustrations, & a variety of helpful indexes /
Adam Thirlwell. — 1st American ed.
        p.   cm.
    Includes bibliographical references and index.
    ISBN-13: 978-0-374-13722-9 (hardcover : alk. paper)
    ISBN-10: 0-374-13722-6 (hardcover : alk. paper)
        1. Fiction—History and criticism.   2. Fiction—Translations—History
and criticism. I. Title.
    PN3491.T55 2007
    809.3—dc22

                                                            2008004533

Designed by Suzanne Dean

www.fsgbooks.com

1   2   3   4   5   6   7   8   9   10

TO ALISON

I still treasure an elegant, elegantly scuffed piece of luggage once owned by my mother. Its travels through space are finished, but it still hums gently through time for I use it to keep old family letters and such curious documents as my birth certificate. I am a couple of years younger than this antique valise, fifty centimeters long by thirty-six broad and sixteen high, technically a heavyish *nécessaire de voyage* of pigskin, with 'H.N.' elaborately interwoven in thick silver under a similar coronet. It had been bought in 1897 for my mother's wedding trip to Florence. In 1917 it transported from St Petersburg to the Crimea and then to London a handful of jewels. Around 1930, it lost to a pawnbroker its expensive receptacles of crystal and silver leaving empty the cunningly contrived leathern holders on the inside of the lid. But that loss has been amply recouped during the thirty years it then traveled with me – from Prague to Paris, from St Nazaire to New York and through the mirrors of more than two hundred motel rooms and rented houses, in forty-six states. The fact that of our Russian heritage the hardiest survivor proved to be a traveling bag is both logical and emblematic.

Vladimir Nabokov, American *Vogue*, 15 April 1972

The Delighted States

Mademoiselle O

INDEX OF MAIN CHARACTERS AND
THEIR MAIN LOCATIONS

Tristram Shandy
Walter Shandy
Uncle Toby
Corporal Trim
Emma Woodhouse
Parson Yorick

Sonia
Leo Tolstoy

IN NEW YORK
Isaac Bashevis Singer
Saul Steinberg

IN PARIS
Sylvia Beach
Mademoiselle de la Chaux
Louise Colet
Denis Diderot
Edouard Dujardin
Gardeil
Ernest Hemingway
James Joyce
Valery Larbaud
Stéphane Mallarmé
Adrienne Monnier
Vladimir Nabokov
Daniel Prince
Mme Reymer
Gertrude Stein
Tanié

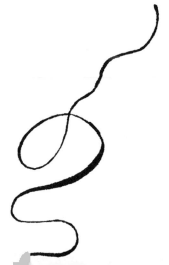

IN THE POLISH PROVINCES
Bruno Schulz
Bruno Schulz's Mother and Father

IN PRAGUE
Bohumil Hrabal
K
Joseph K
Franz Kafka
Jan Mukařovský

IN RIO DE JANEIRO
Machado de Assis
Brás Cubas

IN ROME
Nikolai Gogol
Juvenal

IN ST PETERSBURG
Akaky Akakievich Bashmachkin
Akaky Akakievich Bashmachkin's mother
Vladimir Nabokov

Mademoiselle O
Eugene Onegin
Alexander Pushkin

IN THE SPANISH PROVINCES
Sancho Panza
Alonso Quixano, aka Don Quixote de la Mancha

IN TRIESTE
Signor Aghios
Signora Aghios
James Joyce
Italo Svevo

IN ZURICH
Robert Walser

1 franc 25 centimes à l'étranger

GUSTAVE FLAUBERT

—

MADAME

BOVARY

— MŒURS DE PROVINCE —

—

I

PARIS

MICHEL LÉVY FRÈRES, LIBRAIRES-ÉDITEURS

RUE VIVIENNE, 2 BIS

—

1857

VOLUME I

BOOK I

Mikey

This all begins in private, with Gustave Flaubert's correspondence.

On 24 April 1852, Gustave Flaubert – an unpublished novelist, who had abandoned one novel, and recently begun another – wrote a hopeful letter to his mistress, Louise Colet.

'I've imagined a style for myself,' he told her, 'a beautiful style that someone will write some day, in ten years' time maybe, or in ten centuries. It will be as rhythmical as verse and as precise as science, with the booming rise and fall of a cello and plumes of fire'. And five years later, on 12 December 1857, after his first novel, *Madame Bovary*, had finally been published, Flaubert was writing to a fan, whose name was Mademoiselle Leroyer de Chantepie, and still saying roughly the same thing: 'You say that I pay too much attention to form. Alas! it is like body and soul: form and content to me are one; I don't know what either is without the other.'

Ever since Gustave Flaubert finally published his first novel, some novels have been explicitly as well written as poetry; they have shown the same care as poetry for style, and form. Every word in these novels has the same weight and poise as a word in a poem. And this is not without its problems.

The novel is an international art form. As soon as a novel becomes as well written as poetry, therefore, as soon as style is everything, then the translation of a novel becomes not a peripheral problem, but a central one. Or, as Milan Kundera wrote in the introduction to the fourth, but still only penultimate, English-language translation of his first novel, *The Joke*: 'Once prose

Portrait of Louise Colet by Marie-Alexandre Alophe, dit Menut. Photo © RMN/Gérard Blot.

makes such a claim, the translation of a novel becomes a true art.'

This book – which I sometimes think of as a novel, an inside-out novel, with novelists as characters – is about the art of the novel. It is also, therefore, about the art of translation.

Chapter ii
Warsaw, 1937: Witold Gombrowicz Writes a Review

In 1937, the Polish novelist Witold Gombrowicz wrote a piece for a Warsaw magazine – *Kurier Poranny* – on the French translation of James Joyce's novel, *Ulysses*. Sorrowfully, he did not think that *Ulysses* was really translatable. Meditating wistfully on the happier position of the English-speaking reader, he offered his own paradoxical and contrasting position, that while the 'perfection and power of this complex style' made it obvious how good – even in translation – *Ulysses* was, the dual language gap still prevented 'more intimate contact'. And Gombrowicz ended his piece with an irritable flourish: 'It is annoying to know that somewhere over there, abroad, a previously unknown method of feeling, of thinking and of writing has been born whose existence renders our methods completely anachronistic, and to tell oneself that only purely technical obstacles prevent us from having a deep knowledge of so many new inventions.'

Ulysses had made Polish novelists outdated: Gombrowicz could see that: but in French, his second language, he could not precisely see how. The technical details, he argued, escaped him.

But I am not sure that this is true. If style were purely a matter of technique – if form and content, as Flaubert sometimes thought, were the same thing – then perhaps Gombrowicz might be right. But style is not purely a matter of technique, which is why translation is still possible.

That is the subject of this book.

Often, I wonder if the idea of the untranslatable is really hiding a secret wish for translation to be a perfect fit, and this wish conceals a corresponding wish for style to be absolute. Whereas there are no perfect translations, just as there are no perfect styles. Something is still translatable, even if its translation is not perfect.

Like the example of Witold Gombrowicz himself.

About ten years later, Gombrowicz would be in exile – from the Nazis, and then the Communists – in Buenos Aires. In 1945, his friend Cecilia Benedit de Benedetti gave him an allowance to translate his novel *Ferdydurke* into Spanish. *Ferdydurke*, which had come out in 1937, the same year as his essay on *Ulysses*, had made him famous in Poland. This translation eventually became the preserve of a dedicated group, led by the Cuban novelist Virgilio Piñera and the Cuban writer Humberto Rodríguez Tomeu, as well as Gombrowicz, over eighteen months. The translation took place during sessions in the chess room on the second floor of the Café Rex, Gombrowicz's favourite café in Buenos Aires. According to one of his early collaborators, Adolfo de Obieta, the translation was therefore inherently amusing: it was charmingly amateur – 'transposing from Polish into Spanish the book of a Polish author who barely knew Spanish, assisted by five or six Latino-Americans who scarcely knew two words of Polish'.

No Polish-Spanish dictionary existed at the time. 'It was an experimental translation in macaronic Spanish,' recalled Tomeu. 'At that time, he already knew some Spanish. Later, he spoke it well but always with a very strong accent. We therefore discussed each sentence under every one of its aspects: choice of words, their euphony, their cadence and their rhythm. Witold's observations were always pertinent.' The translation came out in April 1947, accompanied by a defensive note from Piñera, who worried that the unwarned Spanish reader might impute the language's oddness to a lack of competence on the part of the translators. No no, he argued. It was all a matter of Gombrowicz's new and different

manner of envisaging language in the original Polish. (Which Piñera, of course, could not read.)

But he did not convince the public: *Ferdydurke* was not a success. It bemused its new Latin-American public.

The history of the novel is, simultaneously, a history of an elaborate and intricate international art form – and also a history of errors, a history of waste.

Chapter iii
Paris, 1930: James Joyce in Paul Léon's Living Room

While Witold Gombrowicz, in Warsaw, was fretting at the French translation of *Ulysses*, James Joyce was making things even harder. In Paris, Joyce was completing the novel which was being serialised in the small magazine *transition* as *Work in Progress*, but which would finally be called *Finnegans Wake*. Famously, this novel is hardly even written in English: itself a description of a dream, Joyce wanted the English of his novel to mimic, in its language, the operations of a dream. Just as the images in dreams are dense with overdetermination, so the language in *Finnegans Wake*, therefore, Joyce hoped, was unstable, impacted, polyglot. So that the reader of its first instalment would have been unpleasantly surprised to discover a style that made puns with more than one language, and had a sentence like this: 'What clashes here of wills gen wonts, oystrygods gaggin fishygods!'

Maybe, with *Finnegans Wake*, Joyce had reached a point of stylistic density which could not survive any transition to another language – a realm of pure poetry, a nonsense style. Perhaps Gombrowicz was right. Maybe translation was finally impossible.

But maybe not.

In 1930, Joyce agreed to supervise a translation into French of the *Anna Livia Plurabelle* section of *Work in Progress*: the translation had been begun by Samuel Beckett and his French friend Alfred Péron. Beckett, however, had gone back to Ireland after completing a first version of the opening pages. His work was then revised by a group of Joyce's friends: Eugene Jolas, the editor of *transition*; Ivan Goll, a poet; and Paul Léon.

Léon (whose wife, Lucie, was a family friend of Vladimir Nabokov) was a Russian émigré, who had left Russia in 1918: he had first gone to London, and then, in 1921, had arrived in Paris. He was a lawyer by training, and literary in his tastes. He soon became a kind of secretary to Joyce.

At the end of November 1930, after the first draft of the French translation had been completed, the French Surrealist writer Philippe Soupault was instructed to meet Joyce and Léon in Léon's flat. At Léon's round table, they would sit for three hours, starting at 2.30 every Thursday, and go through the translation.

(And I hope that the Léons kept this table for a while, because then it would be the same table at which, eight years later, in 1938, Nabokov would sit with Lucie – as she helped him with the English of his first novel written directly in English, *The Real Life of Sebastian Knight*.)

Joyce smoked in an armchair; Léon read the English text and Soupault read the French, at the same time, breaking off to consider any problems. After fifteen of these meetings, they reached a final draft. This was sent to Jolas and Adrienne Monnier – Joyce's friend, who had published the French translation of *Ulysses* – who suggested further changes. The finished translation of *Anna Livia Plurabelle* was published in the *Nouvelle Revue Française* on 1 May 1931.

There is no need to understand French to hear how talented this translation was. A lack of French is fine. Joyce shocked everyone with his care for sound over sense. In its new language, he was more concerned to preserve the form than the content.

Anna Livia Plurabelle falls asleep

Can't hear with the waters of. The chittering waters of. Flittering bats, fieldmice bawk talk. Ho! Are you not gone ahome? What Thom Malone? Can't hear with bawk of bats, all thim liffeying waters of. Ho, talk save us! My foos won't moos. I feel as old as yonder elm. A tale told of Shaun or Shem? All Livia's daughtersons. Dark hawks hear us. Night! Night! My ho head halls. I feel as heavy as yonder stone. Tell me of John or Shaun? Who were Shem and Shaun the living sons or daughters of? Night now! Tell me, tell me, tell me, elm! Night night! Tellmetale of stem or stone. Beside the rivering waters of, hitherandthithering waters of. Night!

Anna Livia Plurabelle falls asleep, this time in French

N'entend pas cause les ondes de. Le bébé babil des ondes de. Souris chance, trotinette cause pause. Hein! Tu n'est past rentré? Quel père André? N'entend pas cause les fuisouris, les liffeyantes ondes de, Eh! Bruit nous aide! Mon pied à pied se lie lierré. Je me sens vieille comme mon orme même. Un conte conté de Shaun ou Shem? De Livie tous les fillefils. Sombre faucons écoutent l'ombre. Nuit. Nuit. Ma taute tête tombe. Je me sens lourde comme ma pierrestone. Conte moi de John ou Shaun. Qui furent Shem et Shaun en vie les fils ou filles de. Là-dessus nuit. Dis-mor, dis-mor, dis-mor, orme. Nuit, Nuit! Contemoiconte soit tronc ou pierre. Tant riviérantes ondes de, courtecourantes ondes de. Nuit.

Occasionally, the sense, and its connotations, has to alter. But this is so that the rhythm of the words, the sentences' musicality, can still remain. The style, even of this work in progress, is still there.

Yes, the history of the novel is a history of an elaborate but international art form.

Chapter iv
Paris, 1929: Samuel Beckett Writes an Essay

And it is also a history of waste.

The first mistake in this book was Witold Gombrowicz's. The next, related mistake was made by Samuel Beckett.

As he was writing *Work in Progress*, Joyce decided that a campaign might be necessary in order for his impossible novel to receive the criticism and reception it deserved. Or any reception at all. A group of his friends and fans in Paris therefore wrote a small, if dense, book of essays – *Our Exagmination Round His Factification for Incamination of Work in Progress* – which was published in 1929, ten years before *Finnegans Wake* finally came out.

In his contribution to this book, Samuel Beckett – who was fluent in both French and English – wanted to show how *Work in Progress* was, contrary to popular opinion, not difficult to read at all. Beckett's idea was that the bourgeois, unintelligent reader was probably baffled by the novel's reinvention of the twin relations between language and reality, and between content and form. Normally, according to Beckett, in conventional novels, the form and the content were different things – but in Joyce's *Finnegans Wake*, he argued, his prose tetchy with italics, 'form *is* content, content *is* form'. And so he came up with this catchy conclusion: 'His writing is not *about* something; *it is that something itself.*'

But Beckett's conclusion is not just catchy: it is also impossible.

A sign is not the same as the thing it represents. Because this is the case, it is possible to create more and more precise signs – since the gap between the sign and real life is infinite. And this is why there are values in literature – marking the moments when novelists working in the art of the novel invent more precise styles. Often, it is true, the more precise a style, the more form and content are inter-related. But this intertwining of form and content does not entail that a style is so precise in its relation to real life as to be the thing it is describing. All novels, after all, are smaller than real life. They are all miniaturisations. They are never real life itself. Real life is always elsewhere.

And this is why translation is always still possible. The style of a novel, and a novelist, is a set of instructions, a project: it is never able to create an entirely unique, irreplaceable object.

The novel – this art of the precise, the authorial, the deliberate – is also an art of repetition, of reproduction.

That is why I prefer the hopefulness of less programmatic, more carefree experimentalists than Samuel Beckett.

In 1930, the Czech writer Adolf Hoffmeister came to see Joyce in Paris. He wanted permission to translate *Anna Livia Plurabelle* into Czech. And just as Joyce had preferred a translation of sound over sense in French, he advised Hoffmeister to do the same thing in another new language: 'poeticise it with the greatest poetic freedom that you can give it.' The crucial thing was to re-create the dazzling effect: 'Create a language for your country according to my image. Viktor Llona in *transition* posited the thesis: language can be made by a writer. In this case, also by the translator.'

A translator, like a novelist, needs to have not just a talent for languages. A translator also needs talent.

All styles are systems of operations on a language for the contrivance of effects: they are like machines. And these stylish machines are therefore also portable. Machines, after all – like cars, or typewriters – can be imported anywhere.

Chapter v
St Petersburg & Rome, 1842: Akaky Akakievich Bashmachkin

The hero of Nikolai Gogol's story (or novella, or short novel) called
Coat – which Gogol wrote in Russian, while living in Rome – is
called Akaky Akakievich Bashmachkin.

This name – this *name!* – requires translation. This name must
always be sadly remembered, whenever a reader becomes hopeful
that translation is happily possible.

In Gogol's *Coat*, Akaky Akakievich Bashmachkin's mother is
presented with various suites of names for her newborn baby, all
of which she rejects. These names form a crescendo, an
accelerando. At first, the three names are Mokky, Sossy and Khoz-
dazat. Then she is offered Triphily, Dula and Varakhassy. But she
rejects these as well. When she is finally offered Pavsikakhy and
Vakhtisy she, understandably, snaps, and decides to simplify. So she
gives the baby his father's name – Akaky, thus becoming Akaky
Akakievich – Akaky, son of Akaky.

If these lists are compared with the lists in Gogol's drafts for this
story, then the precision of Gogol's comic sound-effects can be
heard more clearly, in surround sound. The first trio (Yevvul, Mokky
and Tevlogy) and the second trio (Varakhasy, Dula and Trephily)
were not so different. But the final duo, in the draft, was Pavsikakhy
and Frumenty. And Frumenty is much less funny than Vakhtisy –
it does not have the musical repetition, the ugly clash of conso-
nants, which Gogol invented in his final draft of Pavsikakhy and
Vakhtisy: it is much too normal, and various.

Gogol put a lot of care into his hero's names. And Akaky's name,
the most ordinary thing in this story, is untranslatable, because it
is the root of so many jokes in the Russian, which are not jokes in
any other language.

The story of *Coat* is all about the most ordinary of characters, an office-worker, a copyist. He is unoriginal, Akaky. And in the same way, *Coat* is a story whose music is based on small words; these small words are normally unnoticed, like Akaky himself; but Gogol noticed them.

There is, for instance, the Russian word как. There are many possible translations of как. Its simplest is 'how', although it is occasionally 'what'. It is one of the tiniest words – the most over-used, the least individual. Its close relative in the world of words is так, which means 'so', or 'in this way'. And it is these words' shared '*ak*' sound which is there to be heard in Akaky Akakievich's stammering first name. He is a particle. He is the lowest linguistic unit there is.

More oddly, it is the word which is there to be heard as well in Akaky's troubled speech.

Akaky talking to himself in Russian (but not in Cyrillic)

Vishel na ulitsu, Akaky Akakievich bil **kak** vo sne.

  – Etakovo-to delo etako**e** [. . .] – **tak** vot **kak**! Nakonets vot chto vishlo, a ya, pravo, sovsem i predpologat ne mog, chtobi ono bilo et**ak**. – [. . .] – **Tak** et**ak**-to! Vot **kak**oe uzh, tochno, ni**kak** neozhidannoe, tovo . . . etovo bi ni**kak** . . . et**ak**oe-to obstoyatelstvo!

In any other language, his name and his speech will be nothing to do with each other. Whereas Gogol made them the same thing. It was therefore not a normal world, and yet this world seemed normal: that was the linguistic world which Gogol created.

The majestic and orthodox nineteenth-century English trans-lator, Constance Garnett, translated these sentences like this – quite reasonably translating the content, and not the form:

Akaky talking to himself in English (I)

When he got into the street, Akaky Akakievich felt as though he was in a dream. 'So that is how it is,' he said to himself. 'I really did not think it would be this way . . .' and then after a pause he added, 'So that's it! So that's how it is at last! and I really could never have supposed it would be this way. And there . . .' There followed another long silence, after which he said: 'So that's it! well, it really is so utterly unexpected . . . who would have thought . . . what a circumstance . . .'

It is reasonable, but I am not so sure that it is a truly accurate translation. It does not quite do in English what Gogol wanted to do in Russian. Another way of translating this story would be to translate it imprecisely – by translating the form, and not the content, and inventing a new name for Akaky. In this story about Akaky, it may turn out to be braver and better to just give him a new and ordinary name, like Mikey. So that then the sentences might sound like this:

Akaky talking to himself in English (II)

On the street, Mikey felt like he was dreaming.

– Crikey, so that's how it is, – he was saying to himself, – I really didn't think that it'd turn out like . . . – and then, after a small silence, added: I mean like. There it is. So it turned out like that in the end, but I really and truly couldn't have imagined that it would have happened like that. – Then yet another long silence followed, after which he carried on: – But like that! You could strike me down with . . . I mean like . . . what a thing to happen!

The intertwining of form and content is relational: it does not create an irreducibly unique linguistic object. And so in Gogol's story *Coat*, it's not so much important that the main character's name is Akaky: it's more important that his name sounds like a minor part of speech.

Mikey, therefore, will also do.

Gogol's story gave a poetic structure to the dowdiest things. It organised them into a comic beauty. And this is one of the things that novels are good at (especially novels with wishful thinkers at their centre) – what Nabokov called 'the dazzling combinations of drab parts'. Gogol came up with a style which was entirely original, one based on the contamination of reality by the words used to describe it. And it is precisely this uniqueness which makes the translations of his work (and the translations of all other dazzling combiners of drab parts) so complicated, and intricate, and exhausting for the translator. It means that the idea of a literal translation may have to be slightly revised.

Even Akaky's surname is a problem. His last name was originally Tishkevich, not Bashmachkin – it was an ordinary name, not an extraordinary one. Only later did Gogol further reduce his hero into singularity, giving him first the name Bashmakevich, and finally Bashmachkin – Mr Bootlet, Mr Cloggle.

In Russian, this name Bashmachkin is comic, a perpetual giggle. Whereas in Uzbek, or Italian, if left as it is, it is only Russian. It is only a frown.

Chapter vi
Croisset, 1852: A Short Essay on Style (I)

In 1852, while writing *Madame Bovary*, Flaubert made a wish: 'May I die like a dog rather than try to rush through even one sentence before it is perfectly ripe.' This wish is a motif in Flaubert's correspondence. His sign for style was always the sentence. So that in 1857, after the furore of *Madame Bovary*, he told Mademoiselle Leroyer de Chantepie that he was 'almost back in my old routine, so uneventful and so peaceful, where sentences are my adventures'. And twenty years later, the motif is still a motif: 'I can't stop myself, even swimming, I test my sentences, despite myself.'

Ever since Gustave Flaubert, some people have thought that a style was the same thing as the way of constructing a sentence; that a style was equivalent to its individual sentences.

But I am not sure how absolutely Flaubert's statements about sentences should be taken. They are more of a shorthand. His sentences should not be taken less teasingly than they are written. As well as working on his sentences, after all, Flaubert also worked on their construction, on the transitions between the sentences; on the silences. 'I'd like to be working on books,' Flaubert told Louise Colet, 'in which the *writing* of sentences (if I may put it that way) was all I had to do, just as you only need to breathe the air in order to stay alive. What vexes me are the clever tricks of composition, the arranging of effects, all the backstage calculations which are nevertheless Art, because the stylistic effect depends upon them, exclusively.'

Flaubert's different definition of style means both the style of sentences, and the style of these sentences' arrangement.

But I am not sure it can even stop there. A style may be as large as the length of a book. Its units may well be more massive, and more vague, than I would often like.

A style, in the end, is a list of the methods by which a novelist achieves various effects. As such, it can seem endless.

In fact, it can become something which is finally not linguistic at all. For the way in which a novelist represents a life depends on what a novelist thinks is there in a life to be represented. A style is therefore as much a quirk of emotion, or of theological belief, as it is a quirk of language.

A style does not entirely coincide with prose style, or formal construction, or technique.

According to Marcel Proust, style 'has nothing to do with embellishment, as some people think, it's not even a matter of technique, it's – like colour for a painter – a quality of vision, the revelation of the particular universe that each of us sees, and that other people don't see.' And this is abstract, obviously, but I think that this abstract definition is the best anyone can do. Like Flaubert's metaphorical, experimental definition: 'Just as the pearl is the oyster's affliction, so style is perhaps the discharge from a deeper wound.'

Real life does not exist – not abstractly. It only exists when it has been given a particular form, when it has been defined by the technical quirks and physiological constraints of a style.

Chapter vii
Paris, 1931: A Short Essay on Style (II)

The end of James Joyce's *Anna Livia Plurabelle* seems like a game with sound, an exercise in pure phonetics, in the sounds of sentences, but this is not quite true. It is also one of Joyce's most delicate representations of sleepiness.

The only relative of this finale occurs in the finale to the penultimate section of *Ulysses* – when the novel's hero, Leopold Bloom, is falling asleep. And because he is falling asleep, the language is suddenly repetitive, mistaken, rich with musicality:

Leopold Bloom falls asleep

Womb? Weary?
He rests. He has travelled.

With?
Sinbad the Sailor and Tinbad the Tailor and Jinbad the Jailer and Whinbad the Whaler and Ninbad the Nailer and Finbad the Failer and Binbad the Bailer and Pinbad the Pailer and Minbad the Mailer and Hinbad the Hailer and Rinbad the Railer and Dinbad the Kailer and Vinbad the Quailer and Linbad the Yailer and Xinbad the Phthailer.

When?

Going to a dark bed there was a square round Sinbad the Sailor roc's auk's egg in the night of the bed of all the auks of the rocs of Darkinbad the Brightdayler.

Joyce is a realist. His style is a calm comprehensiveness, a patient determination to be accurate. One consequence of this is Joyce's realisation that, to be calmly comprehensive, to be true to his style, it is possible to have more than one prose style. Because style is not just linguistic. It is more amorphous than that. It exists prior to language: it is biological as much as formal – in a person's teeth, the arteries, the kidneys, in the left and right ventricles.

Joyce could no more relinquish his style by altering his prose style than he could make himself taller.

In the same way, in another medium, when Ernst Ansermet, Stravinsky's conductor, asked Picasso why he varied his style and medium so much, Picasso replied: 'But can't you see? The results are the same.' And he was right.

For instance. Using a drying-up cloth as a canvas, Picasso's *The Painter and His Model*, painted in August 1914, shows a seated painter gazing happily at the exposed vulva of his naked model, who has conveniently lowered a towel below her genitals. Behind them, there is an easel, with a landscape painting propped on it. A table with a fruit bowl is on the right.

The painter, part of the easel, and the table are all simply drawn in crayon. The model, however, and the painting behind her, are painted delicately in oils.

It is a kind of collage – a painting of a collage.

On the back of the man's hand, there is a thickly crayoned patch of hair. Because the man is crayoned in black and white, with very little modelling, the patch is coarsely described. It is quickly read as hair. But the girl's pubic hair is different. Black paint has been dabbed on lightly, sparsely, so that the pink flesh tone blurs through.

It has been dabbed on so that it is darker than shadow, but still light enough to match the sparseness of pubic hair as it fades towards the stomach.

The painting included two different ways of representing hair. The results, however, were the same – they were both precise descriptions of real life. And they are both in Picasso's style. In both cases, Picasso discovered visual equivalents. He discovered accurate signs.

There is no need for a style to have a single style.

Anna Livia Plurabelle's finale, and Leopold Bloom's finale, are precise and different ways of representing the state called sleep. Since no one falls asleep in the same way, there is no need for sentences to sound the same, to be consistent, either. Anything is possible, since real life is infinite. Anna falls asleep thinking of her family. But Leopold has other things on his mind.

The last sentence, we find out from Leopold's wife, Molly, represents Leopold's last words in *Ulysses*: 'Going to a dark bed there was a square round Sinbad the Sailor roc's auk's egg in the night of the bed of all the auks of the rocs of Darkinbad the Brightdayler.' In this last sentence, he requests breakfast in bed, with eggs.

Chapter viii
Prague, 1920–61: A Quick Life of Jan Mukařovský

In the 1920s and 1930s, while James Joyce, in Paris, was finishing *Ulysses*, and then beginning *Finnegans Wake*, Jan Mukařovský was a literary critic in Prague. And Mukařovský was a very intelligent literary critic: he thought more precisely than most other people about the forms which literature takes.

Mukařovský was not happy with the idea that all artistic opinion is subjective. Instead, he argued, it was quite possible to tell if a work was good or bad – there was no problem in determining if a literary work had a value or not. A work 'appears as a positive value if it in some respect regrouped the structure of the preceding stage; it will appear as a negative value if it took over the structure without changes'.

Mukařovský made things simple, and incontrovertible.

A style is not national, that much is easy. It is also something which is not identical to prose style: that much is easy, too. But a style is only a start. Some styles are more interesting than other styles: it is only the styles which renew the history of the art which have a value – only the originals, who regroup an art's structure.

As a result of this simplicity, Mukařovský was also clever about what literary history looked like: it was always different from the front or from the back. 'A living work of art always oscillates between the past and future status of an aesthetic norm.' If every new work regroups the preceding ones, then it initially seems original – but it then seems too fixed, when a new new work comes along. The paradox of the aesthetic, then, is that it is a process which constantly claims not to be a process at all: 'every struggle for a new aesthetic value in art, just as every counter-attack against it, is organised in the name of an objective and lasting value.'

Mukařovský made things objective, and complicated.

And then Mukařovský gave up on objectivity. Soon after the February 1948 Communist takeover of Czechoslovakia, he recanted all his previous literary opinions. Only Marxism was a true science. His previous work on aesthetic value, he declared, was just 'a furtively masked and hence the most dangerous idealism.' He gave up writing on aesthetics, became the Rector of Prague University – and was a central figure in the university's purging to align it with Communist doctrine. In 1961 he published a collection of essays, arguing that the only criterion of literary value was *lidovost* – popularity. So that 'the most popular authors are the greatest authors,' and 'a work that is alien to the people ceases to be a work of art.'

Whereas the aesthetic is elsewhere: it has nothing to do with popularity, and victories.

I find this story moving because it is so tense with contradictions. Mukařovský begins his career by asserting the objective and timeless nature of literary value. But he then complicates this by pointing out how each new literary value believes that it is the only literary value. The process of literary history is a continual redefinition of what constitutes literary value at all. And yet he then decides that this subtle, true literary theory is only bourgeois, and irrelevant – that the only literary criterion is popularity. Only the masses matter. He becomes a socialist realist.

And it is possible to make this story even more poignant, since just as Mukařovský was deciding that the only history of literature was a socialist literature, the novelist Bohumil Hrabal, at the same time, was proving him wrong, and developing the art of the novel in Czech, via Adolf Hoffmeister's translation into Czech of James Joyce. And Hrabal himself would eventually be forced into silence, by the Communist regime.

It is moving because it is so sad, and so common – this depressing contrast between novels and politics. But, unlike Mukařovský, the novelists in this book refuse to accept the superior value of politics. They will not believe in the value of its history, above the value of their art. The art is always more important.

In reply to a query on 17 September 1932 from a woman known only as H. Romanova – working for the International Union of Revolutionary Writers in Moscow – asking what impact the October Revolution had made on James Joyce as a writer, and what it meant to him as a man of letters, Joyce, masquerading as his secretary Paul Léon, wrote this letter:

A letter from James Joyce to H. Romanova

Dear Sirs, Mr Joyce wishes me to thank you for your favor of the 17th instant from which he has learned with interest that there has been a revolution in Russia, in October 1917. On closer investigation, however, he finds that the

October Revolution happened in November of that year. From the knowledge he has collected up to now it is difficult for him to judge of the importance of this event and he wishes only to say that judging from the signature of your secretary the changes cannot amount to much. Yours sincerely, Paul Léon.

That, I think, is the right kind of attitude.

'There can be no question,' Vladimir Nabokov told an interviewer, 'that what makes a work of fiction safe from larvae and rust is not its social importance but its art, only its art.'

And this is one thing I would like to believe as well. Although it is a history of ephemeral inventions, the novel's history is also a history of objects whose value is durable, and timeless. Sometimes I believe this. Sometimes I want to nod in agreement with the grand French critic Paul Valéry, who pointed out how 'today we say Stendhal and Napoleon. But who would have dared to say to Napoleon that one day people would say: Stendhal and Napoleon?'

That is my personal form of romanticism. That is the romance of this book.

Chapter ix

Moscow & Nice, 1889–98: This Is Not a Novel

In 1889, Anton Chekhov, a writer of short stories and plays, suddenly came up with an original idea: 'I am writing a novel, I have already outlined ten characters. What an intrigue! I call it "Stories from the lives of my friends", and I write it in the form of separate complete stories, closely connected by the general intrigue of the novel, by its idea and by the same characters. Each story has a separate title ... I can hardly manage the technique.' For the next decade, as he moved from Moscow to Nice and back to Russia again, Chekhov kept on referring to this possible novel, always worrying that he had not found the right form.

Eventually, nothing came of it. But three stories from Chekhov's drafts were published: 'A Man in a Case', 'Gooseberries' and 'On Love' – these were the 'fragments of the intended novel'.

And this was a lost chance in the history of the novel. Because it did not just describe one life. As written, this novel described three lives, and the various lives surrounding them. Chekhov had chanced on a new form, which he did not develop into a finished object. All three stories contain the same theme – that all our desires are ironised; all our wishes, even when they come true, do not come true.

The story called 'A Man in a Case' began with two friends – Ivan Ivanovich and Burkin – who were staying the night in a barn after a day's shooting. Burkin was a schoolteacher and, to while away the time, he told the story of Belikov, the classics teacher at his school. Belikov was the title's man in a case – repressed, fearful, introverted. He lived alone, with his male cook – sleeping in a four-poster bed with the blanket over his head. There was a plan that he should marry Barbara, the sister of a new teacher. And this plan was progressing, Belikov was enticed, until the moment when he saw Barbara riding a bicycle. He could not cope with the indecency. He went to her brother, the new teacher, to remonstrate with him; but the brother simply kicked him downstairs, where he landed, unfortunately, at the feet of the sister, who had just returned home. Mortified by Barbara's mocking laughter, Belikov went home and died a while later.

'Gooseberries' was told by Ivan Ivanovich, after he and Burkin had reached the house of their friend Alyokhin. Having bathed, and admired the beauty of Alyokhin's maid Pelageya, Ivan Ivanovich told the story of his brother, a civil servant. All his brother ever wanted was a country estate on which to grow gooseberries. His brother married a rich widow, who died three years later. With the money, he bought his estate and planted gooseberry bushes. When Ivan Ivanovich had tried them – praised by his brother as delicious – he had found that they were sour and unripe.

Alyokhin told the final story: 'About Love'. He began by mentioning the fact that the beautiful maid Pelageya was in fact in love with the fat cook, Nikanor. He could not understand it: and so he came up with this maxim: 'What seems to explain one instance doesn't fit a dozen others. It's best to interpret each instance separately, in my view, without trying to generalise. We must isolate each individual case, as doctors say.' And he also told his own story. He had fallen in love with a pure and wonderful woman called Anna, the wife of a friend, but had never dared tell her that he loved her, even when alone with her in the railway carriage as they said goodbye to each other forever.

The three friends then fell silent. Burkin and Ivan Ivanovich went outside to admire Alyokhin's view. 'And they imagined how stricken that young woman must have looked when he had said good-bye to her in the train, kissing her head and shoulders. Both of them had met her in town. Burkin, indeed, had been a friend of hers and had thought her very good-looking.'

Every life is the same – but the stories are not a series. There is no unified plot. They are three separate variations.

But Chekhov never finished it, this new experiment, this new invention in the history of the novel.

Chapter x
London, 2007: An Aurora Borealis

A different way of describing the timeless yet ephemeral nature of novels is this sentence from one of Vladimir Nabokov's interviews. 'One of the functions of all my novels', said Nabokov, 'is to prove that the novel in general does not exist.' It is the same argument, in a different form, as the argument of the young Jan Mukařovský. All original novels are one of a series and – simultaneously – entirely new objects.

Like this idea for a novel, which Nabokov described in a 1937 lecture on the Russian novelist and poet Alexander Pushkin – a lecture delivered in Paris, to an audience which included James Joyce and the Hungarian football team: 'What an exciting experience it would be to follow the adventures of an idea through the ages. With no wordplay intended, I daresay that this would be the ideal novel: we would really see the abstract image, perfectly limpid and unencumbered by humanity's dust, enjoying an intense existence that develops, swells, displays its thousand folds, with the diaphanous liquidity of an aurora borealis.'

This book, with its dictionaries, its tourism, is about the invented and international art form of the novel. It is an atlas.

And its heroine, its theme, is Miss Juliet Herbert.

In 1856, an Englishwoman called Juliet Herbert was living with Gustave Flaubert (and Gustave Flaubert's mother) as the governess of his niece, Caroline. Her previous address had been Chelsea, just off the King's Road.

In a letter to his best friend Louis Bouilhet, Flaubert praised the curves of Juliet's breasts: 'at table my eyes willingly follow the gentle slope of her breast. I believe she perceives this. For she blushes five or six times during the meal.' In another letter, again to Bouilhet, he praised the curves of her bottom: 'I hold myself back on the stairs so as not to grab her behind.'

She was born on 27 April 1829. She arrived in Croisset, as Caroline's governess, in 1854, when she was twenty-five.

Caroline, however, was not Juliet's only pupil. Miss Herbert also gave Flaubert English lessons: and he believed that these lessons were going very well, since he was on to *Macbeth*, he wrote, and therefore would 'soon understand all Shakespeare'. And on 30 April 1856, Flaubert finished writing his novel, *Madame Bovary* – which reinvented the idea of style.

As part of his instruction in the art of the English language, Gustave and Juliet made translations to and from English. One was of Byron's poem 'The Prisoner of Chillon', the manuscript of which, dated 1857, survives. But Byron and his romanticism are not so interesting, not in themselves: they are interesting only as a romantic motif. The other thing they translated, from French into English, working from the fair copy of the manuscript, was *Madame Bovary*.

Miss Herbert was an inverse, unromantic, English Madame Bovary.

In May 1857, Flaubert wrote to his publisher, Michel Lévy, stating that an 'English translation which fully satisfies me is being made under my eyes. If one is going to appear in England, I want it to be this one and not any other one.' But nothing happened. Five years later, in 1862, Flaubert wrote to his friend Ernest Duplan, commenting on the phrase 'translation rights reserved'. According to Flaubert, this phrase was 'a bitter joke': 'I had one of Bovary (in English) made under my eyes which was a masterpiece. I had asked Lévy to arrange to have it published with a London publisher. Nothing doing!'

A few months after Flaubert had finished *Madame Bovary*, Juliet Herbert returned to England. Packed into her suitcase was this first translation of *Madame Bovary*; and this translation disappeared.

That is why Miss Herbert is the theme of *The Delighted States*: her story is a story about style and translation.

In homage to Miss Herbert, therefore, *The Delighted States* speaks ten languages. As for me, I only speak three – with my fluent English, quixotic French, and hobbyhorsical Russian. Since style is international, after all, it is possible to read or translate a novel in an unknown language. There is no need to be worried.

This book is my version of Nabokov's ideal novel – which is not really a novel. It has recurring characters; with a theme, and variations; and this theme has its recurring motifs. It just has no plot, no fiction, and no finale. It is a description of a milky way, an aurora borealis.

Chapter xi
Prague, 1992: The Golden Tiger Pub

Like the story of Jan Mukařovský, many of the stories in this book – about the Polish Jewish American novelist Isaac Bashevis Singer, or the Russian American French Swiss novelist Vladimir Nabokov, or the Polish novelist Witold Gombrowicz in Buenos Aires (or the one about Nikolai Gogol in Rome, or Denis Diderot in St Petersburg) – could be read as sad stories. They are often fractured by politics, by invasions and revolutions, by Nazis and by Communists. But according to the logic of *The Delighted States*, no story is really sad. These miniature biographies, with their politics, and exile, and mistakes, are not as important as the biographies of the novelists' styles. And style is timeless, and placeless. 'The very term "émigré author"', wrote Vladimir Nabokov, who had already been an émigré for over twenty years, 'sounds somewhat tautological. Any genuine writer emigrates into his art and abides there.'

For instance, this is one of my favourite stories, about Bohumil Hrabal, in the Golden Tiger pub in Prague.

Bohumil Hrabal was a Czech novelist in the twentieth century. One of his last books was a collection of autobiographical letters to an American girl called April Gifford, christened Dubenka by the drinkers in the Golden Tiger pub, since April, in Czech, is *duben*, the oak month. And April herself came up with her own reciprocal pun in translation, when the drinkers in the Golden Tiger pub asked her where she was from – 'Ze "Spokojeneých" státù . . . From the "Delighted" States . . .' Because normally the United of the United States, in Czech, would be *spojené* – without the extra spike of *spokojeny* – the Czech word for happy.

In one of his letters, Hrabal told her the story of why he did not sign an anti-Communist declaration in 1989. Although Václav Havel was paying personal visits to Hrabal, coming to find him in the Golden Tiger pub, Hrabal's regular hang-out, Hrabal still would

Bohumil Hrabal in the Golden Tiger pub, courtesy of Tomas Mazal and the Twisted Spoon Press

not sign the petition 'A Few Sentences'. And although he was called a collaborator, says Hrabal, he still told Havel that he would not sign. He cared more about looking after his novel, *Too Loud a Solitude*, which was about to be published, than about the freedom of the Czech people.

The reason why Bohumil Hrabal does not sign a petition in Prague

Because I wouldn't swap that signature on 'A Few Sentences' for eighty thousand copies of my *Too Loud a Solitude*, due in November, I won't swap 'A Few Sentences' for the eighty thousand afterwords by Milan Jankovič . . . I mean, Dubenka, the only purpose of my being in this world has been to write this *Too Loud a Solitude*, that *Solitude* which Susan Sontag in New York said was one of the books, the twenty books that would form the image of the writing of this century . . . So I didn't sign . . .

In its wilful comic egotism, with its calm at the idea of collaboration, its display of Hrabal's delighted commitment to his novel, *Too Loud a Solitude*, not to other people's politics, this story proves Nabokov's point.

Hrabal was not an emigré, but he was a kind of émigré. He was elsewhere, even in Prague, in the Golden Tiger pub. He was happy, in the delighted states.

BOOK 2

Jeanne de Lamare

One March, in the nineteenth century, some time after 1835, but a while before 1857, a new doctor arrived at the village of Yonville-l'Abbaye, in Normandy. His name was Dr Charles Bovary, and he was accompanied by his second wife. There to meet the new couple, at the village inn, were Madame Lefrançois, the mistress of the inn; Monsieur Homais, the pharmacist; the village curé; and Monsieur Léon Dupuis, a young clerk. In the parlour of the inn, they all talked of this and that – the inconvenience of carriage-journeys, love of travel, the climate in the area, the possibility of walks. And then a conversation developed between the young man, Léon, and the young woman, Madame Bovary.

At first they shared their mutual adoration of the sea:

A conversation about the sea

– Oh, I adore the sea, said Monsieur Léon.

– And do you not feel, replied Madame Bovary, that the mind drifts unfettered upon that immensity, whose contemplation raises up the soul and feeds a feeling of infinity, of the fabulous?

They moved on to a shared appreciation of mountain scenery, and music. And then they discovered their mutual passion: reading. Madame Bovary's favourite reading matter at the moment was not prose but poetry: 'I detest common heroes and temperate feelings, the way they are in life.' And Léon agreed that the true end of Art was not accuracy but romance: 'So lovely, amid life's disappoint-ments, to be able to dwell in fancy on nobility of character, pure affections and pictures of happiness.'

And they continued to talk of other things, while, intimately, Léon rested his foot on one of the bars of the chair in which Madame Bovary was sitting. For they were falling in love, these romantics, by the fire. They shared a provincial dislike for all that was provincial, ordinary, domestic: they both believed that a dull life was not a life, that the only true thing was poetry, and feeling.

Real life, they believed, was elsewhere.

And although this is only the beginning of Madame Bovary's life in Yonville-l'Abbaye, it is also the beginning of the end. For Léon will become her lover, because of her romanticism, because of her poetic idea that life is poetry, and should be full of passion. And this romanticism will also make her have another lover, and lovers cost money – and so her romanticism will cause her to get into debt and this debt will make her so anguished and melancholy that eventually she will commit suicide by arsenic poisoning.

But that is in the future. At the moment, there is just the romance for Madame Bovary. At the moment, this romance is happy.

Chapter ii
Angers, 1857: A Letter from Mademoiselle Leroyer de Chantepie

Some years later, in another province of France, in Angers, Made-moiselle Leroyer de Chantepie, an heiress in her mid-fifties, picked up her pen and began to write to Gustave Flaubert, the author of *Madame Bovary*. She wanted to tell him how accurate his portrait of Madame Bovary had been, that his description of Madame Bovary's life was 'exactly how it is in the provinces where I was born and have spent my life'. 'From the beginning,' wrote Made-moiselle Leroyer de Chantepie, about her new love, Madame Bovary,

Mademoiselle Leroyer de Chantepie by Ellebé, Rouen, courtesy of Musée Flaubert, Croisset

'I recognised her and I loved her as though she were a friend. I so identified with her experiences that it was just as though she was me.'

This was a fan letter, but also an unhappy one – perturbed by the pain of recognition: 'Where have you acquired your perfect knowledge of human nature, it's a scalpel applied to the heart, to the soul, it is alas the world in all its hideousness?'

Mademoiselle Leroyer de Chantepie's scalpel is the point of this small chapter. Because the scalpel will turn up again, in Flaubert's *Dictionary of Received Ideas* – a dictionary of clichés which he collected throughout his life – where the entry for 'Novel' includes this detail: 'Some novels are written with the tip of a scalpel (*Madame Bovary*, for example).'

This letter presented Gustave Flaubert, the novelist (whose novel had not been uniformly well received, had gone down so badly, in fact, that he had been in court on charges of obscenity), with a conundrum: what was he to do with his fan, Mademoiselle Leroyer de Chantepie? Perhaps she was unhappy, perhaps she was depressed, but depression and unhappiness are unfortunately no guarantee of accuracy; they are not guards against getting things wrong.

Like the heroine of his book, Flaubert's welcome fan was a romantic. And, according to Flaubert's definition, a romantic was always a misreader; a romantic was only an average reader.

Mademoiselle Leroyer de Chantepie had made a crucial mistake.

On 9 October 1852, Flaubert wrote to his romantic girlfriend Louise Colet about his unpublished novel: 'I am in the act of composing a conversation between a young man and a young woman about literature, the sea, mountains, music, and all the other so-called poetic subjects. It may all seem to be seriously meant to the average reader, but in point of fact the grotesque is my real intention. It will be the first time, I think, that a novel appears where fun is made of the leading lady and her young man. But irony does not impair pathos – on the contrary, irony enhances the pathetic side.'

The conversation was the one which Léon Dupuis had with Emma Bovary about reading, while, intimately, Léon rested his foot on one of the bars of the chair in which Madame Bovary was sitting.

Another part of the same conversation

– You melt into the characters; it seems as if your own heart is beating under their skin.

– Oh, yes, that is true! she said.

– Has it ever happened to you, Léon went on, in a book you come across some vague idea you once had, some blurred image from deep down, something that just spells out your finest feelings?

– I have had that, she answered.

Flaubert's conundrum was this: Mademoiselle Leroyer de Chantepie was in love with his book through misreading it. She loved it because she identified with the characters, because she took them seriously, and believed in their poetry. And therefore she was following an outmoded form of romantic reading. The sad thing was that this mode of reading had been outmoded precisely by the novel she was enjoying so much.

Flaubert's new style invented a new way of reading. Instead of just following the characters, he wanted the reader to have the extra and more complicated pleasure of observing the techniques. Rather than losing oneself in the characters, this new reader was meant to be alert to the pattern of clichés, their collage.

It subject was romantic, but its style was not.

But this type of reading is difficult. Think, for instance, of poor André Gide, who agreed with Flaubert, but who also explained the problem: 'Allow only the indispensable to subsist was the rule I imposed on myself – nowhere more difficult and dangerous to apply that than for the novel. This amounts to counting too much

Cairo by Maxime du Camp, courtesy of Bibliothèque Nationale, Paris

on that collaboration which the reader will supply only when the writer has already been able to secure it.' There is a vicious circle in Flaubert's method – since the more reticent and elegant a novelist wants to be, the clunkier he or she might simultaneously have to become, in order to make sure that the reader has noticed the novel's reticence. Too much reticence can go unnoticed.

A week after Flaubert's reply to her letter, he received a parcel containing a portrait of Mademoiselle Leroyer de Chantepie, three volumes of her unpublished writings, and a letter affirming that she loved Emma like a sister.

Chapter iii
Egypt, 1849: The Pyramids

On the other hand, we should not think that Flaubert was arrogant, or superior. We should not think that Flaubert was never a romantic himself.

In 1845 – domestic, Norman, homebound – Flaubert was twenty-four. And because he was domestic, Norman, homebound and twenty-four, in his first novel which would never be published he therefore imagined himself on top of a pyramid, because that would give him an insight into what it would be like to be the opposite of domestic, Norman, homebound and twenty-four. It would make him oriental, and Egyptian.

But in Flaubert's account of the view from this pyramid, there is something a little unusual, a little unrealistic: having reached the apex, apparently, with hands torn and knees bleeding – because the traveller will have ascended on his hands and knees, not been hauled up by two hired Egyptians – this traveller will look around and see not the ramshackle outskirts of Cairo but 'cities with domes of gold and minarets of porcelain, palaces of lava built on plinths of alabaster, marble-rimmed pools where sultanas come to bathe their

Possibly Gustave Flaubert in Egypt, by Maxime du Camp, courtesy of Bibliothèque Nationale, Paris

bodies at the hour when the moon makes bluer the shadow of the groves and more limpid the silvery water of the fountains'.

Four years later, in December 1849, Gustave Flaubert, still the author of no published work, but suddenly less of a romantic, was a genuine tourist in Egypt. Accompanied by his best friend, Maxime du Camp, he visited the Pyramids: this time, the view was less apocalyptic, more suburban: 'an immense, delightful expanse of green, furrowed by endless canals, dotted here and there with tufts of palms'.

It was here, in these travel notes, that everything began. For Flaubert's first description of a pyramid, Pyramid 1, only had someone else's style. It only had sultanas. Whereas Pyramid 2 is Flaubert's: he has found the comedy of romanticism; his style is piquant with detail. Outside, there is a business card: 'On the side of the Pyramid lit by the rising sun I see a business card: *'Humbert, Frotteur'* fastened to the stone. Pathetic condition of Maxime, who had raced up ahead of me to put it there; he nearly died of breathlessness.' Inside the pyramid, there are other tourists: 'As we emerge on hands and knees from one of the corridors, we meet a party of Englishmen who are coming in; they are in the same position as we; exchange of civilities; each party proceeds on its way.'

It was here, then, that the European novel found its symbolic centre – with Flaubert on top of and inside the great Egyptian pyramid of Cheops.

And is it therefore possible that Vladimir Nabokov borrowed his most famous hero, Humbert Humbert, from this Humbert on the business card? Or is it too mischievously sentimental to imagine that here, on top of a pyramid, life was trying to live up to art: life was trying to invent its own thematic echoes and reflections? Sometimes I like to think that this is Humbert Humbert in a previous and unconscious incarnation – the Humbert who later liked to rub Lolita, not parquet floors.

Characters are eternal. This is one thing which does not seem obviously true, but which may well be true. Their genealogies are nothing to do with language, and nothing to do with time. In French, or English, or Russian, in America and Egypt, a character can migrate across novels, but still remain the same.

Chapter iv
Egypt, 1849: Irony

On his trip to Egypt, Flaubert slept with a prostitute called Kuchuk Hanem (although even this name was a translation: it was not her real name, but a Turkish euphemism, an assumed identity – *küçük hanim* is Turkish for 'little lady').

Afterwards, in his journal, Flaubert wrote this up, excitedly mixing his tenses. 'She falls asleep with her hand in mine. She snores. The lamp, shining feebly, cast a triangular gleam, the colour of pale metal, on her beautiful forehead; the rest of her face was in shadow. Her little dog slept on my silk jacket on the divan. Since she complained of a cough, I put my pelisse over her blanket.'

In Egypt, Flaubert discovered that the oriental was in fact domestic; because everything was always domestic. Realism is everywhere. That is why it is realistic. Nothing is ever pure, like a romance.

One feature of Flaubert's ironic style is that two things happen simultaneously which do not happen simultaneously in romantic literature, like the coupling of sex and the snore. Or the coupling of sex and the cockroach. In Flaubert's original notes on his night with Kuchuk Hanem, he added other details.

Gustave in bed with Kuchuk Hanem

To shield herself from the lighted charcoal, she put the blanket over her head.
'Ia Zeinab, ia Zeinab,' with the first syllable accented.

My face turned toward the wall, and without changing my position, I amused myself killing cockroaches on the wall.

When Louise Colet, who was still Flaubert's mistress, read this, the cockroaches distressed her. Perhaps more precisely, the cockroaches were what she said distressed her. She did not dwell on the fact that the difficult man she was in love with once spent time with Egyptian prostitutes. And Flaubert replied: 'You tell me that Kuchuk's bedbugs degrade her in your eyes; for me they were the most enchanting touch of all. Their nauseating odour mingled with the scent of her skin, which was dripping with sandal-wood oil. I want a touch of bitterness in everything – always a jeer in the midst of our triumphs, desolation even in the midst of enthusiasm.' That last sentence is Flaubert's description of his new literary form: the novelistic scene, the anti-lyrical poem.

Irony is all about the juxtaposition of opposites. And Flaubert's style would exploit as tense juxtapositions as possible. After all, 'irony does not impair pathos', Flaubert had written: 'on the contrary, irony enhances the pathetic side.' It would be like a collage. It was an ironic form of poetry, which took over from poetry the need to be as alert as possible to language, while destroying the cliché of poetry that poetry had to be lyrical.

So that while eight years earlier, in 1842, Flaubert had thought things like this – 'Oh, to be bending forward on a camel's back! Before you a deep red sky and deep brown sand, the flaming horizon stretching ahead, the undulating ground . . .' – now, he was noticing things in sentences like this: 'Here and there, about every two or three leagues (but irregularly spaced), large plaques of yellow sand that look as if they were varnished with *terre-de-Sienne* – coloured lacqueur; these are the places where the camels stop to piss.'

In Egypt, he had grown up. He was no longer romantic and immature. He was on to a new concept of style. This style was

ironic. And a description of Flaubert's style would therefore have to include the following elements (but would not be exhausted by them): two things happen simultaneously which do not happen simultaneously in romantic literature; always a jeer in the midst of our triumphs, desolation even in the midst of enthusiasm; the novelistic scene, the anti-lyrical poem. These things constitute, approximately, an abbreviated checklist of Flaubert's style.

Chapter v

Normandy, 1850s: A Short Essay on Style (III)

A couple of years after his trip to Egypt, Flaubert was writing more letters to Louise Colet. In these letters, Flaubert told her about the agonies of style. He explained his theory that style was an immature, evolving thing. And so he sent letters including his wish for a style 'as rhythmical as verse and as precise as science, with the booming rise and fall of a cello and plumes of fire'.

This is not, of course, a precise description of any style, let alone Flaubert's: no style possesses cellos, or plumes of fire. But I am not so sure that this should be upsetting. It is not that, for Flaubert, style had to be grandiose and melodramatic. No, the important thing is that Flaubert was talking about style in a letter. And every letter is inflected by the fact that it is a letter – there is always a plot behind it; there is always a strategy.

I have a theory, an unprovable theory, about Flaubert's tactics in his letters to Louise Colet.

Flaubert's agonies over style were perhaps not meant to be taken as seriously by the eavesdropping and posthumous reader as they were meant to be taken seriously by Louise, who wanted him to leave his house in Normandy and come to live with her in Paris. So that Flaubert's famous melodrama of style was also an indirect way of telling Louise that he did not love her, that he did not want to leave his comfortable study and live with her in Paris.

Many of Flaubert's agonies about this thing called *style*, which are taken so seriously, are partly agonies caused by the problem that it is very difficult telling a girl whom you like but do not love that you do not love her. From Croisset, in Normandy, Flaubert continued to tell Louise Colet that style was an absolute, that he was engaged on the creation of an object for which the distinction between form and content was irrelevant; he continued to impress on his romantic girlfriend the sanctity of his romantic calling.

So that he wrote love letters that did not sound like love letters, but like this:

Part of another letter from Gustave

What I'd like to do is a book about nothing, a book with no external attachment, one which would hold together by the internal strength of its style, as the earth floats in the air unsupported, a book that would have no subject at all or at least one in which the subject would be almost invisible, if that were possible.

This statement is often taken as a precise description of Flaubert's style, as an accurate guide to his project; but it is not a very useful guide, when thinking about what Flaubert meant by style. Its meaning is not, let's be frank, immediately clear. It is hyperbole.

On other occasions, Flaubert's metaphors for writing were less grandiose, and were all about much smaller things, like decoration, or flower-arranging: they likened the making of sentences to the making of napkin rings.

This, I think, is a more useful way to understand what Flaubert did to style.

Flaubert's agonies of style were much less to do with trying to turn words into things, but were instead the agonies of arrangement, the conundrums of *placement*. For rather than being precise about reality, he wanted to be precise about how calmly people were imprecise about reality. The words he used were therefore often second-hand, they were often clichés; whereas the arrangement of these clichés was beautiful. The drab parts were combined in a dazzling way.

Flaubert did not use words in the same way as they had been used in novels before. Instead of stating, he quoted. Flaubert discovered the idea that all language in a novel could be a form of quotation, always at one remove. If that happened, then the manner of writing became the thing that the reader was reading, and style in a novel became the arrangement of ugly things. So that in *Madame Bovary*, say, when Flaubert approaches Madame Bovary, the prose becomes stormier, more romantic: 'The next day, for Emma, was one of mourning. Everything seemed to be wrapped in a confusion of shadows drifting over their surfaces, and sorrow plunged into her soul with a muffled howling.'

According to this new definition, a style is no longer just the literal sound of the sentences, the individual precision of words. It is also the way in which these sentences are arranged, the talent for melodically framing clichés.

In this way, Flaubert's style makes form and content closer than they have ever been before. This does not mean that words, in a novel, magically become the things they describe. It instead means that the novelist has become a ventriloquist, a mimic, and that the reader is meant to be reading about the characters through these various styles, these various clichés.

It means that the art of the novel is now based on parody. Parody is the closest linguistic operation to the art of Flaubert's novel. In a parody, the form and content are aspects of the same thing – the content which the reader is meant to be noticing is the form itself.

The techniques of this new style are therefore ways in which Flaubert can signal, indirectly, that a romantic cliché is a cliché. His characters are romantics, but his style is not. Flaubert's technique is invented to intertwine as deftly as possible the beautiful and the pathetic, the parodic and the sincere. This creates the weird effects of a novel like *Madame Bovary*, which is, so often, simultaneously comic and moving. Both these effects stem from his reticent arrangement of clichés: because it would not be so moving if a romantic cliché were explicitly pointed out; but nor would it be so funny, as well.

Flaubert's style is a very fragile instrument. It is not a rejection of romanticism. It incorporates, while ironising, romanticism.

And that is another way of describing Flaubert's style. Techniques, for Flaubert, are visible invisibilities.

(Just as Flaubert once invented his personal rule that the innocent reader of his *Dictionary of Received Ideas* would constantly have to ask whether Flaubert was writing sincerely or parodically, and that at no point would the reader be able satisfactorily to reply.)

But this created a problem for Flaubert. The more he wanted to make his effects invisible, the more work had to be done. So that on 25 June 1853, at one in the morning, Flaubert wrote to Louise Colet, informing her of his progress with *Madame Bovary*, and mentioning his worry that 'this book will have one great defect, which is: its lack of *material* proportion.' The artistic problem was a simple problem of maths: 'I already have 200 pages and all they contain is preparations for the action, expositions of character more or less disguised'. A style was a massive, architectural thing.

A story by Flaubert is a form which is desperately pretending not to have a form at all. In this sense, it is trying to be true to real life.

Chapter vi
Normandy, 1857: Cupid, or A Theme

I can take, for instance, three random moments from Flaubert's description of a real, if fictional, life – Emma and Charles Bovary's wedding cake; the lawn of the notary's house in Yonville l'Abbaye; and a Rouen hotel room, where Emma meets her lover Léon.

All three of these random descriptions also contain a random Cupid.

Three Cupids in the life of Emma Bovary

The Wedding Cake: 'finally, on the upper platform, a green field with rocks and pools of jam and boats made out of nutshells, there was arrayed a little Cupid, perched on a chocolate swing, its two poles finished off with two real rose-buds, just like knobs, on the top.'

The Lawn: 'a white house across its circle of lawn embellished with a Cupid, his finger on his lips; two urns in cast-iron stand at either side of the front-steps; the brass plates gleam on the door; this is the notary's house and the finest in the district.' (But when Emma comes to beg for money from the notary, frantic at the end of the novel, Emma does not notice this Cupid, or the iron urns, the brass plates.)

The Hotel Room: 'On the clock there was a little bronze Cupid, smirking as he held out his arms under a shining garland.'

The cake, the garden and the hotel room are all punctuated by a Cupid. Cupid is a visible invisibility.

And Cupid is there because he is the image of cutesiness in love. Cupid is love's kitsch. (And so Cupid is therefore related to Madame Bovary's artificial rose which she wears to a ball, complete 'with artificial dew-drops on the tips of the leaves'.) Cupid is everywhere, and he is nowhere in this novel – he is a theme, pointed out by Flaubert with a finger laid vertically over his horizontal lips.

Chapter vii
Paris, 1883, & London, 1888: Artlessness (I)

One of Flaubert's friends was the mother of a boy called Guy de Maupassant.

Since Maupassant wanted to be a novelist, Flaubert looked after him: he gave him advice on the art of the novel.

And Maupassant therefore learned from Flaubert his idea that style was the most important thing in a novel. But, most importantly, Maupassant also learned how a style should look as much like real life as possible: 'What a piece of machinery it is, artlessness,' wrote Flaubert to Louise. 'And to what stratagems one is driven, in the name of telling the truth.'

The more a sign looks as if it's real, the more it will have to be artificial (like the interior monologue in James Joyce's *Ulysses*, or Pushkin's decision to call the hero of his novel, Eugene Onegin, his friend). And so the opposite will also be true. The less artifical a sign is, the less likely it is to be convincing. The truest poetry is the most feigning. This was Flaubert's lesson. And Maupassant was a very good pupil.

In March 1888, the cosmopolitan and American novelist Henry James published an essay (in English) on Maupassant, after Maupassant had published most of his major works. It was a review piece, a career summation. But his opinion of Maupassant's first novel, *Une Vie (A Life)*, was that it was formless. It was too much like a life, and not enough like a novel.

'He has arranged, as I say, as little as possible,' wrote James; 'the necessity of a "plot" has in no degree imposed itself upon him, and his effort has been to give the uncomposed, unrounded look of life, with its accidents, its broken rhythm . . .' So for Henry James the novel was not really one for the general reader: it was not for the beach. Instead, it was 'especially to be recommended to those who are interested in the question of what constitutes a "story", offering as it does the most definite sequences at the same

time that it has nothing that corresponds to the usual idea of a plot'. OK. So this was the story.

Chapter viii
Paris, 1883: The Life of Jeanne de Lamare

In the nineteenth century, having left the convent at which she had been educated, Jeanne Le Perthuis des Vauds married a man called Monsieur le Vicomte de Lamare – whose first name was Julien. They honeymooned in Corsica. They then lived together in Jeanne's family home in Normandy – Les Peuples. There, Julien was unfaithful with Jeanne's maid, Rosalie. Meanwhile, Jeanne had a baby, called Paul. Julien was unfaithful with Jeanne's best friend, the Comtesse de Fourville. Her husband, the Comte de Fourville, discovered this, and murdered both Julien and the Comtesse. Then Jeanne's mother died. Jeanne's son Paul left home, acquired large debts, set up with a prostitute. He asked for more and more money. Jeanne's estate was ruined. Then Jeanne's father died. The maid, Rosalie, returned to nurse Jeanne. Paul's girlfriend gave birth to a baby girl and then died, also. Rosalie went to Paris to recover the child, and brought it back to live with her and Jeanne.

And that was how Guy de Maupassant described the life of Jeanne de Lamare, *née* Le Perthuis des Vauds: he did not begin at the beginning, and he did not end at the end.

Chapter ix
Paris, 1883: Artlessness (II)

Perhaps this truncation of the beginning and end of Jeanne's story should have made Henry James, as he reread this novel five years later, pause on his accusation that Maupassant's novel was formless, and too much like a life. It was quite like a life, but it was not amorphous. This life was full of stratagems to give it form. It was written in Maupassant's style.

A theme, in a novel, is a variable category. It can be an object, like the Cupid which was a minor theme in the life of Madame Bovary. But it can also be something larger, and more comprehensive.

Form in a novel is a matter of composition, of architecture. It is based on the repetition and variation of specific elements, not the unity of a linear story. This can mean that a novel can dispense with a plot almost entirely, so that Milan Kundera can state, about his novel *The Book of Laughter and Forgetting*, that the 'coherence of the whole is created *solely* by the unity of a few themes (and motifs), which are developed in variations'. In this way, its closest analogue is the composition of a piece of music, which is also a successive presentation of elements, structured on a basis of theme and motif.

These three terms – theme, motif and variations – are musical in origin. But when applied to a novel, they slightly change.

Musically, the distinction between a theme and a motif is relatively simple. A theme is a longer version of a motif: both are repeated elements whose variation constitutes the basic form of a piece of music. But in a novel, these terms are slightly more fraught. In music, there is pure form. But pure form can never quite exist in a novel. No novel can be about nothing. Unlike music, the art of composition in the novel is hampered, and made more interesting, by the complications of subject matter: the attempt to be true to the mess which is real life. A theme in a novel is therefore much messier, more capacious, than its musical equivalent.

In this way, therefore, memory is a major theme in the life of Jeanne de Lamare.

Having returned from her honeymoon, Jeanne goes on a walk with her father: and they 'went through the wood where she had walked on her wedding-day, then completely at one with the person whose life-long companion she was in the process of becoming – this wood where she had received her first caress'. Much later, after her mother's funeral, she stands in front of the window in her bedroom: 'And Jeanne suddenly recalled that night she had spent standing at the window when they had first arrived at Les Peuples. How distant that was, how everything had changed, how different the future looked now!'

When she stood at her bedrom window, Jeanne imagined what life would be like with her future and perfect love:

Jeanne imagines her future love

On they would go, hand in hand, cleaving tightly to one another, listening to each other's heart beat, feeling the warmth of the other's shoulder, mingling their love with the balm of a limpid summer's night, so completely at one that by the simple power of their tender devotion they would be able to penetrate each other's innermost thoughts.

And things would always be thus, in the serenity of an indestructible affection.

That final, single, alienated sentence is the ironic statement of Maupassant's subject, and it is part of Maupassant's ironic style. As said by Jeanne, it is sincere. As said by Maupassant, it is only sarcastic.

This story had a plot, after all: its plot was the graph of Jeanne's disillusionment. Things, obviously, would only be thus for a moment. Only in utopia, only in a romance, would things be so perfect forever. Elsewhere – in Normandy, or London, wherever – a character would have to make do with memories.

Towards the end of her life, and towards the end of *A Life*, Jeanne returns to Les Peuples and wanders round her home for the last time. 'Two armchairs still stood by the fireplace as though they had just been vacated', and all at once, 'in a sudden hallucination born of her one, single, overriding memory, she thought she saw, in fact she did see, as she had so often seen them in the past, her father and mother warming their feet by the fire.'

Maupassant's novel was about the sad impossibility of prediction, the mismatch between the past and the future. But it did not want to say this: its form was a visible invisibility.

So that there is the irony of the novel's form, produced by the story's linear yet repetitive arrangement, the mismatch between statements at the start of the novel and events everywhere else. The novel's form is a theme with variations. These variations lead to deliberate contradictions, ambiguities, so that a character's theory or idea is never shown to be absolutely wrong or right but enmeshed in particulars.

But this is not the only visibly invisible technique which Maupassant uses to tell the story of Jeanne de Lamare: there is also the drift into stylised vocabularies.

Maupassant is adept at ventriloquising the characters and their internal mistakes. And, since this is a linguistic medium, he does it through ventriloquising the characters' styles. Because, obviously, this is not Maupassant's idea of good style, it is not quite how he would put it himself, if he had to describe two people in love – 'mingling their love with the balm of a limpid summer's night, so completely at one that by the simple power of their tender devotion they would be able to penetrate each other's innermost thoughts'. It is Jeanne's romantic idea of style instead.

And this is something else which Maupassant learned from Flaubert – his technique based on the manipulation of cliché. Sometimes, Flaubert had even made it easier for the less acute reader: the character's vocabulary was picked out, in a new typeface, for particular delectation: so there are Madame Bovary's romantic inclinations – 'She often spoke to him about the bells at evening or the *voices of nature* . . .' – or, most grotesquely, there are the pharmacist Homais's plans for Madame Bovary's tomb: 'First he proposed a broken column with drapery, then a pyramid, then a temple of Vesta, a sort of rotunda . . . or else a *mass of ruins.*'

This is the art of the novel, in Paris, in the nineteenth century: the dazzling combination of drab parts.

Chapter x

Paris, 1883: Subject Matter

In one of Vladimir Nabokov's lectures to his literature students at Cornell University (lectures which he wrote on the boat to America from Europe, as he escaped from the Nazis in Paris, having initially escaped to Berlin from the Communists), Nabokov gave his students a useful formula: 'Form (structure and style) = Subject Matter: the why and the how = the what.'

For Nabokov, technique was everything. Quite rightly, he was unimpressed by more earnest readers, who wanted to see a novel as a moral lesson or a political document. He wanted to reduce the number of readers like Mademoiselle Leroyer de Chantepie, Flaubert's fan, who believed in the characters and identified with them.

But there is a problem. Nabokov's formula is reversible.

A style is not just a matter of technique, it is also intimately and dirtily conditioned by a novelist's choice of subject matter.

Good novelists (or, maybe more honestly, the novelists I like) are often not just avant-garde in terms of technique; they are morally avant-garde as well. They are disrespectful (for one definition of cosmopolitan, after all, is the refusal to know one's place). They see distinctions and complications where other novelists had observed no such distinctions and complications. They are therefore libertines (even if, like Jane Austen, they do not seem like libertines).

One of the discoveries which Maupassant made, and which Henry James did not think he should have made, was the discovery of sex. Maupassant's style is inflected and deliberately coarsened by the startling calmness in the way he describes how people have sex with each other. When Julien comes to Jeanne's bedroom, for instance, on their wedding night, Maupassant is expert at the awkward details of undressing. As Jeanne lies in bed, she listens to 'the rustle of clothing as he undressed, the clink of money in his pocket, the successive clatter of boots being removed': 'And all at once, dressed only in underwear and socks, he darted across the room to place his watch on the mantelpiece.' Or Maupassant is more tenderly, but just as originally, adept at the childishness of intimacy: 'As Jeanne slept on the right, her left nipple was often exposed when they awoke. Julien noticed the fact and christened it "the Outdoor Type", while the other one became "Lover Boy" because the pink flower at its summit seemed more responsive to kisses.'

I am not sure that these sentences could have been written by anyone else before Maupassant in the history of the novel. It's true that in their calmness they were not possible without the prior example and tutoring of Gustave Flaubert, but Flaubert himself could not have written them. They are not his style.

The frustration of writing about style is that two words always exist – like form and content, or style and subject – when only one word, really, is necessary. Readers, and novelists, have to use two concepts to explain the complications of a single thing.

Chapter xi
Paris, 1919: A Review by Marcel Proust

Nearly thirty years after Flaubert's death in 1880, on 14 August 1919, a French critic called Louis de Robert, writing in a soon-to-be-defunct little magazine, *La Rose rouge*, published an article called 'Flaubert Wrote Badly'. His argument was not stylistic: instead, according to Louis de Robert, the problem with Flaubert was grammar; Flaubert's syntax was sloppy. This article then began a strange debate among French *littérateurs* – with some people defending the master, and other people gleefully attacking him. The tone was raised when Marcel Proust, who was forty-eight, and in December 1919 had just won the Prix Goncourt for the second part of his novel *In Search of Lost Time*, decided to state his own opinion in a grander small magazine, the *Nouvelle Revue Française*. Proust moved the question away from grammatical mistakes and into stylistic innovation.

In his article 'On Flaubert's Style', Proust noted the new things that Flaubert did with the arrangement of words – Flaubert, 'a man who by the entirely new and personal use he has made of the past tense, the imperfect tense, the present participle, certain pronouns and certain prepositions, has renewed our vision of things almost as much as Kant . . .' The main thing Proust wanted to point out was Flaubert's repeated use of the 'eternal imperfect': over and over again Flaubert would use the imperfect tense, denoting a repeated action in the past, where other writers had been happy to use a more conventional series of verbs in the simple past tense. The plot becomes less a description of a single extraordinary event, and more a description of habitual ordinary events. In Flaubert, therefore, nearly everything is habit. Singular events are rare. This, according to Proust, was the centre of Flaubert's style. This was the root of his 'background effects': in order to be truer to the repetitiveness of lives, Flaubert had to spend most of a story not telling a story at all: just as Flaubert had written to Louise Colet – 'it seems to me that life is rather like that. The event lasts for a minute, having been expected for several months. Our passions are like volcanoes: they are always rumbling, but they only erupt now and again.'

The second thing Proust noted was how this use of the imperfect tense was central to Flaubert's habit of letting the sentences speak the characters' own languages – it was part of his method of 'using the least speech-marks possible'.

And the third thing was Flaubert's odd relationship to the word 'and': 'The conjunction "and" in Flaubert does not at all have the function which grammar assigns to it. It marks a pause in the rhythmical structure and divides up a scene. In effect everywhere where one would put "and", Flaubert suppresses it.' And on the other hand, added Proust, 'where no one would think to use it, Flaubert puts it in.'

This article by Proust has become justly celebrated as a piece of literary criticism. Carefully, and cleverly, Proust was trying to be precise about this thing called *style*.

But however careful and clever Proust was, the specifications he produced for Flaubert's style were, like my own list, comic in their brevity – a novelist's style is not absolutely defined by the use of an imperfect tense, a lack of speech-marks, and an unusual relationship to the word 'and'.

No. A style, like a life, is infinite.

BOOK 3

Pierre Menard

On top of and inside the Great Pyramid of Cheops, Gustave Flaubert discovered the art of detail. He discovered that the oriental was always domestic, too. In fact, the oriental did not exist. This was the lesson of his first published novel, *Madame Bovary*, and the lesson of his novelistic technique.

But the ordinary, the domestic, was not just Flaubert's discovery. At other points in the history of the novel, other novelists have come up with their own similar findings.

A few years after *Madame Bovary* was published in Paris, Leo Tolstoy began the third part of the Second Book of *War and Peace* with one of his many theories. Opening with a brief summary of the political situation in Russia and France in 1808–9, he soon became ironic: instead of a theory of history, Tolstoy developed a theory of real life. According to Tolstoy, real life was repetitive, unremarkable – the realm of the hobby, the everyday. It was the opposite of history. So that while the Emperors Alexander and Napoleon held meetings, and discussed the possibility of diplomatic marriages, 'Life meanwhile – real life, with its essential interests of health and sickness, toil and rest, and its intellectual interests in thought, science, poetry, music, love, friendship, hatred, and passions – went on as usual, independently of and apart from political friendship or enmity with Napoleon Bonaparte and from all the schemes of reconstruction.'

Tolstoy was unimpressed by the grand; he was unimpressed by the romantic. Just as in the same way, a hundred years later, the

French novelist Georges Perec wrote an essay called 'Approaches to What?' in which he came up with his own related theory. While Tolstoy had seen real life as the opposite of history, Perec saw real life as the opposite of newspapers: 'What's really going on, what we're experiencing, the rest, all the rest, where is it? How should we take account of, question, describe what happens every day and recurs every day: the banal, the quotidian, the obvious, the common, the ordinary, the infra-ordinary, the background noise, the habitual?'

With their different styles, Georges Perec and Leo Tolstoy were saying the same thing as Gustave Flaubert. Because what is real? The only thing which is real is not the extraordinary, not the historical or surreal or romantic: it is prosiness, it is the everyday.

But I can go back further than Leo Tolstoy.

Chapter ii
La Mancha, 1605: This Is Real Life (II)

In Part I, Chapter 4 of *The Life and Exploits of the Ingenious Gentleman Don Quixote de la Mancha*, the Spanish novelist Miguel de Cervantes describes how, some time towards the beginning of the seventeenth century, a man whose real name was Alonso Quixano, but who had called himself Don Quixote, because he thought he was a knight errant (but was not), leaves an inn and enters a wood. He hears someone crying out. He goes on a few paces, and sees a mare tied to an oak, and beside this oak a boy tied to another oak, being beaten with a belt by a 'lusty country-fellow'. And so Don Quixote, naturally, because he is noble, because he is a knight errant, challenges this man to a duel by jousting. And so, also naturally, this man, because he is normal, thinks he is being attacked by a madman, and tries to placate him. He explains to Don Quixote that the boy is his servant, employed to look after his sheep, but the boy has been so careless that he loses a sheep a day, and yet still accuses him of holding back his wages out of covetousness, not redress.

Don Quixote is not convinced by this specious explanation, and orders the man to pay the boy his wages and let him go. And so, naturally, the man unties the boy. Don Quixote then demands that he pay back the missing wages immediately.

A conversation in La Mancha about money

'The mischief is, Señor Cavalier,' quoth the countryman, 'that I have no money about me; but let Andres go home with me, and I will pay him all, real by real.'

'I go with him,' said the lad; 'the devil a bit: no, Sir, I design no such thing; for when he has me alone, he will flay me like any Saint Bartholomew.'

'He will not do so,' replied Don Quixote; 'it is sufficient to keep him in awe, that I lay my commands upon him; and upon condition he swears to me, by the order of knighthood which he has received, I will let him go free, and will be bound for the payment.'

What is funny? Sometimes a novel finds things funny which people are not used to finding funny. The novel about Don Quixote, for instance, might require a less libertine and malicious reader to revise his or her sense of humour.

Many chapters later, walking along the road, Don Quixote and his sidekick Sancho Panza meet the boy again. And, smugly, perhaps, Don Quixote explains that this boy is an example '"of what importance it is that there should be knights-errant in the world to redress the wrongs and injuries committed in it by insolent and wicked men."' But the boy is not so sure of the importance of knight-errantry: instead, he explains that as soon as Don Quixote left, his master had '"tied me again to the same tree, and gave me so many fresh strokes, that I was flayed like any Saint Bartholomew; and, at every lash he gave me, he said something by way of scoff or jest upon your worship; at which, if I had not felt so much pain, I could not have forborne laughing."' And, concludes the boy, this was all Don Quixote's fault: "'for had you gone on your way, and not come where you was not called, nor meddled with other folks' business, my master would have been satisfied with giving me a dozen or two lashes, and then would have loosed me, and paid me what he owed me."'

The structure of this episode is a series of doublings-back: it is a kind of origami. The first fold is the moment when the reader realises that Don Quixote's knight-errantry has backfired. The good action has turned out not just to be not good, but to have created even more harm. The second fold, however, is the counter-realisation that this boy is mildly ungrateful: he is full of the unjustified confidence of the unjustly retrospective. There is no reason to believe him, when he says that the situation was made worse, since he could not definitively predict what the situation would be. And then the final fold is the fact that, whether or not the consequences of Don Quixote's actions were bad or not, it is a basis of our morality that an action is not judged on its ends: we judge an action on its intrinsic merits. And in this moral universe, in this heaven, it will always be right to save a boy who is being savagely beaten.

This is one version of comedy – the juxtaposition of chivalrously good intentions with the prose of real life. And its form is detail; its form is the description of the everyday.

Chapter iii
Paris & Zurich, 1771: This Is Not a Story

A hundred and fifty years after Cervantes's novel about Don Quixote, *né* Alonso Quixano, the French novelist and philosopher Denis Diderot wrote a short story called 'The Two Friends from Bourbonne'.

This story has two sections. The first section is a story about

two friends from Bourbonne. But I'm not so taken with that. The second section, at the end, is a digression on literary theory, where Diderot classifies narratives, or *contes*, into three essential types: first, the *conte merveilleux* (a story which contains the sublime and supernatural); then the *conte plaisant* (a kind of light and delicate and frothy fantasy); and finally the *conte historique* – a story which I would call *realistic*.

And at this point, Diderot's story becomes interesting.

In order to make a story seem historical, in order to make it seem true, argues Diderot, the writer will pepper the story with minute details 'with such simple, such natural features, but which are nevertheless so difficult to imagine yourself, that you will be forced to say to yourself: God that's true: you can't invent things like that . . .' And Diderot offers the less agile reader a comparison, with art:

Diderot's theory of detail

A painter depicts a head on a canvas. All its forms are strong, majestic and regular; it has the most perfect and rare unity. As I consider it, I feel respect, admiration, fear. I look for its model in nature, and do not find it; in comparison, everything is weak, little, petty; it is an ideal head; I feel that, I say to myself. But just let the artist make me perceive a faint scar on the forehead of this head, a wart on one of his temples, an imperceptible cut on the lower lip; and, ideal as it was, in an instant the head becomes a portrait; a smallpox scar at the corner of the eye or beside the nose, and this face of a woman is no longer that of Venus; it is the portrait of one of my neighbours.

In 1771, Diderot – with his faint scar on a forehead, his wart on a temple – had also discovered the considered art of detail.

In Cervantes's novel, the everyday detail of the boy's beating was simply comic. It pointed the ironic juxtaposition of Don Quixote's invented reality and the boy's prosaic reality. In Diderot's theory at the end of a story, the emphasis has shifted. Detail is not just funny; it is also true. It is a reality effect. And this is because all reality is full of comic mistakes, and imperfections. Reality is structured ironically. Irony – or real life – is everywhere.

The truth about humans is by nature ironical. It is therefore a sad kind of comedy, perhaps, but it is still a form of comedy. This is why many novels which are also comic masterpieces do not look like comic masterpieces. Often, they look quite sad. They do not make the reader laugh out loud. But laughter, I think, is not the only criterion of comic value.

There is no reason why an ironic comedy should not make a reader sad, as much as it might make a reader laugh. This version of truth is not always happy. It often makes the reader confused. In this subtler form of comedy, the emotions become complicated. Just when the reader thought that he could be lushly distressed, something comic occurs. Or, just when she thought she could laugh, something distressing occurs.

And the structure of this comedy, the sign of its truthfulness, is detail.

Diderot's proof of his avant-garde theory of detail was a new story, published two years later, in 1773. This story was called 'This Is Not a Story'. Before Magritte's pipe which was not a pipe, but a painting, there was Diderot's story which was not a story, but the truth. It was the opposite of previous stories, a new literary object.

One meaning to Diderot's title, that this is not a story, is because it is quite literally not a story; it is fact instead. It was first published in Melchior Grimm's *Correspondance littéraire* – a magazine circulated among friends. This story is not therefore addressed to a public audience. It is addressed in a kind of semi-privacy, where everyone knows the characters themselves.

The story's first editor, Jacques-André Naigeon, in 1798, said that Diderot's story was 'literally true'. The novelist Honoré de Balzac, who loved it, said that it 'sweated truth from every sentence'. Even the street names are real. Madame Reymer and Tanié have an apartment in the rue Saint-Marguerite, Gardeil lives on the rue Saint-Hyacinthe, Mlle de la Chaux lives on the place Saint-Michel, while Diderot himself, who is a character, is on the rue de l'Estrapade.

But there are different kinds of truth. Two of the story's main characters (Tanié, Madame Reymer) have left no trace in any record; and yet some of the minor characters (le comte d'Hérouville, the actress Lolotte, Jean-Baptiste Gardeil and the doctor Le Camus) are definitely real.

This story is not quite literally true; it is a game with ideas of fiction and truth. It is true in other ways.

At the beginning, Diderot announces that he is going to make up a surrogate reader within the story, who can play the part of the reader outside the story. This reader can interrupt and interject. The reader, in Diderot's head, turns out to be a cantankerous, recalcitrant man whose main theory is that all stories say the same thing – that both man and woman are immoral animals.

The essence of Diderot's story which isn't a story is to agree with this cantankerous statement, and then make it irrelevant.

Like a football match, this story is in two halves – the first half about a good man in love with a bad woman, and the second half about a good woman in love with a bad man. The meaning of the stories is reducible to the surrogate reader's theory that both man and woman are two immoral animals. Diderot's literary football match ends, ethically, in a tie.

The abstracted morality of many novels is often simple. In paraphrase, it is often saying no more than Diderot's story: that morality is complicated. This kind of abstract statement can seem banal. (But banality is endless, banality is universal.) What makes a novel interesting is less its extractable moral, than the precision with which this moral is described. The main criterion for making a story seem more truthful than another is the precision of its detail.

So that when Mademoiselle de la Chaux asks her lover, Gardeil, to tell her why he no longer loves her, he answers brutally, and honestly. His reply is impolite with realism: 'I don't know. I only know that without knowing why, I began to love you, and now I feel that it is impossible that this feeling should ever return.' And this emotional detail is then complicated by Diderot, since later on Mademoiselle uses the same argument, upside down, to explain to her doctor, Camus, why she cannot love him. The feeling simply will not come, she tells him politely, brutally; it is unavailable to her.

That is the other reason why Diderot's story is not a story, but the truth. It is an allegory about detail.

In Anton Chekhov's story 'The Chorus Girl', an enraged upper-class wife bursts in on her husband's chorus-girl mistress, Pasha, while the husband overhears their conversation in the next room. And 'Pasha felt that on this lady in black with the angry eyes and white slender fingers she produced the impression of something horrid and unseemly, and she felt ashamed of her chubby red cheeks, the pock-mark on her nose, and the fringe on her forehead, which never could be combed back.'

At the centre of Chekhov's story is a comparison. There is a sexual and surface comparison, between Pasha and the wife. But there is also a more primal and private comparison, between the beautiful person and the ugly person. For Pasha has been younger and better-looking. She does not only feel bad because she is less attractive than her sexual rival. She feels bad because she is not as attractive as she once was: she looks common. And this is only as convincing as it is because of the chubby red cheeks, the recalcitrant fringe, the pock-mark on the nose.

And I like the fact that the crucial detail is a smallpox scar – because there it is in Diderot's theory of detail: 'a smallpox scar at the corner of the eye or beside the nose'. I do not reckon Chekhov had read Diderot. But there is no need to be troubled by such sublunary problems as that. Through *The Delighted States*, they're friends.

Chapter iv
Constantinople, 1850: Three Lives

Towards the end of his travels in Egypt and the Middle East, on 14 November 1850, Flaubert wrote from Constantinople to his best friend Louis Bouilhet: he wanted to tell him that he had thought of three stories – one about Don Juan, another about a woman who wants to sleep with the dog god Anubis, and a third about a girl who is a mystic and dies a virgin – but he could not start writing any of these stories, because he was worried that they were 'perhaps one and the same'. They all had the same theme: the overlap between mystical and sexual love.

As he remains undecided in Constantinople, before abandoning his three stories and beginning *Madame Bovary*, it is possible to say one final thing about what Flaubert meant by style. He did not see the world sequentially, but thematically.

(Just as Vladimir Nabokov, in his autobiography, describes how a friend of the family, General Kuropatkin, once showed the young Vladimir a magic trick with matches. Then, fifteen years later, fleeing the Bolsheviks, Nabokov's father came across Kuropatkin in disguise, asking for a light: 'What pleases me', continued Nabokov, 'is the evolution of the match theme': 'The following of such thematic designs through one's life should be, I think, the true purpose of autobiography.')

In Egypt, Flaubert had discovered that only detail was interesting. But he then discovered something else – that detail was not irreducibly specific, but could be arranged into themes.

Flaubert's underlying metaphysical theory – that everything can be related to everything else, that everything can be a variation on a theme – was not one which ever left him. And its literary effect was that the importance and machinations of a linear plot became diminished. Just as, according to Gogol's friend Annenkov, Gogol 'used to say that for the success of a story or, in general, of any narrative, all the author must do is describe a familiar room and a familiar street'. And just as Jane Austen wrote that '3 or 4 Families in a Country Village is the very thing to work on', sending novelistic advice to her niece, Anna Austen, after being sent three of Anna's books. There is really very little plot anywhere, in this world. Plots, like places, are fabrications. And so Vladimir Nabokov can say: 'in Gogol's books the real plots are behind the obvious ones . . . His stories only mimic stories with plots.'

And I remember the poet, editor and critic Craig Raine – in one of our many conversations, which are one of this book's motifs – explaining how in James Joyce's *Ulysses* background and foreground are reversed. So that a plot element – a letter arranging an appointment to have a singing lesson, but implicitly to have adulterous sex – is lost in among the bedclothes, the breakfast things, the early-morning conversation. Because life itself is plotless.

But it is not just plot which becomes less important. There is also the setting.

After telling Louise Colet about his difficulties with the background effects he was having with his novel *Madame Bovary*, Flaubert concluded that if everything turned out well, 'I will have established by the very fact of doing it the following two truths, which I hold as axiomatic, namely first that poetry is purely subjective, that there are no beautiful subjects in literature, and that Yvetot is therefore as good as Constantinople; and that you can therefore write well about absolutely anything at all.' As soon as detail becomes everything, then all subject matter is equal. There is no hierarchy; there are no better or worse places to write about. And the art of the novel centres not on authenticity, but truth. And truth is a fabrication.

Its source is pock-marks, and chubby cheeks.

The same story could take place in Constantinople, or in Yvetot. It could take place anywhere. Because real life is everywhere.

Chapter v
London, 1738: Rome

But there is a problem. To illustrate this problem, I need to introduce some extra characters.

On 12 May 1738, Samuel Johnson, who had not yet published his dictionary, and had not yet had his biography written by James Boswell, published a poem called *London* – a translation of the Roman poet Juvenal's third satire. This was less a translation than a rewriting: it was a variation on Juvenal's theme: an imitation.

Whenever Juvenal had written *Rome*, Johnson translated this as *London*. While Juvenal lamented the pernicious influence of Greek customs on the manly Romans, Johnson similarly lamented the wily French.

This poem called *London* made Samuel Johnson very popular, with its political updating of Juvenal's poem, its translation of Rome into London. But for all its social success, there were literary problems, too, which were problems of translation.

It might be true that, as Flaubert thought, from the point of view of a subject's treatment, everywhere was everywhere. But Rome, to take a relatively easy example, is not quite London.

Initially, Johnson insisted that the sections of Juvenal's Latin poem which he had followed closely 'must be subjoined at the bottom of the page, part of the beauty of the performance (if any beauty be allowed it) consisting in adapting Juvenal's sentiments to modern facts and persons'. But the problem was still there in the solution – how can a poem stand on its own as a contemporary poem, if it is borrowing the form of a classical poem? If a writer tries to reproduce the effect, even if everywhere is everywhere, is it still the same object in translation? Nearly fifty years later, in 1781, in his 'Life of Alexander Pope', Johnson implicitly attacked his own much earlier poem, and much earlier self, arguing that 'between Roman images and English manners there will be an irreconcilable dissimilitude, and the work will be generally uncouth and party-coloured; neither original nor translated, neither ancient nor modern'.

One view of translation is that only a literal translation is morally and philosophically possible. Another view, however, is that if the important thing is translation of effect, then a translation might have to be updated and reworked: a translation will have to be a form of variation. And, therefore, will no longer, strictly, be a translation at all. 'We must try its effect as an English poem;' said Samuel Johnson, arguing against himself: 'that is the way to judge of the merit of a translation.'

These, then, are the two opposing views. And these are not just eighteenth-century problems; they are forever.

London is universal. It is also, for instance, Buenos Aires.

Chapter vi
Buenos Aires, 1939: The Story of Pierre Menard

Two centuries after Samuel Johnson's *London*, Jorge Luis Borges, in Buenos Aires, wrote a story which pretended it was not a story, but an essay, called 'Pierre Menard, author of the *Quixote*'. In this essay which is not an essay, Borges describes the hypothetical life of a fictional early twentieth-century poet and philosopher, Pierre Menard – the author of various poems and translations and tracts and, most importantly, of an unpublished draft of Cervantes's *Don Quixote*. On his death, Menard had completed 'the ninth and thirty-eighth chapters of the first part of Don Quixote and a fragment of chapter twenty-two'.

Borges explains the task which Menard set himself: 'He did not want to compose another *Quixote* – which is easy – but the *Quixote itself*. Needless to say, he never contemplated a mechanical transcription of the original; he did not propose to copy it. His admirable intention was to produce a few pages which would

co-incide – word for word and line for line – with those of Miguel de Cervantes.'

His two completed fragments are therefore very strange objects. And the oddest things they do are to content and form.

'It is a revelation to compare Menard's *Don Quixote* with Cervantes's,' states Borges. When Cervantes had defined truth – 'whose mother is history, rival of time, depository of deeds, witness of the past, exemplar and adviser to the present, and the future's counsellor' – this was simply 'rhetorical praise of history'. But when Menard writes the same sentence, at the beginning of the twentieth century, 'the idea is astounding'. Yes, continues Borges, historical truth for Menard 'is not what has happened; it is what we judge to have happened.' In the twentieth century, it is an entirely new definition. In the same way, the two styles (which are also the same style) are now radical opposites. 'The archaic style of Menard – quite foreign, after all – suffers from a certain affectation,' continues Borges, wittily. 'Not so that of his forerunner, who handles with ease the current Spanish of his time.'

This story is an allegory of style and interpretation, whose secret meaning is the uncomfortable fact that the novels which form the timeless history of the novel are also absolutely conditioned by their historical time and place.

But this conclusion can lead to another conclusion. While Diderot's story which is not a story is an allegory of detail, Borges's essay which is not an essay can be read as an allegory of detail in translation. For translation always involves a shift not just in place, but in time as well. It is an art of relativity.

There are two clichés which Borges is implicitly having fun with in his story about Pierre Menard. He is having fun with the idea of the literal translation: no translation can be literal, for some details will not be transportable. They will seem alien, where they were really only domestic. But he is also having fun with the idea of imitation. It is impossible, after all, to imagine what Juvenal might have written, had he been an eighteenth-century Londoner. It is only a thought-experiment, a hypothesis. A twentieth-century Cervantes is philosophically impossible.

It is a sad story, this fictional life of a man called Pierre Menard.

However comprehensive an imitation might be, it will still reveal the writer who is imitating. Because style is inescapable, and singular. It is impossible to reproduce the same subject. Every representation of the same subject will be inevitably, and charmingly, unique.

According to Borges, with his rewrite of Cervantes, Menard 'has enriched, by means of a new technique, the halting and rudimentary art of reading: this new technique is that of the deliberate anachronism and the erroneous attribution.' But this technique is only a game, a game which only proves one thing – that no one can reproduce a past work precisely. Anachronism is only fun because it is also illogical.

That is the problem with the idea that everywhere is everywhere, that only style matters. No style exists abstractly; it is bound up with its subject matter. And all subject matter is crammed with detail, which is helplessly historical. It is intrinsic to a specific time and place.

Chapter vii
Buenos Aires, 1939: London

But there is another possible interpretation of Borges's story, which is less stern, and more comic. This story about a new version of *Don Quixote* is also an allegory of *Don Quixote*. Because who else is Pierre Menard, if not a laughable idealist? He is full of the poetry of good intentions. The person who has really rewritten *Don Quixote* is therefore not Menard, but Borges. He has created a new variation on the theme of the hopeless romantic.

And this more comic interpretation makes me think that a less pessimistic conclusion is also possible.

It is obviously true that all novels are specific to the date and place in which they are written. But this does not mean they are only specific. Somehow, it is possible for a twenty-first-century person in London to read and be amused by roughly the same jokes as a seventeenth-century person in Madrid. (Although, as Nicholson Baker notes about Samuel Johnson, never with the same honking abandonment with which one laughs at a joke by someone who is alive.) The history of the novel, and the history of translation, is happy with the idea of mistakes – a more haphazard definition of accuracy.

A form does not need to be reproduced precisely, in order to be understood. Variations are possible.

This book, therefore, is written with a full acceptance of mistakes, the complications of anachronism. The lack of a perfect translation, after all, does not mean that there is such a thing as the untranslatable.

Chapter viii

Croisset, 1857: A Short Definition of Marxism

I need to return to Miss Juliet Herbert, and her translation of *Madame Bovary*.

This translation, which is lost, is therefore Platonic now – a heavenly shimmer. And, if Flaubert were right in his letters to Louise Colet, it might seem that a translation of *Madame Bovary* would always be a heavenly shimmer, since how can a translation be made out of something whose form and content are the same thing?

But a novel is a project: a novel is a set of instructions. All the novelistic techniques which Flaubert had perfected by the time he met Juliet Herbert, which he used in *Madame Bovary*, are translatable. All of his jokes and patterns, the musical arrangement of cliché, his visible invisibilities, can be preserved. The style, his ironic form of poetry, can be reproduced in another language.

There are still, it's true, the rhythm and the sound of the sentences – but even the sentences are not impossible. The sentences are projects too. So maybe I can still imagine this shimmer of a translation.

Everywhere is everywhere. Even Rouen.

In Croisset, Gustave and Juliet were faced with a description of a romantic woman, in the unromantic town of Rouen, romantically watching an opera-singer singing an aria set in the romantic location of Italy:

A sentence by Gustave Flaubert in French

Emma se penchait pour le voir, égratignant avec ses ongles le velours de sa loge.

Even if Juliet Herbert had understood no French, she would only have needed to read it out loud to hear the problem. You cannot translate the deft economy with '*o*'-sounds, the slide from *ongles* to *velours* to *loge*. These are not the same sound: they are only smudgily similar.

It is only a minor sentence in *Madame Bovary*, but its minor status is important: Flaubert was happy to confer a delicately patterned form on the most irrelevant of sentences.

When Eleanor Marx-Aveling, the daughter of Karl Marx, translated this novel for the first time into English (although it was not the first time; the first time, of course, was by Juliet Herbert), she rendered this sentence, correctly, as:

A sentence by Gustave Flaubert in English (I)

Emma leant forward to see him, clutching the velvet of the box with her nails.

But I think there is something wrong with a translation that does not transmute the sounds of *égratignant avec ses ongles le velours de sa loge*, a translation which is content with the bland sound of 'clutching the velvet of the box with her nails'.

In my cartoon of musical notation, the tempo of the last sentence, in Flaubert's French, is:

A sentence by Gustave Flaubert in (British) musical terminology

Quaver two quavers quaver two quavers quaver crochet quaver quaver crochet quaver quaver crotchet.

Whereas the Marx-Aveling sentence is all quavers: there are no rhythmic effects at all. It is a monotone. But the tempo and sound of Flaubert's sentence is part of the point.

The shimmer that is Juliet and Gustave's translation (which is now mine) can do something more entertaining: it may not be able to repeat the trick with '*o*'-sounds, but it could use, as an alternative, '*u*'-sounds: so that then it would sound like this:

A sentence by Gustave Flaubert in English (II)

Emma leaned forward to see him, scrunching with her nails the plushness of her box.

It isn't perfect; but it's a start.

And I like the fact that my translation is therefore more Marxist than Marx-Aveling's – since it was Karl Marx, along with Friedrich Engels, in the *Communist Manifesto*, who stated his utopian vision of how 'the intellectual creations of individual nations become common property. National one-sidedness and narrow-mindedness become more and more impossible, and from the numerous national and local literatures there arises a world literature.'

In that sense, and only in that sense, this book is a Marxist book. That is the only way in which its realism is socialist realism.

Chapter ix
Paris, 1773: A Short Essay on Brand Names

I think I can be more precise about the universal nature of ephemeral things.

Denis Diderot's story 'This Is Not a Story' is full of real people, and real street names. It is full of ephemera. And the problem, obviously, with ephemera is that they are so ephemeral. Their meaning is only local, both in space and time.

But a story without ephemera would not feel like a story at all. Without Diderot's stray references to real people – like Monsieur d'Hérouville; or Monsieur de Montucla, who wrote a history of mathematics in 1758; or Gardeil, the anti-hero of Diderot's second story, who lived from 1725 to 1808, and made a translation of Hippocrates – his story would not sound like real life.

The ephemeral is not the same thing as the irreducibly private, the comprehensively gnomic. It is, instead, a category which everyone can recognise as intrinsic to the everyday and universal. And therefore many details can still fulfil their basic function, even if they are not understood – like people's names, or brand names.

In James Joyce's *Ulysses*, Leopold Bloom, an advertising salesman, is professionally struck, as he glances through the newspaper, by an advertising slogan:

What is home without
Plumtree's Potted Meat?
Incomplete.
With it an abode of bliss.

It is a kind of poetry. To Leopold Bloom, it is definitely poetry. To the more discerning reader, it is also a form of poetry, because it has been incorporated, musically, into the collage-like structure of Joyce's novel. And it is a poetry which is happily comprehensible – even to a reader who has never heard of Plumtree's Potted Meat, or even potted meat itself. Everyone is familiar with advertising jingles. They are a fact of life – like mistranslation, and call centres.

The brand name is simply an accelerated example of a common phenomenon: that all details, eventually, will be out of date. They will be out of date superficially. But their substance is universal. Without them, no account of real life can hope to outlive rust and larvae – and become, precariously, immortal.

Chapter x
London, 1864: This Is Not a Story

After Juliet Herbert had returned to London, Flaubert did not relinquish her friendship. In 1864, Juliet returned to Croisset to visit him. In 1865, he visited Juliet Herbert in London, in the summer: they went to the pleasure gardens together, they saw the fireworks, the tourist sights. In 1866, Flaubert returned for another holiday.

At certain points, Juliet seems to be mentioned in Flaubert's letters to other people. Occasionally, he refers to a person who is sending him cuttings, ironic commentaries, destructions of the English literary scene.

Someone in England was as clever as he was.

It is possible therefore to conjecture a more painful reason for the disappearance of the manuscript of their translation; that its disappearance was not accidental; it was Juliet's refusal to allow there to be any romance. For it was not just the translation that is lost: none of their letters survive, either.

Perhaps it is possible to invent an explanatory theory. Juliet was an ordinary foreigner. She was the opposite of a romantic; she was practical. That is why nothing survives. She did not want their privacy invaded.

The suitcase containing this translation, and this possible love affair, is lost. It is burned; or perhaps it is still alive, in the suburbs, in an attic in Shepherd's Bush, west London, where Juliet Herbert died, on 17 November 1909, of 'disease of Heart, duration unknown, syncope 10 days'.

This is not a story. This is real life.

Her effects were worth £5,329.

Chapter xi

Paris, 1919: A Short Essay on Pastiche

Towards the end of his article on Flaubert's style, Proust paused for a moment and described the effect that a stylist can have on the reader – on the reader's internal voice. He observed that, after finishing a book with a distinctive style, the reader's voice wants to continue talking in this voice – to continue to sound like Balzac, or Flaubert. And Proust's advice was that the reader should let it do this, 'let the pedal prolong the note'. The reader should 'make a voluntary pastiche, so that you can become original again afterwards, rather than making involuntary pastiche for the rest of your life.'

But I think there is another use for pastiche as well. It is not just a game with originality; it is also a game with style.

The secret mechanism of a pastiche is the fact that a style is not just a unique set of linguistic operations: a style is not just a prose style. A style is also a quality of vision. It is also its subject matter. A pastiche transfers the prose style to a new content (while parody transfers the prose style to an inadmissible and scandalous content): it is therefore a way of testing out the limits of a style. It is a form of map-making.

And this becomes more acute in translation. Every question of style can also become a question of translation; every theory of the relation between form and content contains its corresponding theory of how these might be reproduced. And another description of an accurate translation, I think, can be a voluntary pastiche, a reproduction of the style.

But translations are often acts of fragile restoration. Because there is nothing style can do about time, nothing it can do about the possible comic and unpredictable betrayals.

In translation, for instance, a style is often an anachronism. It is in thrall to its ephemeral subject matter.

As a trial run, I could invent a hypothetical translation of Diderot's story 'This Is Not a Story', done by an invented translator called *Jean Bull, philosophe* – which was James Boswell's nickname for the cosmpolitan yet nationalist thinker, Samuel Johnson.

Jean Bull would have his problems.

First, there is the problem of Diderot's detail. Since Diderot has been superseded by other novelists, in the twenty-first century his style doesn't now quite resemble his style in the eighteenth century. This is partly because later novelists have been braver with their detail: they have been more libertine with literary convention. Beside Maupassant's Julien, naming Jeanne's nipples, Diderot may seem a little tame when he talks about relationships. But it is also because, conversely, Diderot now seems both a little hysterical and a little formal. The detail Diderot offers is there to flesh out emotions which seem strangely arcane, in excess of their object. Where Diderot must have seemed to his eighteenth-century readers shockingly intimate, and out of control, he now seems sadly mannered, and theatrical – 'At these words a deathly paleness spread across her face; the drops of a cold sweat which were forming on her cheeks mingled with the tears which descended from her eyes; they were closed; her head fell onto the back of her chair; her teeth chattered; all her limbs shivered; after this shivering followed a

weakness . . .' It is melodrama. And yet at the same time, his characters are strangely polite, they observe the proprieties in a way
which is only out of date.

The problem of anachronism is the problem of translationese. It
is the problem that, oddly, many translations begin to sound like
each other, consistently awkward, poised between the contemporary
and the old-fashioned. And this creates the strange dialect in which
many translations are written – a hybrid, impossible language.

But Jean Bull would still be able to reproduce the central and
delightful effects of Diderot's story: the ephemeral could still
become the universal. And this would be possible if the story were
left in Paris, in the eighteenth century, but it would also be possible
for Jean Bull to imitate Samuel Johnson and relocate the story to
the twenty-first century, in London. The zaniness of Diderot's inter-
locutor, the story's oddly interruptable form would transfer without
any trouble. While the shock of real names, and real streets, would
be even more abrupt in their revamped version.

Diderot's story is designed to make the reader feel like he or she
is eavesdropping. And that is an unusual form, and style: it is still
an unusual style, in Jean Bull's imaginary English translation.

Although it is ephemeral, it is still a true and permanent version
of real life. And so it could therefore also be true to Pierre Menard,
and Juliet Herbert.

BOOK 4

L Boom

Early in the day, at a funeral in Dublin, a journalist on the local paper approaches Leopold Bloom as the mourners drift away from the grave:

– I am just taking the names, Hynes said below his breath. What is your christian name? I'm not sure.

– L, Mr Bloom said. Leopold.

Much later in the day, Mr Bloom happens to pick up the local paper, in its early edition, in the small hours of the morning. Casually, he reads the report of the funeral. And then he notices a mistake: not in his unknown first name, but his surname. In this paper, he is now 'L Boom'.

This misprint is the artistic proof that James Joyce's story, describing a day in the life of Leopold Bloom and his wife, Molly, is true. It proves that Joyce is describing real life.

After all: 'But just let the artist make me perceive a faint scar on the forehead of this head, a wart on one of his temples, an imperceptible cut on the lower lip,' Denis Diderot had written – 'and, ideal as it was, in an instant the head becomes a portrait; a smallpox scar at the corner of the eye or beside the nose, and this face of a woman is no longer that of Venus; it is the portrait of one of my neighbours.'

While for James Joyce, his version of real life was the misprint. So that even earlier in the day, before the funeral, as Stephen

Dedalus is walking on the beach, he recalls, to himself, a telegram he had been sent by his father. He was living in Paris; his father and mother were in Dublin: and the telegram read:

– Nother dying come home father.

An artistic misprint which the original publishers mistook for an inartistic misprint: and so they edited it out.

Chapter ii
Zurich, 1916, & Paris, 1922: James Joyce Sits Down to Write

Before he arrived in Paris to finish *Ulysses*, Joyce's working method for each episode of his novel had been to write a first draft; he would then add to this from sheets of notes he had taken – crossing through the note in coloured crayon when it had been used. These notes have become mythical. Joyce would take these notes on 'little writing blocks, specially made for the waistcoat pocket', wrote Joyce's friend Frank Budgen, who knew Joyce in Zurich: 'I have seen him collect in the space of a few hours the oddest assortment of material: a parody on the *House that Jack Built*, the name and action of a poison, the method of caning boys on training ships, the wobbly cessation of a tired unfinished sentence, the nervous trick of a convive [dinner guest] turning his glass in inward-turning circles, a Swiss music-hall joke turning on a pun in Swiss dialect, a description of the Fitzsimmons shift.'

These note-sheets are small shopping lists, things which Joyce needed: for instance, he took about forty pages of notes for the episode set late at night in a cabman's shelter, where Leopold Bloom picks up the evening paper – an exhausted episode, whose language is also exhausted, built out of cliché. His notes are therefore scraps of depleted vocabulary:

globetrotters

containing the habitual

in the shape of solid food

got into hot water (O'Call)

slouchy

make matters worse

to benefit his health

a new lease of life

you can safely say

then an incident happened (sailor goes out)

on the spur of the moment

in its most virulent form

cured of his partiality

turning money away

he could truthfully state

extraordinary interest was aroused at the time

affectionate letters passed between them

Of these, only 'turning money away' was turned away.

When he had finished transferring these notes into his first draft, Joyce made a final draft written out in longhand; this draft was sent to a typist, who made three copies, one original and two carbons; Joyce would then make additions and corrections on one or two copies, and send two of the three to the poet and literary editor Ezra Pound – to be sent to the *Little Review* and the *Egoist*, the magazines in which the novel was being serialised in the US and in Britain.

Having arrived in Paris and found a publisher for the whole book, Joyce began a new process. Before sending a manuscript to be set up in the finished book, he found the serialised typescript and then made further emendations.

But it got worse.

Joyce would then receive back what the French printer called *placards* (*épreuves en placard*) – very large sheets on which eight pages were printed at once, four on each side, in descending order. Joyce received three copies of each of these drafts, or 'pullings', making changes on only one copy. He then sent this copy back, when he had emended it, and received in return page proofs, which he further emended. This process of correction, in some cases, was repeated eight or nine times. So that the proofs, in his friend and publisher Sylvia Beach's description, are 'all adorned with the Joycean rockets and myriads of stars guiding the printers to words and phrases all around the margins. Joyce told me that he had written a third of *Ulysses* on the proofs.'

There was the serialised version, then, which had already gone through three drafts. And then the book proofs were revised at least three more times – and sometimes eleven or twelve times, in all.

That is one way of describing the effort which might go into describing real life.

Chapter iii

Paris, 1920–22: James Joyce Finishes His Book

On 11 July 1920, in Paris, three days after arriving off the train from Trieste, Joyce – whose new novel *Ulysses* was being serialised in the American magazine the *Little Review* – met Sylvia Beach, an American woman who ran Shakespeare and Company, an English bookshop and lending library. And they made friends.

Unbeknown to either Joyce or Beach, in September 1920 a copy of the *Little Review*, containing an episode from *Ulysses* in which Leopold Bloom surreptitiously masturbated on a beach, was sent to the daughter of a New York attorney. Consequently, John Sumner, the secretary of the New York Society for the Suppression of Vice, filed an official complaint. A warrant was sworn out against the Washington Square bookshop where Sumner had bought confirmatory, incriminatory copies. The US postal authorities agreed to hold up mailing of the issue.

Valery Larbaud

On 15 February 1921, Sylvia Beach sent *Ulysses* to Valery Larbaud, who was ill, and in bed. Beach had introduced Larbaud to Joyce at Christmas. Valery Larbaud was a collector of toy soldiers (he bought Sylvia Beach a set to guard the window of her bookshop: 'what we all want, our own army') and, more importantly, was a novelist and poet. But his main schtick was translation. He was the Parisian intellectual and anglophile: influential, clever, generous, and easily influenced. Larbaud had a nice line in cosmopolitanism, and a nice line in self-mockery – calling himself the 'prospector for foreign literatures, the introducer of future international classics': a European literary businessman.

Now, in February, Beach sent him the March 1918 to September 1920 issues of the *Little Review*, which included the first thirteen episodes of *Ulysses*. On 22 February 1921 Larbaud wrote to Beach:

A letter from Valery Larbaud

71, rue du Cardinal Lemoine. Ve

Monday

Dear Sylvia, I am raving mad over 'Ulysses'. Since I read Whitman when I was 18 I have not been so enthusiastic about any book. I have read all there is in the Little Review (but I want to keep it a little longer – to read a few other things – may I?) and I am reading now the typescript of Episode XIV. I think I should like to translate a few pages for 'La NRF' or, if they don't want it, 'Les Écrits Nouveaux'. Perhaps the place where Mr Bloom is in the Restaurant. Just 8 or 10 pages in all, just to show how wonderful it is. But I shall want time for that. Will you ask Joyce about it, I mean will he allow me?

Yours,

V Larbaud

It is wonderful! As great as Rabelais; Mr Bloom is an immortal like Falstaff. As grand.

Meanwhile, Joyce had reached the final episodes of *Ulysses* – which he worked on in earnest from March 1921, after Italo Svevo, his friend, who was a paint manufacturer, and a novelist, delivered a suitcase containing Joyce's notes, which he had left behind in Trieste.

On Thursday 31 March 1921, in Sylvia Beach's bookshop, Joyce received a press cutting from the *New York Tribune* reporting the trial of his book for obscenity, and the subsequent banning of *Ulysses*'s publication in America – and, by extension, the English-speaking world as a whole. According to Sylvia Beach, she immediately offered to publish his novel instead, in a first printing of 1000 copies, proposing a printer in Dijon, Maurice Darantière.

And Joyce said yes.

Two pieces of publicity were then planned. A presentation of Joyce and *Ulysses* by Valery Larbaud would take place in Adrienne Monnier's bookshop. (Adrienne Monnier ran a French bookshop and library on the rue de l'Odéon. She was the impresario of Paris's literary projects; it had been her idea that her friend Sylvia should set up her English-language equivalent.) And, with an original design by Monnier, a four-page prospectus was published. On the second page there was a photo of Joyce in profile, looking aesthetic, and much younger than he now was, above '*Advance Press Notices.*'

These press notices were very funny:

– THE OBSERVER – . . . whatever may be thought of the work, it is going to attract almost sensational attention.
– THE TIMES – . . . . . . of the utmost sincerity . . . complete courage.

On the facing page, there was an announcement: 'ULYSSES suppressed four times during serial publication in "The Little Review" will be published by "SHAKESPEARE AND COMPANY" complete as written.'

James Joyce with Sylvia Beach and Adrienne Monnier, by Gisèle Freund, © the Estate of Gisèle Freund

This is what makes a good marketing campaign, after all: a combination of authority and scandal.

On 3 June 1921, the Joyces moved into Larbaud's flat, vacated specially for them, at 71 rue du Cardinal Lemoine. Joyce continued to work on the final two episodes. On 10 June he received the first sheets to be proofed from the printer Darantière. By July, the first six episodes had been set up. By 7 September he had revised around half the book.

Page proofs of the penultimate episode were pulled on 19 January 1922, and of the last episode a day or two later. On 23 January Joyce described them as being in 'uncorrected semifinal form' and returned them that week with more alterations – sending back the last episode on 31 January. The printer Darantière therefore reset both episodes in about two days, in order to meet the publishing date of 2 February.

And why was this a deadline? Because it was Joyce's birthday.

On 2 February 1922, *Ulysses* was published. Joyce had spent eight years writing it, living in three cities – Trieste, Zurich and Paris – at nineteen addresses.

Chapter iv
Paris, 1921: Valery Larbaud Gives a Lecture

Valery Larbaud's lecture on James Joyce's new novel was scheduled for 9 p.m. on Wednesday, 7 December. '*We do warn the public*', ran the advert, '*that certain pages to be read aloud are written in an uncommonly strong style which could quite legitimately shock the listener.*' Places had to be booked in advance, at 20 francs each, and were limited to a hundred.

Two hundred and fifty people turned up. And they made the right choice, that evening. Because, as lectures go, this lecture was a masterpiece.

Larbaud began by placing the initial emphasis on the mass of detail in the book. And it is fun to revive the sheer avant-garde fascination, the courage, of Larbaud's contented list, as he describes the start of Leopold Bloom's day: 'we begin with him when he rises, we accompany him from the bedroom where he has just left his wife, Molly, half-asleep, to the kitchen, into the hall, to the earth-closet where he reads an old newspaper and lays his literary plans while he eases himself; then to the butcher's, where he buys kidneys for his breakfast [although, actually, it is only one kidney]; and on the way home he is excited by the form of a servant-girl. Again in his kitchen he puts the kidneys [kidney] in a frying-pan and the pan on the fire; he goes upstairs to take his wife her breakfast; lingers to talk to her; a smell of burning meat; he redescends to the kitchen in haste; and so on.' Joyce's novel had discovered the joy of thoroughness, and Larbaud rightly shared this joy of thoroughness in his lecture. His criticism, for a moment, became a form of paraphrase.

Next, Larbaud mentioned the key technical element in the novel – the interior monologue. Because of this technique, claimed Larbaud, 'in this book, all the elements are constantly melting into each other, and the illusion of life, of the thing in the act, is complete: the whole is movement.'

The problem with real life is that it is not like a novel: real life has no formal organisation at all. That is why novelists often seem impatient or embarrassed or perplexed by the novel. In their effort to describe the everyday, novels can often seem so clunkily made up. Instead, the most artificial techniques are necessary to make a novel seem as if it resembles real life, like the sentences by Flaubert which were written in the characters' language. And a more extreme example of this technique was James Joyce's use of interior monologue.

James Joyce's passport photo, © the Poetry Collection of the University Libraries, SUNY Buffalo

Leopold Bloom goes for a walk

Fingering still the letter in his pocket he drew the pin out of it. Common pin, eh? He threw it on the road. Out of her clothes somewhere: pinned together. Queer the number of pins they always have. No roses without thorns.

Flat Dublin voices bawled in his head. Those two sluts that night in the Coombe, linked together in the rain.

O, Mary lost the pin of her drawers.
She didn't know what to do
To keep it up
To keep it up.

It? Them. Such a bad headache. Has her roses probably. Or sitting all day typing. Eyefocus bad for stomach nerves. What perfume does your wife use? Now could you make out a thing like that?

To keep it up.

But as well as giving the illusion of real life, Joyce's novel had a hidden form. And so Larbaud finally got to the structure: 'We begin to discover and to anticipate symbols, a design, a plan, in what appeared to us at first a brilliant but confused mass of notations, phrases, data, profound thoughts, fantasticalities, splendid images, absurdities, comic or dramatic situations; and we realise that we are before a much more complicated book than we had supposed, that everything which appeared arbitrary and sometimes extravagant is really deliberate and premeditated; in short, that we are before a book which has a key.' According to Larbaud, this key was the title, *Ulysses*.

At this point I need a small digression.

Joyce himself came up with a complicated schema, for Larbaud to use in the lecture, where events in his novel could be correlated to events in Homer's epic poem, the *Odyssey*. He had used this

schema as he wrote the novel. But very soon, these correspondences also become confused. Molly Bloom, for instance, according
to the schema of *Ulysses*, is both Calypso and Penelope. Unlike
Penelope, she is unfaithful. The reason why Joyce wanted to place
such emphasis on the key was not because the Homer was definitively important: instead, he was guiding the international reader
to the fact that this book had a form at all; it had a web of interlinking correspondences.

So: I can go back to Larbaud in the rue de l'Odéon, at about
9.30 p.m. 'It is a genuine example of the art of mosaic. I have seen
the drafts. They are entirely composed of abbreviated phrases
underlined in various-coloured pencil. These are annotations
intended to recall to the author complete phrases; and the pencil-
marks indicate according to their colour that the underlined phrase
belongs to such or such an episode. It makes one think of the boxes
of little coloured cubes of the mosaic workers.' And so Larbaud
could conclude: 'This plan, which cannot be detached from the
book, because it is the very web of it, constitutes one of its most
curious and fascinating features.'

Some readings from *Ulysses* then followed Larbaud's lecture –
translated by a young friend of Adrienne Monnier called Jacques
Benoist-Méchin, and revised by Larbaud. At the end, Joyce was
called forward to bow. Larbaud hugged him. And Joyce – records
Sylvia Beach – Joyce blushed.

Chapter v
Paris, 1922: Artlessness

In Paris, as he finished his novel, Joyce was doing two things at
once: he was writing the final episodes, and he was revising the
episodes he had already written.

As he began to finish his book, Joyce found that the interior monologue was the perfect vehicle for the production of repeatable motifs. In the final episodes, and as he revised the proofs, these motifs became decorated with more and more detail.

Leopold Bloom, for instance, was stung by a bee on 23 May 1904. In the fair copy, this bee-sting existed in two episodes.

In September 1921 it was then added to the final episode – 'Whit Monday is a cursed day too no wonder that bee bit him' – then in October to the penultimate one: 'He compressed between 2 fingers the flesh circumjacent to a cicatrice in the left infracostal region below the diaphragm resulting from a sting inflicted 2 weeks and 3 days previously (23 May 1904) by a bee.' And it was added back in to earlier episodes – so that this bee-sting recurs across the space of almost the entire gargantuan novel: 'Still gardens have their drawbacks. That bee or bluebottle here Whitmonday'; 'Nice young student that was dressed that bite the bee gave me. He's gone over to the lying-in hospital they told me'; 'Still I got to know that young Dixon who dressed that sting for me in the Mater and now he's in Holles street where Mrs Purefoy. Wheels within wheels.'

When Nabokov lectured his American students on *Ulysses*, he made a stern point about Joyce's proliferation of thought: 'This book is a new world invented by Joyce. In that world people think by means of words, sentences. Their mental associations are mainly dictated by the structural needs of the book, by the author's artistic purposes and plans.' Joyce, argued Nabokov, was using language to represent something which was not linguistic at all: thought. And this is a reasonable reservation, but it does not quite understand Joyce's method. Joyce never wanted to make words stand in for thought, and then hope that no one would notice. Instead his method was based on the inverse idea that people are so verbal: their consciousness is so often unoriginal. A mind is a scrapbook; a mind is a suitcase. Everyone – like Madame Bovary – has their own, second-hand, style.

The artistic artlessness of Joyce's form coincides with the inartistic artlessness of his characters' day.

In an essay for the small French magazine, the *Mercure de France*, Ezra Pound noticed that Joyce had systematically removed quotation marks from his text, and said that the interior monologue was simply interior speech, without the speech marks – 'voilà tout.' (Just as Proust had said the same thing, about Flaubert.) But I think that something more precise is going on. Joyce's novel is a development of the novelistic art of collage. It is based on a perception that if people's perceptions are conditioned by linguistic habits, borrowed styles, then it is more accurate to remove quotation marks. The outer world of dialogue and the inner world of thought are much more similar than quotation marks might suggest.

'I am quite content to go down to posterity as a scissors and paste man,' Joyce told the American composer George Antheil – 'for that seems to me a harsh but not unjust description.'

Chapter vi
Paris, 1922: A Short Story About Love

Let us try to recap the end of this long day.

Finally, Leopold Bloom is on his way home. With him is Stephen Dedalus – a failed poet, and jobbing secondary-school teacher. They go back to Mr Bloom's house at 7 Eccles Street, where Mr Bloom's wife, Molly, is asleep upstairs (having been unfaithful with a man called Blazes Boylan that afternoon). They make cocoa, they have a chat, and Stephen leaves, having refused Bloom's offer of a bed for the night. Then Bloom potters around in his house, before going upstairs to bed, where he wakes Molly up, and is questioned about his day – questioning to which Bloom only offers an edited version – expurgating, for instance, his visit to a brothel. And then Bloom falls asleep.

While Bloom falls asleep, Molly is still awake. And the rest of what happens in the novel is purely internal – it is thinking. And this is the most important event in the novel. For this is the end of the day, and once someone has read *Ulysses*, all the information embedded in this episode leaks back into the earlier episodes.

In bed, Molly remembers herself and Bloom; this is not always simultaneous: sometimes Bloom disappears, but he always reappears. In this way, the patient reader finds out that Molly loves Bloom. Although she has just been unfaithful, although Bloom has been avoiding the house all day, she loves him. And therefore the reader also finds out, if the reader did not know this already, that love is complicated.

This avant-garde experimental novel is strangely sweet, and old-fashioned. The reader knows that Molly has been unfaithful, and knows that this does not matter.

The last two episodes of *Ulysses* are remarkable for two apparently contradictory things: they are comprehensive, and reticent. On the one hand, these episodes are huge, and full of detail. But these episodes refuse to make any form of selection among detail. And this is why they are also reticent: this mass of detail does not respect any detail's relative importance. Some of the most important things are therefore barely said.

Leopold and Molly Bloom's sex life

What limitations of activity and inhibitions of conjugal rights were perceived by listener and narrator concerning themselves during the course of this intermittent and increasingly more laconic narration?

By the listener a limitation of fertility inasmuch as marriage had been celebrated 1 calendar month after the 18th anniversary of her birth (8 September 1870), viz, 8 October, and consummated on the same date with female issue born 15 June 1889, having been anticipatorily consummated on the 10 September of the same year and complete carnal intercourse, with

ejaculation of semen within the natural female organ, having last taken place
5 weeks previous, viz. 27 November 1893, to the birth on 29 December 1893
of second (and only male) issue, deceased 9 January 1894, aged 11 days, there
remained a period of 10 years, 5 months and 18 days during which carnal
intercourse had been incomplete, without ejaculation of semen within the
natural female organ.

This mass of information, about Leopold and Molly's sex life which
is now a sad sex life, since the death of their son – a coitus which
is always interrupted – is all about love and its attendant heartbreak
and complications, but love is never mentioned. The effect of this
information is to make the reader realise how much has been only
implicit in this seemingly encyclopaedic novel. Everything has been
oblique. A sentence which looked like something else – a random
detail, say – was actually the tiniest of stories.

Earlier in the day, Bloom had got a little tipsy on a glass of
Burgundy at lunchtime; and because he was tipsy, and maudlin, he
began to think about sex. In a pub, at lunchtime, he thought about
kissing his wife.

Leopold eats an erotic sandwich

Pillowed on my coat she had her hair, earwigs in the heather scrub my hand
under her nape, you'll toss me all. O wonder! Coolsoft with ointments her
hand touched me, caressed: her eyes upon me did not turn away. Ravished
over her I lay, full lips full open, kissed her mouth. Yum. Softly she gave me
in my mouth the seedcake warm and chewed. Mawkish pulp her mouth had
mumbled sweet and sour with spittle. Joy: I ate it: joy. Young life, her lips
that gave me pouting. Soft, warm, sticky gumjelly lips. Flowers her eyes
were, take me, willing eyes. Pebbles fell. She lay still. A goat. No-one.
High on Ben Howth rhododendrons a nanny-goat walking surefooted,
dropping currants.

And then about twelve hours later, 800 pages later, Molly is thinking to herself as she goes to sleep.

Molly falls asleep

the sun shines for you he said the day we were lying among the rhododendrons on Howth head in the grey tweed suit and his straw hat the day I got him to propose to me yes first I gave him the bit of seedcake out of my mouth and it was leapyear like now yes 16 years ago my God after that long kiss I near lost my breath yes he said I was a flower of the mountain yes so we are all flowers all a womans body yes that was one true thing he said in his life and the sun shines for you today yes that was why I liked him because I saw he understood or felt what a woman is and I knew I could always get round him and I gave him all the pleasure I could leading him on till he asked me to say yes and I wouldnt answer first

At lunchtime, the detail of the seedcake is a moment in Bloom's memory, an episode in his romantic and pornographic autobiography. It is only at the end of the book, when the reader has forgotten all about it, that the reader also discovers that this moment Bloom remembered was also the moment he proposed to Molly. He is not just thinking about sex. He is thinking about marriage as well.

But none of this was obvious. Everything has to be pieced together, restored from the oblique state in which Joyce left it. The story is there in the text, but it is not there, as well.

Chapter vii
Paris, 1924: The Everyday

According to Sylvia Beach, her friend Ernest Hemingway came specifically to Paris in time for the publication of *Ulysses*, to meet James Joyce; and it was Hemingway's illegal contacts who worked out a smuggling operation to get *Ulysses* to its American subscribers via the Canadian border. And this seems proper, and artistically true, because Hemingway's stories, *in our time*, first published in 1924, were the first fictions to realise what Joyce was up to in *Ulysses*. While sounding nothing like Joyce in tone, Hemingway invented stories which borrowed his indirect, oblique method:

A short story by Ernest Hemingway

They shot the six cabinet ministers at half-past six in the morning against the wall of a hospital. There were pools of water in the courtyard. There were wet dead leaves on the paving of the courtyard. It rained hard. All the shutters of the hospital were nailed shut. One of the ministers was sick with typhoid. Two soldiers carried him downstairs and out into the rain. They tried to hold him up against the wall but he sat down in a puddle of water. The other five stood very quietly against the wall. Finally the officer told the soldiers it was no good trying to make him stand up. When they fired the first volley he was sitting down in the water with his head on his knees.

The everyday can only be expressed with more and more indirect techniques. That is one tradition of the novel. It leads from Gustave Flaubert, via James Joyce and Ernest Hemingway, to the lists of Georges Perec – which seem to be only detail, but in fact are distorted by stories, by hidden meanings. So from a Saul Steinberg drawing called *The Art of Living*, realised Perec, can be drawn the plan for a novel, which is really a list.

Part of Georges Perec's list for The Art of Living

9 rooms where the floor is no doubt covered with moquette

3 rooms with tiled floors

1 interior staircase

8 pedestal tables

5 coffee tables

5 small bookcases

1 shelf full of books

2 clocks

5 chests of drawers

2 tables

1 desk with drawers with blotting-pad and inkwell

2 pairs of shoes

1 bathroom stool

11 upright chairs

2 armchairs

1 leather briefcase

1 dressing gown

1 hanging cupboard

1 alarm clock

1 pair of bathroom scales

1 pedal bin

1 hat hanging on a peg

1 suit hanging on a hanger

1 jacket hanging on the back of a chair

washing drying

3 small bathroom cabinets

several bottles and flasks

numerous objects hard to identify (carriage clocks, ashtrays, spectacles, glasses, saucers full of peanuts, for example)

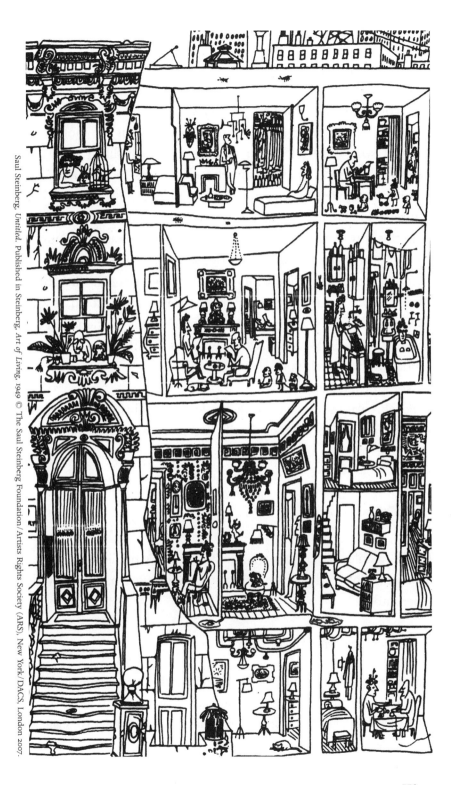

'Examine the drawing a bit more closely', says Perec, 'and the details of a voluminous novel could easily be extracted from it.'

According to Perec's theory, every detail is always a miniature narrative: 'The woman doing nothing very much is the mother of the girl who is sitting down and it's extremely likely that the gentleman leaning on the mantelpiece, a glass in his hand and looking somewhat perplexedly at the Calder-style mobile, is her future son-in-law.' Everything conceals a potential narrative.

In this way, Perec worked on the plan for his last and best novel, *La Vie mode d'emploi* (*Life: A User's Manual*), a title which in its vacuous pragmatism flaunts its refusal of the idea that literature should teach, should be a moral or everyday guide. Instead, it was an affirmation of real life, of the multiple novels contained in an apartment block. Which is why, as well as its title, Perec added a subtitle to his novel: *Romans*.

Not a novel: *Novels*.

For this was the discovery of James Joyce, with his multiple styles, structured on a network of detail. The everyday was infinite.

Chapter viii
Paris, 1921: Utopia

In the middle of the preparations for *Ulysses*'s publication, on 21 September 1921, Valery Larbaud wrote to Sylvia Beach, in his private esperanto:

Another letter from Valery Larbaud

Indeed, as you say, after that we are bound together for La Postérité. (Do you know where it is?) When I think of that, la mano mi trema, no sé come decir what I feel, and I do not so en que idioma estoy writing! We shall be the wonder ad il pasmo dei futuri centuries.

And it is true. In any language, everything is possible.

And, for thematic reasons, it seems fun to be able to add that Hemingway's other hero was Gustave Flaubert. But, according to his reader's card at Shakespeare and Company, Hemingway could not read Flaubert in French: he read his fiction in translation.

BOOK 5

The Fluke

It is possible to close this volume with a coda, an allegory. It is possible to end with a story about a fluke.

In 1887, in Paris, lived Edouard Dujardin. This man was a lover of beauty, of rare things, a connoisseur. He was a Symbolist, a man of letters. And in 1887, he wished to add to the store of rare and beautiful things by writing a novel called *Les Lauriers sont coupés* (*The Laurels Are Cut Down*), a title which in its first English translation was transformed into *We'll to the Woods No More*. Which is not, obviously, a literal translation, but is an accurate translation of the title's wistful and literary regret. For *Les Lauriers sont coupés* is a quotation by Dujardin from an elegiac poem by the French romantic poet, Théodore de Banville, whose first line is 'Nous n'irons plus au bois, les lauriers sont coupés'. Just as *We'll to the Woods No More* is a quotation from an elegiac poem by A. E. Housman, whose first two lines were a direct translation of Banville: 'We'll to the woods no more / The laurels all are cut' – published in 1922, thirty-five years after Dujardin's novel.

Dujardin's novel would be rare and beautiful not because of its content, but because of its style. Its content was just banal, and tiny: a day and a night in the life of a man called Daniel Prince, trying to seduce the woman he has been trying to seduce – an actress called Leah D'Arsay – for some months now. The plot was unoriginal, but the style was not.

This novel was published, in serial form, in the elegant small magazine *La Revue Indépendante*.

The style which Dujardin chose, and which would mark this book as beautiful, was a style which had not been used in a book before. There had, until now, been two ordinary ways of doing things. The first, most normal way had been to orchestrate the narrative in a story from a point outside the story. Which did not mean, of course, that there could not be small forays and ingressions, small incursions, into the thoughts and psychologies of the characters. This had led to sentences like: 'Had they nothing else to say to one another? Their eyes indeed were full of a more serious conversation; and, while they were struggling in search of banal phrases, each felt assailed by the same langour; it was like a murmur from the soul, profound, unbroken, eclipsing the sound of their voices.' On the other hand, it had been permissible for characters to narrate the events of the story, either because it was their own story, or because it was a story which they had somehow gained information about – which led to sentences like this: 'Whether I shall turn out to be the hero of my own life, or whether that station will be held by anybody else, these pages must show. To begin my life with the beginning of my life, I record that I was born (as I have been informed and believe) on a Friday, at twelve o'clock at night. It was remarked that the clock began to strike, and I began to cry, simultaneously.'

Dujardin thought up a new way.

This story would not be narrated from a point outside the story, nor would it be narrated by a character. This story would be inferred from the represented thoughts and sensations of one character, and nothing else: it would therefore be an exercise in pure subjectivity. The story would be told by someone who was not aware they were telling a story at all.

And so it sounded like this:

Daniel Prince thinks while eating a sole in a restaurant

What's that waiter up to? Coming now with the sole. Funny things soles. About four mouthfuls in this one and there are others would make a meal for ten people; of course they eke it out with sauce. Let's start on it anyhow. A shrimp-and-mussel sauce would be a distinct improvement. That time we went shrimping at the sea-side; a rotten catch, boring performance it was and my feet were sopping, though I was wearing those stout tan shoes I bought near the Bourse. What an endless business it is picking away at a fish . . .

Chapter ii
Paris, 1888: A Letter from Stéphane Mallarmé

One of Dujardin's friends, and fans, was the famously stylish poet Stéphane Mallarmé. In his retrospective essay 'Interior Monologue', written in 1930, Dujardin wistfully remembered Mallarmé's praise for his novel. 'I shall always regret that Mallarmé *said* to me but never *wrote* to me what he had thought of the book on its serial publication': according to Dujardin, Mallarmé had been the only person at the time 'to feel what Joyce was to discover later on: the enormous possibilities of interior monologue. I recall his phrase "the moment gripped by the throat . . ."'

For all his preciousness, Mallarmé was aware of the everyday; like Tolstoy, he was a connoisseur of the hobby, the non-political pleasure. As the (anonymous) editor of *La Dernière Mode*, a fashion magazine, Mallarmé described the wish to capture 'life, immediate, dear and multiple, our own life with its serious nothings'. And I like this phrase, 'serious nothings', I like its commitment to the ordinary.

But I am not so sure that Mallarmé was quite as clever as Joyce.

Dujardin also quotes a letter from Mallarmé – 8 April 1888 – in which Mallarmé stresses how for him the delight of Dujardin's invention was not aesthetic, but journalistic:

A letter from Stéphane Mallarmé translated into English

I can see you have set down a cursory method of notation that turns upon itself, whose sole aim, independent of large-scale literary structures, poetry or decoratively convoluted phraseology, is to express, without misapplication of the sublime means involved, everyday experience which is so difficult to grasp.

Mallarmé was, and is, celebrated for the intricacy of his technique, the complications of his delicate and obscure poems. And Mallarmé can be therefore, while I contine to let Daniel Prince eat his lunch, a useful comparison with Dujardin's adventure in the art of prose.

Mallarmé's technique remained the same, whether in his more ambitious poems, or in his lighter poems sent as gifts to friends. For instance, in the copy of his poem 'L'Après-midi d'un faune' which he sent to Dujardin, Mallarmé wrote this quatrain, entreating the faun of the poem to float away and thank his Norman brother, Dujardin:

A poem by Stéphane Mallarmé in French

Faune, qui dans une éclaircie
Vas te glisser tout en dormant,
Avec quatre vers remercie
Dujardin, ton frère normand.

There are, in this quatrain, two internal rhymes on *é*, and four internal rhymes on **air**:

Faune, qui dans une é*clair*cie
Vas te glis*ser* tout en dormant,

Avec quatre vers remercie
Dujardin, ton frère normand.

The technical name for these rhymes is *rime normande*. And
Dujardin, from Normandy, is a *norman* too. The rhyme scheme is
therefore personal to Dujardin. The poem's form is an analogue
for its addressee, and vice versa.

Dujardin himself had found a form which was obviously less
precious than this, but was not as inartistic as Mallarmé therefore
thought. Although he liked Dujardin's novel so much, Mallarmé
did not notice that Dujardin had not just found a form which was
brilliant at describing the everyday, the things of this world. He had
also found a form based on motif, on the repetition and echo of
minuscule elements – the scraps of Daniel Prince's interior monologue. Dujardin had found a new way of making prose poetic, of
organising it formally. For the more discrete a unit is made – of a
novel or a poem – the easier it is to balance themes, to create visible
(and less visible) patterns and relations.

Chapter iii
Buenos Aires, 1947: Against Poets

Let's turn this another way round.

On 28 August 1947, Witold Gombrowicz gave a talk, in Spanish,
called 'Contra los poetas': 'Against Poets'. It was delivered at a bookshop called Fray Mocho, in Buenos Aires.

Gombrowicz's argument was simple. 'Even though we have
come to doubt practically everything, we still venerate the cult of
Poetry and Poets and this is the only deity which we are not
ashamed to worship with great pomp, low bows, and inflated
voice . . .' But, argued Gombrowicz, we should not worship poetry.
We should not worship anything so careful about its cleanliness.

For Gombrowicz, poetry was the epitome of style. And he distrusted style. Or, more precisely, he was a stylist who distrusted the complacency of lesser stylists, for whom style was a refuge, an alibi. No, argued Gombrowicz, in his problematic Spanish, 'We should never lose sight of the truth: that all style, every distinct attitude forms itself through elimination and is, basically, an impoverishment. Because of this, we should not allow any attitude whatsoever to reduce our potential, becoming a gag . . .'

Gombrowicz therefore split writers into two categories: those who are happy to reduce their potential, whom he called, for convenience, poets; and those who instead try to refuse restrictions of any kind. In other words, a writer could either be an ironist or a romantic, a novelist or a poet. But the best stylists would be able to be both. A stylist should always be hospitable to the things which might destroy a style – which, in Gombrowicz's case, was the world of the serious, the pretentious, the poets (just as Saul Bellow, in the same year, in Chicago, was failing to include things into his style which he would manage to include a few years later: the comic, the streetwise, the immature). 'My art', asserted Gombrowicz, 'has shaped itself not in confrontation with a group of people related to me, but in relation to the enemy and confrontation with the enemy.'

That was Gombrowicz's argument, against poets, in Buenos Aires. And I think it is universal. It is just as applicable to the Paris of the 1880s as to the Buenos Aires of 1947. Mallarmé, a poet, wanted a style as restricted as possible. He did not think it was compatible with everyday experience. Whereas Dujardin had discovered a way of writing which was open to real life. It was a form which could be stretched to its limits.

Chapter iv
Paris, 1888: Interior Monologue

Dujardin's style, it's true, had its faults. The main problem was the usual problem of any exclusive and limited technique – it had to be warped to serve the needs of exposition of plot; so that at a certain point Daniel Prince quite unnecessarily decided to reread an entire cache of letters, which was very convenient for Dujardin, but less convenient for poor Daniel Prince; and at other points Daniel Prince was less thinking to himself than narrating to an imaginary audience: 'And that's the end of my documentary evidence. A pity! For that's only the beginning of the story. Next Saturday what happened? Ah, that was the day she . . .'

But this style was very good at other things, like character, so that Daniel's idle throbbing nondescript sexual imagination could be lightly intimated: 'A woman in front; tall, slim, heavily scented; shapely figure she has, flashing red hair; wonder what her face is like; handsome, probably.' And it could be flexible enough for momentary detail, which even a realist like Gustave Flaubert had not quite managed to fit in: 'Now why is the stair carpet turned up at the corner here?'

(Although, I've just realised, Tolstoy had: in *War and Peace*, the pedantic character Berg 'rose and kissed Vera's hand, and on the way to her straightened out a turned-up corner of the carpet.' Tolstoy, as so often, was exceptional.)

But the central effect of Dujardin's new style was that he used the interior monologue to break moral limits on content in literature: it could be an excuse for comprehensiveness. So my favourite moment in this little novel is towards its end.

Leah told Daniel to wait in the drawing room while she undressed for bed. And this would be, it must be, thought Daniel Prince, his moment: this would be when she would finally sleep with him. But as he let his imagination linger on the details, he was struck by a more practical thought: 'must be nearly six hours since that lavatory in the Boulevard Sébastopol; the privy here is on the left of the hall; one should feel at ease on these amorous occasions; mind not to make a noise though, mustn't be heard going out; the hall lamp should be lit, anyhow I have matches; open the door now; hush, no noise; tip-toe out; good business, the light's on; door's ajar; remember gentlemen are requested to adjust; for this relief – and very needful it was; I leave the door ajar as I found it; the drawing-room door; softly does it; here we are; capital, no one can have heard me; and now let's take it easy for a while in this armchair.'

As well as descriptive comprehensiveness, however, even more acute and edgy was Dujardin's moral comprehensiveness. While Daniel waited and waited in the drawing room, his thoughts became less romantic, and more financial.

Daniel Prince waits for Leah to undress

That's enough of it; this evening, damn it, we sleep together; it would be too silly for words, a love affair that's been going on so long and cost so much, to lead to nothing; all that time and money wasted just for the pleasure of gazing at the charms of a young woman who is playing a small part at the Nouveautés; it's pure folly; it's worth a couple of hundred francs and that's all; this high-falutin' business is out of place; I know that sort of girl, exhibits herself on the boards every night and when she's hard up goes on duty at some establishment in nighttown.

This is one of the most daring passages I can think of in nineteenth-century literature, in its sheer blunt accuracy and refusal to be likeable. It marks Dujardin, a symbolist aesthete, as a more rigorous realist than more publicised realists, like Émile Zola.

The novelty in this novel was not just the interior monologue itself – since this had been done before, though not in such truncated sentences. The novelty was also the fact that Dujardin wrote a novel which was only interior monologue. In this way, he used the technique as a means to comprehensiveness. Dujardin could pretend that he no longer had the politic luxury of choice. He had to describe things which a previous writer might not have wanted to describe, in order to be convincing. And this was an advance, therefore, this novel called *Les Lauriers sont coupés* – which no one seemed to have noticed, as it drifted out of print, at the end of the nineteenth century.

Chapter v

Paris, 1907: Gertrude Stein's Theory of the Twentieth Century and Paris

But I am not sure that this thing called the nineteenth century needs to exist in *The Delighted States*: I am not sure the time or date is relevant.

This is one reason why it is not very easy, defining what is avant-garde and what is not – what is a work with a value, and what is a work which is justly neglected. Because Dujardin, in Paris, had come up with what the young Jan Mukařovský, in Prague, would later have called a literary value. But in 1888 no one, apart from Stéphane Mallarmé, who had not understood it anyway, had noticed.

In *The Autobiography of Alice B. Toklas*, which is not written by Alice B. Toklas but by her lover, the novelist Gertrude Stein, Stein mentions Gertrude Stein's theory of new countries and old countries.

This theory of new countries and old countries is also the same as her theory of new literature and old literature. They are often topsy-turvy. And so her theory is a theory of America.

Gertrude Stein's theory of America

Gertrude Stein always speaks of America as being now the oldest country in the world because by the methods of the civil war and the commercial conceptions that followed it America created the twentieth century, and since all the other countries are now either living or commencing to be living a twentieth century life, America having begun the creation of the twentieth century in the sixties of the nineteenth century is now the oldest country in the world.

In the same way she contends that Henry James was the first person in literature to find the way to the literary methods of the twentieth century.

When considering literary history, it helps to remember Gertrude Stein's definition of America as the oldest country in the world. It is her way of pointing out the fact that literary history is always subject to jet lag.

The novel is not a simultaneous genre. Sometimes, it takes a while to catch up with itself. That is why there is such a thing as the avant-garde. It is a category of objects whose value is only visible retrospectively.

Chapter vi
Paris to Trieste, 1902: James Joyce Reads on a Train

The first English translation of Dujardin's novel came out in 1938. In this English translation, the literary reader would have come across a sentence which may have sounded familiar: 'and softly, yes softly she'd whisper Yes'. This sentence was very similar to the final sentence of James Joyce's *Ulysses*: 'and his heart was going like mad and yes I said yes I will Yes.' And there were other tiny Joycean moments in this 1938 translation, like Dujardin's apparent use of truncation: 'Again; no, imposs. It won't do to drop these bits of

'Dejeuner Ulysse, June 24, 1929,' © the Poetry Collection of the University Libraries, SUNY Buffalo

card on the floor . . .' – just as Bloom felt qualms about the letter he was writing to a woman who was not his wife: 'Lovely name you have. Can't write. Accept my little pres. Play on her heartstrings pursestrings too. She's a. I called you naughty boy'; or the mention in Daniel's thoughts of 'nighttown' – the name Joyce gave Dublin's red-light district in *Ulysses*.

Dujardin's novel was translated by the Joycean scholar Stuart Gilbert. This translation was done with Joyce occasionally helping out.

The reason they were doing this was that in 1902, on the train between Paris and Dublin, a much younger James Joyce had read Dujardin's novel, the centrepiece of a collection Dujardin had made of his prose and verse. And this book was the technical prompt for *Ulysses*. It introduced Joyce to a new technique.

I like this story, this allegory. Literary history is odd – that is what this story proves – it is small-scale, local, minuscule, and international.

ULYSSES BY JAMES

MERICAN EDITION, PU

EW YORK, 1934. COF

Y MARGARET CAROL

934, BY THE MODERN

OUND IN U. S. A. BY H.

RNST REICHL. FOURT

VOLUME II

BOOK 6

Monsieur Sterne

This second volume is an upside-down version of the first.

In the first volume, real life was described in the various styles of Gustave Flaubert, Guy de Maupassant, James Joyce and others – all of whom were trying to be as indirect as possible. They were trying to pretend not to be artful at all. And this represents, for many people, a grand tradition of the novel.

But there are other ways of describing real life, and still being accurate. Another way is to be as open and exhibitionist as possible. This other tradition of open exhibitionism flaunts its digressions, its diagrams: it forms a succession of stylists who are often not seen as a tradition at all. They are often seen as too bizarre. This second volume of *The Delighted States* therefore has two themes: the first is how a stylist might be accurate to real life, while being interfering, flippant, full of tricks; and the second is how a tradition might be defined at all. Because a tradition does not have to be major, in order to be a tradition. It can be as small as the movement from Edouard Dujardin to James Joyce – or as haywire, in this case, as the movement from Laurence Sterne to Denis Diderot and on to Bohumil Hrabal, via Machado de Assis and Italo Svevo.

This volume of marginal novelists can therefore start on the margins, the edge of things. It can begin in Yorkshire, in the eighteenth century, where a man called Uncle Toby is talking to his manservant, Corporal Trim.

Trim is about to tell Uncle Toby his story about 'a *King of Bohemia and his seven castles*'. He has to announce this title five times in the same chapter because he is interrupted five times by the distractions and questions of Uncle Toby before he can advance beyond it. Finally, things work out. He gets to the first sentence. And is then interrupted again.

The King of Bohemia and his seven castles

Now the king of Bohemia with his queen and courtiers *happening* one fine summer's evening to walk out – Aye! there the word *happening* is right, Trim, cried my uncle Toby; for the king of Bohemia and his queen might have walked out, or let it alone: – 'twas a matter of contingency, which might happen, or not, just as chance ordered it.

King William was of an opinion, an' please your honour, quoth Trim, that every thing was predestined for us in this world; insomuch, that he would often say to his soldiers, that 'every ball had its billet.' He was a great man, said my uncle Toby.

The Corporal's first name is James. Some years later, across the sea in France, a man called Jacques is chatting to his Master:

Jacques. My Captain also used to say that every bullet shot out of the barrel of a rifle had its billet.

Master. And he was quite right.

In England, meanwhile, Trim attempts to carry on. According to him, 'if it had not been for that single shot, I had never, an' please your honour, been in love.' But this last comment is fatal. Because Uncle Toby will always prefer a love story concerning Trim to a story concerning the King of Bohemia. And so the story of the King of Bohemia and his seven castles is finally abandoned for good, while Trim tells the story of his love life, without any major interruption or digression, until its conclusion four chapters later.

Over in France:

Laurence Sterne, a rake: by Joshua Reynolds © National Portait Gallery, London

Jacques and his Master have a chat

Jacques. For instance, if it hadn't been for that shot, I don't think I'd ever have fallen in love, or walked with a limp.

Master. So you've been in love?

Jacques. Have I been in love!

Master. And all on account of a shot from a rifle?

Jacques. All on account of a shot from a rifle.

Master. You never mentioned it before.

Jacques. No, I don't think I did.

Master. Why was that?

Jacques. Because it could not have been said before nor after this moment.

Master. And that moment has now come and you can speak of being in love?

Jacques. Who can tell?

Master. Take a chance. Make a start.

And that is how Denis Diderot's novel *Jacques the Fatalist and His Master* begins – where the nineteenth chapter of the eighth volume of Laurence Sterne's novel *Tristram Shandy* had begun. But after that, it lingers. It tells the story of Jacques's only love. No, it tells the story of Jacques *trying* to tell the story of his only love. And it ends where the twenty-second chapter of the eighth volume of *Tristram Shandy* ended.

Denis Diderot expanded four chapters by Laurence Sterne into a novel.

Chapter ii
Paris, 1981: A Tradition (I)

In Milan Kundera's essay 'Introduction to a Variation' – which introduces his own theatrical variation on Diderot's novel *Jacques the Fatalist and His Master*, published in Paris in 1981, six years after he

had left Communist Czechoslovakia – Kundera discusses the originality of Laurence Sterne's novel *Tristram Shandy*. According to
Kundera, the novel's 'wisdom and its beauty' are inseparable from
'its ludic origins'. In Sterne's novel, argues Kundera, everything is
submitted to comic doubt. And yet, he continues, this novel is still
surprisingly unusual in the history of the novel: 'No one followed
him. No one – except Diderot.' And then Kundera comes up with
his theory of originality, based on this odd relationship between
Laurence Sterne and Denis Diderot. For only Diderot 'was responsive to this invitation to new paths. It would be absurd on this
account to devalue his originality. No one denies the originality of
Rousseau, Goethe or Laclos because they owed (they and the whole
development of the novel) so much to the example of naïve old
Richardson. If the similarity between Sterne and Diderot remains
so striking, it's because their common enterprise has remained
completely isolated in the history of the novel.'

In order for a writer to seem original, it helps to be one of a
series. It helps to be unoriginal. Only then will a writer's originality
be detected. Whereas the attempt to invent a new series, a new
tradition, means that Diderot looks more like Sterne than he in
fact is.

The history of an art is based on a paradox: a new work only
makes sense if it is part of a tradition, and yet it only has a value
in that tradition if it does something new. That was the lesson of
Jan Mukařovský, in Prague. This means that an art form is a direct
confrontation of a problem which is not just a problem in art, but
in life: what is the difference between a repetition and a variation?
At what point is an imitation original?

In the second volume of his aphorisms, collected under the title
Human, All Too Human, Friedrich Nietzsche devoted a section to
Laurence Sterne – '*The most liberated writer*'. For Nietzsche, Sterne
was 'the great master of *ambiguity*'. Lovingly, Nietzsche noted the
'"endless melody"' of Sterne's style: 'in which the fixed form is

constantly being broken up, displaced, transposed back into indef-initeness, so that it signifies one thing and at the same time another.' This endless melody meant that everything was double.

I like Nietzsche's description of Sterne's style. It is patiently precise to the oddness of Laurence Sterne. But the thing which intrigues me the most is Nietzsche's immediate turn to Diderot. He is expert at describing the paradoxes of originality: 'It is strange and instructive to see how as great a writer as Diderot adopted this universal ambiguity of Sterne's: though he did so, of course, ambiguously – and thus truly in accord with the Sternean humour. Was he, in his *Jacques le fataliste*, imitating Sterne, or was he mocking and parodying him? – it is impossible finally to decide: and perhaps precisely this was Diderot's intention.'

An ambiguous homage to ambiguity: that is the style of Denis Diderot's novel *Jacques le fataliste*.

Since Jacques, and therefore *Jacques*, covers the same distance as Sterne but in a longer time, Diderot's rewriting can be seen as a variation which slows down Sterne's tempo. And yet the opposite is also true. Sterne's novel *Tristram Shandy* is remarkable for the slowness of its narratives, their clogged and dilapidated texture. But Diderot has chosen for his variation perhaps the quickest narra-tive of all the clogged narratives in *Tristram Shandy*. Since it is not Tristram narrating, the story of Trim in love is a cartoon inserted into Tristram Shandy's novel, a wistful moment for the exhausted reader – a glimpse of a faster technique that is forever unavailable. And now Diderot slows it down again. So there is a simultaneous effect, in Diderot's variation, of speeding up and slowing down.

A style in Paris is not the same as a style in Yorkshire. To the people who accused him of plagiarism, of writing a weak imita-tion, Diderot would have been able to feel secretly proud. Because he was an original, Diderot: he was extending an international art.

Chapter iii
Paris, 1762: Laurence Sterne Does a Publicity Tour

In 1762, Laurence Sterne, who had so far published six volumes of his novel *The Life and Opinions of Tristram Shandy, Gentleman*, arrived in Paris to have fun, and see the sights. But he did not see so many of the sights. Instead, as the new English literary sensation, he was lionised. Writing to his friend David Garrick, the famous actor, Sterne informed him that he had so far received invitations from Michel-Étienne Lepeletier, comte de Saint-Fargeau; the Baron D'Holbach; the Graf von Limburg-Styrum; and Claude de Thiard, comte de Bissy. The duc d'Orléans commissioned a sketch of Sterne, to be added to his collection of notable foreign visitors to France. Just like his friend David Garrick, Sterne was famous too.

In Paris, Sterne became a friend of Crébillon *fils* – an elegant, erotic, playful writer of short novels. They were such good friends, who understood each other's projects so well, that they came up with a witty plan: Crébillon was to write a letter attacking 'the indecorums of T. Shandy' which Sterne would reply to 'by recrimination upon the liberties' in Crébillon's novels as well. The two letters would then be printed together and sold, with the profits split between the authors.

But Sterne's most important meeting in Paris, the one I really care about, was with another writer of stories: Denis Diderot.

During his stay in Paris, Sterne wrote to his London publisher, Thomas Becket, asking him to send some English books for his new French admirers in Paris: among these books were 'the 6 Vols. of Shandy'. These volumes were for Sterne to give to Diderot.

By September 1762, Diderot was writing to his friend Sophie Volland, describing *Tristram Shandy* as 'the maddest, the wisest, the gayest of all books'. This novel, thought Diderot, had reinvented the novel as an art.

Tristram Shandy is a melancholy man, whose family comprises his mother, his father – called Walter – and his uncle, called Toby.

At the time of Tristram's birth, Uncle Toby's main pastime – aided by his manservant, Corporal Trim – is to build a mock-up replica of the Siege of Namur, the siege at which he had been wounded in the groin. And yet his character is one of gentleness, not militarism. He does not only dwell on military matters; one other siege preoccupies him – that of Widow Wadman's heart: a neighbour, and a looker.

Walter, on the other hand, is a more go-getting personality: he is a man of schemes and science. He believes in meticulous planning.

But the fate or creator or chance that determines the life of Tristram Shandy does not seem to believe in meticulous planning. From the moment of his conception, to the birth itself, and the days following the birth, including his baptism, everything that could go wrong goes wrong – whose symbolic apex is reached with the moment when a sash window falls brutally onto the young Tristram's penis.

And so, sat down as he was with the full intention of fully describing the story of his life, Tristram had only managed, by the time Diderot read his autobiography, to venture not much further than his birth. He constantly found himself sidetracked by the million mishaps of his early years – and these mishaps could not be missed out: for Tristram has a theory that life is a chain of infinite causes. And if life is a chain of infinite causes, then no cause is too small to be ignored. Everything is relevant.

This means, also, that events which are not strictly related to the plot have to be described, in full. So that the reader receives a sermon delivered by Corporal Trim – as well as an obscure and possibly obscene story about a nose (a theme which Nikolai Gogol, many years later, writing in Russian, would pick up on in his story called *Nose*.)

As well as the story of his early years, however, in both its relevant and irrelevant forms, this book also contains – interwoven, interrupting – the story of the older Tristram's attempt to tell the story of his early years. (Because no cause is too small to be missed out.) His book therefore contains descriptions of his travels, accounts of his worries about his health, hints as to his possible relationship with a girl called Jenny, boasts of his friendship with the actor David Garrick, elaborations of his views on acting, and so on.

But no. It's fun, the content of the book, but it's not the real fun. It's not really what is so mad, so wise and so gay about *Tristram Shandy*, by Laurence Sterne. That's something else entirely.

Chapter v
London, 1759: The Musical Novel (1)

To begin again, at the beginning.

Tristram begins the story of his life and opinions with an opinion about the beginning of his life. If only, he thinks, his parents had thought about what they were doing when they conceived him. For Tristram possesses the unusual theory that the exact course of 'the animal spirits' at the moment of conception could determine a person's character. In what remains of his first paragraph, he therefore describes this theory at length. And then the second paragraph, abruptly, is this:

Mrs Shandy interrupts Mr Shandy

'Pray, my dear, quoth my mother, *have you not forgot to wind up the clock?* —— *Good G –!* cried my father, making an exclamation, but taking care to

moderate his voice at the same time, —— *Did ever woman, since the creation of the world, interrupt a man with such a silly question?* Pray, what was your father saying? —— Nothing.'

This first chapter only has two paragraphs. And already Denis Diderot, in 1762, reading the first chapter, would have known that across the English Channel, in English, Sterne was on to something new.

This beginning is not a beginning at all. As Tristram would say, it needs an explanation. And so gradually the reader discovers that Tristram's father and mother were involved in something which was similar to a conversation, perhaps, but was still a very different thing. This, it turns out, was the moment when Tristram was conceived – a moment of comedy, where at the important moment, Tristram's father Walter was distracted by domestic concerns. But to explain that – to explain the beginning – Tristram has to backtrack. Constantly, throughout the novel, Tristram has to backtrack.

The opening sets up a theme which is the centre of Sterne's book. Tristram is trying to write an ordinary book, which begins at the beginning, and goes happily through to the end. But there are two drawbacks to this plan, which are the end and the beginning.

The essence of Sterne's novel is the way, deadpan, he makes Tristram a character who is stricken by a mania for comprehensiveness. To describe this type of mania, Sterne came up with the word *hobbyhorse*. Sterne's style is predicated on the hobbyhorse. All his destabilising of beginnings and endings (and everything in between) are part of his way of describing character: a construction helplessly at its own mercy, in thrall to compulsions of its own making. And Tristram's mania for comprehensiveness creates havoc with the book.

Tristram takes his life so seriously that his *Life* becomes impossible. For Tristram discovers that no beginning is ever a beginning. Every description of a beginning requires another description, of the beginning's beginning, and so on. Therefore, although Tristram's *Life*, in its final state, takes up around 600 pages, he has still not managed to get past the first few months of his life: he is still stuck on the story of his father and mother, and his uncle Toby's romance with the Widow Wadman. There are always more stories which need to be told, in order to explain the stories themselves. So *Tristram Shandy* becomes one of the earliest, and one of the most complicated, examples of a novel with no plot. Or, equally, a novel which is a collection of miniature plots.

This hobbyhorse for comprehensiveness has one crucial formal effect: rather than possessing the luxury of effacing himself behind the story, like Gustave Flaubert, Tristram is a vociferous stage manager, chivvying his characters. He has to keep interrupting himself to keep explaining his explanations: it is a vicious circle, a line circumscribing itself.

Which creates kinks like this.

Having left his mother eavesdropping on his father and uncle Toby, 'holding in her breath, and bending her head a little downwards, with a twist of her neck – (not towards the door, but from it, by which means her ear was brought to the chink)', so that Tristram could backtrack and 'bring up the affairs of the kitchen', six chapters later Tristram remembers he has left her still bent over at the door: 'I am a Turk if I had not as much forgot my mother, as if Nature had plaistered me up, and set me down naked upon the banks of the river Nile, without one.'

Gradually, mismatches emerge between the order of events in the story itself, and the order of events as they actually occur in the novel. In a conventional novel – a novel about the birth, education and death of its hero, say – the two will be the same: the order of events will be the same as the order of their telling. But not in *Tristram Shandy*. Because of Tristram's darting comprehensiveness, the reader ends up with tense juxtapositions of tenses: 'a cow broke in (tomorrow morning)'.

The Life and Opinions of Tristram Shandy is such an entertaining novel because it discovered that there was no reason to start a story from the beginning – since, in fact, all beginnings are arbitrary – and so it discovered a new unity for a novel. Rather than being unified by a plot, the novel was unified by thematic echoes: its unity was formal.

This novel was musical.

That is why Diderot was content, in Paris, in 1762, having read the first two volumes of his new friend's novel.

Chapter vi
Paris, 1796: A Tradition (II)

Diderot's novel *Jacques the Fatalist and His Master* tells the story of Jacques (a fatalist), who believes that everything is written on high, that our lives are predetermined. As he wanders round France with his master, he tries to recount the story of his love for a girl called Denise: but he is constantly interrupted. Finally, Jacques seems to be about to come to the conclusion of his love life – he is just coming to the point in his story when his love for Denise will be consummated or not, as she tends to him on his sickbed (because this story about love is a story about sex) – when he is arrested, and his master runs off in flight. And so Jacques's story, abruptly, ends.

At this point, with a couple of pages to go, the narrator of the novel, described as the editor of its manuscript, admits that 'by resorting to published memoirs', he 'could supply what's missing here, but what would be the point? You can only be interested in what you think is true.'

The reader is only interested if a story seems like real life.

Nevertheless, wearily, he promises to go back and reread these memoirs, and returns one week later to inform the reader that three paragraphs in some other published memoirs concerning the same story do not correspond to his manuscript.

This novel about the overlap between chance and causation is also a display of variation, a way for Diderot to show off how much he understood what Sterne was up to with his new way of writing a novel – with his digressions, impossible endings, interruptions, his private chats with the reader – and how much Diderot himself could do it differently too. It was an exercise in originality.

That is one reason why Diderot ended with three different endings.

Ending number 1

Jacques and Denise made protestations of love, with Jacques promising that sex was not what he wanted, absolutely not, and so the two of them lived happily ever after.

Ending number 2

This second ending was copied out from *Tristram Shandy* – 'unless, that is, the conversations of Jacques the Fatalist and his Master predate that work, in which case the Reverend Sterne is a plagiarist, though I don't believe that for one minute, for I have a particular regard for Monsieur Sterne . . .' In *Tristram Shandy*, James Trim's account of his love affair had ended with Denise rubbing Trim so tenderly that Trim seizes her hand –

'– And then thou clapped'st it to thy lips, Trim, said my uncle Toby – and madest a speech.

Whether the corporal's amour terminated precisely in the way my uncle Toby described it, is not material . . .'

But the editor of Diderot's novel includes an imaginary reader, who is not happy with Tristram's insouciance: 'You're wrong, you slandering swine, I won't finish it the way you have. Denise was a good woman.' But Diderot also lets Tristram riposte with the obvious response: 'Who's saying different? Jacques grabbed her hand and put it to his lips: his lips. You're the one with the dirty mind, you hear things no one is saying.'

In this way, Diderot was showing what a good reader he was. He was repeating one of Sterne's running gags.

Sterne's favourite joke throughout *Tristram Shandy* was 'that ornamental figure in oratory, which Rhetoricians stile the *Aposiopesis*' – where a sentence is abruptly broken off, leaving the reader to complete it, like Tristram's description of Trim himself, who 'now and then, though never but when it could be done with decorum, would give Bridget a –' This kind of sentence was overtly obscene. But Sterne then made the game more amusing by changing the rules, since he loved inventing sentences which the reader could believe had been completed, and were not obscene, but which looked very much like sentences which had not been completed, and which were in fact obscene – like this: 'My sister, I dare say, added he, does not care to let a man come so near her * * * *. I will not say whether my uncle Toby had completed the sentence or not.'

Sterne had invented a new literary game which went something like this: Tristram pretends to give the reader more freedom than they had previously had when reading a novel, and yet he worries constantly that the reader may be taking too much freedom, and not reading the book in the way that Tristram wants – in particular this reader may well be reading obscenities into sentences which Tristram does not intend; and yet the final irony is that Tristram, obviously, is well aware of these obscenities, since there are so many clues to their presence that the reader is, in effect, being told to read obscenely.

How much freedom does anyone have? That is one of the

questions which Sterne is playing with, in fictional form, in *Tristram Shandy*. How independent are we from our compulsions? It is this concern with freedom, and with the loopy prisons people invent for themselves, which is explored by the formal tricks of Sterne's style.

And which Diderot also developed in his multiple endings.

I therefore need to finish with Diderot's finish.

Ending number 3

According to the third ending, Jacques, in prison, was rescued by a gang of bandits, roamed the countryside with them, and then, one day, recognised his Master in one of the houses they were robbing, along with the love of his life, Denise. And they all lived happily ever after – 'for that is how it is written on high.'

Obviously, there is an irony here. Nothing is written on high. This narrative about a person who believes in absolute order, absolute predetermination, is characterised by zaniness, multiple endings, interruptions, unfinished stories; like *Tristram Shandy*, it is a mayhem of caprice. But a second irony, the one I am most interested in, takes this even further. All of it is predetermined, because all Diderot is doing is copying a story from a book that has already been published by Laurence Sterne. And all of it is improvised, since Diderot the narrator is constantly, overtly, rewriting Sterne's text. He is constantly demonstrating his new freedom.

Chapter vii
London, 1759: A Chapter upon Chapters

As the fourth volume of *The Life and Opinions of Tristram Shandy* begins, the reader discovers Tristram's father Walter in an attitude of dejection – on his bed, with one arm flung over the side, where his hand rests gently, domestically, and realistically, on the handle of a chamber-pot. He is recovering from the news that in using a forceps to bring Tristram into this world, the doctor has crushed Tristram's nose. For it is one of Walter's comical but seriously held opinions that a man's character depends on the nobility of his nose: a crushed nose is no use at all. And so from his bed he lectures his brother Toby on the 'cross-reckonings and sorrowful *items* with which the heart of man is overcharged'. Faced with the sorrows of this world, and with the fact that his son now does not possess the one thing – a splendid nose – which might counterbalance the forces of evil, Walter decides that urgent measures are now called for: as he begins to go downstairs, he announces to his brother Toby that his son's name will have to be Trismegistus – after Hermes Trismegistus, the great alchemist and philosopher.

And he descends the staircase.

He descends the staircase, and continues to talk to his brother: 'What a chapter of chances, said my father, turning himself about upon the first landing, as he and my uncle Toby were going downstairs – what a long chapter of chances do the events of this world lay open to us!' And then Tristram takes over again – because Tristram rarely lets his characters take over for long: he adopts his father's chapter of chances, and changes its meaning completely. 'What a lucky chapter of chances has this turned out! for it has saved me the trouble of writing one express.' Poor Tristram is always behind with his promises – earlier, he had vowed to give the reader a chapter of knots, two chapters upon the right and the wrong end of a woman, a chapter upon whiskers, a chapter upon wishes, a chapter of noses – and a chapter upon chapters. Finally, therefore, he can fulfil at least one of these premature vows.

But at this point, I am going to take over from Tristram myself. Because I also want to talk for a moment about chapters.

A chapter, before Laurence Sterne and Tristram Shandy got hold of it, was a way of splitting up a narrative into its narrative units.

It was the unit of an event, like a man saving a boy from being whipped by his master. As such, it had a reasonable length.

However:

The Life and Opinions of Tristram Shandy, Gentleman: IV. 5

Is this a fit time, said my father to himself, to talk of PENSIONS and GRENADIERS?

This chapter in one sentence, while Walter is still on his bed, and has not yet descended the staircase, is not, obviously, the description of a significant event. It is just an idle moment of thought.

That is the new thing Laurence Sterne did to chapters.

On the one hand, Tristram seems to shift chapters in a purely arbitrary manner, because in this way he can be true to what he and his creator, Laurence Sterne, see as real life – something subject to chance, punctiform, disastrous. But there is another principle behind these zany chapter divisions. Rather than dividing up chapters according to events, Sterne divides them according to themes. His chapters are more reminiscent of musical phrases than theatrical scenes. They are what permit the musicalisation of form – a structure of developed themes and motifs.

The chapter, for Sterne, is his central formal unit, and it balances two opposing forces in this universe: the force for entropy, formlessness, the anarchy of chance; and the force for form, permanence, the perfection of a pattern.

With his father still on the first landing of the staircase, Tristram begins a new chapter with a possible reader's complaint: 'Is it not a shame to make two chapters of what passed in going down one pair of stairs? for we are got no farther yet than to the first landing, and there are fifteen more steps down to the bottom.' And to this impatient reader, Tristram offers his explanation: he cannot help it: 'let that be as it will, Sir, I can no more help it than my destiny:

– A sudden impulse comes across me – drop the curtain, Shandy
– I drop it – Strike a line here across the paper, Tristram – I strike
it – and hey for a new chapter!'

Is a man to follow rules, or are rules to follow him? That is the
question of this tenth chapter, which is, Tristram suddenly informs
us, 'my chapter upon chapters'. That is its theme. His essay on
form is really an essay on freedom. For some questions of form
are also questions of real life.

What a long chapter of chances do the events of this world lay
open to us! Real life consists in all the cross-reckonings and
sorrowful items with which the heart of man is overcharged.

The Life and Opinions of Tristram Shandy, Gentleman, IV. 11

We shall bring all things to rights, said my father, setting his foot upon the
first step from the landing – This Trismegistus, continued my father, drawing
his leg back, and turning to my uncle Toby – was the greatest (Toby) of all
earthly beings – he was the greatest king – the greatest lawgiver – the greatest
philosopher – and the greatest priest – and engineer – said my uncle Toby.
– – – – – – In course, said my father,

And that is where this chapter ends, with a comma. The comma is
crucial. It is a mute demonstration of Sterne's new idea of the chapter.
For in this chapter, Sterne's theme is the silent fact that everyone is
on their hobbyhorse – Walter with his dreams of grandeur, Toby
with his dreams of military fortifications. The comma is a haywire
way of showing how a chapter does not need to end with the end
of a scene: it can end with the end of a theme. For anyone reading
this book knows the tragedy in wait for Walter, the cross-reckoning
in store. This book is not narrated by Trismegistus Shandy. Somehow,
Trismegistus never happened: the narrator of this novel, this autobiography, does not take his name from an alchemist, but instead from
a name which means unhappiness itself.

Chapter viii
Rio de Janeiro, 1881: A Tradition (III)

But I am not sure that Milan Kundera needed to be so depressed, when considering the truncated tradition begun by Laurence Sterne. It is not quite true that this tradition only consists of two lone novelists. At the very least, it is a threesome.

In 1881, the Brazilian novelist Machado de Assis published *The Posthumous Memoirs of Brás Cubas*. It was his fifth novel, written when he was forty-one. But Machado's earlier novels did not sound like this one: they were not so exhibitionist, or skilful. They were not original.

Narrated from beyond the grave by Brás Cubas, these posthumous memoirs describe a small, minor plot – Brás's affair with the wife of one of his friends. Her name was Vírgilia.

But the plot, as so often for my characters, my novelists, is a pretext: the novel's real concern is for truth. It is all about real life. And so in the first version of the novel, serialised in the magazine *Revista Brasileira*, there was an epigraph from Shakespeare's *As You Like It*: 'I will chide no breather in the world but myself; against whom I know most faults.' Because that is the theme of this novel: it is about the infinite and elusive charm of honest self-critique.

Although this may mean that the reader has to revise his or her idea of charm.

'Now, as I write this,' says Brás, 'I like to think that the compromise was a fraud, that compassion was still a form of selfishness and that the decision to go console Vírgilia was nothing more than a suggestion of my own suffering.' Or, when Vírgilia's husband is about to be sent as an ambassador to Dalmatia, and thus she too will live in Dalmatia – wherever, wonders Brás, Dalmatia is – a revolution breaks out in that minuscule country. 'The revolution was bloody, painful, formidable.' This does not upset Brás. 'Inside

I blessed the tragedy that had removed a pebble from my shoe. And, then, Dalmatia was so far away!'

This man is likeable, Brás Cubas: he is a charmer. And his ancestor is Tristram Shandy: Tristram is his best friend, his closest relation.

But I need to be clear here what I mean by a relation, and a tradition.

A tradition is not formed by repetition: it is not maintained through comprehensive copying. A tradition is a more complicated series, where certain elements are maintained, while other elements are morphed into new variations.

It is a messy process, evolution.

And so Tristram and Brás resemble each other in the way they choose to tell a story, full of interruptions and digressions, a story which emerges from its doodlings; and in the fact that Tristram has only been born for a few days, just as Brás has only been dead for a few days; and in Brás's pet project for a patent for 'an anti-hypochondriacal poultice, destined to alleviate our melancholy humanity' which is so similar to Tristram's advertised wish 'to drive the *gall* and other *bitter juices* from the gall-bladder, liver and sweet bread, of his majesty's subjects, with all the inimicitous passions which belong to them, down into their duodenums.'

And the most important resemblance is a self-conscious frankness. Both narrators are impatient with emotional and fictional clichés. 'Perhaps I'm startling the reader', says Brás, 'with the frankness with which I'm exposing and emphasizing my mediocrity. Be aware that frankness is the prime virtue of a dead man . . . in death, what a difference! What a release! What freedom! . . . There's no more audience. The gaze of public opinion, that sharp and judgmental gaze, loses its virtue the moment we tread the territory of death.' Tristram and Brás are expert in this kind of paradoxical sentence – where the lack of an audience is announced to a primed audience of uncomfortable readers. They are both connoisseurs of caprice, noting their own 'slackness of will, the rule of whim.'

But this is where the similarity ends. Because one consequence of Brás's zany freedom from beyond the grave is what he does to narrative form: he is full of impatient and bright ideas to make a book shorter, more economical, less boring.

After all, if Laurence Sterne ends up in Brazil, you don't end up with Laurence Sterne. You end up with something else entirely.

That is what a tradition means.

Chapter ix
Rio de Janeiro, 1881: Artlessness

In Rio de Janeiro, everything speeds up.

Rather than developing background effects, like Gustave Flaubert in Normandy, thirty years earlier, Brás simply advertises his transitions from one subject to another: 'And now watch the skill, the art with which I make the greatest transition in this book. Watch. My delirium began in Vírgilia's presence. Vírgilia was the great sin of my youth. There's no youth without childhood, childhood presumes birth, and here is how we come, effortlessly, to that day of October 20, 1805, on which I was born. See? Seamlessly, nothing to divert the reader's calm attention, nothing.'

Or he substitutes a chapter describing a funeral with a quick list of notes ('bier, candle holders, invitations, guests slowly entering, stepping softly') 'for a sad and banal chapter that I won't write.' Or there is this comic substitution for dialogue, where Machado realises that for certain conversations, like 'the old dialogue of Adam and Eve', there is no need for words: the punctuation will do:

Brás Cubas

....................?

Vírgilia

....

Brás Cubas

....

....

Vírgilia

.......................!

Brás Cubas

....

Vírgilia

....

.......................?...................

....

....

Brás Cubas

....

Vírgilia

....

Brás Cubas

....

....

.................................!...

..!.......................................

....!

Vírgilia

.......................?

Brás Cubas

.....................!

Vírgilia

.......................!

Which is a new way – I can't deny it – and a witty way, of doing dialogue.

A novel can be much shorter than people had previously thought. That is the basis of Machado de Assis's new style. He took the form of Sterne's musical novel, and then concentrated the effects.

Chapter x
Paris, 1925: The Musical Novel (II)

In 1925, in Paris, André Gide published his novel *Les Faux-Monnayeurs* (*The Counterfeiters*) about a novelist, Edouard, writing a novel called *The Counterfeiters*. Two years later, Gide also published the journal he kept as he was writing *The Counterfeiters*, in which he addressed the problems he was having with the novel's composition.

As he considered the problems of form, as he worried at his structure – with its competing, contradictory, inclusive aesthetic – his vocabulary became tinged with musical terms. So that the journal begins with Gide's fretting at the multiplicity of his material:

André Gide begins a notebook

I'm sure it's crazy to group together in a single novel everything which life has presented me with and taught me. As stuffed as I want this book to be, I can't dream of putting everything into it. And yet it's this desire which still embarrasses me. I'm like a musician trying to juxtapose and interweave an andante motif and an allegro motif, like César Franck.

I think I've got material for two books and I'm beginning this notebook so that I can try to extract the tonal elements which are too different.

Gide wanted a more precise terminology for the art of the novel. Especially since, for him, the novel was an art of juxtaposition. It was an art of irony, and collage. And it seems natural that since the novel is an art of composition – whose elements occur in succession, like a piece of music, not simultaneously, like a painting – it should borrow its terms from music. The sketched precision it seems to offer, reasoned Gide in his journal, allows a more specific description of the composition's problems.

At the centre of Gide's novel there is a tea party, where Edouard, the fictional novelist, explains his theory of the novel. What Edouard would like to do, he explains, 'is something like the art of fugue writing. And I can't see why what was possible in music should be impossible in literature . . .' Like André, he would like to write a musical novel. And yet, at this point, I am not sure that we should be taking Edouard so seriously.

In a fugue, a theme is stated and then repeated by a new voice, or a new instrument. So I can see what Edouard means, with his theory of a musical novel: he means that a story could be constructed where a theme is developed through different characters. He means that a novel could have the thematic unity of a fugue.

But perhaps there is a problem with this.

A fugue is not really a form. A fugue is just mechanical: a system of adaptations, repetitions. The musical form Edouard would really like is the art of theme and variations – where a theme is stated and then embroidered harmonically, or rhythmically, or melodically. A theme and its variations is the most basic, most minimal form possible.

The desire for complete musicality is a romantic idea. A novel can never be a fugue: a fugue is too precise. At best, it can only borrow the scrappier form of variations. For music is just a metaphor for fiction. It is an experiment, an exploratory idea.

Unlike music, the art of composition in the novel is hampered, after all, by real life.

Chapter xi
Rio de Janeiro, 1881: The Sentimental

Once upon a time – Brás Cubas tells the reader, in a digression, apparently for no reason – he was thrown from his mule, and was saved by a muleteer who ran up, grabbed the reins, and calmed the animal. In his emotion following his near-death experience, Brás thought he would give the muleteer three of the five gold coins he was carrying. But as he went over to his moneybags, he decided that two coins would be sufficient.

Maybe even one.

Finally, he gave him just a silver cruzado. As he left, he looked back: 'the muleteer was bowing deeply to me as an obvious sign of contentment.' This caused a worry in Brás's soul: 'maybe I'd paid him too much.' He felt in his waistcoat and found some copper coins. These, he thought, were what he should have given the muleteer. 'I called myself prodigal. I added the cruzado to my past dissipations. I felt (why not come right out with it?), I felt remorse.'

There is an acute diminuendo in this episode of the muleteer – from the character's impulse to prodigal generosity to his remorse at his prodigality, a remorse at dissipation, which is in fact a new way of describing his miserliness. And it is also part of Machado de Assis's technique to make this episode, which seems to be a digression, part of the narrative. It is progressive, and digressive, at the same time.

Like Laurence Sterne, Machado de Assis wrote a novel musically: which is to say, he wrote it in the form of a theme subjected to minute variations. In *The Posthumous Memoirs of Brás Cubas*, the digressions are often smuggled allegories, they are steeped in the story's thematics – they are clues as to how to read the sections which do not seem like digressions at all.

One romantic cliché is that man is noble, that his emotions are grand and beautiful. Instead, unimpressed, Machado de Assis shows that this is not true.

That is the point of the musical novel. Through its tricksy arrangement, where one episode cancels out another, the more true a novel will be. It will resemble the ironic, imperfect form of real life.

There is therefore a relationship between novelists who try to write musically, who write ironically, like a collage – with sections juxtaposed intensively and intently, so that an allegro motif sits beside an andante motif – and their subject matter, which is often a variation on sentimentality and lyricism. Through their technique of juxtaposition, the lyrical can be made to look comic, can be made to seem unnaturally absolute. The lyrical, in the musical novel, is revealed to be a mistake.

And so I like the fact that the same misunderstanding was made as with Laurence Sterne (and as would be made with Leo Tolstoy and Anton Chekhov). Poor Machado de Assis suffered the same indignity: an anthology was made of his grand thoughts, which were not grand thoughts at all, but fictional and comic instead.

There are some motifs which can be planned. Others just turn up, when considering real life. A motif I did not expect, when I began this book, is the theme of anthologies.

In the memoirs of Brás Cubas, Machado de Assis, in Rio de Janeiro, gathers together a variety of forms which seem hopelessly outdated – old-fashioned rhetorical forms: the anecdote, the vignette, the apologue, the caricature, the puzzle, the portrait, the preface. They are forms of nineteenth-century public address – pompous, ungainly. Yes, Machado de Assis loved using second-class novelistic material. But this does not mean that they signify the second-class. Instead, Machado was interested in turning forms which seemed outdated into live, fizzy instruments.

Dazzlingly, Machado de Assis arranges his drab parts.

The reason for this variety – this digressive, intrusive, parodic voice – is related to the reason why Flaubert invented an opposite kind of voice, a voice which was as impersonal as possible, as fluent and reserved. Both styles – with their very different inflections – derive from a contempt for ideas, for the human wish to institute generalities.

And this also shows how difficult it is to equate moral categories with aesthetic ones. Although Flaubert's style is characterised by what looks like reticence, this is not the same as humility. And while Machado de Assis's exhibitionist techniques, his accelerated structures, seem egotistical, they are really expressions of shyness. They are wary of pride.

His talent was for showing the ironic impurity of grandiose feelings. It was an attack on the sentimental, the romantic, the serious.

BOOK 7

The Fluke

But maybe I need to return to Laurence Sterne, and his formal inventions. I need to be more detailed about digression.

With his technique of multiple digression, Sterne invented a novel which seemed formless, but which in fact was musical with thematics. Long before André Gide's novel *The Counterfeiters*, it resolved contradictory elements. It managed to be both artless and artful at the same time. And Sterne was proud of this invention. So, towards the middle of the book, in the sixth volume, Tristram decided to give some sketches of the narrative line of his book.

Tristram draws his book

I am now beginning to get fairly into my work; and by the help of a vegitable diet, with a few of the cold seeds, I make no doubt but that I shall be able to go on with my uncle Toby's story, and my own, in a tolerable straight line. Now,

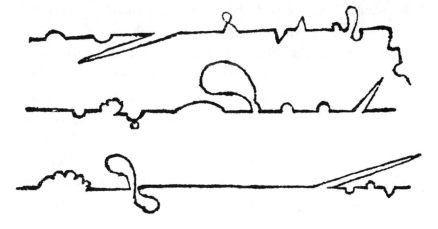

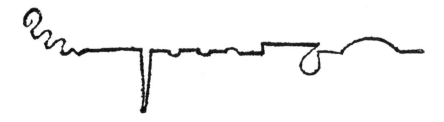

These were the four lines I moved in through my first, second, third, and fourth volumes. – In the fifth volume I have been very good, – the precise line I have described in it being this:

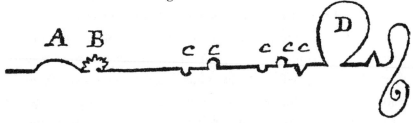

These diagrams were a new aspect of Sterne's playfulness. They were there to point to the novel's musical innovations of form (because what else is that at the end of the final line, but a treble clef?). They were a personal homage to his form based on digression.

Superficially, these diagrams represent a frank admission that Sterne's novel is formless, a squiggle. In fact, for the delighted reader, they are a joke at the expense of more conventional readers, who equate linearity with form. They are there to assert that Sterne's idea of form is something else entirely.

I am not sure that *digression* is the right word to use, when thinking about what Sterne did to the telling of a story. Digression implies that a central thread exists, from which the novelist diverges. But with these wonky lines, Sterne was saying something else. The lines are all drawn in one go, however wonky they are. The seemingly extra, redundant overmatter which Tristram gives his reader is not superfluous, but is exactly what the reader is meant to be reading. 'In a word', commented Tristram at one point, 'my work is digressive, and it is progressive too, – and at the same time.' As Nietzsche noted, Sterne's style is an '"endless melody"' – 'His digressions are at the same time continuations and further developments of the story; his aphorisms are at the same time an expression of an attitude of irony towards all sententiousness, his antipathy to seriousness is united with a tendency to be unable to regard anything merely superficially.' Tristram's chat was careful, it was thematically precise.

A digression can be anything. It can be an explanation, a change of subject, a clarification, a memory, a relevant joke. The subject, however, is always the same: the subject is Tristram, and his galloping hobbyhorses.

Sterne's subject is digression. Therefore, in the end, no digression can digress from the subject: in Sterne's novel, digression becomes impossible.

Chapter ii
London, 2007: Not a Digression

At this point, I could carry on in two directions. From these diagrams, it would be possible to talk about other pictures and pictorial games in Sterne's novel *Tristram Shandy*. It would be possible, for instance, to mention the flourish which Corporal Trim makes, with his stick, in the air, to demonstrate the freedom of a bachelor:

But I need to wait a while: I need to stay with digression. For digression is not just a technical quirk. No technique is only a quirk. Sterne discovered digression as a value. It was also about real life. The essence of digression, as for Sterne, is that it allowed a more precise description of real life: it became an instrument of ironisation.

Yes, the diagrams will have to wait a while.

Digression, for Sterne, was a feature of real life. Everyone, in Sterne's vision, is evasive, unsure of what was meaningful in a life, and what was meaningless. A life's plot so often escaped the person who was living it. What was a true cause, and what was an imaginary one? That is one question which Sterne's digressions allowed to be asked.

Chapter iii
Calais to Paris, 1768: A Short Sentimental Journey (I)

As recorded in Laurence Sterne's second and final novel, *A Sentimental Journey Through France and Italy*, published in London in 1768, an English parson called Yorick, in the eighteenth century, goes on a trip to the continent.

The title, however, is slightly misleading, since Yorick never makes it to Italy and, to be honest, does not get very far through France. The real plot of this journey is not travel, but sex: for Yorick is far more alive to the possibilities of sexual tourism than he is to the possibilities of cultural tourism. The plot, therefore, does not provide the reader with examples of Christian generosity and altruism, as Yorick thinks, or wants the reader to think: this plot, instead, is all about girls.

Sterne's digressions set up surfaces which are constantly leaking what they are trying to hide. They are deliberately imperfect machines.

And this has disturbed some people.

In 1782, fourteen years after his death, an anthology was published in London called *The Beauties of Sterne*. Its full title, as laid out on the dramatic title page, was *The Beauties of Sterne Including All his Pathetic Tales, and Most Distinguished Observations on Life Selected for the Heart of Sensibility*. And I dislike this title. It is much too serious and sickly for the selected works of the comic and mischievous Laurence Sterne.

The reason why the title page was problematic is also the reason why the whole anthology was problematic.

The writer of the 'Preface' to *The Beauties of Sterne* expressed sadness that the '*chaste* lovers of literature' had been 'deprived' of the possible 'pleasure and instruction' to be derived from the works of Laurence Sterne – since they could not risk encountering the 'obscenity which taints the writings of Sterne': 'his *Sentimental Journey*, in some degree, escaped the general censure; though that is not entirely free of the fault complained of'. The purpose of *The Beauties of Sterne* was therefore to give the reader an expurgated version of the works of Laurence Sterne. But this is not an easy task, to expurgate the work of Laurence Sterne – because it is not easy, turning an unserious novel into a serious extract.

The second extract chosen by the editor of *The Beauties of Sterne* was titled 'The Pulse' – a chapter title from *Sentimental Journey*.

Asking for directions in Paris

Hail ye small sweet courtesies of life, for smooth do ye make the road of it! like grace and beauty which beget inclinations to love at first sight; 'tis ye who open this door and let the stranger in.

– Pray, Madame, said I, have the goodness to tell me which way I must turn to go to the Opera comique: – Most willingly, Monsieur, said she, laying aside her work –

I had given a cast with my eye into half a dozen shops as I came along in search of a face not likely to be disordered by such an interruption; till at last, this hitting my fancy, I had walked in.

The problem, of course, is that there is a sexual subtext to this passage. It is not, as the anthologist wishes, about the innocence of love at first sight. No, as Craig Raine once mischievously and precisely taught me, this novel is all about knowing which girl to pick up.

Sentimental Journey was not a difficult novel. It was an unambiguous novel about ambiguity – a story of sexual tourism where the narrator pretended that it was a story about morality. All the joy of the writing was in this disjunction – between what seemed important, and what was actually important. It was not a story about the 'small sweet courtesies of life'. It was about chat-up lines, which 'open this door and let the stranger in'.

Sterne was exploiting the fact that sexual vocabulary does not quite exist; it mimes the ordinary vocabulary of sociability. A person can talk about sex while pretending to talk about niceness. A person can talk about sex without ever mentioning sex: the point of flirting, its utilitarian benefit, is that it allows for deniability.

Sterne's novel was ambiguous, a double thing. His great novelistic talent was for the implicit. Without saying everything, he says everything.

The author of *The Beauties of Sterne*, for instance, wanted to include two episodes concerning Yorick's encounter with a monk. But these upend him, also.

Early on in his journey, in Calais, Yorick meets a French monk. But he is not impressed, John Bullishly, by the mendicant Christian. He is stubborn and careful with his money, in this Popish country.

Yorick, however, then has a problem, which is sex. Having just met a woman he likes, Yorick sees the monk again. First he sees him in conversation with the woman he is after, and is suddenly struck by the worry that the monk is informing on him, and telling her about his selfishness. Then, out walking with the woman, Yorick sees the monk for a third time.

Suddenly, because he is attracted to this woman, Yorick also feels generous to the monk. His generosity, of course, is purely selfish, and self-interested – designed to placate the monk and impress the woman. But Yorick is not to be deterred by such moral squeamishness. Theatrically, he gives the monk his snuff-box, as a present, apologising for having used him unkindly before. 'The poor man blush'd as red as scarlet. Mon Dieu! said he, pressing his hands together – you never used me unkindly. – I should think, said the lady, he is not likely. I blush'd in my turn; but from what movements, I leave to the few who feel to analyse.'

Sterne (and possibly Yorick) is enjoying the fact that we have to use a physical vocabulary for non-physical things. This creates happy ambiguities – like Yorick's 'movements', which are the stirring of a penis, much more than they are the stirring of a generous soul.

The editor of *The Beauties of Sterne* therefore had a lot of work to do in order to make the passage concerning Yorick and the monk sound moral, and not obscene. His two techniques were the eternal ones of subtraction and addition. He cut the intervening material between the two episodes of the monk, so that the woman is hardly mentioned. Thus the sexual motive for the moment of spiritual good is deleted; the reader is left with a story which demonstrates the sudden conversion of a soul to moral probity, from moral stubbornness. And he added a sermon. The next extract chosen from the works of Laurence Sterne was from Sterne's sermon on 'Fellow-Feeling', which praised, hopefully, 'a certain generosity and tenderness of nature which disposes us for compassion, abstracted from all considerations of self'.

This is how the anthologist wanted his readers to read the episode of the monk, and it is not a correct way. For the novel contradicts the sermon, the novel knows more than the sermon: it knows that it is rarely possible to abstract all considerations of self.

The anthologist was a romantic: he was sentimental. Whereas, like Machado de Assis, Sterne was an analyst of the sentimental, he was not sentimental himself.

Chapter iv
1861, Trieste: Europiccola

As soon as Sterne's technique is made more precise, as soon as the ironic, careful precision of his digressions and formal games, rooted in real life, is understood, then it becomes more possible to see his various descendants. His tradition of geeks and oddballs emerges from the darkness, like a Polaroid. There is Denis Diderot, and Machado de Assis. But there is also another odd person: Italo Svevo.

Italo Svevo was a quiet family man who was not really called Italo Svevo: his real name was Ettore Schmitz. But his pen name was Italo Svevo. In 1861 Ettore, or Italo, was born in Trieste.

But Trieste was not quite a simple thing either. For the same reason that Svevo's name was complicated, Trieste was complicated. Both of them were simultaneously Italian and Austro-Hungarian. That is why Schmitz invented his pen name – to be true to the dual allegiance of his city, its Italianate status in the Austro-Hungarian Empire.

Schmitz, or Svevo, was also Jewish. But his Jewishness was not, perhaps, so important as his city. '"It isn't race which makes a Jew," said Svevo sadly, "it's life!"' (Just as Franz Kafka wrote in his diary: 'What do I have in common with the Jews? I don't even have anything in common with myself.')

James Joyce's name for this city, which he arrived in as an English language teacher in 1904, was Europiccola. And this is lovely, but is not a name which is unique to Trieste. Europiccola is everywhere. It is the same place as Bohumil Hrabal's Delighted States.

Schmitz, then, was an Austro-Hungarian Italian, who worked in the submarine paint industry. Italo Svevo was a novelist.

In 1892, Svevo published a novel, *Una Vita*. He published another novel, *Senilità*, in 1898. These were coolly received by the critics, if received at all.

And then, since his business often took him to England, in 1906 Svevo began English lessons with James Joyce, who was finishing a book of short stories called *Dubliners*. Joyce's main teaching method was to ask his pupils to make descriptions. One pupil, Boris Furlan, remembered being asked to describe an oil lamp. Furlan tried, and failed. His teacher took over, and with what Furlan called 'descriptive lust', showed him how to do it.

And this method of language teaching is the same, perhaps deliberately, as the way Flaubert taught his protégé, Guy de Maupassant, how to write: Flaubert would send him out and order him to describe a grocer or a concierge or a cab-rank '"in such a way that I shan't confuse them with any other grocer or any other concierge; and you must make me see, with a single word, in what way one cab-horse is totally unlike fifty others that go before and after it."'

Svevo's task was even harder. He had to describe his teacher. This was both an exercise in English, because Schmitz's grasp of English was shaky at best, and an exercise in novelistic technique, the art of character in prose.

Mr James Joyce described by his faithful pupil Ettore Schmitz

When I see him walking on the streets I always think that he is enjoying leisure a full leisure. Nobody is awaiting him and he does not want to reach an aim or to meet anybody. No! He walks in order to be left to himself. He does also not walk for health. He walks because he is not stopped by anything. I imagine that if he would find his way barred by a high and big wall he would not be shocked at the least. He would change direction and if the new direction would also prove not to be clear he would change it again and walk on his hands shaken only by the natural movement of the whole body, his legs working without any effort to lengthen or to fasten his steps. No!

In 1919, over twenty years after his previous novel, and presumably having improved his English, Svevo began what was to be his final novel, *La Coscienza di Zeno* (*Zeno's Conscience*), which was published at the end of May 1923 (by which time Joyce had moved from Trieste to Paris). Again, its reception was cool.

The mechanics of what then happened were a miniature reproduction of what had happened a year earlier with the publication of James Joyce's *Ulysses*. It received its first fame, and first serious criticism, in another language – French – in Paris, through a campaign organised by Valery Larbaud, and facilitated by Adrienne Monnier.

In November 1925, happy at his burgeoning success, Svevo began to write his last work, an unfinished novella, *Corto Viaggio Sentimentale* (*Short Sentimental Journey*), about a man on a train trip from Milan to Trieste. On 1 February 1926 Monnier's magazine, *Le Navire d'Argent*, published a eulogistic essay on Svevo, along with 40 pages of translation, including the finale of Svevo's second novel *Senilità*, and the opening of *La Coscienza di Zeno*, with its first chapter, 'Il fumo' – 'Smoke'.

And Svevo became slightly famous.

But, in a way that sees biography collusive with literature, just as Svevo was experiencing success and confidently writing his *Short Sentimental Journey*, his life was ended prematurely, in a car accident. His biography became a story of defeat.

Chapter v
Trieste, 1925: A Short Sentimental Journey (II)

Short Sentimental Journey is about a man called Signor Aghios, a bourgeois family man and businessman, returning from Milan to Trieste on the train.

Like Sterne, Svevo was in love with characters who were clever at enjoying their own repression. In this curtailed sentimental journey, Svevo lavished attention on people who are adept at contradiction.

At the opening of Svevo's *Short Sentimental Journey*, Signor Aghios is at the Milan train station. And Signor Aghios is a man of complication and contradiction. The acuity of Svevo's style is in the psychology. It is in the way sentences end up disrupting each other, as they process past, in succession. Everything seems amiable, digressive, unimportant: whereas everything, in fact, is pointed and precise.

So that there comes a moment when Signor Aghios, unsettled without his wife, requires a porter, since he cannot find his train.

But no – since Svevo was a friend of James Joyce, I will not call him Signor Aghios; nor will I call his wife Signora Aghios. In my paraphrase, derived from Beryl de Zoete's more authoritative version, this couple can be borrowed from *Ulysses*, and become Mr and Mrs Leopold Bloom.

Because characters are eternal.

After all, I speak no Italian. But I can, on the other hand, speak bad English. I can be true to the dullness of Svevo's Italian – with its corporate pompousness, its fussiness, its lapses into cliché – at the same time as the acuity of his style.

Bloom, lost in the station, sees a porter: 'He gave him the little suitcase which he could just as easily have carried himself and asked about the train. He felt the need to excuse himself: "It's light, but it's heavy for me because I'm old."'

Svevo sets up a miniature situation. Then he allows the thoughts to form a cartoon bubble above it.

'The porter, a neat fat man, smiled and mumbled something which Mr Bloom did not understand. It was good that he smiled and Mr Bloom, with goodwill and at a swift pace, followed his friend who, with the small suitcase in his hand, ran in front of him. He followed him and already loved him. What a beautiful invention tips were!' And this is where Svevo begins the baroque psychological and moral ramifications which he helplessly, deftly describes.

A theory of tipping

Especially small ones, which do no one any harm. For he was quite miserly, since if you gave everything away in one fell swoop, the pleasure was all too brief and left one paralysed for a long time. His wife was more generous and when she found a need which could not be alleviated except by a substantial sum, she gave it. But it was a way of disposing of other people's possessions, since to other people in need one could then say: 'I've already disposed of what was rightfully yours.' Only on rare occasions did he dip deep into his pockets, because his wife wanted him to, just as he did many other things when she wanted him to do them.

Svevo's subject, as always, is pleasure. More precisely, it is the contradictory nature of pleasure.

I need to backtrack.

Chapter vi
Trieste, 1923: Pleasure

The plot of Svevo's third and most successful novel, *Zeno's Conscience*, was Zeno's description of a failed course of psychoanalysis: in the process of describing this, Zeno also described his efforts to give up smoking, his father's death, his marriage to the least pretty of three sisters, his mistress, and his business affairs.

But these subjects were not the subjects of Svevo's novel, even if they were the subject of Zeno's conscience, and consciousness. The subject was instead the contradictions of feeling: this novel was also a sentimental journey.

It may seem formless, but in fact it possesses a delicate structure.

And therefore I like the fact that in 1932, after Svevo's death, Joyce came up with this dust jacket idea for Svevo's novel in English translation, ridiculing the philistine love of practical moral purpose – which Georges Perec would still be satirising many years later – at the expense of aesthetics:

a coloured picture by a Royal Academician representing two young ladies, one fair and the other dark but both distinctly nicelooking, seated in a graceful though of course not unbecoming posture at a table on which the book stands upright, with title visible and underneath the picture three lines of simple dialogue, for example:
   Ethel: Does Cyril spend too much on cigarettes?
   Doris: Far too much.
   Ethel: So did Percy (points) – till I gave him Z E N O .

The first chapter of Zeno's novel, called 'Smoke', is a short one, but it functions like an overture. The motifs of Zeno's smoking habit, the reader gradually discovers, are motifs of his life in general. Everything is out of date, and melancholy. Zeno's preferred brand of cigarettes, for instance, has been discontinued. His life is marked by oblivion, forgetfulness: the kids he once smoked with when very young have now disappeared in his memory: 'Two pairs of short socks that stand erect because there were then bodies inside them, which time has erased.' (Just as Nabokov, ten years later, having arrived in Paris to read a story about – or memoir of – his French governess, would admit that 'her portrait, or rather certain details of her portrait, seem to me to be lost forever'. And just as one of Chekhov's characters, Marya, possesses a photograph of her mother of which, and of whom, only the eyebrows remain.)

Zeno's first chapter is the history of Zeno's smoking. But, since Zeno wants to give up smoking, it means that it is also the history of his decisions to give smoking up. Pleasure is complicated, it is comically voracious and contradictory: this is one of Svevo's, and Zeno's, discoveries. There is a pleasure in the decision to have no more pleasure – and there is also a pleasure in breaking that decision once more. Pleasure is migratory. So that Zeno is acute enough to notice how useful cigarettes are to him: 'If I had stopped smoking, would I have become the strong, ideal man I expected to be? Perhaps it was this suspicion that bound me to my habit, for it is comfortable to live in the belief that you are great, though your greatness is latent.' (Just as one of Bohumil Hrabal's narrators explains that 'a fortune teller once read my cards and said that if it wasn't for a tiny black cloud hanging over me I could do great things and not only for my country but for all mankind'.) In smoking, as in life, Svevo's Zeno takes his pleasure where he can. He can make do with anything.

And now, after the pleasure involved in the complications of smoking, Svevo had discovered the contradictory feelings involved in the act of tipping, of donating – like Machado de Assis's Brás Cubas, or Edouard Dujardin's Daniel Prince. Or Sterne's Parson Yorick, in Calais.

Signor Aghios, aka Mr Bloom, had a method: 'he began by paying less than the going rate. Normally the other person did not protest, but remained looking, amazed, at the little coin which he was holding in his open hand. Then Mr Bloom put small coins one after the other into this hand, until the hand closed and a smile appeared on the porter's face. And so this smile, which was slow to appear, was stamped all the more in Mr Bloom's memory and softened his road for miles. Sometimes, before he had reached the point of giving the whole tip, the porter gave up and walked away with a blunt word. Mr Bloom then walked away with the tip in his hand, but could nevertheless pronounce himself completely satisfied because he had fallen out with an enemy, but not with a stranger.' This is not, obviously, a description of generosity: it is a description of how much pleasure might be self-ishly derived from generosity.

Svevo's meandering, amiable style is also a rigorous dissection of sentimentality: it is cruel to the noble animal. That is why Svevo could also come up with a laughable description of a man in love.

Chapter vii
Milan, 1923: A Short Definition of Love

Finally, Mr Bloom gets onto his train. His wife, who has come back to the platform partly to see him off, partly to remind him to look in on a jeweller's in Venice, and partly – since he cannot be trusted – to check that he still has a large amount of money in his inside breast pocket, waves him goodbye: 'And, advancing into his solitude, looking at this slender figure, he wanted to have one precise and sincere thought and he thought: "The further I go away from her the more I love her". Then he felt his conscience at peace. For a moment, in a word, he found himself at one with human and divine law, for he, sincerely, could truthfully state that he loved his own wife.'

But this is not the end of the story's beginning. The end is sadder. Happy at his new congruence with human and divine law, happy at his romanticism, Mr Bloom looks back at his wife again:

Was he seeing right? His wife had put her hand to her breast with an exaggerated gesture. It was not possible that she, such a well-balanced person, would have wanted to display to strangers an exaggerated grief at being left on her own. And yet it seemed that this grand gesture was accompanied by a scream.

Italo Svevo with his wife, Livia, courtesy of Museo Sveviano, Trieste

Italo Svevo with his wife, Livia, courtesy of Museo Sveviano, Trieste

Then, when he could no longer see her, he had a moment of inspiration. With that gesture she wanted to give him a final reminder to look after the money he had in his breast-pocket. Much better! He smiled and, obediently, to lessen the remorse he felt at loving his wife more now that he could not see her, patted with great energy his breast pocket. The wallet, stuffed with notes, was still there.

That is how the start of this sentimental journey finishes – with a man consoling himself for the fact that the less he sees his wife, the more he can happily love her. Like Laurence Sterne's radical description of tourism, Svevo's journey is not, in the end, sentimental at all.

Chapter viii
Paris, 1931: Anachronism

Like life, literature is lived forwards, and understood backwards. A tradition can develop anywhere. It is unpredictable. The same novel can be a reference point for more than one tradition.

Honoré de Balzac's novel *La Peau de Chagrin* (*The Wild Ass's Skin*) is about how a melancholy young man, Raphaël de Valentin, having decided to throw himself into the Seine, goes into a curiosity shop on the river bank. He is shown a piece of ass's skin, with Sanskrit lettering on the hide, which informs the reader that whoever owns the skin will have all his wishes fulfilled, but that his life will decrease for every wish he asks for.

Obviously, he buys this magic skin. And so all of Raphaël's wishes come true, but his life becomes unlivable.

The theme of this novel is a simplification: life is corrupted precisely by what makes it interesting: people are trapped by the limitlessness of their own freedom. The novel is an allegory.

When Balzac's novel was first published, in Paris, in 1831,

Corporal Trim's flourish was reproduced as the epigraph to the novel. Oddly, however, it was laid on its side, and without the final flourish, so that it more resembled Sterne's narrative diagrams.

(Although this resemblance would only have been fortuitous, if Balzac was reading Sterne in French translation: since the French translation, for unknown reasons, cut all of Tristram's narrative diagrams.)

I have a theory about Balzac's epigraph.

It is obviously possible that Balzac used Trim's flourish as a way of signalling that *Tristram Shandy* was a novel on a similar theme to his own – a novel of freedom and compulsion. But I think that it is also, and more importantly, a literary advertisement. It is an assertion on Balzac's part, this author of 'la grrrrrande Comédie Humaine', that he belongs to Sterne's tradition in the art of the novel.

And this may seem a surprise – that Balzac, the most famous nineteenth-century realist, whose technique was all to do with exhaustive detail, should see himself as part of Sterne's family. But I am not sure that this contradiction really exists – not when Sterne's novel was so carefully progressive and digressive at the same time, so content to flip between length and concision.

Good novelists may well be bad historians. Instead of attending to the historical specifics, they may well attend to what can be generalised in previous novels, and reused. They steal techniques which may have been adapted for historically specific and now irrelevant reasons.

One word for this is anachronism: but another word is timelessness.

Chapter ix
Piedmont, 1795: The Side Effect

And that is the lesson of the final story in this odd series: the story of Xavier de Maistre.

Born in Chambéry, Savoy, in 1763, Xavier de Maistre – whose parents were French – served in the Sardinian Army when Savoy was expatriated to France in 1792. Arrested for duelling, he was sentenced to remain in his room for forty-two days. As a result, he wrote *Voyage autour de ma chambre* (*A Journey Around My Room*) which was finally published in 1795.

The nineteenth-century French critic Sainte-Beuve, who was a tetchy friend of Gustave Flaubert, wrote an admiring essay on de Maistre, in which he admitted that he was intrigued by de Maistre's *manière de confession d'ailleurs*, his style of confession by other means. According to Sainte-Beuve, de Maistre had managed to invent a novelistic form which told a personal story – a doomed romantic love affair – but in which the personal story only seemed to emerge by chance.

It was a masterpiece of digression.

Xavier de Maistre opened his short novel with a simple announcement: 'I have undertaken and completed a forty-two-day journey around my room. The interesting observations I have made, and the continual pleasure I experienced en route, filled me with the desire to publish it . . .' It was not really a novel at all, he was implying. It was much too factual for that. And yet, obviously, it had to be a novel, it had to be a comedy, since no journey around a room can last for forty-two days.

De Maistre's journey begins at the armchair, moves on to the bed – via the pictures on the walls – mentions his dog in passing, before he walks over to the desk, and ends by the fire. In one sense, that is the plot of his short novel. But the real story is about a love affair, which may well be a doomed love affair, with a woman called Madame de Hautcastel. So that just as in Georges Perec a description of a room can become a description of a life, so in de Maistre a description of a dried rosebud can fade into a description of a romance: 'it's a carnival flower from last year. I myself went to pluck it from the greenhouses of the Valentino, and in the evening, one hour before the ball, full of hope and in a state of agreeable turmoil, I went to present it to Mme de Hautcastel.'

But she ignores the rose, just as she ignores the lover who brought it to her. She is more interested in checking her carnival outfit in the mirror.

It is very difficult – distinguishing anachronism from timelessness.

In one way, de Maistre's novel is happily eighteenth-century. It is a neat variation on Laurence Sterne's technique. But it also feels in some way more contemporary, more recent. Like these domestic sentences: 'Once you've left my armchair, walking towards the north, you come into view of my bed, which is placed at the far end of my room: it's a most agreeable sight. It is situated in the most pleasant spot imaginable: the first rays of the sun come to disport themselves on my bed curtains. – I can see them, on fine summer days, advancing along the white wall as the sun slowly rises: the elm trees outside my window break up these rays in a thousand different ways, and make them sway on my pink and white bed, which sheds the charming hue of their reflections on every side.'

I am not sure how many descriptions of a bed and, especially, a bedspread there had been in previous novels. It has the effect of making de Maistre sound daringly avant-garde, since it makes him sound like James Joyce, or Gustave Flaubert. But this modernity is obviously unintended.

De Maistre's central joke is at the expense of more grandiose travel narratives, to the wilds of Patagonia. The details of the bedspread are therefore unintentionally avant-garde in their domestication, their humdrum nature. They are merely products of his irony.

Yes, his pink and white bedspread, which I like so much, is a side effect.

BOOK 8

But Sterne's diagrams veer in another direction as well.

At Laurence Sterne's request, the artist William Hogarth made two frontispieces for Sterne's novel *Tristram Shandy* – one of Corporal James Trim reading a sermon, and another of Tristram's christening. Partly, Sterne made this request because he was impressed by the fact that Hogarth was a celebrity. Sterne admired celebrity. He could stand a lot of celebrity. But there was also a less unlikeable reason: both Hogarth and Sterne shared a taste for curviness.

Hogarth's book of aesthetics, *The Analysis of Beauty*, was published in London in 1753. Its new idea in aesthetic theory was the curvy Line of Beauty:

This line, according to Hogarth, was the most aesthetically pleasing form of a line. It was digressive, and its pleasure was the pleasure of pursuit. Hogarth's treatise was a book in praise of curls and loops.

But I think that, as well as being an ally in praise of digression, Hogarth was important to Sterne for another reason.

Although his paintings and engravings are crammed with so much urban detail, Hogarth was also famous for his economy: he was famous for his caricatures. With three lines, he could achieve the same result as with three hundred. Like Sterne, he was not overly impressed with his chosen medium.

Chapter ii
London, 1759: Economy!

'Imagine to yourself', writes Tristram, 'a little squat, uncourtly figure of a Doctor *Slop*, of about four feet and a half perpendicular height, with a breadth of back, and a sesquipedality of belly, which might have done honour to a serjeant in the horse-guards.

'Such were the outlines of Dr Slop's figure, which – if you have read Hogarth's analysis of beauty, and if you have not, I wish you would; — you must know, may as certainly be caricatured, and conveyed to the mind by three strokes as three hundred.'

Like Hogarth, Sterne was bored by the idea that a representation should pretend to be descriptively exhaustive. He was interested in the truth of shortcuts. And the proof of this, the quiet hint, is that Dr Slop looks like a 'serjeant'.

According to a contemporary biographer, Hogarth used to enjoy the fact that the signs needed to represent a person are much fewer than they might think. In fact, he used to argue, a Sergeant with a pike, going into an alehouse with his dog, could be represented simply by three straight lines:

Hogarth boafted that he could draw a Serjeant with his pike, going into an alehoufe, and his Dog following him, with only three ftrokes ;—which he executed thus:

A. The perfpeétive line of the door.
B. The end of the Serjeant's pike, who is gone in.
C. The end of the Dog's tail, who is following him.
There are fimilar whims of the *Caracci.*

This is also a portrait of Dr Slop.

The art of caricature is the same as the art of character. This is what Sterne wanted to prove. Just as Chekhov would prove, as shown in the following volume, that there is no structural difference between the short story and the novel, there is also no structural difference between a sketch and a more detailed description. Length is an optional extra.

(And so, two hundred years later, Françoise Gilot observed the way Picasso arrived at his 1946 *Woman Eating Sea Urchins.* 'The *Woman Eating Sea Urchins* was begun one afternoon in a realistic manner. Everything about the portrait was a recognisable representation of the woman as we knew her: pug nose, corkscrew curls, man's cap, and the dirty apron in which she enveloped herself. Then, when it was finished, each day Pablo eliminated a few more naturalistic details until there remained only a very simplified form, almost vertical, with just the plate of sea urchins in the middle to remind one of what she looked like.')

In his essay 'The Two Chekhovs', written in 1914, the Soviet poet Vladimir Mayakovsky argued that in Chekhov's style 'the urgent cry of the future is felt: "economy!"' But Sterne was already the future, in 1759. Even at 600 pages, he was economical.

The art of representation is much more paradoxical, thought Sterne, than people seemed to think. It was both hospitable to dense detail, and also to bare sketches. The central aesthetic principle – of Sterne's chapters, and his descriptions, and his pictures – is that something can be both lavish and economical (progressive, and digressive) at the same time. A novel can both frankly admit its artificiality, and still be realistic.

Like Tristram's attempt to describe Corporal Trim attempting to describe the life of the bachelor:

Whilst a man is free, – cried the corporal, giving a flourish with his stick thus –

A thousand of my father's most subtle syllogisms could not have said more for celibacy.

And this picture is playful. It is a nonchalant admission that it is far easier drawing a flourish than describing one. So Sterne, unembarrassed, draws one.

Another way of looking at Sterne's pictures is to turn the problem inside out, and compare it with an artist in a different medium: Pablo Picasso. Sterne included pictures and diagrams in a novel; Picasso included words in a picture.

Talking to the photographer Brassaï, Picasso said: 'I always aim for likeness. A painter has to observe nature, but must never confuse it with painting. It can be translated into painting only with signs.' In other words, there are no natural signs. A picture is no more real than a novel. No art work is ever the thing itself. It is always inflected by a style.

In Picasso's 1912–13 collage called *Bottle and Glass*, the bottle is outlined in charcoal. And this bottle is half full. We know it is half full because a tapering piece of newspaper, that has been cut out and pasted within the bottle's outline, fills half of the shape of the bottle.

A painter has to observe nature, but must never confuse it with painting. It can be translated into painting only with signs. The newspaper does not look like wine, but we read it as wine. The charcoal outline, which is unmistakably the outline of a bottle, means that we mentally abstract the newspaper print. So a piece of newspaper becomes the sign for wine. It is a metaphor.

'You do not invent a sign,' Picasso added, talking to Brassaï. 'You must aim hard at likeness to get to the sign.'

'The *papier collé* was really the important thing', Picasso told his wife, Françoise Gilot. 'The sheet of newspaper was never used in order to make a newspaper. It was used to become a bottle or something like that. It was never used literally but always as an element displaced from its habitual meaning into another meaning.' Like a metaphor, or a row of asterisks, the newspaper in Picasso's collage, with its printed words, did two things at once. It was there to show how much the eye could ignore and simplify in search of a realistic resemblance. It was a joke that confirmed the picture's irreducible style – and, simultaneously, its realistic precision.

It was economical.

In the same way, Sterne's pictures and diagrams are a way of confirming that everything, in the end, is just a sign. A novel is no more real than a picture. But they are simultaneously more playful, less clinical. They are wilful, comic ways of confirming his novel's attempt to be true to real life. They have made the discovery that, since nothing can be perfectly realistic, since it can never be the thing itself, there may well be shorter ways, or extra ways, of describing something accurately.

Chapter iv
Moscow, 1859: A Map

Sterne's first unexpected nineteenth-century descendant was Honoré de Balzac. And now I think it is possible to detect another, perhaps even more surprising one: Count Leo Tolstoy.

One of Tolstoy's earliest works was an unfinished translation – from French – of Sterne's novel *A Sentimental Journey*, which Tolstoy began in the 1850s. (Just as a translation of *Sentimental Journey* from English into French was a project begun by the young Gustave Flaubert, but which would only survive as a ghostly allusion in the title of his later, more celebrated novel: *Sentimental Education*.) And it is interesting that 'Having read Le Voyage Sentimental par Sterne,' according to his wife, Tolstoy 'once sat at the window, stirred and excited by his reading, and watched what was going on in the street. "There comes a baker: what sort of person is he, what is his life like? . . . And there is a carriage driving by: who may be inside,

where is he going, not thinking of anything in particular, and who lives in that house over there, what is its inside life? . . . How interesting it would be to describe these things and what an interesting book could be written on this."' Tolstoy, therefore, was not worried by Sterne's tricksiness: for Tolstoy, there seems to have been no contradiction between formal tricksiness and realism: that mistake still needed to be invented.

No, Tolstoy understood that unusual bits and pieces – a sketch of a battleground, for instance – could be both playful and realistic at the same time.

In Tolstoy's *Voina i Mir* (*War and Peace*) the battle of Borodino, which will mark the high point of Napoleon's campaign against Russia, is about to be fought. It marks the high point of the campaign, but arguably, argues Tolstoy, it also marks the low point, since this battle will be fought with such attrition, and lead Napoleon to make so many tactical mistakes, that it is also the beginning of the end for Napoleon.

This battle, therefore, as Tolstoy set it up, is ironic: it is all about mistakes.

As he arrives at this point in his story, Tolstoy digresses from the narrative, but does not digress from his theme: he embarks on a chapter which is an essay on mistakes, examining the question of why exactly the battle of Borodino was fought. 'There was not the least sense in it for either the French or the Russians.' For the Russians, it led to the destruction of Moscow; for the French, it led to the destruction of their army. No one would win. Tolstoy's mini-essay is therefore about the impossibility of making correct predictions. One definition of being human, in Tolstoy's opinion, is to be incapable of predicting the future. Even within the battle itself, the positions taken up by the armies were entirely different from their expected positions.

And then Tolstoy added: 'A rough outline of the plan of the intended battle and of the battle that actually took place is given.'

And suddenly, in the middle of all this text, a drawing appeared – by Tolstoy, from his research:

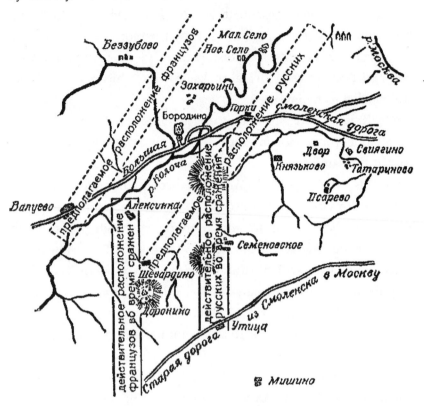

This map was a mess. Deliberately, it was a smudge: the two lines of the armies' intended positions were blurred by the two lines of their actual positions. This created a skew-whiff map, an angular line of beauty, a kink. It was a stark visual representation of the novel's central theme: how everyone, always, gets things wrong.

Chapter v
New York, 1942: Saul Steinberg and the Art of Writing

The novel is an artificial art form; but that does not mean its subject is not real life. That is what Sterne was intimating, with his novel

which contained drawings and diagrams. His art was the same as the opposing art of William Hogarth.

In the same way, when asked about the influence of Paul Klee on his art, Saul Steinberg replied that they both shared a 'Bauhausy philosophy of transforming writing into drawing . . .' Like Klee, he also once said, he used the line 'as a form of writing'.

Let's rehearse the early and international life of Saul Steinberg, from the ages of nought to twenty-eight.

Saul Steinberg was born in 1914, in Romania. In 1933, he moved to Milan, where he studied at the Architectural Faculty in the Reggio Politecnico. In 1940, trying to escape the Fascist anti-Jewish laws which had been passed from 1938, he tried to get a visa to the US. He succeeded as far as getting a visa to the Dominican Republic, via Lisbon; but in September 1940 he was sent back by the Portuguese to Italy. In November, his Romanian passport expired, thus rendering him stateless. Having hid in friends' apartments, and been arrested and interned between May and June 1941, Steinberg reached Lisbon again, via Barcelona. This time he was allowed to leave. In July he arrived in the Dominican Republic – and again tried to get a US visa. In May 1942 he was finally successful. He landed in Miami on 12 June 1942, and got on a bus for New York.

That was Steinberg's early life. But the art is more important. And Steinberg's idea of his artistry was that he was a writer: 'My idea of the artist, poet, painter, composer, etc, is the *novelist*.' Steinberg's art is characterised by an inversion, so that marks on flat paper are treated as real, whereas people and objects are unreal – they are just handwriting, calligraphy.

The real comparison is not with Klee, but Picasso. From Picasso, Steinberg learned that all signs are conventional: everything can be made to look like everything else: it just takes imagination. And so, in his 1961 drawing 'Erotica I', a number 5 has sex with a question mark, lusciously intertwined on a bed. The picture is both a joke, and seamy, pornographic. Or there is his 1954 'Graph Paper

Architecture' – where graph paper becomes a realistic portrait of a skyscraper, with its precise windows, simply with the drawn addition of an awning over its doorway onto the pavement. Or his 1954 drawing 'The Line', where a single line – which runs for 33 feet – is a bridge, a shop window, a horizon, a ceiling, a table edge, the meniscus of a swimming pool, a line of laundry, and then finally the line itself being drawn by a line-drawing of a hand.

Steinberg's art is an art of literalisation, where signs are literalised: this is why, unsurprisingly, one of his favourite stories was Nikolai Gogol's novella, *Nose*, where the impossible becomes realistic.

Steinberg was a novelist who happened not to write a novel. He tried to come up with economical ways of describing real life.

His art was an art of cropping.

Towards the end of his life, in 1989, Steinberg was working on photographs of European towns: Bucharest, Brest, Buzau, Moscow, Heidelberg, Lille, Avignon. But these were not ordinary photographs: in the first place, they were reproductions of antique postcards; and secondly, they were blown up. A portfolio of these postcards was put together by Steinberg with the title 'DOGS'. In each blown-up picture, each street scene, could be observed a random detail, a random dog. The dogs were not part of the subject. They were accidental.

And I like these dogs very much. Because this canine project was Steinberg's final version of the art of detail – his homage to the truth of the cropped, enlarged and artificial image. A truth which was first invented by Laurence Sterne.

Chapter vi
Dessau, 1925: Europiccola (III)

But my final curve is even cheekier. It is more of a joke in this tradition. This final line belongs to Paul Klee himself.

In 1925, Paul Klee opened his Bauhaus *Pedagogical Sketchbook* with a line:

An active line on a walk, moving freely, without goal. A walk for a walk's sake. The mobility agent is a point, shifting its position forward:

It was Hogarth's Line of Beauty, having a rest, on its side. But Klee then proceeded to draw Sterne's Trimian flourish:

The same line, circumscribing itself:

I am not sure if either of these lines was an allusion to Laurence Sterne, or even William Hogarth. But this final line, and its description – a line circumscribing itself – is a neat summary of Laurence Sterne, and his useful inventions in the international art of the novel.

BOOK 9

Hrabalovština

One way of becoming happier with the history of an art is to realise that every work, as an aesthetic value, is never quite irrelevant. At any point, it can become part of a new and miniature tradition. It can turn out to have been a move in a right direction. It can have side effects.

There is no need to be prescriptive when it comes to form, or style. There is no reason for there to be any limiting terms to the novel. Everything is up for grabs. My favourite definition of a novel is Henry Fielding's non-definition of his new prose form, which we now call the novel, his 'comic Epic-Poem in Prose' – two oxymorons cancelling each other out.

In this way, I can finish this volume on Laurence Sterne, and tradition, with a description of the Czech novelist Bohumil Hrabal. Like Sterne, Hrabal was a writer of hectic digression, with a thematic musical structure. Like Sterne, his writing was an ironisation of the sentimental, the lyrical, the romantic.

But I am not sure Laurence Sterne was important to him. His most important international influence was from another tradition entirely. It was James Joyce.

Techniques, after all, are diminutive, portable devices. They can therefore crop up in multiple places.

Chapter ii
Brno, 1914: Bohumil Hrabal Is Born

Bohumil Hrabal was born in 1914, in Brno, a town which was part of the Austro-Hungarian empire. By the time Hrabal was thirty, however, and had become a novelist, he had also become a citizen of a country called Czechoslovakia, which was then to be invaded by the Nazis, and which, following the Second World War, was about to become part of the Soviet Communist empire.

I can understand, therefore, why Milan Kundera simply calls this country Bohemia.

Although dates and places are not really very important, not in the history of the novel, they can still be useful as a quick code. They symbolise, in Hrabal's case, a sad problem.

When he grew up, and became a novelist, Bohumil Hrabal would have to think about Socialist Realism. And Hrabal was the opposite of Socialist Realism. He was the opposite of sentimentality.

Chapter iii
Moscow, Prague, Budapest, etc., 1917–89; A Short Definition of
Socialist Realism

Socialist Realism, in Vladimir Nabokov's summary, is another variant of romanticism: it is the ability to think up only sentimental novels.

A Socialist Realist story

The plot thickens and when the climax is reached and the villain is unmasked by the strong silent girl, we find out what we had perhaps suspected – that the man who was wrecking the factory is not the ugly little old workman with a trick of mispronouncing Marxist definitions, bless his little well-meaning soul, but the slick, easygoing fellow well versed in Marxian lore; and his dark secret is that his stepmother's cousin was the nephew of a capitalist.

Although Socialist Realism, as a term, sounds terse, and blunt with accuracy, it is much more romantic than its name suggests: its conventions are those of slushy fiction. It tries to sound like the future – but the conventions it aspires to are old-fashioned, flimsy and twee.

A break-up in the Soviet Union

Olga was silent.

'Ah,' cried Vladimir, 'Why can't you love me as I love you.'

'I love my country.'

'So do I,' he exclaimed.

'And there is something I love even more strongly,' Olga continued, disengaging herself from the young man's embrace.

'And that is?' he queried.

Olga let her limpid blue eyes rest on him, and answered quickly: 'It is the Party.'

The Czech novelist Josef Škvorecký, who emigrated from Communist Czechoslovakia to Canada, came up with a neat euphemism for a novelist who adheres to these conventions – 'a realist with an adjective attached'. And any novelist with an adjective attached is a conventional writer. Good novelists have nothing to do with slogans.

This is why dates and places are never so important, when trying to be clear about novels and their international histories. Socialist Realism, it's true, was a particular problem for novelists living in Communist countries in the twentieth century. But it is just a particular variant of a constant danger, whether in a socialist regime or not (because everywhere is everywhere).

This danger is sentimentality.

In Czech, there is a word for Hrabal's style. This word is *Hrabalovština*. *Hrabalovština* is a comic display of vocabulary, of headlong words and invented syntax – it is a system which is forever trying to put off its own demise. But Hrabal's own word for his style was *palavering*, and palavering is a much more useful and precise concept for this style, this new invention in the art of the novel. Palavering is an art, and it is committed to deferral, to a comic refusal to be polite, and stop talking. It is, according to Hrabal, 'my defence against politics, my policy in fact'. And this word policy is important. It shows how considered and meditated was Hrabal's apparently natural style. Because the truest poetry is also the most feigning. Against the direction and drive of ideas, Hrabal offers the more vulgar luxuries of digression, and of free association.

An example of Hrabalovština

Just like I come here to see you, young ladies, I used to go to church to see my beauties, well, not exactly to church, I'm not much of a churchgoer, but to a small shop next to the parish house, a tiny little place, where a man by the name of Altman sold second-hand sewing machines, dual-spring Victrolas from America, and Minimax fire extinguishers, and this Altman he had a sideline delivering beauties to pubs and bars all over the district, and the young ladies would sleep in Altman's back room, or when summer came they set up tents in the garden and the dean of the church would take his constitutional along the fence and those show-offs

But this makes me think something else.

No style is just a style: it is its subject matter as well. And the subject of Hrabal's palavering is complicated: in its delight and fun and lightness, it is an example of deliberate immaturity. This style is happy with naughtiness, with its whimsical lack of seriousness and gravity. The narrators of Hrabal's palavering, the exponents of *Hrabalovština*, are all grown-ups who have not grown up.

Once the reader gets used to this style, then it becomes possible to analyse various specimens of immaturity. The example I just quoted is the opening of Hrabal's novel in one unfinished sentence, which lasts for around a hundred pages – a serpentine, joky, scratchy sentence, an accordion of a sentence: *Dancing Lessons for the Advanced in Age*. The comedy here is all in the narrator's chutzpah, his cheeky obsession with sex and pleasure over the more questionable values of politics or religion.

(But even here, there is an inaccuracy. The history of translation is the history of mistakes. Hrabal's title in Czech is *Taneční hodiny pro starší a pokročilé*, which is more like 'Dancing Lessons for the Older and More Advanced'. And I prefer this more ambiguous, sadder title. Because there is no reason – that is what the little letter *a*, meaning *and*, is saying – that the older should be the same as the more advanced. Everyone is always immature, and inexperienced. Even the mature, and experienced.)

As well as religion and politics, however, there are more mundane examples of immaturity. There is also, for instance, the human animal's relationship with driving.

Hrabal's story 'The Driving Lesson' is narrated by a man called Hrabal, and describes a motorbike lesson. But it also describes something else. As they drive round Prague – Hrabal in front, his instructor perched on the back – Hrabal tells his instructor stories about his father, a man in love with machines. While Hrabal wobbles his way round the city, the pleasure of the story is in the palavering anecdotes which Hrabal tells – the crashes, the near misses, the hospital visits. Its title is a driving lesson, but its subject is the comedy of Hrabal's father's love of driving. It is a story about idealism. Even Hrabal's instructor is a romantic too. Charmed by the tales of Hrabal's father, he wafts round Prague with Hrabal at the controls, praising the danger, the romance of injuries and wounds.

There are dancing lessons, and driving lessons. And there are more varieties of lesson in Hrabal's stories. It is a theme which recurs, musically, throughout his fiction. His new brand of romanticism is the lesson. The lesson, for Hrabal, is the epitome of seriousness, and therefore the epitome of comedy (a lesson which Hrabal could well have learned from the lecturing characters of Laurence Sterne, with their tenacious theories). Because in Hrabal's stories, lessons are always given to people who cannot be taught, by people who have no authority to teach.

Everyone is always incorrigible, and immature. That is what *Hrabalovština* means.

Chapter v
Prague, 1930–32: A Golden Shower for Maria Weatherallová

Back in 1929, in Book 1, Adolf Hoffmeister visited James Joyce in Paris to ask permission to translate the *Anna Livia Plurabelle* section of *Finnegans Wake* into Czech. But it was not just *Finnegans Wake* which, because of Hoffmeister, made its way to Prague. Following Hoffmeister's visit to Paris, a translation of *Ulysses* came out in 1930, in three volumes – volumes 1 and 3 by Ladislav Vymětal, volume 2 by Jarmila Fastrová. A synopsis was published simultaneously, written by Zdeněk Vančura. And in 1932, Hoffmeister, with Maria Weatherallová and Vladimír Procházka, completed their version of *Anna Livia Plurabelle.*

The international history of the novel in Czech, therefore, was set up very nicely. And then Communism happened.

Nearly thirty years later, in 1959, a translation of Joyce's early book of short stories, *Dubliners*, was published in Prague by Zdeněk Urbánek. Its introduction, an essay on Joyce's writing, was not the normal translator's eulogy; instead, it was slightly more guarded. Its aim was obviously to try to placate the Socialist Realists, with their rather more limited and old-fashioned ideas of what a novel should be. According to Urbánek, therefore, Joyce's writing loitered too dangerously on the 'path of destructive experimentalism'.

And this depresses me. It is always the same objection: always, the romantics (who in this case were dressed up as Socialist Realists) want to believe that only real life can be realistic. Whereas the opposite is so often true. So often, tricksiness enables the novel to be true to real life. Truth is experimental. And it is precisely Joyce's experimental precision which Bohumil Hrabal loved, and which was not destructive.

I've proposed a grand progression of Sterne to Diderot, and then Machado de Assis. That is one form of a tradition. And now I have another progression – from Edouard Dujardin, to Joyce, and on to Bohumil Hrabal – as well. It is much more friendly, literary history – much more like a café than people normally think.

Or, in Hrabal's own idea, literary history is like a giant game of ping-pong, where the talented players 'hit smashes over the nets formed by the borders of States and nations'. And ping-pong is fine with me too. Why not both together? A café where everyone's playing ping-pong: that's my new definition of literary history. Zany, yes, and competitive, but with espresso.

Bohumil Hrabal spoke no English. But speaking English is no problem for the international history of the novel.

It is no problem, certainly, for the international motif of urine.

Towards the end of *Dancing Lessons for the Advanced in Age*, the narrator mentions how 'you should have seen what Olánek did when we wished him a happy fiftieth birthday and asked him how his health was holding up, right there in the main square he pulled out his member – he had ten beers in him at the time – and drenched the advertisement for Náchod Mills all the way to the accent over the *a* while the local notary public passed under the stream and wished us a pleasant day'. And I like to think that this tremendous achievement is an achievement for which Leopold Bloom has been practising – for in *Ulysses* we discover that Bloom's schoolboy arc of urine was unbeatable: 'capable of attaining the point of greatest altitude against the whole concurrent strength of the institution, 210 scholars.' And, what's more, according to Joyce's adapted system of parallels between his *Ulysses* and Homer's *Odyssey*, this arc corresponds to Odysseus's famed bow with which he killed Penelope's suitors.

A Greek bow, therefore, became an Irish-Jewish arc of urine, and finally fell to earth, in Czech. It was a golden shower. That is one way of paying homage to Maria Weatherallová, the translator of James Joyce, whose name I like very much.

Chapter vi
Paris, 1922–25, & Prague, 1964: On Punctuation

But, in this small tradition I'm trying to be precise about, the urine is not quite so important as Hrabal's digressive, stream-of-consciousness form.

Dancing Lessons for the Advanced in Age is narrated by a man who is often called a shoemaker, but there is no more reason to call him a shoemaker than a brewer or a soldier, among other things, since these are also some of his previous professions. The novel is his autobiography – and, in particular, his sexual autobiography.

An example of flirting by Bohumil Hrabal

I was walking along the river one day when Libuška rode up to me on her bicycle – practically knocked me over, in fact – and said, When are you going to bring me another bunch of roses, another bouquet? and for an answer I upped and kissed her, just like Hans Albers in the steamship scene, and she screamed, My God! and I laughed and said, Not your God but your man, which made her laugh and practically knock me over again and opened the way to another adventure, which I was man enough to take advantage of

But the reason for the fun is not the sex: the sex is fun, but it is not everything. The everything is the structure of the massive engorged sentence, enlarged to the length of a novel.

And so this time, I need to go back not to Laurence Sterne, but to the end of the day in *Ulysses*.

As Bloom drifts off to sleep, his wife, Molly, lies there thinking. And the way she thinks is a series of nine unpunctuated sentences – without commas or apostrophes, and with only occasional capital letters – each forming a single unpunctuated paragraph. These sentences without any punctuation have clauses, but they also have non sequiturs and sudden changes of subject. They skitter.

Molly Bloom thinking about men

he never can explain a thing simply the way a body can understand then he goes and burns the bottom out of the pan all for his Kidney this one not so much theres the mark of his teeth still where he tried to bite the nipple I had to scream out arent they fearful trying to hurt you I had a great breast of milk with Milly enough for two what was the reason of that he said I could have got a pound a week as a wet nurse all swelled out the morning that delicate looking student that stopped in No 28 with the Citrons Penrose nearly caught me washing through the window only for I snapped up the towel to my face that was his studenting hurt me they used to weaning here

till he got doctor Brady to give me the Belladonna prescription I had to get
him to suck them they were so hard he said it was sweeter and thicker than
cows then he wanted to milk me into the tea well hes beyond everything

The first and recurring *he* in this passage is Molly's husband,
Leopold. But there is another *he* lurking – who is Molly's
lover, Blazes Boylan. And this is one aspect of Joyce's sense of
humour: these *he*s contain the secret of Molly's horizontality. The
digressions mask the sameness of her character – her practical, self-
important, mischievous, irreplaceable self.

And the horizontality is contained in Joyce's decision to remove
most of the conventional punctuation. It was not a superficial effect.
It was so careful, in fact, that Joyce came up with an equivalent in
its first translation.

The first published translations into French of *Ulysses* came out
in 1925, in the first issue of a new magazine, called *Commerce*, edited
by Valery Larbaud with Paul Valéry and Léon-Paul Fargue, and
published by Adrienne Monnier, with the help of the presumably
rich Princesse de Bassiano.

Commerce was a deliberately European journal, in line with
Larbaud's European ideals. Along with the translations from *Ulysses*,
the first issue contained extracts from Larbaud's essays on English
literature. It was cosmopolitan, polyglot: it had international
contributing editors, like the poets T. S. Eliot and Giuseppe Ungaretti.

The translations were done in conference, in a threesome of
Larbaud, Sylvia Beach and Adrienne Monnier. According to
Larbaud, the main problem was finding the right tone for the extract
from Molly's bedbound thoughts. 'My *femme de ménage* in Paris said,
talking about her concierge: She's a horror of a woman. Do you
see a place where that can go?', Larbaud wrote to Monnier. 'Molly
has a fine vocabulary, alive and plastic, vulgar but not to the point
of excluding literary words, – in the end the vocabulary of *Mallarmé*.'

One way of approximating Molly's uncapitalised and apostrophe-less speech was therefore to print her monologue without any French accents. Just as her English was denuded, unbuttoned, so was her French. This precipitated a minor kerfuffle: the more conventional printer replaced the accents; when he heard about this, Joyce insisted that they be removed again. Monnier wearily objected, but Larbaud agreed with Joyce.

Finally, Joyce won.

And I think that he was right: he was being faithful to the principle of Molly's artistic artlessness. One of my favourite things in Joyce's notes for *Ulysses* is a list he made in preparation for Molly's final section, her rambling sleepy unedited thoughts.

Some of James Joyce's notes for Mrs Marion (Molly) Bloom thinking

LB have I offended you? MB silent
MB got LB promoted
why? and why?
For any excuse to touch her (Mulvey)
Innocent boy (SD) now?
what did he mean?
LB took off her stockings
LB thanked her for frig
LB made her cry ?might be was someone else
a kiss in eye of glove & in openwork sleeve
How did my foot excite him?
Is he thinking of me?

The cleverness of Joyce's finale to *Ulysses* was the way he included these small details in a fluent surge of swerving, tacking digressions. He invented a new way of showing how someone might think.

And then, in Prague, writing *Dancing Lessons for the Advanced in Age*, Bohumil Hrabal developed it as a way a person might talk: he developed the art of the imaginary monologue, using Molly's interior monologue.

Writing a novel in one sentence let Hrabal show off, and create a hidden taxonomy of form. As the reader continues to read this single sentence, the more he or she begins to notice verticalities, differences, structural links and gaps. The more uniform the apparent technique, the more various and intricate the actual technique becomes.

This novel in one sentence seems to be characterised by constant digression. Its danger is therefore monotony of surprise. But in fact, Hrabal varies his digressions, delicately. It is therefore possible to compile a partial taxonomy of these digressions – a lecturing, ludicrous list of Hrabal's style.

Chapter vii

Prague, 1964: A Partial Taxonomy of Digression

I The Narrator's Character

  i – *attempt at autobiography*

  ii – *desire to give advice*

  iii – *penchant for expanding on an anecdote to prove a passing point*

  iv – *comprehensive memory*

II The Narrator's Idea of a Good Story

  i – *desire to give detail*

  ii – *desire to pay due attention to rumour*

  iii – *description of relatives*

  iv – *improvised portrait*

III Things Not Included in the Above Two Categories
  i – *non sequitur masked by a hinge word*
  ii – *stray thought leading to associative anecdote leading to
       minor character's future*

Chapter viii
Prague, 1964, Sofia, 1980s, & Dublin, 1904: Immaturity (II)

More serious people might find Hrabal's sense of humour blas-
phemous, and misplaced. He is amused by all the noble and
admirable human sentiments, like innocence, or hopefulness.
Hrabal is a connoisseur of the naïve.

And this is something else which Hrabal shared with James Joyce.
Like Hrabal, Joyce knew about kitsch: even in 1922, in Trieste and
Zurich and Paris, he was already an expert on Socialist Realism.

'When I was in Sofia some years ago,' recorded Hrabal, 'there
in front of my hotel stood the man it was named after. Stalin
himself. The citizens were considerate, they said, with the onset of
winter women came in the afternoons to dress Stalin in some warm
long-johns and a nice warm shirt, and a fur cap with flaps, so that
Stalin wouldn't catch cold here in Bulgaria'. And then Hrabal
remembers something else: 'In the same way, James Joyce sadly
tells in his *Ulysses* of Mr Leopold Bloom remembering the coffin
his little son Rudy lay in, and how his mother, Mrs Marion Bloom,
had knitted him a long warm jersey, so that her little son wouldn't
get cold in the grave.'

Kitsch is everywhere. The sentimental harries us.

But this does not quite exhaust Hrabal's sense of humour. The
method Hrabal most enjoys to create his comic effects is accumulation. This is one reason why he loves digression as a technique.
The joke becomes funnier and funnier, and sadder and sadder, the
more it is repeated.

In his story 'A Driving Lesson', before Hrabal gets onto the bike, he waits while the instructor has a last conversation with his previous pupil – a person who is the opposite of Hrabal, and Hrabal's father. He is not entranced by the magic of motorbikes; his passions are elsewhere. Instead of the machinery, this boy loves girls, he loves dancing, he loves the music he can get on the radio. He has no time for the niceties of the highway code.

Before presenting the motorbike romantic, therefore, Hrabal presents us with an inverted romantic, a romantic of other forms. But this also means that the instructor's idealism and passion emerge in relief – as the pupil invents more and more excuses for not reading the highway code, the instructor becomes more and more passionate about why reading the highway code is so important.

Then Hrabal gets on the bike.

The structure of the lesson which follows is in the form of accumulation. Hrabal's stories are a series of crashes, punctuated by more and more admiring interjections from his instructor. Like the monologue of *Dancing Lessons for the Advanced in Age*, this conversation proceeds through association. It is a joke at the expense of people's private and public passions.

But what is so funny about passion? It is funny because it is the epitome of seriousness. And gravity is funny. For, as well as being the epitome of seriousness, a passion is also the epitome of the arbitrary. A passion can latch on to anything. There is no difference, in the end, between a passion and a hobby. And if this restores the idea of the hobby to its grandeur, it also demotes the idea of a passion. Passion is not grown-up; it is not adult. It believes that the things of this world should be seen as things of an eternal world, where they are permanent, and have value. But the things of this world are just the things of this world. They are not permanent; they do not last.

Chapter ix
Kladno, 1951: On Collage

There is another way of describing Hrabal's sense of humour. To understand this, it helps to go back to the beginning, to when Hrabal's style was still immature.

Often, prose is the opposite of poetry; it is an attack on the lyrical. But this is because novelists often conceal within themselves the ghosts of repressed and lyrical poets. The attack is often personal.

And so it was that in the winter of 1951 Bohumil Hrabal was working in an iron works – in Kladno, Czechoslovakia. If Hrabal had needed to classify himself as a writer, in the summer of 1951, he would have described himself as a poet. More precisely, for the last fifteen years he had been a surrealist poet. But by the winter, in Kladno, he became a novelist. 'In Kladno, I broke with poetry. I began to write a sort of reportage which we even classified as total realism. Put roughly, I was moving beyond psychic automatism by returning to lived events. That was *Jarmilka*, mistress of the forge, as we called her.'

Jarmilka is a story told in the first person, set in an iron works, written during the winter of 1951–2. Jarmilka is the name of a girl who works in the canteen, and who is not married, and is pregnant. She is the heroine of *Jarmilka*. But *Jarmilka* is not just about Jarmilka. There are also the stories told by Hannes Reegen, one of Hrabal's co-workers, who had been in a Nazi concentration camp; and there are also the muted stories of the political prisoners interned by the recent Communist government, who have been sentenced to work in the same iron works.

So: there are right-wingers interned by left-wingers; left-wingers interned by right-wingers: and Hrabal and Jarmilka, in the middle.

None of these stories interlink explicitly. They comment on each other, silently. There is a conspiracy of details. The story is a mockery of the official, the serious, the grand. It is an ironic collage.

Via collage, Hrabal came up with a way of satisfying a poetic instinct for form, while rejecting his more suspect instinct for the lyrical and the inflated.

Another way of seeing this art of collage, following André Gide, is to see it as the art of variations. Lecturing his American students, Nabokov explained how, in a novel, 'just as in a musical fugue one theme can be imitated in parody of another'. And this is Hrabal's musical technique: he mutely shows how everything is involved in a game of mutual parody. Themes swap places, swift but structured – like the bubbles in a boiling pan of water. That is Hrabal's version of a fugue.

In Hrabal's fiction, therefore, there is no safe ground on which power can establish its authority.

A good worker

As for me, I follow Jarmilka from a distance and I compare her to every woman I've ever known . . . and I look at Jarmilka with admiration . . . I look at our little Jarmilka and I see how gutsy she is . . . perhaps it was for her that Stalin himself wrote that sentence you see suspended from his moustaches: A good worker is a worker who fears no difficulties . . . And Jarmilka really doesn't fear difficulties, she fights and triumphs . . . I eat my soup as slowly as possible, until I'm alone with Jarmilka.

In this, Hrabal's first novel, the juxtapositions are slightly too obvious. But, in miniature, this structure of juxtaposition, of collage, will be Hrabal's novelistic technique.

Hrabal's narrators are marked by their smallness, their ontological marginality. And this precision of marginality is because Hrabal himself is marginal: he is an eavesdropper of genius. His style is a polyphony of eavesdropping, which is doing its best to look as improvised and haphazard as possible. But, obviously, it is not improvised at all. Improvisation is an invention.

These collages, for instance, involved Hrabal in a lot of active work. He did not only need a typewriter to create his fiction. He also needed scissors and glue: 'I take a pair of scissors, a cutter, and I proceed like a film editor, it's the best moment'. That was how he came up with comic walks like this.

A walk in Czechoslovakia in 1948: a collage

We leave the shadows for the light of the streetlamps and the factory radio illuminates our path from on high: . . . thus we have taken the path towards a radiant future, it only befalls each of us to perform our labour, it is our . . . Jarmilka turns her head in its direction and cries to the heavens: Fuck off, with your sweet talk . . . yeah right, I'm on my way to a radiant future! . . . I wanted to buy a car, 4000 crowns, and I'm meant to find them where, I just harvest them? . . . And for the birth, huh, sweet-talkers . . . But the voice on high didn't hear the voice of Jarmilka and continued: . . . we have the best salaries and the best insurance schemes in the world, and so if only through gratitude, we should produce more . . . But Jarmilka once more cries towards the heights: . . . you what? What are you on?

Hrabal wrote *Jarmilka* on a Perkeo typewriter, made in 1905, which he had picked up from some Soviet soldiers during the Second World War. But Perkeo is a German manufacturer. This means that there was a problem for the young Czech novelist and poet. A Perkeo was not adapted to the complicated system of Czech accents. In fact, it possessed none whatsoever. Hrabal's text, his first novel, was therefore written in Czech, but without any Czech accents.

This Perkeo is an inadvertent perk for me – Hrabal's historian. It is an anticipatory proof of this particular game of ping-pong.

James Joyce, after all, happily called himself a scissors-and-paste man. And it was through reading Joyce that Hrabal discovered a way of developing his style, of inventing more and more digressions and interruptions, weaving shapes around the skeleton of his

underlying ironic structure. So it is amusing, and moving, to remember that in the French translation of Molly Bloom's monologue, the accents were left off, at Joyce's request.

Chapter x
Rio de Janeiro, 1857: The Problem of the Small Language

But the story of Bohumil Hrabal requires a coda, a qualm. This qualm involves the problem of writing in a small language.

As a metaphor, a simile, the story of Bohumil Hrabal can be placed beside the story of Machado de Assis.

While Machado de Assis was becoming a writer in Rio de Janeiro, he earned some money by doing translations from the French.

His translations were pulp, they were work.

Since Machado de Assis needed money, he translated the writing which the public in Rio de Janeiro wanted to read. They wanted romance, so he gave them romance. He translated the poetry of French romantic poets, like Lamartine. He also translated the bad libretti of bad romantic operas. When the public wanted the poetry of the Polish romantic poet, Adam Mickiewicz, Machado de Assis gave it to them. And as he grew older, he continued to translate – more of the French romantics, Baudelaire's translation of Poe's romantic poem 'The Raven', more romantic sentimental poetry.

Everything came via French, and everything was romantic. It was just like Socialist Realism.

The history of Machado de Assis's translations demonstrates the problems of provincial taste: they show what he was up against. Like every novelist, he had to cope with his own provinciality, and learn an international technique.

The opposite of his work was his library.

Machado de Assis owned a French edition of the works of Jonathan Swift called *Opuscules humoristiques*, translated by Léon de

Wailly, published in Paris in 1859. In French, he had everything: Diderot in an 1880 two-volume *Oeuvres choisies* published by Garnier; Balzac, Flaubert, Stendhal. He owned the French nineteenth century.

The point of this abbreviated tour round Machado de Assis's library is to show how much this library, built up over a lifetime, differs from the romantic libretti which he was translating when he was younger: the gap between them and the cosmopolitan library is an image, in miniature, of his learned technique. This library is an allegory. Gradually, through hard work, he stopped being provincial: he became unique, and international.

For instance, when considering what Machado de Assis did to the forms invented by Laurence Sterne, we should remember that he could not read Sterne in English (because he could not read English) or in Portuguese (because there was no translation into Portuguese until the twentieth century). He read Laurence Sterne in French. He owned an 1849 edition of Sterne's *Tristram Shandy* and an 1861 edition of *Sentimental Journey*.

Since the French edition Machado owned was printed in 1849, this means that it is possible he owned the translation which had been done a year earlier, by Léon de Wailly. But it could have been, more plausibly, perhaps, simply the standard reprinted translation from the 1770s. And this detail is quite important, because if it was de Wailly's, then Machado de Assis would have been reading a good approximation to Sterne's text. If, however, it was the 1770s translation, then he would have been reading something less exact than an approximation – more like graffiti.

That is another problem of living in Rio de Janeiro, and developing the art of the novel in the 1880s. Sources are haphazard. It is the same problem as living in Warsaw, or in Prague.

In 1937, Witold Gombrowicz had recently published a book of short stories and a novel, which had made him famous in Poland. He was an *enfant terrible*.

He therefore decided to write about another formally experimental novelist, James Joyce, whose French version of *Ulysses* had come out eight years earlier, in 1929, but which Gombrowicz had only read recently.

Just as Machado de Assis could not read Sterne in Portuguese, Gombrowicz could not read Joyce in Polish. Both of them, therefore, ended up compromising, with French.

And, as I mentioned in Book 1, Gombrowicz was not happy with reading a translation in a secondary language. But I want to linger on Gombrowicz's article for a little longer.

His French, he said, was fine for a conversation, but faced with this translation, produced by a committee of experts, he felt left out, and on edge. For *Ulysses*, like all good novels, was something which bathed entirely in its language, 'attached to it by organic links, a work rooted in its language, even, and created by it.' And yet handicapped as he was by translation, and his imperfect language skills, Gombrowicz could still see what was good about *Ulysses*. There was its innovation, and its technical agility. These made him want a Polish translation – which would be more valuable for Polish literature, he thought, than yet another mediocre novel whose original language was Polish. For if, in these mediocre novels, 'the plot varies, nothing or almost nothing changes, to be frank, in its treatment.' Whereas Joyce himself 'would be able to inject these authors with a dose of elasticity, to inculcate in these lazy organisms the art of adapting themselves, of reforming themselves and in the end inspiring them not so much with inspiration as, more simply, with vigour.'

Joyce, argued Gombrowicz, was a high-quality masseur, a much-needed foreign coach for the Polish literary team.

Still, however, Gombrowicz's conclusion continued to be depressed. The innate advantages possessed by the English-speaking reader depressed him. But his gloominess is both reasonable and unfounded. Naturally, not everything survives its transportation. Yet just as most of a style survives a talented translation into one language, because it is a quality of vision, expressed in more than one technique, it survives its talented translation into a further language, as well. Style is international.

And this is lucky.

There is an inverse problem to the problem of the small language. It is true that the small language may suffer from a lack of translations from larger languages, like Laurence Sterne and James Joyce's English. But, in the same way, the larger language may suffer from the lack of translations from the smaller languages – like Machado de Assis's Portuguese.

Or Bohumil Hrabal's Czech.

Some things, like *Dancing Lessons for the Advanced in Age*, are translated into English. But other things, like 'A Driving Lesson', are not available in English. Like Machado de Assis and Witold Gombrowicz, I can read them only in French. Somehow, therefore, I am asserting the timeless value of Hrabal's prose, although I have never read it in either Czech, Hrabal's first language, or English, my own. And this may seem to some people, who are gloomy like Gombrowicz, a little unreasonable. But I am not so sure about this. I am not convinced that a style is so linguistic.

Just as Hrabal got on a bike in Prague and had a driving lesson, everyone else can get on a scooter, in Paris, or Sofia. Hrabal, just like Joyce, can be a masseur, as well. He can help people develop their mockney in London, their outer-borough accent in New York, their *mat'* in Moscow (a mockney, an accent, a patois which are the opposite of translationese).

Palavering is international. There is no need for the history of the novel to always a history of waste. It is possible to translate a story whose language translator does not speak.

Hrabalovština can become – why not? – *Thirlwellovština*.

It can become anyone's. Try it for yourself. Try it on the beach.

ВОЙНА И МІРЪ

III.

ИЗДАНІЕ ЧЕТВЕРТОЕ.

ИЗДАНІЕ НАСЛѢДНИКОВЪ БР. САЛАЕВЫХЪ.

МОСКВА.

АФІЯ С. ОРЛОВА, У БОРОДИНСКАГО МОСТА, Д. СО

1880.

VOLUME III

BOOK 10

Nicola Tolstoy

For Witold Gombrowicz, in Argentina, a stylist should always be hospitable to the things which might destroy a style. 'My art', asserted Gombrowicz, 'has shaped itself not in confrontation with a group of people related to me, but in relation to the enemy and confrontation with the enemy.' For Gombrowicz, a good style was an anti-style: it was doing its best not to be a style at all.

Throughout these discussions of Gustave Flaubert and James Joyce, or Laurence Sterne and Denis Diderot, I have been conscious of this. It is possible, Gombrowicz was saying in Buenos Aires, to develop a precious theory of style. It is possible to become too exclusive.

I think I therefore need to be more precise about the idea of an anti-style: a style which is almost not a style at all. And so, as a symbolic introduction, I can begin with two similar stories, whose theme is mistakes.

In 1902, a man called Mr Ettinger – in tune with the contemporary vogue for the sayings of great men – wanted Chekhov's publisher to produce a volume of aphorisms that Mr Ettinger had culled from Chekhov's works. This book was to be called 'the thoughts and reflections of Anton Pavlovich Chekhov'. Chekhov, rightly, dismissed the project as 'completely childish': 'All these "thoughts and reflections" are not my own but my heroes', and if a character in one of my stories or plays says that one should kill or steal, that certainly doesn't give Mr Ettinger the right to present me as the advocate of theft or murder.'

It is important to trust Chekhov on this. The unhappy Mr Ettinger had made a mistake – like the unhappy anthologist of Machado de Assis, or the unhappy anthologist of Laurence Sterne.

The novel is not romantic; it does not allow the novelist lyrically to express himself. The statements contained in novels are relative, particular to the characters. The novel is an art of comedy, and relativity.

Like characters, however, mistakes are often eternal, too.

The first translation into English of Tolstoy's novel *War and Peace* was not really a translation at all. Effected by a man called Huntington Smith from a French version of the novel, this book was in fact two sequences of selected passages: the first, 'Napoleon and the Russian Campaign', recounted events after the battle of Borodino, through to Napoleon's retreat from Moscow. The second, 'Power and Liberty', collected together some of Tolstoy's historical essays on chance and necessity. The two were published under the general title: *The Physiology of War*.

It was an anthology.

Oh, these anthologies are everywhere! There was poor Laurence Sterne, with his book of beauties, then Machado de Assis, and Chekhov, and now Tolstoy – who had apparently not written a novel, but a handbook of military tactics instead. Once again, a novel with a complicated form was gutted for its ideas.

An anthology is the paradigm of bad fictional reading, because it believes in reading as a way of gathering information. And this is not true in a novel. The facts in a novel are not like other facts: they have a place in a larger form. But an anthology destroys this form.

In Huntington Smith's preface to the book which Tolstoy did not write, *The Physiology of War*, he felt moved to attack those who wished to see Count Tolstoy return to fiction. Smith, instead, was content with the two 'polemical works' he was presenting to the public. According to Huntington Smith, Tolstoy was not an artist, he was a politician: 'What has led to the significant and rapid rise into popular esteem of Count Tolstoï? It was felt at once that he had a message to deliver, a message worth hearing, and the world has shown itself ready to hear.'

And this depresses me. I will not believe that this is the secret of Tolstoy's popular esteem. It depresses me more than the fact that in the first translation of Tolstoy to appear in English, in 1862 – a translation of his first novel, *Childhood and Youth: A Tale*, by Malwida von Meysenbug – Tolstoy's first name was given as Nicola, not Nikolaievich. Which was, in any case, his second name.

Chapter ii
Moscow, 1865: The History of Mistakes

In *War and Peace*, a short while into her engagement to Prince Andrew Bolkonsky, Natasha and her childhood friend Sonya are playing a game with a mirror. They are trying to see if the mirror will grant them a vision of the future. Natasha is not so successful; Sonya, however, is.

Sonya has a vision

'Oh, Natasha!' she cried.

'Did you see? Did you? What was it?' exclaimed Natasha, holding up the looking-glass.

Sonya had not seen anything, she was just wanting to blink and to get up when she heard Natasha say, 'Of course she will!' She did not wish to disappoint either Dunyasha or Natasha, but it was hard to sit still. She did not herself know how or why the exclamation escaped her when she covered her eyes.

'You saw him?' urged Natasha, seizing her hand.

'Yes. Wait a bit . . . I . . . saw him,' Sonya could not help saying, not yet knowing whom Natasha meant by *him*, Nicholas or Prince Andrew.

'But why shouldn't I say I saw something? Others do see! Besides, who can tell whether I saw anything or not?' flashed through Sonya's mind.

'Yes, I saw him,' she said.

'How? Standing or lying?'

'No, I saw . . . At first there was nothing, then I saw him lying down.'

'Andrew lying? Is he ill?' asked Natasha, her frightened eyes fixed on her friend.

'No, on the contrary, on the contrary! His face was cheerful, and he turned to me.' And when saying this she herself fancied she had really seen what she described.

'Well and then, Sonya? . . .'

'After that, I could not make out what there was; something blue and red . . .'

Some years later, when Prince Andrew is on his deathbed, Sonya and Natasha go to look at him. And Sonya has a shock. She remembers the vision she saw, a long while before.

Sonya remembers a vision

'I saw him lying on a bed,' said she, making a gesture with her hand and a lifted finger at each detail, 'and that he had his eyes closed and was covered just with a pink quilt, and that his hands were folded,' she concluded, convincing herself that the details she had just seen were exactly what she had seen in the mirror.

She had in fact seen nothing then but had mentioned the first thing that came into her head, but what she had invented then seemed to her now as real as any other recollection. She not only remembered what she had then said – that he turned to look at her and smiled and was covered with something red – but was firmly convinced that she had then seen and said that he was covered with a pink quilt and that his eyes were closed.

'Yes, yes, it really was pink!' cried Natasha, who now thought she too remembered the word pink being used, and saw in this the most extraordinary and mysterious part of the prediction.

A little later on, Nicholas Rostov – Natasha's brother – is wondering how he might be released from his promise to marry Sonya, now that he is in love with Princess Mary, Andrew Bolkonsky's sister. Miraculously, he thinks, at this precise point, his valet Lavrushka hands him a letter from Sonya, releasing him from his promise to marry her.

But the real reason for Sonya's letter was not voluntary: the countess, Nicholas's mother, had asked Sonya to write to Nicholas. And Sonya had only consented to do it because of the recent fake fulfilment of her vision of Prince Andrew. She was suddenly feeling spiritual and grandiose, and therefore generous.

There are therefore various misinterpretations in this collage of episodes: Nicholas's misinterpretation of Sonya's letter; Sonya's misinterpretation of her vision; and Natasha's misinterpretation of Sonya's vision.

And there is also the final irony. The vision which was fakely fulfilled was not even a genuine vision at the time. The fakely fulfilled vision was a fake itself. There was nothing; and when something emerged, this something was not – like the cover on Andrew Bolkonsky's bed – pink.

It is possible, therefore, retrospectively, to put the story like this. If Sonya had not made her vision up, and if Andrew had not been wounded, then she would not have written her letter to Nicholas Rostov, and so she would still have been implicitly engaged to Nicholas.

There are too many causes, there are too many beginnings. No one, in this novel, knows all of them. Real life, according to Tolstoy, is by its nature too continuous and complicated to be understood comprehensively. This means that everyone's opinion on everything is always inadequate in relation to the totality of facts.

It is this thematic and formal emphasis on ignorance which is the way Tolstoy constructs his ironies. Ignorance deflates all vanities, all the characters' opinions and certainties. This is true for Sonya, and it is true for Napoleon. And so James Joyce was right, when he was twenty-three, to write (from Trieste) to his brother in defence of Tolstoy: 'Tolstoy is a magnificent writer. He is never dull, never stupid, never tired, never pedantic, never theatrical!'

This is also why Tolstoy did not win the Nobel Prize. According to the Nobel Committee's report on Tolstoy, he was 'an author who in his otherwise magnificent *War and Peace* attributes to blind chance such a decisive role in the great events of world history . . . and who in countless of his works denies not only the church, but the state, even the right of property.' He was not serious enough.

Tolstoy was not just a sage. He was also an aesthete, who distrusted sentimentality and theatricality. He was more of a dandy. 'The aim of an artist is not to solve a problem irrefutably,' he wrote, 'but to make people love life in all its countless inexhaustible manifestations. If I were to be told that I could write a novel whereby I might irrefutably establish what seemed to me the correct point of view on all social problems, I would not even devote two hours' work to such a novel . . .'

Chapter iii
Sevastópol, 1855: On Style (I)

In 1855, while Gustave Flaubert was thirty-four, living with his mother in Croisset, avoiding Louise Colet and writing *Madame Bovary*, Leo Tolstoy was twenty-seven, in the more macho position of being a Russian soldier in the siege of Sevastópol, on the Black

Sea – defending the town against the combined forces of the French, English and Turkish armies in the Crimean War.

But Tolstoy was writing too. They were just sketches he was writing, but their style was also a new thing in the history of the novel.

In May 1855, in Sevastópol, writes Tolstoy, a Russian officer called Kalugin is on his way to the bastion. And this character Kalugin is noted for his courage, the aristocratic nature of his soul. As bombs float up above the barricades, he continues to walk calmly through the town. But then 'another bomb rose in front of him and, it seemed, was making straight for him.' At this point, Kalugin no longer belongs to an aristocracy of courage: 'he suddenly felt scared: he quickly ran forward a few steps and threw himself onto the ground.' Each sentence begins a new perception. The previous sentence described fear. The next pointed sentence describes a different kind of fear – a more social form of anxiety. 'When the bomb fell, far away from him, he began to feel horribly annoyed at himself, and he got up, looking round to check that no one had seen him fall to the ground, but there was no one there.' And yet, because he is petrified, he still cannot walk: he ends up crawling down the side street on all fours. But once more, social anxiety reasserts itself: 'Suddenly he heard footsteps in front of him.' He straightens himself. And so when a sailor points out a bright spot thickening and descending in the air, and shouts to him to lie down, Kalugin simply inclines his neck, just as the bomb falls close by. So that the sailor thinks to himself, '– He's brave, that one'. But the sailor is wrong. It's not bravery: it's mute insensibility. Finally, arriving at the bastion, 'the same stupid fear overcame him; his heart began to beat more strongly, and he had to cross the last remaining distance at a skittering run.' Which allows for Tolstoy's last moment of social comedy: '– Why are you so out of breath? – asked the General, after Kalugin had reported his orders.'

'– I walked very fast', replies Kalugin.

Tolstoy's sentences do not adhere to the conventions of literary taste. At the same time as Flaubert was working on his background effects, Tolstoy was coming up with a style breezily based on his genius for direct presentation, a style avant-gardely impatient with the requirements of good style. It is happy describing things which other nineteenth-century novelists considered unrepresentable.

On the same night, at the bastion, a bomb falls, but does not go off, beside two other officers, Mikhaylov and Praskukhin. 'Mikhaylov fell to the ground. Praskukhin involuntarily bent down and screwed up his eyes; he only heard that the bomb had crashed down on the hard earth close by.' Finally, he opens his eyes, and 'was pleased to see Mikhaylov, whom he owed money at cards, much closer, lying without moving at his feet. But at that moment he caught sight of the glowing fuse of the bomb which was spinning on the ground, very close.'

This is the secret of Tolstoy's style: it is omnisicient, unashamedly violating the characters' privacy, and therefore omnivorous. It will not reject anything – however domestic – like Praskukhin's mental note of his debt at cards. And so he remembers

(Praskukhin about to die)

the twelve rubles he owed Mikhaylov, remembered also another debt in Petersburg that should have been paid long ago; and the gipsy song, which he had sung that evening, came into his head; the woman he loved appeared in his imagination, wearing a cap with lilac ribbons; he remembered a man who had insulted him five years ago and on whom he had not yet had his revenge, and yet, together with all these and a thousand other recollections, the present thought – the expectation of death – did not leave him for an instant. 'After all, perhaps it won't explode,' he thought and with a desperate decisiveness he wanted to open his eyes. But at that instant a red flame pierced through his still closed eyelids, with a terrible crack something struck him in the middle of his chest; he began to run somewhere, stumbling over the gun that got between his legs and he fell on his side.

This is what it is like to be about to die.

And then Tolstoy tells us what it is like to die. It means that it does not feel like dying. How could it? No one knows what it feels like. '"Thank God! I'm only bruised," – was his first thought, and he wanted to touch his chest with his hand, – but his arms seemed tied to his sides and something like a vice was squeezing his head. Before his eyes flitted soldiers – and without thinking he counted them: "One, two, three soldiers, and there's one without any shoes," he thought.'

Tolstoy is a master of estrangement – because it is only human not to know what you are doing. Everyone is always inexperienced, and immature. It is all too human to be amateurish. We are always, initially, oustripped by our experience.

Praskukhin dies

He felt how wet it was around his chest, – this sensation of being wet made him think about water, and he longed to drink even the thing that was making him feel wet. 'I must have made myself bleed when I fell,' he thought, and beginning to give in more and more to his fear that the soldiers who kept flitting past might trample on him, he gathered all his strength and tried to shout, 'Take me with you!', – but instead of that he groaned so terribly that he was terrified, listening to himself. Then some other red fires began dancing before his eyes, – and it seemed to him that the soldiers put stones on him; the fires danced less and less, the stones, which they had put on him, pressed down more and more heavily. He made an effort to push off the stones, stretched himself, and then he saw, heard, thought and felt nothing more. He had been killed on the spot by a bomb-splinter in the middle of the chest.

(And poor Praskukhin will have to die again, with the new name of Andrey Yefimitch, in Chekhov's story 'Ward No. 6':

Andrey Yefimitch dies

Andrey Yefimitch understood that his end had come, and remembered that Ivan Dmitrich, Mihail Averyanitch, and millions of people believed in immortality. And what if it really existed? But he did not want immortality, and he thought of it only for one instant. A herd of deer, extraordinarily beautiful and graceful, of which he had been reading the day before, ran by him; then a peasant woman stretched out her hand to him with a registered letter . . . Mihail Averyanitch said something, then it all vanished, and Andrey Yefimitch sank into oblivion forever.)

There is a calm arrogance to Tolstoy's sentences, engrossed in precision. So that he then has the intelligence and talent to juxtapose Praskukhin's way of dying with Mikhaylov's. Mikhaylov is less nostalgic, more superstitious: he 'began to count: one, two, three, four, deciding that if it burst on an even number, then he would survive, on an odd number – then he would die. "It's all over – I'm dead!" – he thought when the bomb burst (he did not remember whether it was on an odd or even number), and he felt something hit him and a sharp pain in his head.'

But Mikhaylov does not die. He gets away with a head wound.

Chapter iv
London, 1861: The History of Mistakes (III)

When the young Ernest Hemingway was browsing for books in Paris, in Shakespeare and Company, he naturally ended up with Constance Garnett's translations:

Hemingway browsing in Shakespeare and Company

I started with Turgenev and took the two volumes of *Sportsman's Sketches* and an early book of D. H. Lawrence, I think it was *Sons and Lovers*, and Sylvia told me to take more books if I wanted. I chose the Constance Garnett edition of *War and Peace*, and *The Gambler and Other Stories* by Dostoyevsky. 'You won't be back very soon if you read all that,' Sylvia said.

Constance Garnett introduced Russian literature to both Britain and America. She was a great translator. But her translations of Tolstoy's style are not without their complications.

Predominately because of Garnett's translations, there is a cliché in English that Tolstoy's style is simple, that his prose style is a folk style, transparently universal. But this is not true. It is true of his style, overall; but it is not true, on the other hand, of his prose style. And this is partly because of Garnett's own idea of prose style, but it is also because of her talent: she understood that some-times translating accurately may not be the accurate thing to do. Tolstoy in English is not always the same thing as Tolstoy in Russian: the effect may not reproduce, in a precise translation.

And this is complicated.

Although Constance Garnett never wrote anything publicly about Tolstoy, it is possible to glean two theories of his style from her letters. Her first argument was that her English version was better than Tolstoy's Russian version: Tolstoy, she wrote, 'makes no attempt to write good Russian – and more than that – he seems wilfully to go out of his way at times in not doing so.' Her version of Tolstoy's novel *Anna Karenina*, wrote Garnett, 'is clearer and more free from glaring defects of style than the Russian original.'

Tolstoy's sentences are not always written in smooth Russian. This is certainly true. His style is not always simple. Styles are rarely simple. All styles, even the ones that may look simple, however portable they may be, are complicated machines. Having lectured his students with the simple mantra that 'No major writer is simple', Nabokov went on to describe one aspect of Tolstoy's style – based on what Nabokov called 'creative repetition', toying with words in a sentence, regrouping them, reworking them. Tolstoy especially enjoyed elongating his long sentences through simple repetition, letting a sentence sway on a repeated hinge, like terza rima. It may not be entirely charming, this way of writing, but that is what Tolstoy did.

The twin elements of Tolstoy's sentences are length and repetition. Tolstoy can therefore often seem not in control of his long sentences; too often they flop and flail. Garnett's Tolstoyan sentences, on the other hand, are often short and less repetitive. Her decision, presumably, was based on a correct idea that Russian could accommodate this ungainliness in a way that English could not. A precisely Russian Tolstoy in English would therefore not be precise at all.

In the same way, in the preface to her own translation of two stories by Tolstoy, Ann Pasternak Slater gave a literal translation of some sentences from Tolstoy's story 'Master and Man' – to show how ungainly Tolstoy could be in Russian, which was why he was so difficult to reinvent in English. His repetitions were often not so much creative as habitual, and dispiriting.

A literal translation of three sentences by Tolstoy

The thought came to him that he might, and very probably would, die that night, but this thought didn't seem particularly unpleasant to him, nor particularly frightening. The thought didn't seem to him to be particularly unpleasant because his whole life hadn't been a perpetual holiday, but on the contrary an uninterrupted round of hard labour, which was beginning to tire him. Nor was the thought particularly frightening because, apart from the masters he served here, like Vassili Andreyich, in this life he always felt himself dependent on the main master, the one who sent him into this life, and he knew that even in death he would stay in this master's power, and this master would not treat him badly.

And yet, on the other hand, it is still possible to defend Tolstoy's length and ungainliness. Often, they are deliberate. Long sentences mean that he can reword and rethink an idea in mid-sentence, so that it proceeds, slowly, implacably, towards the most precise description. Tolstoy's style is a swarming precision. Anton Chekhov – Tolstoy's friend – once wrote, 'Have you noticed Tolstoy's language? Enormous periods, sentences piled one on top of another. Don't think that it happens by chance or that it's a short-coming. It's art, and it only comes after hard work.'

But Constance Garnett wrote that 'Tolstoy's simple style goes straight into English without any trouble. There's no difficulty.' This was her second, slightly contradictory theory of Tolstoy's style. It means she can also write that Tolstoy is 'the easiest author going. I could translate him in my sleep.'

Both Chekhov and Garnett are right, I think; and both of them are wrong.

Chapter v
New York, 1958: Vladimir Nabokov's Theory of Translation

In the foreword to his translation into English of Mikhail Lermontov's nineteenth-century Russian novel *A Hero of Our Time*, Nabokov defined the task of the 'honest translator': 'In the first place, we must dismiss, once and for all, the conventional notion that a translation "should read smoothly", and "should not sound like a translation".' Instead, maintained Nabokov, 'any translation that does *not* sound like a translation is bound to be inexact upon inspection; while, on the other hand, the only virtue of a good translation is faithfulness and completeness. Whether it reads smoothly or not depends on the model, not on the mimic.' But I am not so sure about this.

Nabokov is confusing two things here which should not be confused. It is true that smoothness depends on the model, not the mimic: but this means that some translations, to be accurate, should not sound like translations at all. If the original is stylistically neutral, the translation should be too. A problem then arises when it is not always obvious what the original effect was in the first place. Nabokov concluded his discussion by stating some facts about Lermontov's crude Russian sentences: 'his similes and metaphors are utterly commonplace; his hackneyed epithets are only redeemed by occasionally being incorrectly used. Repetition of words in descriptive sentences irritates the purist. And all this, the translator should faithfully render, no matter how much he may be tempted to fill out the lapse and delete the redundancy.' And he is right about Lermontov; but Tolstoy is trickier.

Every theory of translation is a theory of style. And Nabokov's idea of style is perhaps too limited to prose, to the internal structure of sentences.

Tolstoy's style is based on his idea that truth is more important than elegance or convention. This means that his prose style is often prolix, ugly, repetitious. Sometimes, this seems deliberate – a studied piece of artistic artlessness. But on other occasions, it does not: the clumsiness just seems clumsy.

That is why it is difficult to be accurate about the accuracy of translations from Tolstoy. It is not easy, working out how much of his muddled prose style was part of his accurately, acutely muddled style.

Chapter vi
Moscow, 1865: On Style (II)

In his preface to an early version of *War and Peace* Tolstoy confesses that in this new novel he has been 'hampered by traditions both of form and content. I was afraid to write in a language which would not be the same as everybody else's; I was afraid that what I wrote would not fit into any category, whether novel, short story, poem, or history.' It was a constant worry for Tolstoy with this novel – that his writing was too avant-garde. In a discarded preface to the novel's first edition, called *1805*, Tolstoy explained how 'Russians generally speaking do not know how to write novels in the sense in which this genre is understood in Europe, nor is the projected work a long short story; no single idea runs through it, no contention is made, no single event is described; still less can it be called a novel with a plot, with a constantly deepening interest, and with a happy or unhappy dénouement.'

The reasons he did not think this novel was a novel were, then, that it had no definite plot, and no known conclusion; and that it was generically impure, containing different registers – the fictional, and the philosophical.

(Although there was, in fact, a tradition to Tolstoy: the two most important novels for Tolstoy's impure form were Sterne's two novels: *Tristram Shandy* and *Sentimental Journey*; and, via Sterne, Pushkin's chatty novel in verse, *Eugene Onegin*.)

But Tolstoy's form was an attempt to be true to his central theme in *War and Peace* – that nothing can ever be truly known about the past, whether the historical past or a fictional past, because there are always too many causes to every event. The theme of Tolstoy's novel – which is not a novel, not a conventional novel – is the human capacity for misinterpretation, the ability to see a meaning in an event which is merely accidental. This is what is behind the two main innovations in the text: the expansion of detail, and the inclusion of historical essays. They are both ways of representing the same thing: they are there to help Tolstoy approach his subject precisely.

In one of the many essayistic sections of *War and Peace*, Tolstoy stated his problem abstractly, directly: 'Historical science in its endeavour to draw nearer to truth continually takes smaller and smaller units for examination. But however small the units it takes, we feel that to take any unit disconnected from others, or to assume a *beginning* of any phenomenon [. . .] is in itself false.' It was an essay about the problems of writing history: but it was also a guide to the reading of *War and Peace*.

This essay was part of the same investigation behind the story of Sonya's false memory. It is a continuation of the same perplexed experiment with the problem of beginnings.

Both parts, the essay and the story, were part of Tolstoy's anti-style. But an anti-style is still a style.

This might seem unpersuasive: it would not have persuaded Nabokov, who dismissed Tolstoy's *War and Peace* as 'a rollicking historical novel', and added: 'In terms of artistic structure it does not satisfy me. I derive no pleasure from its cumbersome message, from the didactic interludes . . .' Perhaps this is my own anachronistic reading of Tolstoy's essays; I am not sure that Tolstoy would have agreed with it, either. Perhaps the essays were not as delicate as I like to think. But on this occasion, I am going to disagree with Tolstoy, and Nabokov.

The Delighted States, let's remember, is written with a full acceptance of the mistake, the anachronism, the side effect.

Chapter vii

Paris, 1839: A Short Definition of an Anti-Style

According to the French novelist Henri Beyle – one of whose pseudonyms was Stendhal – the battle of Waterloo was a mess. It was not, as his hero Fabrizio thought, a romantic and grand event.

Fabrizio at the battle of Waterloo

The sergeant came over to Fabrizio. At this moment our hero heard someone behind him say, quite close to his ear: 'That's the only one still fit to gallop.' He felt someone grab his feet; they were lifted out of the stirrups at the same time that his body was seized under the arms, and he was raised over the horse's tail and let slide to the ground, where he landed in a sitting position.

The aide-de-camp took Fabrizio's horse by the bridle; the general, with the sergeant's help, mounted and galloped off, rapidly followed by the remaining six men. Fabrizio stood up, furious, and began running after them, shouting: 'Ladri! Ladri!' (Thieves! Thieves!) What a farce, to be running across a battle-field after horse-thieves!

The style of this battle represents a new literary value. It is the first unimpressed description of a battle. It is not inflated. And it has comedy. That is why it appealed to Tolstoy.

(And so it is also useful to remember that Stendhal was there himself as a bewildered French soldier when Moscow was burned – the burning which is central to Tolstoy's historical novel, *War and Peace*. He was there, just beyond Tolstoy's narrative, his fiction.)

Leo Tolstoy discusses Fabrizio at the battle of Waterloo

I owe it to him that I understood war. Just realise in *The Charterhouse of Parma* the account of the battle of Waterloo. Who before him had described war like that, as it really is? Do you remember Fabrice crossing the field of battle without understanding 'a single thing' and how smartly the hussars made him get over the hindquarters of his horse, his fine 'general's horse'? Later in the Caucasus my brother, an officer before I was, confirmed to me the truth of these descriptions by Stendhal; he loved war but wasn't one of those simpletons who believe in the bridge of Arcole. 'All that,' he told me, 'is *panache* – and there is no *panache* in war.' Shortly afterwards in the Crimea I had only to look to see with my own eyes. But, I repeat, for all I know of war my first master is Stendhal.

An anti-style is still a style. It is just not as stylish as other people's styles. It will not allow itself the luxury of elegance. In the same way, the Italian novelist Giuseppe di Lampedusa noted how in Stendhal's fiction there was no memorable dialogue – and this was a mark of his talent, not his inability. He was so accurate that his prose was unremarkable, formless – like the everyday. 'The defect of so many novels (including some of the best!), which is to reveal people's inmost thoughts through what they say, has here disappeared.' No, according to Lampedusa, making his point with italics, 'his work contains no famous passage of dialogue.'

Stendhal's style was the opposite of what was considered appropriate, in the elegant nineteenth century. It preferred the deliberately factual, the rhetorically depleted: 'Young girl murdered beside me,' he noted in his journal. 'I run up to her, she is in the middle of the street; a foot from her head a small lake of blood about a foot in diameter. It's what M. Vor Hugo calls being bathed in one's own blood.' M Vor Hugo is Stendhal's quick, deflating notation of the romantic poet Victor Hugo. And Stendhal was not impressed by Hugo: he was not impressed by his style of exaggeration.

In Stendhal, there is no panache. And Tolstoy was clever enough to borrow this distaste for exaggeration from Stendhal's French, and rework it in Russian.

That is one of the benefits, therefore, of having more than one language – it allows for multiplicity of effects. It gives stylistic evolution.

Tolstoy, however, went further than Stendhal in his deflation of panache. His imagination was more comprehensive. Only Tolstoy could precisely and ironically imagine what it was like to be a boy on a battlefield ('The wounded crept together in twos and threes and one could hear their distressing screams and groans, sometimes feigned – or so it seemed to Rostov') for whom battlefields up till then had only been imaginary, and which still seemed imaginary, still unreal.

Chapter viii
Paris, 1880: A Letter from Gustave Flaubert

The problem with Tolstoy proving that the truth about man is by
nature ironical, that everything is impure, is that sooner or later people
accuse a novelist of not understanding about form, or style. In his
effort to be true to impurity, therefore, Tolstoy ended up looking
impure. So that Henry James (who called Tolstoy's novel *Peace and
War*) could number it as one of many 'large loose baggy monsters'.

Or this could happen.

On 24 January 1880, Ivan Turgenev, who lived in France and who
was Tolstoy's friend, wrote to Tolstoy in Russia, copying out a
passage from another of Turgenev's friends, Gustave Flaubert: '"I
am grateful that you gave me the opportunity to read Tolstoy's
novel. It is first-rate! What an artist and what a psychologist! The
first two volumes are sublime, but the third goes downhill, dread-
fully. He repeats himself. And he philosophizes. In a word, here
one sees the gentleman, the author and the Russian, whereas hith-
erto one had seen only nature and mankind.'" And Turgenev added,
Parisianly: 'I think *en somme* you will be satisfied . . .'

However.

Repetition, yes: lazy repetition is bad. It's an objective formal
fault. But what is so wrong with philosophy?

There is a danger, it's true, to the essayistic in the novel – the
essays will overtake the characters, will chivvy them into order too
neatly, too bossily. This is what Flaubert disliked. But they can also
allow the characters to relax, to do their own thing, untinged by
the unconscious pressure to live up to the novelist's need to be a
sage, a thinker. They can relieve the characters of a burden. And
they can also form doodles around the characters' actions – if
arranged with irony, with counterpoint. They can offer the novelist
different routes to the same destination.

In response to Flaubert I can make Tolstoy say what he said to his friend N. N. Strakhov: 'In everything or almost everything I have written, I have been moved by the need to bring together ideas which are closely knit, in order to express myself, but each idea, expressed separately in words loses its meaning, is enormously impoverished when removed from the network around it.' Tolstoy's range of tone and register, moving from the narrative to the essay-istic, is held together by a structure of motif. The philosophy he wrote is not quite – or, maybe more precisely, not always – moral-istic, or preachy, in the way which Flaubert disliked. 'The most important thing in a work of art,' wrote Tolstoy, 'is that it should have a kind of focus – i.e. some place where all the rays meet or from which they issue. And this focus should not be capable of being completely explained in words. This, indeed, is the impor-tant thing about a good work of art, that its basic content can in its entirety be expressed only by itself.' Although Flaubert thought he was more artistically subtle than Tolstoy, this is not quite true. Both Flaubert and Tolstoy were saying the same thing: that in a work of art, form and content echo each other. All they disagreed on were the permitted techniques.

For Tolstoy was investigating the same phenomenon in his story about Sonya's vision, and his essay on the Battle of Borodino. In both cases, he was interested in the impossibility of prediction, and the multiplicity of causes behind any event. The essay and the fiction are complementary.

No, unlike Flaubert, I am not sure there needs to be any limit on the permissible techniques. Everything is up for grabs. The novel in general, after all, does not exist.

Tolstoy's innovation was to invent a form which was able to be true to chance. It represents a new value in the history of the novel. But so many innovations in form at first look like lack of form. It can take time for them to be noticed.

Chapter ix
Moscow, 1865: A Letter from Julie Karagin

This structure of motif binds together the essays and the narrative. But it also binds together the massive details of the fiction on its own.

In the twenty-second chapter of the first part of Book One of *War and Peace*, Princess Mary reads a letter from her friend, Julie Karagin. Midway through this letter, Julie writes: 'To say nothing of my brothers, this war has deprived me of one of the associations nearest my heart. I mean young Nicholas Rostov.' And Julie adds: 'I will confess to you, dear Mary, that in spite of his extreme youth his departure for the army was a great grief for me'; and she talks about Nicholas for a while, whom she thinks she is in love with, and then goes on to more important things.

Hundreds and hundreds of pages and many years later, Princess Mary, not Julie, will marry Nicholas Rostov. And it is Tolstoy's delicate artistry to mention them here, unnoticeably together, when Mary is seen for the very first time.

And I like the fact that this tacit linking was a technique which had been used by Gustave Flaubert, in *Madame Bovary*. Early on in the novel, Madame Bovary is seen, in passing, with the money-lender Lheureux whose avarice will lead to her death, as it has led to the bankruptcy of the café owner, Tellier. And this technique was noted a century later by Vladimir Nabokov, who did not notice the same thing in *War and Peace*.

Vladimir Nabokov lectures his American students

'What an appalling disaster!' exclaims Homais, who, says Flaubert ironically, finds expressions suitable to all circumstances. But there is something behind this irony. For just as Homais exclaims 'What an appalling disaster!' in his fatuous, exaggerated, pompous way, at the same time the landlady points across the square, saying, 'And there goes Lheureux, he is bowing to Madame Bovary, she's taking Monsieur Boulanger's arm.' The beauty of this structural line is that Lheureux, who has ruined the café owner, is thematically linked here with Emma, who will perish because of Lheureux as much as because of her lovers – and her death really will be an 'appalling disaster.' The ironic and the pathetic are beautifully intertwined in Flaubert's novel.

Like Flaubert, Tolstoy wanted to intertwine the beautiful and the pathetic. He was an artist, too: he was a writer who was careful with form. It is just that he invented a different kind of form to express his version of real life.

Chapter x
Moscow, 1865: Economy!

The thematic network scribbled across the apparently random detail of *War and Peace* means that Tolstoy's form, which allows for elasticity, is not profligate and wasteful, but neat and economical. Tolstoy should be believed when he criticised his original opening for *War and Peace*, with its traditional full-frontal descriptions of characters, by commenting that 'all these descriptions, sometimes dozens of pages long, tell the readers less about the characters than some casually thrown out artistic detail in the course of an action already in progress between people who have not been described at all.' Writing to Alexander Fet, Tolstoy told him that 'Turgenev's opinion that one can't spend ten pages describing what N.N. did with his hand helped me very much.'

So that while sometimes Tolstoy's details function like Diderot's smallpox scar, or James Joyce's misprint, as proofs of truthfulness ('"May I ask you," said Pierre, "What village that is in front?" "Burdino, isn't it?" said the officer, turning to a companion.

"Borodino," the other corrected him.') some details develop a dual function. They are like those toys called Transformers. In their repetition across the book, they then become meaningful, symbolic; they become part of the machinery. It is never obviously predictable, however, when a detail will become so meaningful – like Sonya's invented vision: the explanatory impetus is always with the characters, and their intricate improvised plot.

Everything in this world is capable of becoming meaningful, retrospectively. It simply depends on chance. This is something which is natural in real life, which was not always natural in the description of real life. Tolstoy, however, found a method which was fluid enough to represent this ambiguity, this state of suspension – most events remain flat in their triviality, and yet, at the same time, every event, however trivial it is, can at any moment become an episode in an adventure. So that of all the details in the letter which Princess Mary reads, it is one which seems irrelevant, the mention of Nicholas Rostov, which many years later will blossom, will be turned from triviality into a story.

Chapter xi
London, 2007: A Short Conclusion About Shortness

Length, I think, is odd.

Because there is Franz Kafka, the author of the shortest stories, who is Tolstoy's opposite – a novelist whose short fictions are crammed, internally elongated with proliferation. And so I will get on to Franz Kafka soon. Whereas Leo Tolstoy, this monster of length, is a writer of exquisite concision. He is a miniaturist.

BOOK II

Weyl & Scampi

Inelegant prose style may still be part of a good style. That is one idea which can be entertained, when thinking about Leo Tolstoy. But other ideas may well then follow.

Conversely, for instance, an elegant, exclusive style may be a hindrance. It may be necessary to come up with ways of infiltrating imperfection, raggedness, into a style. 'An old Rolls Royce', Vladimir Nabokov reminded his reader, 'is not always preferable to a plain jeep.' A good style is often tentative, not authoritative – it is open to its own obliteration.

In Chicago, for instance, in 1951, in a new century, Saul Bellow was in the library, reading up on western literature. And so, for a moment, I am going to leave him there – while I explain what this new character, in a new country, was doing.

While Bellow, the son of Russian-Jewish immigrants, was writing his early novels, one of the ways in which he made money was to work on the *Syntopicon*. The *Syntopicon* was subtitled *An Index to the Great Ideas*. It was a cross-referenced system of all the ideas in the Chicago Great Books series – a summary of Western culture. Its first edition came out in 1952, one year before Saul Bellow's third novel (but the first with his own style), *The Adventures of Augie March*.

The preface to the *Syntopicon* stated the book's underlying idea: 'This great conversation across the ages is the living organism whose structure the *Syntopicon* tries to articulate. It tries to show the many strands of this conversation between the greatest minds of western civilization on the themes which have concerned people in every epoch and which cover the whole range of humanity's speculative inquiries and practical interests. To the extent it succeeds, it reveals the unity and continuity of the west.' But the ideas themselves in the *Syntopicon* are not very interesting. I don't really think that ideas are ever interesting, not fictionally. Instead, ideas are more like embarrassing extras to a personality, evolutionary redundancies – like the male nipple. After all, the first ten ideas of western culture, according to the *Syntopicon*, are Angel, Animal, Aristocracy, Art, Astronomy and Cosmology, Beauty, Being, Cause, Chance, Change.

You see? Abstractly, an idea hardly exists at all.

And in a way I like to think of this abstract list as the opposite of the list of objects in an apartment block, from which Georges Perec drew out his novels:

1 pedal bin

1 hat hanging on a peg

1 suit hanging on a hanger

1 jacket hanging on the back of a chair

washing drying

3 small bathroom cabinets

several bottles and flasks

numerous objects hard to identify (carriage clocks, ashtrays, spectacles, glasses, saucers full of peanuts, for example)

In his book on Dostoevsky, André Gide – who could not read Dostoevsky in Russian – noted an odd thing about the ideas in Dostoevsky's novels. 'The ideas are, as it were, the *product* of a special and transitory state of his characters; they remain relative . . .' For a novelist, noted Gide, it would be crazy to write according to general principles: 'Certainly, psychological axioms appear to Dostoevsky what they really are, special definitions of truth. As a novelist (for Dostoevsky is no mere theoretician, he is a prospector), he steers clear of induction and knows what an imprudence it would be (on his part, at least) to try to formulate general laws.'

It is the word *prospector* that I like especially. It fits the author, for instance, of the novel called *The Counterfeiters*. So that in that novel Gide could come up with the nested ironies of a situation in which a fictional novelist writes a theory of love in his journal, a theory of the complications of true feeling: 'In the domain of feeling what is real is indistinguishable from what is imaginary. And if it is sufficient to imagine one loves, in order to love, so it is sufficient to say to oneself that when one loves one imagines one loves, in order to love a little less . . .' And then he ironises further, because the novelist then adds: 'It is by such reasoning as this, that X in my book tries to detach himself from Z . . .' Because all ideas are relative; they are all used by people to confirm or create their own feelings. Ideas, in Gide's novels, are tools, they are boxes of tricks.

But it took some time for Saul Bellow, still sitting there in the library, to come to like this word *prospector*. Instead, for Bellow, in 1951, the novelist was a theoretician.

His solution to the mistake he was making about style was to realise that ideas, themselves, were mistakes.

Chapter ii
Chicago, 1944: A Style

A long time before Bellow was working on Great Books, his first novel, *Dangling Man*, was published in March 1944. Bellow was twenty-eight. Written in the form of a journal, *Dangling Man* describes a guy in Chicago, called Joseph, wondering if he will be called up to fight in the Second World War – while he watches his life and his marriage disintegrate.

The style of this book has dated; it is all too existential.

Saul Bellow by Mitchell Glotzer, courtesy of Maggie Glotzer

Evenings in Chicago

Eventually I learned that Iva could not live in my infatuations. There are such things as clothes, appearances, furniture, light entertainment, mystery stories, the attractions of fashion magazines, the radio, the enjoyable evening. What could one say to them? Women – thus I reasoned – were not equipped by training to resist such things.

'The enjoyable evening'! Because of course, they are unlikeable – those girls who are drawn to the enjoyable evening, as opposed to the existential evening.

Dangling Man was originally called *Notes of a Dangling Man*. That is a clue to the problem I have with this novel. It was influenced by Dostoevsky and, in particular, Dostoevsky's novel *Notes from Underground*, with its earnestly hysterical narrator, intoning his improbable theories. Joseph was a Dostoevskian hero – a failed writer, low-rent, depressive. More precisely, he was Dostoevskian in his psychology, a mishmash of asserted pride and felt humiliation.

The meaning of the novel, therefore, was bald and conventional. Its style was a model of European existentialism.

Joseph does not know how to act. Since everything is permitted, he cannot choose what to do. His pride asserts his independence, and yet his efforts at independence are constantly thwarted. Man, therefore, needs rules. The novel ends with Joseph's cry: 'Long live regimentation!' Just as Dostoevsky's *Notes from Underground* ends with the following conventionally unconventional argument: 'And what is it we sometimes scratch about for, what do we cry for, what do we beg for? We don't know ourselves. And it would be worse for us if our stupid whims were indulged. Just try giving us, for example, as much independence as possible, untie the hands of any one of us, loosen our bonds, and we . . . I assure you we should all immediately beg to go back under discipline.'

Sometimes an influence is not even a direct influence. Often, a writer is not influenced by a true version of another writer, but a fake one – he or she copies the image of another writer. And in this case, Bellow copied a translated, less vernacular, less crazed and subjective, more earnest version of Dostoevsky. Whereas Dostoevsky's underground man is an ironised example of pathology. His theories are not meant to be taken seriously as objective truths. Dostoevsky, after all, was a prospector.

Unfortunately for Bellow, he had not read André Gide. Or if he had, he hadn't understood.

Chapter iii
Chicago, 1949: A New Style

Five years after *Dangling Man*, the May 1949 issue of the small magazine *Partisan Review* contained a story by Bellow called 'A Sermon by Doctor Pep'. In it, Bellow was trying out a new way of writing sentences. He was trying to make seriousness more obviously funny. So his new style was slightly cracked, dizzy, jazzy, with sentences like this: 'Now since I've mentioned hamburgers, I'll lead with them straight into my subject of disease and health, and true and false nourishment, out of my readings in Galen and Hippocrates and even further back in time.' It created a zany quality by combining two things which, previously, Bellow had kept separate – the learned and the streetwise; hamburgers and Hippocrates.

But although 'A Sermon by Doctor Pep' nearly sounded Bellovian, although it nearly sounded how Bellow came to sound in his third novel, *The Adventures of Augie March*, it was not quite there. Although it was trying to be cool, it was still slightly wordy, too nervous about its learning. It was too defensive. Its important invention was not a style but a character – the educated gangster, whose great example would be Augie March, an autodidact thief, casing the bookcases: 'It was a big Jowett's *Plato* that I took'. But the speechy voice was still missing. There was verbosity, but the sentences were too syntactically taut, too measured. The tone was too portentous. This 'Sermon' was a sermon.

There is the problem of jet lag in literary history; but the problem of the time lag occurs in the history of an individual novelist, as well. It might be nice for everything to turn up at once – the subject and the characters and the sentences – but this is not always true. The right character might turn up without the style in which it needs to be expressed. Or the style is there, but with nothing to talk about.

Over a year later, the November–December 1950 issue of *Partisan Review* contained something by Bellow called 'The Trip to Galena'. An asterisk drew the reader to a note at the bottom of the page: 'This is a chapter from a novel in progress called *The Crab and the Butterfly*'.

'The Trip to Galena' featured two convalescents, called Weyl and Scampi, talking to each other in a hospital. But no, that is not quite an accurate description. In 'The Trip to Galena', Weyl talked and Scampi listened. And Weyl was properly Bellovian – he could talk, no doubt about it – 'What say? Your feet have the habit of shoes; your lords and masters give you a pair taken from a man who dies under the impression that he was going to get a shower-bath. You have the shoes two days and they're the darlings of your feet. What's that – treachery from the feet? What do you want? They're not the Michelangelo feet of Evangelists or of the saints treading the air to Paradise, but the street-formed feet of an ordinary, humble, lousy Darmstadt meter-reader with yolky bunions and bursitis bumps.' But he was not yet in a Bellovian novel. There was still a time lag. That 'yolky' was good. It was hard-working. But the conversation was not. Its plot was just a pretext – too flimsy, too tacked-on.

Chapter iv
Chicago, 1949–53: Almost a Style

Then, in 1953, Bellow published *The Adventures of Augie March*, a
novel narrated by Augie himself.

Augie

I am an American, Chicago born – Chicago, that somber city – and go at
things as I have taught myself, free-style, and will make the record in my
own way: first to knock, first admitted; sometimes an innocent knock, sometimes a not so innocent. But a man's character is his fate, says Heraclitus,
and in the end there isn't any way to disguise the nature of the knocks by
acoustical work on the door or gloving the knuckles.

Everybody knows there is no fineness or accuracy of suppression; if you
hold down one thing you hold down the adjoining.

This opening is famous. Because it was not written in English. The
opening talked in American. But what does it mean, to write *free-
style*? Four years earlier, the November 1949 issue of *Partisan Review*
had contained 'From the Life of Augie March', by Saul Bellow –
the first chapter of a prospective novel that had then been called
Life Among the Machiavellians. And this was similar but different:

Augie unrevised

I am an American, Chicago born – Chicago, that sombre city – and go at
things as I have taught myself, free-style, and will make the record in my
own way: first to knock, first admitted; sometimes an innocent knock, sometimes a not so innocent. But a man's character is his fate, says Heraclitus,
and in the end there isn't any way to disguise the nature of the knocks by
acoustic work on the door or gloving the knuckles. I'm curious myself to

know what kind of knocks will come up when I set up a bid. I dislike the stickiness of guile you find even in the best intentioned records of lives. And everybody knows there is no fineness or accuracy of suppression; if you hold down one thing you hold down the adjoining. On the other hand, to invite all knocks is a great gamble. You never can tell but what some muscle strengthened grossly by unconscious bad habits and vices may deliver the kind of knock that brings the door down and tears a hole in the side of the house, a much more dangerous kind of knock than the theosophist ones invited by the evening séance, for these are presumably of another world, presumably from over the border of death, by spirits and souls that have passed intact into the host of chatty spooks. But these living knocks may bring to the front something less than comforting, so it's a daring decision to say, 'Okay, slam away, I'm ready.' But that elementary confidence. Man! it isn't too much to ask of myself at the age of forty, or near it. A whole lot less than asking the Seraphim of Isaiah to unveil their eyes before the awful presence. Only a willingness to entertain these knocks.

No free-style is truly free – that is the lesson of this earlier draft. A free-style has to be invented. This earlier 1949 version extended the metaphor too far – clumsily, and bookishly.

Only through revising can a novel look like it is improvised. The free-style version is a consciously edited style.

I can put this more generally, more grandly: all literary values are founded on hard work. The distance between the initial draft and the final style is one way of measuring these values. It is one way of understanding that drafts are nothing: only works count. Literary value resides in the gap between the draft and the work.

And this takes time.

The Adventures of Augie March is the beginning of Bellow's stylistic triumph. But no novelist begins triumphant. Or only rarely. Novelists begin with practice. Bellow's fiction from 1944 to 1953 forms an atelier: a gym, a sparring joint. It was a place where, through repetition and adjustment, Bellow grew his singular muscles. It was not a revolution. If there was a transformation, that transformation was nervous, hard-working, erratic. It was an effort of rereading.

Ambition is much more embarrassing, much more needy and more charming than people often think; it is much less ambitious.

Chapter v

La Mancha, 1605: A Short Essay on Ideas (II)

It is not just me, and André Gide, who are bored by ideas: other people were bored too. When George Sand attacked Gustave Flaubert, writing to him that 'you seek for nothing more than the well-made sentence, it is something – but only something – it isn't the whole of art, it isn't even the half of it', Flaubert replied, as he always did, that for him the well-made sentence was, in fact, everything. And when an interviewer from the BBC asked Vladimir Nabokov why he disliked 'serious' writers, Nabokov replied: 'By inclination and intent I avoid squandering my art on the illustrated catalogues of solemn notions and serious opinions; and I dislike their pervasive presence in the works of others. What ideas can be traced in my novels belong to my creatures therein and may be deliberately flawed. In my memoirs, quotable ideas are merely passing visions, suggestions, mirages of the mind. They lose their colors or explode like football fish when lifted out of the context of their tropical sea.'

But I have an ulterior motive. I am not just attacking ideas for the fun of it.

Ideas are the ultimate in content; they are the high point of subject matter. Understanding how ideas lose their seriousness – how they become relative to the characters, transient, impermanent – is a way of understanding what irony in a novel is, too.

In a novel, irony emerges through a system of juxtaposition. This means that ironic novels often have the structure of a tie.

One of Nabokov's lectures on *Don Quixote* was called 'Victories and Defeats'. In it, he detailed 'the forty episodes in which Don Quixote acts as a knight-errant'. And Nabokov continued: 'Let us now follow him through his forty encounters. In most of them there is a delusion. The delusion ends in either victory or defeat, and the victory is often a moral one. Behind the delusion stands the actual event. We shall count as we go, the winning and losing points. The match starts. Let us see who wins: Don Quixote or his enemies.'

It takes a reader like Nabokov, with his talent for close reading, to decide to make this kind of table. And it takes this kind of talent to reach the happy result: 'So the final score is 20–20, or in terms of tennis 6–3, 3–6, 6–4, 5–7. But the fifth set will never be played; Death cancels the match. In terms of encounters the score is even: twenty victories against twenty defeats. Moreover, in each of the two parts of the book the score is also even: 13 to 13 and 7 to 7, respectively. This perfect balance of victory and defeat is very amazing in what seems such a disjointed haphazard book. It is due to a secret sense of writing, the harmonizing intuition of the artist.'

It is this tie which structures *Don Quixote*'s irony. Don Quixote is a misreader, whose misreading is good at heart. Its motives are moral – their root is gentleness, and kindness. But this misreading is still a mistake. He still makes the mistake of identifying with what he reads, to the extent of trying to live out a romance in reality. And so Don Quixote, who is saintly, is also comic.

The wronged can also be wrong. That is one way in which irony can work.

So this is the story of how Saul Bellow began with international ideas, like football fish; but he ended up with an international style, like a tropical sea.

His first method was to improve his choice of who he robbed.

Chapter vi
Versailles, 1712: The United States of Europe (I)

The Duc de Saint-Simon wrote his memoirs secretly, at night, at the court of Louis XIV. Stendhal liked him; Proust liked him. Witold Gombrowicz liked him. And so did Bellow.

There is not only no such thing as the history of the American novel, or the European novel, there is also no such thing as the history of the world novel, either. There is only a history of novels. And the lesson of the Duc de Saint-Simon's readers is that, often, these novels have contradictory, international influences. Only by developing contradictory influences do novelists develop an individual style.

No formal element is so individual that it cannot be transported, and re-used. Originality more often consists in the new combination of old things, than the new combination of new things. It is often a more complicated construction, driven by the pressure of new material, discoveries in real life. And Bellow had new material. He had all of Chicago, he had all of Jewishness in America.

Influence is a complicated thing. There is copying, and copying is simple, but then there is everything else – the more structural, more abstract, more independent influences. These are less influences than steals. They are an apprenticeship. Reading ambitiously, a writer is on the lookout for techniques to adapt. And this creates some weird genealogies.

There is one overt clue that Saint-Simon is a travestied stylistic presence in *The Adventures of Augie March*. Towards the end, Augie meets a guy called du Niveau in Paris. 'When we met he told me he was a descendant of the Duc de Saint-Simon. I'm always a sucker for lineage, but this du Niveau didn't really look very good.' This is an emblem. It is a way of describing Bellow's style: a sucker for lineage, which is also happy with the down-at-heel, the disinherited.

Saint-Simon's style in his memoirs was an ideal of notation, dense with adjectival description. So that this was Saint-Simon's summary portrait of Madame de Maintenon, Louis XIV's second wife, as she lay on her deathbed:

Madame de Maintenon

She was strong, brave, German to her fingertips, open, upright, moral and generous, noble and superior in everything she did, and meticulous about everything which concerned what she was due. She was uncivilised, always shut up writing, except for the brief periods of court at her establishment; the rest of the time, alone with her ladies; hard, rude, easily developing aversions to people, and to be feared for the attacks she made sometimes, and on anyone at all; no charm, no elegance of wit, though she did not lack wit; no flexibility, jealous, as has been said, with great meticulousness about everything which she was due; the face and yobbishness of a Swiss guard, capable with that of tender and inviolable friendship.

Saint-Simon's prose style was not courtly: it was not stylish. Instead, it allowed itself contradiction, grammatical obscurity, repetition, periphrasis, precision. It was a style based on an impacted note form, a concentrate of information and imagined information whose source was malice, was gossip.

And I can understand that Saint-Simon, at the court of Louis XIV, may seem an implausible influence on the son of Russian-Jewish immigrants in Chicago in the middle of the twentieth century, but that is precisely why it is plausible. Since Bellow was clever with his influences, he was not influenced only by predictable influences.

Let's use a conveniently American analogy: like a baseball pitcher mixing deliveries, Bellow mixed his influences.

A style that is allowable for a memoir is also allowable for a novel. Bellow's perception of this was a minor moment of creativity. And it then allowed the great sharp packed descriptions like these:

'With the holder in her dark little gums between which all her guile, malice, and command issued, she had her best inspirations of strategy. She was as wrinkled as an old paper bag, an autocrat, hard-shelled and jesuitical, a pouncy old hawk of a Bolshevik, her small ribboned gray feet immobile on the shoekit and stool Simon had made in the manual-training class, dingy old wool Winnie whose bad smell filled the flat on the cushion beside her.'

Yes, style is international. It is nothing to do with place names. It is not limited by its provenance in Versailles, or Chicago.

Chapter vii

New York, 1953: A Digression on the Theme of Jewishness (I)

The novelist Isaac Bashevis Singer was born in Poland in 1904, and moved to America in 1935. He wrote his novels in his first language, Yiddish. In America, he continued to write in Yiddish until his death.

Around twenty years after he arrived in America, in 1953, his career in English translation was begun by the American novelist Saul Bellow.

Jewishness in this book is a motif for placelessness. It is the motif for universality, for a happy cosmopolitanism. But in his essay 'Greenhorn in Sea Gate', describing his feelings as an immigrant, Singer was not happy with cosmopolitanism. 'Literature has neglected the terrible trauma of those who are forced to leave their land, abandon their language and begin a new life somewhere else,' wrote Singer. 'Disruption of this kind must be especially painful to artists – writers and actors whose linguistic roots are the essence of their creation.'

But his disruption was not always so ontological; often, it was local, and practical. For instance, it involved notebooks. The printed red line for a margin on the left-hand side of American exercise books – this was a minor hindrance to a writer who jotted notes in Yiddish, from right to left. 'If there wouldn't be this red line,' said Singer, 'I might really have become a genius.'

Saul Bellow's translation of Singer's story 'Gimpel the Fool' was published in 1953 – in the hip yet highbrow magazine *Partisan Review*. A few months later, Bellow published *The Adventures of Augie March*. His translation of Singer's story announced, simultaneously, another great Jewish and American writer. Its first lines were clipped, precise. 'I am Gimpel the fool. I don't think myself a fool.' It was a triumph of translation.

Unfortunately, it was also mistranslated. This is not necessarily a complete contradiction.

In Yiddish, Singer's first sentences were: 'Ikh bin gimpl tam. Ikh halt mikh nisht far keyn nar.' Which, literally, mean: 'I am Gimpel the *tam*. I don't think myself a *nar* at all.' But a *tam* is not quite a fool; in Yiddish, it is more of a holy fool, a naïf, an innocent. Whereas a *nar* is a simple dolt, an idiot.

In the story, Gimpel will be proved to be right: he is an innocent, maybe, but he is not stupid. In this world, however, sweet can appear a little simple. Bellow's speechy repetition of 'fool' – which was lovely in its bluntness – therefore also overemphasised the story's ironic balance from the outset.

That is one of the perils of writing in a small language – and Yiddish is a small language: a novelist is dependent on translators. He or she cannot therefore always control a novel's intended meaning. The micro-tricks of a style can disappear.

And yet Bellow's version of Singer's story is a minor masterpiece. So that the reader without any Yiddish is faced with the uncomfortable idea that, although the micro-tricks were lost in translation, Singer's style was able to accommodate quite a lot of loss and destruction. It was not the delicate thing that a style is meant to be.

Although this book is an attempt to describe the utopian desire for a rustless and larvae-free style, the lost ideal of Miss Herbert, it is not set in a utopia. This section, after all, takes place in the United, not delighted, States. Its subject is not cosmopolitan utopia, but universal imperfection.

Chapter viii
Paris, 1840: The United States of Europe (II)

Saul Bellow, as he tried to invent his style in the early 1950s, was not just on the lookout for fluid ways to do things with sentences. He also needed a fluid form. And one clue to Bellow's new form is in the title. The adventures of Augie March are called *The Adventures of Augie March*. The form is picaresque. It is the same form as the adventures of Don Quixote. But this does not mean that, like *Don Quixote*, it is a ragbag. There is a form, but Bellow uses as minimal a form as possible.

In *The Adventures of Augie March*, Bellow was writing a comedy – where there was a binary opposition between the hard and the soft; between independence and the need to be loved; between feeling which shades into the sentimental, and intelligence which shades into the cynical. 'I certainly looked like an ideal recruit. But the invented things never became real for me no matter how I urged myself to think they were . . .' The novel is about how Augie is everyone's protégé, and how he rejects all his mentors as well.

Rather than being based on one idea, then, *The Adventures of Augie March* is based on two polarities. Within these polarities, a character could occupy any space, or even occupy more than one space.

The Adventures of Augie March is in American. But the voice which Bellow invents, and its helterskelter form, are just as much from Paris as Chicago.

The direct influence here, for instance, on the form, is Stendhal. Just as for Tolstoy, Stendhal provided a useful model of a form which did not seem formal at all.

There is a major clue to Stendhal's influence on the form of *Augie* – which is Bellow's abbreviated note jotted down on the back of the novel's manuscript: 'Doesn't want to be what others want to make of him – Stendhal main example of this.' And this central theme was echoed by Augie himself: 'But what did people seem to me anyhow, something fantastic? I didn't want to be what they made of me but wanted to please them. Kindly explain! An independent fate, and love too – what confusion!'

Some people have a problem with Bellow in the same way as they have a problem with Stendhal. They do not notice the binary form. Because they do not notice, they think Stendhal, or Bellow, cannot organise the detail in a narrative. They think he is too ragged.

Sometimes *ragged* is just the adjective people use for novels whose form is more careful, more implicit than is normally the case. Because Tolstoy was not ragged, and Bellow was not ragged. And nor was Stendhal.

On 25 September 1840, in the *Revue parisienne*, Balzac wrote a rave review of Stendhal's novel *La Chartreuse de Parme* (*The Charterhouse of Parma*); but although it was a rave review, there were still things that Balzac did not like. Balzac was one of the people who thought Stendhal was too ragged. His novel, he thought, lacked method. In Balzac's opinion, there were two main problems – the beginning and the end. Neither was tailored chronologically to the life story of the hero, Fabrizio.

Naturally, this rave review upset Stendhal.

That is because Balzac had misunderstood the novel. Its subject is not Fabrizio. In *La Chartreuse*, there is an opposition between luck and energy. The subject of the novel is how a person can haphazardly overcome luck through their own personal energy.

Stendhal was not writing a conventional novel. And Stendhal tried to explain this. 'We will admit that, following the example of many serious writers, we have begun the story of our hero a year before he is born'. It was Stendhal's helpful allusion to *Tristram*

Shandy. Sterne was the first novelist to realise that there was a way of writing a novel other than chronologically. A novel could be written thematically too.

Stendhal understood, Bellow understood. But Balzac, although he loved Laurence Sterne, did not.

Chapter ix
New York, 1943: Jewishness (II)

In some of Isaac Bashevis Singer's surviving notebooks and diaries there are jotted glossaries. One, dated 19 May, without a year, has a list of English words beside their equivalents in Yiddish. These words are minor, without gravity: like blocks of Lego.

Fuss

Adjust

Snail

Daisy

Spare

Victuals

Sumptuous

Repast

Superb

to Excel

Filch

Indem(nify)

Indemnity

Summary(ily)

In his diaries, on scraps of paper, Singer compiled vocabulary notes – working hard at the English language, its American version.

A style is not just a prose style. It is, said Marcel Proust, a quality of vision. With this idea in mind, I think it is possible to say something new, and surprising.

A style is not identical to the language in which it takes form.

Singer's own attitude to Yiddish was sternly absolute. In 1943, eight years after arriving in America, he wrote two essays on Yiddish: one about Yiddish in the old country, 'Concerning Yiddish Literature in Poland'; and one about Yiddish in the new, 'Problems of Yiddish Prose in America'. The argument of each piece was the same. He rejected the idea of modernity – both in a writer's subject matter and, especially, in the language: 'Americanisms reek of foreignness, of cheap glitter, of impermanence. The result is that the better Yiddish writers avoid treating American life, and they are subjectively (aesthetically) right to do so.' His conclusion was a literary ghetto – 'Yiddish literature', he argued, 'is a product of the ghetto with all its virtues and faults, and it can never leave that ghetto', not without becoming 'a caricature of a language'.

And yet it was also possible for Singer to argue less sternly, less absolutely. According to him, he treated – or said that he treated – the Yiddish original as a rough draft, a preliminary sketch. By 1975, Singer said about his translators, 'I dictate to them in English, my English. They polish my English.' Two years earlier, he called English his 'second original language'. It is not, therefore, clear what language Singer wrote in. It was Yiddish and American, at the same time. 'The English translation is especially important to me,' wrote Singer, 'because translations into other languages are based on the English text. In a way, this is right because, in the process of translation, I make many corrections. I always remember the saying of the Cabalists that man's mission is the correction of the mistakes he made both in this world and in former reincarnations.'

A style is a quality of vision; it is not limited by language.

Chapter x
Chicago, 1953: Bellow's Style

In *The Adventures of Augie March*, Bellow's style becomes playful. It discovers the joys of excess, of the vulgar, the ordinary. And this effort of inclusion is the oddest thing about Bellow's style. Most style is exclusive, it learns what to leave out. Whereas since Bellow started with such a studied refusal of inelegance, he had to learn the opposite. He had to learn how to include, how to stop being so serious – to become a novelist, a prospector, and not an intellectual.

So that now there were similes, like this: '"You weren't going to shoot, were you?" I said. He was reaching inside his sleeve with a lifted shoulder, almost like a woman pulling up an inside strap.' Or sentences crammed with precise adjectives: 'all was rich, was heavy, velvet, lepidopterous'. Or, my favourite, his description of diarrhoea: 'I still had the dysentery bug and in the morning often felt that heavy drape of the guts that made me run to the biffy . . .' (a heaviness which is quite the opposite of Caligula the eagle's 'straight, heavy squirt of excrement'.)

And this dense network of detail meant that finally, finally, Bellow's great ideas went haywire.

This is how ideas lose their seriousness – when they are so embedded in their context that they cannot ever be generally applicable. All their pretensions to truth are undermined.

One variation of irony in a novel is this: *irony* means that somewhere, somehow, an idea in one part of a book is contradicted by an idea in another part of the book. And neither idea is proved to be right.

Like Flaubert's variation, it is based on a system of relentless juxtaposition. The novel is the art of careful collage.

Towards the end of *The Adventures of Augie March*, Augie's friend

Clem Tambow says to him: '"What I guess about you is that you have a nobility syndrome. You can't adjust to the reality situation. I can see it all over you. You want there should be Man, with capital M, with great stature. As we've been pals since boyhood, I know you and what you think. Remember how you used to come to the house every day? But I know what you want. O *paidea*! O King David! O Plutarch and Seneca! O chivalry, O Abbot Suger! O Strozzi Palace, O Weimar! O Don Giovanni, O lineaments of gratified desire! O godlike man! Tell me, pal, am I getting warm or not?"' And this was true self-criticism, on Bellow's part. All the seriousness was being sent up.

Bellow's great invention in *Augie* was to repeat himself, at a higher speed – to intensify all his serious quirks, to draw them on a larger scale and so make them weird and cartoonish. It was not quite a revolution. It was much more gradual. The crucial difference was this: the ideas in *Augie* were all there because Augie liked ideas. He shared the younger Bellow's cute idea that ideas are a good idea.

This means that *The Adventures of Augie March* is a comedy.

'Pretty soon I'll be unassailable,' said Bellow, after *Augie* was published, 'and I can write philosophy like Tolstoy.' And he was right, in a way. He was right in a way which perhaps he did not mean. He had made it – he could write philosophy that wasn't really philosophy at all. Everything was a comedy instead. He had come up with his own ragged careful style, which talked in American, and was also French as well. He had learned how to imitate only himself. Because this is another mark of originality: once a novelist has discovered a style, then he or she has to learn how to repeat it. Once a novelist has a style, the only style left to imitate is itself.

Chapter xi
London, 2007: Anachronism

At this point, maybe I can return to one of my theories.

Tolstoy may not have written his ironic philosophy intentionally. After all, he respected ideas. The irony may have been a side effect of his compendious style, not a deliberate effect. While although Saul Bellow could see the funny side of ideas, the comedy of certainty and earnestness, he also remained enamoured of ideas, simultaneously.

In the case of Tolstoy, therefore, the irony was my invention. In Bellow's case, it co-existed with a respect for ideas as well.

The irony in each case was a little anachronistic: it was a fluke of retrospective reading.

BOOK 12

Мама

On 16 April 1897, recovering from two weeks of treatment in Moscow for tuberculosis, Chekhov wrote a letter. 'Every cloud has a silver lining,' he added, in a postscript. 'I had a visit in the clinic from Lev Nikolayevich, and we had an exceptionally interesting conversation – exceptionally interesting for me at any rate, because I listened more than I spoke. We discussed immortality. He accepts the idea of immortality in the Kantian sense, proposing that all of us (human beings and animals) will continue to live on in some primal state (reason, love), the essence and purpose of which is a mystery hidden from us. However, this primal state or force appears to me to be a shapeless mass of jelly, into which my "I", my individuality, my consciousness, would be absorbed. I don't feel any need for immortality in this form. I don't understand it, but Lev Nikolyaevich finds it astonishing that I don't understand it.'

This person whom Chekhov found so difficult to understand was Lev Nikolyaevich Tolstoy, Chekhov's friend.

There are two things which everyone knows about friendships: they are often surprising, and they are often difficult.

It might seem odd, this friendship between Tolstoy and Chekhov – the fat man and the thin one, the white beard and the dark goatee. Sometimes, it seemed odd to Leo and Anton themselves. In A. B. Goldenveizer's *Talks with Tolstoi*, one entry, from 29 April 1900, records how 'Tolstoi as usual praised Chekhov's artistic gift very highly. The lack of a definite world conception grieves him in Chekhov ...' A friendship is a complicated thing. Because there is

not only love and tenderness in a friendship; there is frustration and cattiness too.

But maybe friendships between writers are slightly different. In the case of Tolstoy and Chekhov, it could well be based on a happy inequality between a great writer and his talented but sometimes wayward disciple. Because friendships are less to do with personality, and more to do with style. The Tolstoy of his novels is not quite the same as the Tolstoy of his conversations – especially not his later conversations, when he had grown his long white beard. It may have been that their conversations were difficult, but conversations are not the only basis of a friendship.

Three years after Tolstoy came to see him in hospital, Chekhov movingly and calmly stated: 'I fear the death of Tolstoy.' In his Chekhovian way, according to his style, he went on to analyse this feeling into its two constituent parts: 'In the first place, there is no other person whom I love as I love him; I am not a religious person, but of all faiths I find his the closest to me and the most congenial. Secondly, when literature possesses a Tolstoy, it is easy and pleasant to be a writer; even when you know that you have achieved nothing yourself and are still achieving nothing, this is not as terrible as it might otherwise be, because Tolstoy achieves for everyone. What he does serves to justify all the hopes and aspirations invested in literature.'

That is why Chekhov and Tolstoy were friends. They admired each other's work. And the work was beyond them. The work was not personal.

And yet, still, something is troubling. What is this thing, 'a definite world conception'? Why should Leo want Anton to have one? Why should Anton not want to have one?

Or even: what is a friendship?

Chapter ii
Nice, 1897: On the Cart (I)

At the end of the nineteenth century, Marya – a spinster schoolmistress – is on her way home from the town where she collects her monthly salary. She is being driven in a horse-drawn cart by a coachman called Simon. It is April, but 'it might be spring, as now. It might be a rainy autumn evening or winter. What difference did it make?' For she is lost in thought.

She thinks about her exams, the brutal school watchman, the problems of obtaining firewood for the schoolroom. She does not think much about her life before she became a schoolteacher, because she does not remember much about it. 'Her father had died when she was ten, her mother soon after.' She is no longer in touch with her brother. 'All she had left from those days was a snapshot of her mother and that had faded, as the schoolhouse was so damp – all you could see of Mother now was hair and eyebrows.'

As they keep driving, the terrain becomes muddier.

They meet a landowner called Hanov, whom Marya knows slightly. He is 'a man of about forty, with a worn face and a bored look, had begun to show his age, but was still handsome and attractive to women.' The schoolmistress, for example, still thinks that Hanov is attractive. The road gets so muddy that Hanov and Simon have to get down and lead the horse. Looking at Hanov, Marya thinks that 'there was a hint of something in the way he walked which showed that he was really a feeble, poisoned creature well on the road to ruin.' And then it strikes her 'that if she was his wife or sister she would very likely give her whole life to saving him.' But she dismisses the romantic fantasy.

Hanov turns off onto another road. The journey is boring, difficult: 'They kept turning back.' They stop at an inn at Lower Gorodishche. There are wagons in the courtyard filled with large bottles of sulphuric acid. On the last leg of the journey they have to cross a river. Simon decides to cross through the water rather than continuing on to the bridge a few miles away. The horse goes in up to his belly. 'Marya's galoshes and boot were full of water, the bottom of her dress and coat and one sleeve were sopping wet – and worst of all, her sugar and flour were soaked.' On the other side, at a railway crossing, the barrier is down. The schoolmistress gets down from the cart, shivering. She can see her village, and 'the school with its green roof'. The train crosses.

A train crosses in Russia

On the small platform at the end of a first-class carriage stood a woman and Marya glanced at her. It was her mother! What a fantastic likeness! Her mother had the same glorious hair, exactly the same forehead and the set of the head. Vividly, with striking clarity, for the first time in thirteen years, she pictured her mother and father, her brother, their Moscow flat, the fish-tank and goldfish – all down to the last detail. Suddenly she heard a piano playing, heard her father's voice and felt as she had felt then – young, pretty, well-dressed in a warm, light room, with her family round her. In a sudden surge of joy and happiness she clasped her head rapturously in her hands.

'Mother,' she cried tenderly, appealingly.

And she bursts into tears, just as Hanov arrives at the crossing. 'Seeing him, she imagined such happiness as has never been on earth. She smiled and nodded to him as to her friend and equal, feeling that the sky, the trees and all the windows were aglow with her triumphant happiness. No, her father and mother had not died, she had never been a schoolmistress. It had all been a strange dream, a long nightmare, and now she had woken up . . .' But this romance is interrupted by the driver, asking her to get back in the cart. 'Suddenly, it all vanished. The barrier slowly rose. Shivering, numb with cold, Marya got into the cart.' They cross over into the village. '"Well, here we are. Vyazovye."'

And that is the end of the standard English translation of the story 'In the Cart', by Anton Chekhov, written in Nice in the same year that Tolstoy came to talk to him in hospital: 1897.

Chapter iii
Nice, 1897: On Style

Chekhov's definition of talent was that a writer should be 'capable of distinguishing between testimony which is important and testimony which is not, be skilled at illuminating my characters and speaking in their language.' His style was not interested in overt and glitzy linguistic effects, instead it was based on a combination of economy and reticence.

But reticence cannot be entirely reticent. An entirely reticent story would be unreadable.

In the standard translation of Chekhov's story 'In the Cart', there is a small mistake. Marya's first glimpse of the woman she thought was her mother made her use the word мат' – мат' is the Russian for mother. But when she cried out, overcome by memories and sadness and happiness, she did not say мат': she said мама.

This word is international. It means mama.

Unlike the English version, in Russian, Chekhov talks Marya's language, he offers one crucial piece of testimony: the shift from мат' to мама.

In Chekhov's story nothing is hidden: it means what it says. Its focus is Marya's dead mother.

Since this story is about Marya's mother, it is about everything that is not her mother. It is about going on living when the people you love are dead: it is structured on the contrast between the drudgery of the present moment and the idyll of her remembered past. The details in this story – the large bottles of sulphuric acid, the wet sleeve – are there as the weight of the present world on

Marya, who cannot forget what she has lost. It must be remembered, said Samuel Johnson, who to my surprise is becoming a major minor character in my book, 'that life consists not of a series of illustrious actions, or elegant enjoyments; the greater part of our time passes in compliance with necessities, in the performance of daily duties, in the removal of small inconveniences, in the procurement of petty pleasures'. Or, as Franz Kafka said, who is only a minor character so far, but is about to become a major one: 'In the battle between you and the world, back the world.' This is the contrast on which Chekhov's story is based: the distressing mismatch between the past and the future; the way in which happiness is only ever a memory, or a fantasy.

Not much description, therefore, is necessary to create a story. And so Chekhov developed his style of reticence and economy: there was no need for anything more. There was no need for more stylistic effects than the small shift to the word мама, which is no longer in Chekhov's language, but in Marya's. All of Marya's fragility and sadness is in her use of the word мама – it describes her helpless yearning to be happy again.

You do not need to be extravagant, in order to be precise. Nor do you need to be clear about everything, in order to be clear. Shortness is fine.

Chapter iv
Moscow, 1888: Economy

Sometimes, people are worried about characters: these characters, in fictions, seem so denuded, so described. This comprehensive description can often make them seem unrealistic – for one definition of a person is a bundle of perceptions and psychologies which cannot be fully known.

But there are two things wrong with this.

The first mistake is ethical. It cannot be voyeuristic or wrong to know about the private life of an imaginary character. A character is not a person. Knowing things that a character does not know is the precondition of an ironic narrative. Without that disjuncture, there would be no irony. The ethical and the aesthetic do not match up, they are incommensurate. A character has no ethical rights. A character, unlike a person, has no right to privacy.

The second objection is aesthetic: it is never true that description is comprehensive. Even in the most explicit of fictions, there are things which are not described, not because they cannot be described, but because they do not need to be described. The first aesthetic principle is economy.

And Chekhov was a great economist.

In a letter to his friend and patron, Suvorin, Chekhov famously repeated his artistic position that a writer should not have an artistic position: 'You are right to demand that an author take conscious stock of what he is doing, but you are confusing two concepts: *answering the questions* and *formulating them correctly*. Only the latter is required of an author.' And I like the fact that this echoes a letter by Tolstoy, his aesthetic assertion that the 'aim of an artist is not to solve a problem irrefutably'. I am not saying that Chekhov ever saw this letter. I am just saying that this is something he had in common – on the level of art, on the level of style – with his older, frustrating friend.

But this shared clarity of presentation seems to have led in two different directions. Whereas Tolstoy, in his fictions, is seen as a monster of hassle, of interruption and shepherding, Chekhov is seen as an angel of discretion, of reticent ambiguity.

In Chekhov's style, however, economy is not the same thing as perpetual ambiguity. It is useful to remember that Chekhov's favourite writer was Guy de Maupassant, and that Chekhov nursed a project to translate Maupassant's stories into Russian. Maupassant's clarity of presentation, the clean lines of his ironies, were Chekhov's model.

I need another moment in Chekhov's correspondence.

On 9 June 1888, Chekhov wrote to his friend Shcheglov: 'A psychologist should not pretend to understand what he does not understand. Moreover, a psychologist should not convey the impression that he understands what no one understands. We shall not play the charlatan, and we will declare frankly that nothing is clear in this world. Only fools and charlatans know and understand everything.'

This might look as if Chekhov disagrees with me about Chekhov, but the crucial thing, as always, is the context. Shcheglov had written to him after reading Chekhov's story 'Lights', on 29 May 1888: 'that finale – "You can't figure out anything in this world . . ." – is abrupt; it is certainly the writer's job to figure out what goes on in the heart of his hero, otherwise his psychology will remain unclear.'

In his answer to Shcheglov, Chekhov was being slightly cheeky; he was deliberately confusing two issues. It is true that no one ever understands everything about someone. And it is also true that no novelist ever knows everything about a character – but in each case what 'everything' means is different. In the case of a person, a totality of facts exists – it is just not known. In the case of a character, this totality of facts does not exist: it is unverifiable. This does not mean that the totality of facts for a character is arbitrary – the facts that might be possible are constrained by plausibility. But there is no way of knowing facts which are outside the story. They are not unknown, just non-existent.

Chekhov's position is therefore not a position of ethical humility: it is aesthetic, not ethical. Aesthetically, there is no need to understand everything about a character. Only the salient details need to be described. That is because it is fiction. In fiction, what is not described is simultaneously infinite and irrelevant.

This is where the similarity, the friendship, between Chekhov and Tolstoy can become more visible. 'Turgenev's opinion that one can't spend ten pages describing what N. N. did with his hand helped me very much', Tolstoy had written. And Chekhov, for his own part, gave this advice to the novelist Alexander Kuprin. 'Your first chapter is taken up with descriptions of people's appearances – again an old-fashioned device; you could easily do without these descriptions. Describing in detail how five people look overburdens the reader's span of attention, and ultimately loses all value. Clean-shaven actors resemble one another like Catholic priests, and they'll go on resembling one another no matter how much effort you put into describing them.'

Chapter v
Hertfordshire, 1815: More Examples of Irony

At the beginning of the nineteenth century, a young girl called Catherine Morland, who has a passion for Gothic novels, is taken to Bath by some family friends, the Allens. In Bath, she falls in love with a man called Mr Tilney. She is invited to stay with Mr Tilney and his sister at Northanger Abbey – where the Tilneys live with their menacing father. Here, Catherine imagines horrific and Gothic events to be taking place, when in fact nothing extraordinary is taking place at all. Eventually, having been cured of her imaginative tendencies, Catherine and Mr Tilney become engaged to be married. And that is how the story happens in Jane Austen's novel *Northanger Abbey*.

Catherine is another name for Don Quixote, or Madame Bovary.

These people, in England or Spain, or Normandy – wherever – are hapless readers: they read romantically. Don Quixote misread chivalrous romances; Catherine misread Gothic novels.

Austen's novel, with its ordinary plot, which its heroine believes is Gothically extraordinary, provides the agile reader with vocabulary lists, with a dictionary of skewered romantic clichés. This is partly because the novel is an attack on bad style, and on

bad reading. But it is also because reading becomes the most convenient metaphor, in this form whose medium is words, for understanding.

Northanger Abbey therefore becomes a parody of a certain romantic vocabulary.

And so it is possible to make a vocabulary list, from *Northanger Abbey*. It is possible to imagine synonyms, a kind of English to English vocabulary list, or Gothic to English: so that definitions of *balm*, or *disappointed*, can be obtained through the sentences: 'Catherine was delighted with this extension of her Bath acquaintance, and almost forgot Mr Tilney while she talked to Miss Thorpe. Friendship is certainly the finest balm for the pangs of disappointed love.' Or *grand*:

'Had I the command of millions, were I mistress of the whole world, your brother would be my only choice.'

This charming sentiment, recommended as much by sense as novelty, gave Catherine a most pleasing remembrance of all the heroines of her acquaintance; and she thought her friend never looked more lovely than in uttering the grand idea.

(And I like the fact that the word *grand* also troubled Leo Tolstoy: so that in *War and Peace* he growled about *grand*'s imported romanticism: '"*C'est grand!*" say the historians, and there no longer exists either good or evil, but only "*grand*" and "*not grand*". *Grand* is good, not *grand* is bad. Grand is the characteristic, in their conception, of some special animals called "heroes". And Napoleon escaping home in a warm fur coat and leaving to perish those who were not merely his comrades but were (in his opinion) men he had brought there, feels *que c'est grand*, and his soul is tranquil.'

Just as Flaubert had discovered in Egypt that the oriental was already domestic, so Tolstoy knew that there was no reason for the glamour of the foreign; the foreign, after all, is only the domestic, once removed.)

The Gothic, according to this list, is the transposition of a mundane word to a comically inappropriate application.

The irony of *Northanger Abbey* is based on the idea that a character does not know something about the world of the novel which is obvious to the reader. That is the style of these novels' sentences – when the reader knows that a woman is not a romantic heroine, but a doctor's wife, or a nineteenth-century girl, whereas Madame Bovary, or Catherine, does not.

Austen's new style in English (which Flaubert would, unknowingly, perfect in French), where the sentences mime a character's thoughts and speak the character's language, developed a new area – where the reader knows something about the character that the character does not know: the range of possible fictional facts was extended into the internal as well as the external. So that it then becomes easier to describe, with precision, events like this.

At the beginning of the nineteenth century, once more, but this time in Hertfordshire, a clever but cocky girl called Emma decides that she will improve the lives of those around her. Her major project is to set up her friend Harriet with the curate, Mr Elton. Her efforts to bring this about, however, only convince Mr Elton that he and Emma are made for each other. And so this project fails. Meanwhile, Emma decides that the man of her dreams is the dashing Frank Churchill. But then Emma discovers that Frank Churchill is in fact already secretly engaged, just as she discovers that Harriet believes she is in love with Mr Knightley, Emma's most trusted friend, and whom Emma then finally realises she has been in love with all along.

Her story is a story of mistakes. And that is why as well as being Emma, Miss Woodhouse is also Don Quixote. For the way Emma thinks is exactly the way Don Quixote would think, if he were a clever but limited girl from a village in England, who was not very good at knowing who is in love with her: "'I thank you; but I assure you you are quite mistaken. Mr Elton and I are very good friends, and nothing more;" and she walked on, amusing herself in the consideration of the blunders which often arise from a partial knowledge of circumstances, of the mistakes which people of high pretension to judgement are for ever falling into . . .'

Irony, in this story, means that a character makes the mistake of not realising she is making a mistake. The irony, therefore, is not infinite: the ambiguity created by the reticence of the sentences, written in the character's language, is controlled by the precision of the plot. Irony is not the same thing as indeterminacy: it creates a suspension of judgement, not a refusal to accept that any judgement is possible at all.

Just because the novelist's job is not to pass judgement, but present the evidence, this does not mean that a law does not exist.

Chapter vi

Moscow, 1895: Economy (II)

In *The Life and Opinions of Tristram Shandy, Gentleman*, Laurence Sterne, or at least his surrogate narrator, came up with the witty orchestration of Dr Slop's entrance to the Shandy house: 'It is about an hour and a half's tolerable good reading since my uncle Toby rung the bell, when Obadiah was ordered to saddle a horse, and go for Dr Slop, the man-midwife; – so that no one can say, with reason, that I have not allowed Obadiah time enough, poetically speaking, and considering the emergency too, both to go and to come; – though, morally and truly speaking, the man, perhaps, has scarce had time to get on his boots.'

This overlap of two time-frames – the time-frame within the fictional novel, and the time-frame of the real-life reader – was another effect which was only possible because of Sterne's way of not obeying the simple principle that the story should be told in the same order that it happened. And so he could juxtapose not just time-frames within the story, but also the time-frame of the story with the present time-frame of the writer writing, and reader reading, the book. But, once these disjunctions have been admitted – and the admission is central to the art of the novel – other ways become possible of creating narrative form.

One neglected way is cropping.

To Bunin, Chekhov once said: 'When one has written a story I believe that one ought to strike out both the beginning and the end. That is where we novelists are most inclined to lie. And one must write shortly – as shortly as possible.'

There are many anecdotes like this. And I like them – they make me warm to Chekhov more and more, with his charming insouciance. In his *Reminiscences*, Schoukin relates the following advice given him by Chekhov: 'Try to tear up the first half of your story; you will have to change only very little in the opening of the second half, and the story will be perfectly intelligible. And as a rule, there must be nothing superfluous in it. Everything that has no direct relation to the story must be ruthlessly thrown away. If in the first chapter you say that a gun hangs on the wall, in the second or third chapter it must without fail be discharged.'

(Just as in Ernest Hemingway's memoir, *A Moveable Feast*, Hemingway describes his 'new theory that you could omit anything as long as you knew that you omitted and the omitted part would strengthen the story and make people feel something more than they understood.' But it was not a new theory. Chekhov was there first.)

And in Sobolev's memoir of Chekhov, Sobolev records how his friends used to worry that Chekhov's manuscripts should be removed for his own benefit: 'Otherwise he will reduce his stories only to this: that they were young, fell in love, then married and were unhappy.' When Chekhov was told this, he replied: 'But look here, so it does happen, indeed.' Or: 'To the question what would he do, if he became rich, Tchekhov answered with perfect seriousness: "I would write the tiniest possible stories . . ."'

The reason for this, however, is not quite a matter of technique. It is to do with the harshness underneath the meticulous tenderness of Chekhov's imagination. Stanislavsky remembered the anguish of rehearsing Chekhov's plays, subject as they were to Chekhov's sudden and persistent cuts. So that in *Three Sisters*:

In Act IV Andrey, talking to Ferapont, tells him what a wife is from the point of view of a provincial who has come down in the world. It was a superb monologue about two pages long. Suddenly we receive a note saying that all that monologue must be left out and the following words substituted for it:

'A wife is a wife!'

People, unfortunately, are simpler than many of us like to think. It is not out of delicacy or ethical respect for his characters that Chekhov uses such minimal means. It is because it is unnecessary to explain any further.

Not everyone likes this kind of truth. It seems unfair to the human animal. But it's true.

Chapter vii
London, 1768: Characters

No. Not everyone likes this kind of truth.

According to James Boswell, Samuel Johnson's biographer, Dr Johnson preferred the dazzlingly long and adagio novels of Samuel Richardson to the more concise and allegro novels of Henry Fielding. When comparing them, said Boswell, he 'used this expression: "that there was as great difference between them, as between a man who knew how a watch was made, and a man who could tell the hour by looking on the dial-plate." This was a short and figurative state of his distinction between drawing characters of nature and characters only of manners.'

But the precision and depth which Johnson found in Richardson's novels, unlike Fielding's, can be achieved through multiple techniques. It is not the same thing as length.

It is true that everyone likes to differentiate between characters and caricatures, or characters of nature and characters of manners, but these distinctions are often less aesthetic than ethical: they simply refer to a reader's idea of what a self is. Trying to improve his argument, Dr Johnson explained that 'Characters of manners are very entertaining; but they are to be understood by a more superficial observer, than characters of nature, where a man must dive into the recesses of the human heart.' But there is no reason why character cannot be displayed swiftly, through external action.

There is also a more philosophical assumption to Johnson's preferences in the matter of character. Johnson admired Richardson for his Christian perception of a self which was cosseted, internal, which could not be known by external means. It was based on privacy. Whereas Fielding was less sure that such a self was so hived off. His self was also social.

That is why I think that Dr Johnson was making a mistake. For a style cannot be dismissed on ethical grounds. A style is aesthetic only.

Even Dr Johnson – even one of my heroes – in the end, was sentimental. Because everyone is sentimental. He believed in the private complexity of the human animal. That was his version of romanticism.

Continuing his discussion of omission, Ernest Hemingway mentioned his story 'Big Two-Hearted River'. 'When I stopped writing I did not want to leave the river where I could see the trout in the pool, its surface pushing and welling smooth against the resistance of the log-driven piles of the bridge. The story was about coming back from the war but there was no mention of the war in it.' This story was about shell shock. And it does not mention shell shock. That is how you know it is about shell shock.

Often, the shortest things will do.

Chapter viii

Moscow, 1880: On Style (II)

Vladimir Nabokov once wrote that when he thought of Chekhov, 'all I can make out is a medley of dreadful prosaisms, ready-made epithets, repetitions, doctors, unconvincing vamps, and so forth: yet it is his works which I would take on a trip to another planet.' As a stylist, he was bewildered and confused by his love for Chekhov, who was not a stylist. But perhaps he did not need to be so confused. The paradox is that a writer whose sentences are hardly even sentences, just pale arrangements of words, is still a writer with a style. And Chekhov's style, like everyone else's style, is a collection of multiple objects – in his case, it is a fusion of concision, reticence, ventriloquism, and a vicious sense of humour.

Chekhov found things funny which to other people, perhaps, might seem sad. But that is not unusual. Just as when reading Cervantes, or Flaubert, or many other novelists in *The Delighted States*, the rattled reader might have to revise his or her sense of humour and become more accepting, more libertine.

It is easy to make another mistake about using minimal means. This mistake is that it is more delicate to use minimal means. Logically, however, this cannot be true. The fewer signs you use, the more efficient they must be. They must, therefore, be blunter.

And Chekhov can be a very blunt writer.

There is an early story by Chekhov, 'Because of Little Apples', written in 1880, when Chekhov was nineteen. A landowner finds an engaged couple who are otherwise engaged in eating apples from his orchard. The punishment he comes up with is that first the girl must beat the boy and then the boy must beat the girl. When the boy beats the girl, he cannot stop. He enjoys it too much. So the boy and the girl leave the orchard, their relationship irreparably damaged.

Nothing is missing in this story. It means what it says. It is nasty, and funny, but it is not an allegory, or a parable. It is just a description. All the psychological information the reader needs is there. It is a description of one way in which a couple might break up.

It is important to get Chekhov's sense of humour: it was not mild; it was implacable. Its central characteristic is a refusal of cliché. So, in 1880, Chekhov (or, as he used to sign himself, diminutively, Chekhonte) wrote a two-page story which is not a story, but a list of elements from other people's stories: 'What You Nearly Always Find in Novels, Stories etc.' This list (like Flaubert's *Dictionary of Received Ideas*) is full of iciness at the boredom induced by conventional literature.

Things that sometimes happen in real life but far too often in novels

A count, a countess whose face still bears traces of her former beauty, a baron living nearby, a literary man with liberal ideas, a nobleman fallen on hard times, a foreign musician, dull-witted footmen, nannies, governesses, a German estate manager, an English squire and an heir from America. Plain people but with nice attractive personalities. A hero who rescues the heroine from a runaway horse: he has great strength of character and is capable of showing the strength of his fists whenever a suitable occasion arises.

That is what Chekhov found funny: clichés – both in literature, and in real life.

The first story by Chekhov to be published in Britain (in *Temple Bar: A London Magazine*), in 1897 – twelve years after it had come out in Moscow – was translated as 'The biter bit'. Its real title, its Russian title, was 'Overdoing It'.

But I prefer the English translation: it is closer to the concise reversals of Chekhov's style.

The story is simple – it is about a land surveyor called Gleb Gavrilovich Smirnov being driven to an estate thirty or forty versts away from a remote railway station. The driver's name is Klim. He is 'a hefty great peasant' with 'a sullen look and pockmarked face' – 'wearing a torn caftan of undyed cloth and bast shoes'. He is, therefore, bucolically menacing. They set off.

This is another story about a journey on a cart.

Smirnov looks at the landscape. 'It was dusk by the time the cart left the station. To the surveyor's right stretched the dark frozen plain, with no end to it. Go out there and you'd most likely finish up in the middle of nowhere. On the horizon, disappearing and merging with the sky, the cold autumn sun was lazily setting. To the left of the road mounds of some kind rose up in the darkening air: were they last year's haystacks or was it a village?' Smirnov begins to get very scared. He begins, especially, to get scared of Klim. And so he decides, as a precautionary measure, to lie – he assures Klim that he is immensely strong, armed, and, moreover, the friend of every judge. His friends, who are following, as protection, are strong and armed.

They continue silently on their way, to Smirnov's silent satisfaction.

Suddenly, Klim jumps off the cart and runs into the darkness. Smirnov becomes even more afraid, waiting for the attack.

Finally he hears a whimpering sound.

It is Klim. Klim has believed everything he said, and become scared: "'God forgive you, master," grumbled Klim, climbing into the cart. "If I'd known, I wouldn't have taken you for a hundred roubles. I almost died of fright."'

This is, in miniature, the bleak outline of Chekhov's ironic imagination. The style of his stories functions through reversal. In his later writing, the reversals are deftly blurred. All Chekhov's later technique, his continuing concern with reticence and economy, is developed to complicate the simple structures of his plots. But the structure remains the same. It is reckless, precise, comic and economical.

And that is why Anton Chekhov was friends with Leo Tolstoy. Their styles overlapped. They were both adept at concise, yet comprehensive, descriptions of real life.

Chapter x
Trieste, 1923: On Bad Style

When Italo Svevo thought that he might be about to become famous, he wondered if one of the consequences of his fame and money might be that he would then get the opportunity to mend the faults in his Italian. One criticism of his novels that had often been made was the homeliness of their style. But this is one reason to therefore see in Svevo's life story another motif of inadvertent success. Because the interest, the originality, of Svevo is partly to do with his stumbling sentences, his style based on inelegance. Revision would have made him less stylish.

And this is partly to do with Trieste.

Svevo's first language was Tergesteo, the Triestine dialect. His second language was German. His third language was Italian, the language in which he wrote. Some people, of an Italian and stylistically aristocratic disposition, therefore had a problem with Italo. According to them, Svevo had no style – since his Italian, his third language, was the Italian of a salesman, a book-keeper, not a man of letters. So that the poet Eugenio Montale, who loved Svevo's style, had to defend it by asking whether the clunky clutter of Svevo's paragraphs were not 'the sure presence of a style? A commercial style, true, but also the only one natural to his characters.'

I don't see anything wrong with a commercial style. As far as I can see, and I speak no Italian, let alone the Triestine dialect, Svevo managed to invent a style which was also a grumble, which was utterly and happily minor. That was part of Svevo's contribution to the international novel.

There are two mistakes that can be made about style, if stylistic issues are confused with moral ones. The first mistaken judgement is that a simple style is preferable to a complicated one – since plainness is a virtue, and tricksiness is not. But the second mistaken judgement is that a simple style is not preferable to a more literary style – since elegance is a virtue, but inelegance is not. Both of these are wrong. They are both based on moral criteria which are not about style at all. They are not based on the complicated effort to be true to real life.

But there is still a problem with Montale's defence of Svevo. His defence seems to imply that Svevo's style was a deliberate form of bad writing; that it was studiously, consistently inelegant. The sentences in his sentimental journeys are sometimes misshapen, dense with cliché, grammatically disjointed. But this happens so much that the effect is not ungainly: the domestic style is a supple object to describe domestic complication.

On the other hand, it may not have been as deliberate as Montale was arguing.

In another piece on Svevo, Montale returned to the problem of Svevo's language, his pidgin Italian. This time he was bothered by the possible harmonising effect of a well-meaning translation – 'which is bound to lose what I would call the sclerosis of his characters'. Instead, argued Montale, Svevo's sentences were 'both laborious and profound, complicated and free'. So that although a translator might feel the need to 'add some commas, to remedy some anacoluthons', Svevo's style was too inseparable from its mistakes. Correction would only be an imprecise translation. It would not be true to his dowdiness.

Sometimes I agree with Eugenio Montale that Svevo's style was a marvel of workmanship. Other times, I don't. Given Svevo's relief that, if he earned some money from writing, he might be allowed the luxury of correction, it seems as likely that his sentences' sclerosis was simply the product of his hurried, harried improvisation, his bourgeois version of *sprezzatura*. It seems possible that his style only coincided with his subject matter by accident.

In a letter to James Joyce, early on in their friendship in Trieste, after Joyce had given him a copy of his novel *A Portrait of the Artist as a Young Man*, Svevo worried that the emphasis Joyce placed on describing the ordinary and the humdrum would lead to exaggeration: that no style would be possible which would not be forced into a kind of romantic melodrama, in order to make these details interesting, if prolonged on a grand scale. The problem of describing the everyday, thought Svevo, was the danger of hyperbole. And that is why I like Svevo so much, this polyglot writer and friend of Joyce – who I see as a friend of Anton Chekhov's, as well. All of them discovered ways of disproving his letter, and being true to the humdrum: they all discovered styles which were not styles at all.

Even if, in Svevo's case, the luminous form he gave to the everyday was a mistake; a side effect.

Chapter xi
Buenos Aires, 1931: Soul

According to Gustave Flaubert, style was everything in the novel. For Flaubert, the necessary and endless revisions and corrections of a style were what made prose invulnerable to the caprices of time, or politics. The art preserved prose from larvae and rust.

At this point, however, some people might become rather more pessimistic. Such dark moments occurred to Jorge Luis Borges in Argentina, who in 1931 wrote an essay which doubted Flaubert's idea that perfection of style made prose immortal: 'I personally have not experienced any confirmation.' Borges's darker idea was that the opposite was true: the more perfect the style, the quicker that style would disappear. 'The perfect page, the page in which no word can be altered without harm, is the most precarious of all. Changes in language erase shades of meaning, and the "perfect" page is precisely the one that consists of those delicate fringes that are so easily worn away. On the contrary, the page that becomes immortal can traverse the fire of typographical errors, approximate translations, and inattentive or erroneous readings without losing its soul in the process.'

But there is a resolution: it is there in Borges's word 'soul'.

Following Tolstoy and Chekhov in Moscow, or Italo Svevo in Trieste (and Isaac Bashevis Singer in New York), it is possible to state something more brutally and clearly. A style is not just a prose style. Sometimes, it is not even a form of composition. Style is a quality of vision; a soul. This word *soul* is not my favourite word, it is not one I would use if I could help it, but I am not sure I have any choice.

Only with this kind of abstraction is it possible to be precise about the difficult, particular thing called style.

FRANZ KAFKA

IN DER
STRAFKOLONIE

ERZÄHLUNG

VOLUME IV

BOOK 13

K

At this point, it is also important to rethink the idea of real life.

One morning, in Prague, in the twentieth century, a man called Joseph K wakes up to discover that his breakfast routine has been unaccountably altered. Instead of his landlady bringing him breakfast in bed, no breakfast appears; in his landlady's place, two men who seem to be guards come into his room.

Joseph K, however, is quick to set things straight. He establishes friendly terms. 'The strange thing is', says Joseph K, chattily, 'that when one wakes up in the morning, one generally finds things in the same places they were the previous evening. And yet in sleep and in dreams one finds oneself, at least apparently, in a state fundamentally different from wakefulness, and upon opening one's eyes an infinite presence of mind is required, or rather quickness of wit, in order to catch everything, so to speak, in the same place one left it the evening before.'

Or rather, this is what Joseph K said in the novel *Der Prozess* (*The Trial*) before it was deleted by Joseph K's creator, Franz Kafka.

This conversation between Joseph K and the guards who have come to take him away, in which K reports what someone once told him, that waking up is the 'riskiest moment', because after all, 'if you can manage to get through it without being dragged out of place, you can relax for the rest of the day' – this conversation disappeared.

Franz Kafka by Klaus Wagenbach, courtesy of Archiv Klaus Wagenbach, Berlin

Chapter ii
Paris, 1920: Going to Sleep

Unbeknown to him, Joseph K would soon have a friend in Paris, someone who thought in the same way as he did.

At the beginning of the fourth volume of Marcel Proust's novel *A la recherche du temps perdu* (*In Search of Lost Time*) the narrator, whose name is Marcel, rambles into a discussion of sleep. And Marcel is a connoisseur of sleep: he knows all about the precisions of bedtime. At one point, therefore, he begins to wonder about the phenomenon of the truly deep sleep, the leaden sleep. He tries to be true to its perhaps unnoticed surprise. How is it that after a deep sleep one becomes so effortlessly the person one was the night before? The self, thinks Marcel, should be seen for what it is: a perpetual surprise of continuity. 'We call that a leaden sleep, and it seems as though, even for a few moments after such a sleep is ended, one has oneself become a simple figure of lead. One is no longer a person. How then, searching for one's thoughts, one's personality, as one searches for a lost object, does one recover one's own self rather than any other? Why, when one begins again to think, is it not a personality other than the previous one that becomes incarnate in one? One fails to see what dictates the choice, or why, among the millions of human beings one might be, it is on the being one was the day before that unerringly one lays one's hand.'

This fourth instalment of Proust's novel was published on 17 August 1920. Kafka wrote *The Trial* in 1914. It was not published until 1925, the year after Kafka died. As far as I know, Kafka never read any of Proust's novel. And Proust definitely cannot have read Kafka's novel.

This European coincidence is, therefore, a coincidence. But the coincidence helps to prove a useful point.

There is not much difference between the first draft of Kafka's story about Joseph K and Proust's finished novel, narrated by Marcel, considering the nature of sleep, and self. The moment which institutes the difference is Kafka's deletion in the second draft. His second draft is an entirely new way of writing fiction. Rather than speculating on the fact that falling asleep might be ontologically dangerous, Joseph K now wakes up into a world which is exactly like a dream. Like a dream, it does not feel like a dream at all.

Rather than explaining the oddity, the unreality, Kafka lets his characters act out unreal situations as if they are totally real.

In this way, Kafka invents a new use for everyday detail. He creates stories which are literally true, and yet which cannot be literally true. The subject is still real life; it is just a more unusual version than people had previously described. It gave a form to the confused, the minuscule, the contradictory.

The same subject, after all, is never the same subject. That is one consequence of the way in which style works. Going to sleep, and waking up, are infinite operations. They vary from person to person. Each description is unique, and irreplaceable.

Chapter iii
Prague, 1914: A Flirtation

Another day, over a week after Joseph K's bad morning, and having tried to begin the case for his defence, K is in an attic room which he believes adjoins the courtroom: he begins to flirt with the woman he finds there, the wife of a court usher, until they are interrupted by her unwelcome lover, a law student. The student takes her aside, and the student and the woman begin petting and whispering.

This is too much for Joseph K, who begins to tramp up and

down, beside them. 'If you're impatient,' asks the student, reasonably, 'why don't you leave?'

'This remark may have been an outburst of utmost anger, but it contained as well the arrogance of a future court official speaking to an unpopular defendant.' The two men begin to scuffle over the woman, while the student explains to her that the decision to let K wander round freely like this is a grave mistake. Then, 'with a strength one wouldn't have expected', the student lifts the woman with one arm and runs to the door, 'gazing up at her tenderly'. 'A certain fear of K was unmistakable in his action, yet he dared to provoke K even further by stroking and squeezing the woman's arm with his free hand.' K runs after them, but the woman assures him that it is no use, the student will never let her go – '"And you don't want to be freed," yelled K, placing his hand on the shoulder of the student, who snapped at it with his teeth.'

In his rage and disappointment, K shoves the student, who stumbles, but does not fall. And K slowly wanders away.

Joseph K meditates on revenge

He realized that this was the first clear defeat he had suffered at the hands of these people. Of course there was no reason to let that worry him, he had suffered defeat only because he had sought to do battle. If he stayed home and led his normal life he was infinitely superior to any of these people, and could kick any one of them out of his path. And he pictured how funny it would be, for example, to see this miserable student, this puffed-up child, this bandy-legged, bearded fellow, kneeling at Elsa's bedside, clutching his hands and begging for mercy. This vision pleased K so greatly that he decided, if the opportunity ever arose, to take the student along to Elsa one day.

Elsa was the woman whom K thought of as his girlfriend: she was a nightclub dancer, and very possibly a prostitute.

This is not, obviously, your average flirtation. It is not your average version of real life. With Kafka, something new is happening both to the way a novel can be written, and also to the range of subjects which a novel can describe.

In real life, there is a naturally occurring version of real life which is unreal. This version happens at night, when everyone is asleep. And in Central Europe, in the 1920s and 30s, some novelists were trying to develop ways of writing stories about this version of real life: this aspect of real life which is called a dream.

Chapter iv

Croisset, 1876, & Prague, 1914: Utopia

In 1876, twenty years after *Madame Bovary*, four years before his death, Flaubert began a new story, called 'Un Coeur Simple' – 'A Simple Heart'. It was published a year later in his final published book, *Trois Contes (Three Stories)*, whose other stories told the life of a medieval saint and the martyrdom of John the Baptist.

In a slightly morphed form, the book was the culmination of the project he had thought up many years earlier in Constantinople – a triptych of stories about the overlap of body and soul.

'A Simple Heart' describes a girl, Félicité, who faithfully served her mistress in a Normandy village for fifty years. The story is punctuated by a list of the people she loved: a boy who left her for an older woman; then her mistress's two children; then her nephew; then a Polish soldier; then an old man who lives in a sty; then a parrot. But everyone leaves her, or dies. The tension in the story, however, the thing which makes it heavy with a comic sadness, is how delicate Flaubert is with his detail. Everything seems ordinary, and superfluous, and then becomes freighted with meaning and emotion.

When Loulou – Félicité's parrot – dies, she sends it away to be stuffed. In this way, she will be able to keep it near her, even though it can no longer talk. He arrives back 'splendid, upright on a branch, which was screwed into a mahogany base, one claw in the air, his head tilted, and biting a nut which, through love of the grandiose, the taxidermist had gilded.' He is fixed in place in Félicité's bedroom, on a chimney ledge.

And the story continues. Félicité's mistress dies. The house begins to fall apart, since Félicité is too scared to ask for any repairs, in case this draws too much attention to the fact that she is living there. In the village, it is the time for the altars of repose. Félicité, who is now dying, wants to offer something to be placed on the altar. She decides it should be the parrot.

Before Loulou is placed on the altar, Mother Simon, who has been looking after Félicité, brings him to Félicité so she can say goodbye. And suddenly Loulou has changed; he has aged. 'Although he was not a corpse, the worms were devouring him; one of his wings was broken, the stuffing was falling out of his stomach. But, blind now, she kissed him on the forehead, and held him against her cheek.'

Félicité is utopian. She is a believer, a romantic. (And so she is Don Quixote as well – since, after all, characters are migratory: 'A baby could convince him that it's midnight at high noon – and for his simple heart I love him like my own life, and all his eccentricities could not make me leave him,' says Don Quixote's best friend, and faithful companion, Sancho Panza.) So that when Félicité 'breathed out her last breath, she believed she could see, in the open skies, a gigantic parrot, buoyant above her head.'

Real life is not utopia: it is the opposite of utopia. But because it is the opposite of utopia, it is also utopian. It is full of projects not to be real at all. Real life is diet books, time-management plans, timetables, travel brochures, interior-design magazines. It is always wishful.

Real life, therefore, is like a dream. Everything which is ordinary and everyday, like a stuffed parrot, is also latent with transfiguration.

Long ago, in Volume I, Flaubert was a major character, along with his technique for describing a character's psychology. His talent was for realism, and reticence: he could make up sentences about a character which seemed to have been almost written by the character, not the novelist.

Kafka's fictions sound so new and so strange because Kafka took this technique – which had been used by Flaubert to detail the interior life of wishful thinking – and used it to describe a new area. Kafka was an attentive reader of Flaubert. He saw that Flaubert's technique allowed for both banality and fantasy – Flaubert had discovered that the two things shared a secret root. And so Kafka then simply extended it into a new subject: dreams.

Everything is portable.

All developments of form are developments of content. This is also true the other way around. All developments of content are developments of form.

Kafka had the idea that the odd combination of third-person and first-person that marked Flaubert's style – in which a character thought in the first person but was represented in the third person – was a correlative to a certain type of dream, where the dreamer is conscious of dreaming, and unconscious, at the same time. So, in the description of K's argument with the student, from Kafka's novel *The Trial*, Joseph K's dream-logic – his egotistical fantasies, his constant concern for his own pride – infected Kafka's prose. For one of the marks about Joseph K's character was that he was full of wishful thinking. He made decisions based on a mildly insane ability to keep seeing the bright side of his problems. This was the root of the comedy, and his pathos.

He was a secret utopian, too.

Chapter v
St Petersburg, 1836: A Short Interlude on Jetlag

In St Petersburg, in the mid-nineteenth century, Nikolai Gogol – before Flaubert, and long before Kafka – had written his story called *Hoc* (*Nose*), which was Saul Steinberg's favourite story. More harshly, more garishly than his story about Akaky Akakievich Bashmachkin and a coat, this story was about a reality which has morphed into something odd, something dream-like – where a man can lose his nose, and this nose can walk around St Petersburg, as if nothing had happened.

In early drafts of this story, the story was explicitly a dream. But by the time it was finished, there was nothing there to tell its reader it was a dream. All references to a dream had been cut by Gogol.

Gogol did not want to reassure his reader too quickly, too easily. He did not want the reader to be able to dismiss the story as something which was recognisable or familiar. Without the comfort that it was all a dream, the familiarity of the world being described would be queasier, more gruesome than it normally was.

In the small magazine *Areté*, Craig Raine once wrote a short essay on Franz Kafka's *The Trial*. He argued that there had not been enough precision amongst readers of Franz Kafka's *The Trial*. It was not just that the reality was *like* a dream. It was a dream, itself. It was an extended, minute description of a world which behaved, like *Alice in Wonderland*, according to an oneiric, patiently accepted, frighteningly deviant, rationale.

But there was no one there in Kafka's novel to tell his perturbed readers that this was a dream – if it was a dream, in the end, at all. Even the hint – that reality was so difficult to seize, on waking up – was cut. *The Trial* was Joseph's novel about himself, which did not say it was by Joseph at all.

This use of a dream structure, without the structure being

mentioned, was one aspect of Kafka's originality. But it it is not quite – not exhaustively – the originality of the original writer of fictions, Franz Kafka. For Kafka took Gogol's technique, and then developed it even further.

Chapter vi
Prague, 1914; Short Is the New Long

The reason Kafka is such a pleasure to read is that his effects are so small, and muted. Often, the jokes are barely audible. They are packaged up, and stored out of sight.

In his later novel *Das Schloss* (*The Castle*) Kafka wanted to describe what effect official recognition of his title of surveyor would have on his character, K (who may or may not be the same as Joseph K): in his first draft, he had written of this recognition: 'like everything that is spiritually superior, it's also a little oppressive.' The final version of the sentence, however, read: 'And if they believed that with their recognition of his surveyor title, recognition that in itself was certainly spiritually superior, they could keep him in constant fear, they were deceiving themselves; he felt a slight shudder, but that was all.'

The phrase in the final draft – 'keep him in constant fear' – is in K's language: it represents his reaction to the now suppressed generalisation in the original draft, that spiritual superiority is 'a little oppressive'. If its effect is so oppressive then naturally it follows, in K's world, that it must have been meant to make him scared. And so the sentence as a whole is full of Kafka's comedy, where confused characters continue to assert their unfounded belief in their control over unpredictable and incomprehensible events.

The first draft of this sentence is in the old tradition of the novel: it is open about its characters' generalisations. But the second draft is not. The second draft is avant-garde. In Kafka, characters are constantly reacting to assumptions and prejudices which are never explicitly stated. This sentence is therefore a miniature of Kafka's style – the ability to nest interiority in a seemingly neutral way into a third-person sentence. Developing from Flaubert, Kafka learned how to make his sentences fluent yet illogical.

He is a microscopic writer, Kafka – his effects are cumulations of small things. They are there in his sad, comic sentences – like these, in which Joseph K blusters to himself about his power of self-control, and his power to control other people: 'How could she ensnare him? Wouldn't he still be free enough to simply smash the entire court, at least insofar as it touched him? Couldn't he grant himself that small degree of self-confidence?' Which is, after all, not a particularly self-confident way of putting things.

In one of the manuscripts of *The Castle*, there is this vital note, which, obviously, because his technique is based on reticence, Kafka cut: 'What's truly comic is the minute detail'.

The technique of Franz Kafka, who only wrote short things, is massive detail. This detail gives the comic illusion of length. That is another way of describing the *Kafkaesque*.

Chapter vii
Zurich, 1928: Detail

But maybe Gustave Flaubert is too glossily international. There are other, more local influences, too. In his review of Kafka's first book, a collection of short short stories called *Meditation*, the Austrian novelist Robert Musil said that Kafka's style was a special case of the Robert Walser genus.

Robert Walser is much less glossy than Gustave Flaubert, but he has an importance as well.

Robert Walser was a Swiss-German writer of small fictions: he was born in 1878, and died in 1956. He was one of the first writers to reduce the short story, to develop it away from the nineteenth-century bar-room anecdote, the clubman's joke. He was one of the first people to develop the story as a place for linguistic delicacy and experiment.

Like so many other people in this book, he did not see the need for an obvious plot.

Robert Walser's story about a walk

I was walking aimlessly, and while I proceeded on my way a dog crossed my path, and I offered the brave animal a most particular attention as I let my gaze slow down over him for quite a while. Am I not a stupid man? Isn't it stupid to stop on a road for a dog and to lose precious time? But while I was walking aimlessly, I in no way had the impression that time was precious, and what's more, after a moment, I carried on my road without hurrying. I was thinking: 'But it's really hot today', and in fact it really was hot.

From Walser, Kafka learned that a story did not have to tell an ostentatious story. More precisely, perhaps, he learned that a story did not have to have a stated moral. It could be smaller, and more evasive.

In 1928, Walser said that he was 'experimenting in the linguistic field in the hope that there existed in language an unknown vivacity which it is a pleasure to awaken'. It is possible, following this, to locate this vivacity as the centre of Walser's writing. But in fact the interest of Walser's stories is the opposite. Rather than vivacity, Walser was fascinated by the decrepitude of language, its leisurely habits. In Walser, as in Kafka, the writing frames clichés – which are trying to cope with impossible or unmentionable realities.

So in Walser's story about a walk, the interest is all in the shyness of the whimsical, conversational details – the fact that they seem to be a story about something else, more important than a small thought caused by a dog. And yet nothing else, in this story, seems visible. It is as small as it says.

But Kafka developed Walser's technique of inconsequence, his exploitation of the apparently whimsical, into a far more stringent style.

Kafka does this by writing stories which are missing a crucial word. It is the absence of a vital word that creates so much worry and confusion for his characters, but should not do so for his readers.

On the grander scale, Kafka did this in his novels which smuggle in their characters' thoughts and prejudices, in the guise of objective narrative. But the technique is there in Kafka's shorter stories as well. The missing word in Kafka's famous story 'Metamorphosis' – where the travelling salesman Gregor Samsa wakes up to discover he has been transformed into a beetle – is 'dream': if Gregor could only find his way to the word 'dream', then he would be calmed. But it is Kafka's genius never to mention this word. Or, in Kafka's story 'Investigations of a Dog', narrated by a ruminative dog, the word 'human' is never mentioned. For this investigative dog sees everything as a dog: acrobats are criminal dogs, birds are hovering dogs. It is the absence of any term other than 'dog' which creates the dog's scientific and philosophical confusions.

I am beginning to think that detail is a problem when thinking about novels: because all good novelists are expert at deploying detail. But for each novelist, the detail forms part of the overall style. There are therefore multiple ways of using detail.

Most technical terms, in fact, are just generalisations. And yet no generalisation can ever hope to describe a technique. All techniques are individual.

For instance – massive detail, which creates the illusion of length, but which is missing a crucial word. It isn't elegant, but it's a more precise definition of the Kafkaesque.

Chapter viii
Prague, 1914: Tempo

Kafka's use of detail is the reason for his innovations of tempo. With his careful, accumulated particulars, he slows his short narratives down until they seem gigantic.

If speed is distance travelled divided by time taken, a short paragraph which describes one hundred years is very quick, while a novel which describes an entire day is very slow. Simultaneously, there are the intricacies of tempo within a novel itself. A short section describing a long time will be seen as fast, as an allegro – while a longer section describing a smaller amount of time will be seen as slower.

In all of Kafka's prose, the dominant tempo is adagio. He lengthens the description of small things: he goes slow.

This technique of the miniature can be seen, in miniature, in one of Kafka's notebooks, where, considering himself, or imagining a character considering himself, he states: 'If I think about it, I must say my upbringing in certain respects has done me great harm.' Then the character, or Kafka, tries to answer this sentence. He gives various forms of this answer, but its structure always remains the same: it is an extravagant, accurate whine. 'This reproach is aimed at a multitude of people, namely my parents, several relatives, certain house guests, various writers, a certain particular cook who accompanied me to school for a year, a heap of teachers (whom I must bundle together in my memory, otherwise I'll lose one here and there, but having bundled them together so tightly, the whole mass begins, in certain spots, to crumble away), a school inspector, slow-walking pedestrians, in brief this reproach twists like a dagger through society.' Since Kafka is a great master of the miniature, he is also a great master of exaggeration and melodrama. He is aware how quickly the minor proliferates. In another version, therefore, his answer has expanded: it now includes girls from dance lessons, and a swimming instructor.

It is the swimming instructor, the slow pedestrians – these are the pleasure of Kafka's style: they are triumphs of grandiose, banal detail.

'I've had to, you understand,' says the hero of Witold Gombrowicz's novel *Cosmos*, 'have recourse to smaller and smaller pleasures, almost invisible . . . You have no idea how immense one becomes, with these little details, it's incredible how much one grows.'

All of Kafka's writing is a strange exercise in shape, in the attempt to be precise about something. And this creates a style with an unusual tempo.

It is adagio, and massive, and very short.

Chapter ix
New York, 1909: The Portable Library

Gertrude Stein believed in the avant-garde theory of history. She believed that the methods of the twentieth century were in advance of those used in the nineteenth century.

But I am not so sure of this. I tend to think that literary history is haphazard; it is a system of interlinked revisions and inspirations, like Franz Kafka's importation of Gustave Flaubert. All techniques are portable. Yes, I prefer a roll-on, roll-off literary theory.

In 1909, Gertrude Stein, an expatriate in Paris, published her first book, called *Three Lives*. Its original title was *Three Histories* – a homage to Flaubert's collection *Trois Contes*. The collection was published in New York by the Grafton Press, run by a man called Frederick H. Hitchcock. It was Hitchcock who asked Stein to change the title from its Flaubertian one to its less Flaubertian one.

This was not so much out of concern for literary history, and a care for Stein to advertise her originality. It was because the Grafton Press was a vanity press, which specialised in genealogical and historical books. *Three Histories* would therefore look too literal, too factual, worried Frederick H. Hitchcock, as a title for Stein's book of fictions.

The print run was 500 copies.

In 1903, her brother Leo, who wanted to be a painter, had found an apartment in Paris, where Gertrude joined him. As a way of improving her French, Leo suggested that Gertrude should translate Flaubert's story 'Un Coeur Simple' into English. And because Gertrude was a dutiful, diligent person, she obeyed her brother. Meanwhile, she continued to write her own fiction. But none of this fiction seemed to work. It did not seem to be original. In October 1905, however, she began a story called 'The Good Anna', which would be the first story in her collection of three histories, three lives.

This story was not a translation, but it was not an original either. And yet this unoriginal story was a work of fluent originality. It was written in a new style.

The first sentence (which is also the first paragraph) of Gertrude Stein's 'The Good Anna' is: 'The tradesmen of Bridgepoint learned to dread the sound of "Miss Mathilda", for with that name the good Anna always conquered.' And this is a variation on Flaubert's theme, who, in the first sentence of 'Un Coeur Simple' (which is also the first paragraph), wrote how 'For fifty years, the women of Pont-l'Evêque envied Madame Aubain for her servant Félicité.'

This is not a translation; it is a form of recycling. But Gertrude was careful to advertise her independence from Flaubert. So that while in Flaubert's story it is Félicité's relationship with her pet parrot, her subsequently stuffed parrot, which forms the emotional climax of the story, Gertrude's parrot is a momentary detail – a peace offering from the family's daughter, Jane, which Anna likes, but never as much as her dogs. The parrot is unimportant.

Flaubert is portable. That is what Gertrude Stein, in Paris, realised. And just as some writers explained this through techniques and metaphors for writing borrowed from music, Gertrude explained this through metaphors drawn from painting. For André Gide, César Franck was a model of counterpoint; Gertrude Stein's model was the painter Cézanne. 'Cézanne conceived the idea that in composition one thing was as important as another thing', she argued in her 1926 essay 'Composition as Explanation'. 'Each part is as important as the whole, and that impressed me enormously.'

Through her theory of Cézanne's paintings, Stein was able to steal from Flaubert's prose in an original way. Whereas in Flaubert details grouped themselves singly, uniquely, while the verbs were all in the repetitive and habitual imperfect tense, Stein reduced the complexity of tenses, and amalgamated detail with repetition. And this was a more subtle and comprehensive way than a smuggled parrot for Stein to advertise her independence.

The second story in *Three Lives* is called 'Melanctha' – about the love triangle between Melanctha Herbert, who is half black, and in love with Jeff Campbell, who is entirely black, and Melanctha's friend Rose Johnson, who was a 'real black negress but she had been brought up quite like their own child by white folks.' Its motif is confusion. Because this is a story about confusion; it is about the inarticulacy of our feelings.

And this is universal. Confusion, after all, was a feature of the eighteenth century, just as much as it was a feature of the twentieth.

In the 'First Attempt at a Preface' to his book *De l'amour (On Love)*, Stendhal wrote that 'Love is like the heavenly phenomenon known as the Milky Way, a shining mass made of millions of little stars, many of them nebulae. Four or five hundred of the small successive feelings – so difficult to recognise – that go to make up love have been noted in books, but only the most obvious ones are there.'

Stendhal was arguing for a detailed taxonomy of love; for him, an emotion was an accumulation of smaller emotions. Gertrude

Stein, two hundred years later, tried to list some more. Her main innovation was to show, clearly, how often love suffered from a lack of clarity – in short, repetitive sentences, constantly reworking the same words, the same feelings (a style which would influence her friend, Ernest Hemingway).

Jeff Campbell's Milky Way

Jeff never, even now, knew what it was that moved him. He never, even now, was ever sure, he really knew what Melanctha was, when she was real herself, and honest. He thought he knew, and then there came to him some moment, just like this one, when she really woke him up to be strong in him. Then he really knew he could know nothing. He knew then, he never could know what it was she really wanted with him. He knew then he never could know really what it was he felt inside him. It was all so mixed up inside him. All he knew was, he wanted very badly Melanctha should be there beside him, and he wanted very badly, too, always to throw her from him.

And this is real life. It is stylised, but it is messy as well. It is an accurate portrait of minute feelings.

Chapter x
Prague, 1928: An Editor

But the history of the novel is also a history of waste. Although everything is portable, that does not mean that everything is made use of, and reinvented. There is, for instance, the missed opportunity represented by the prose of Franz Kafka.

No one has copied Franz Kafka in the matter of structure. This is partly because no one has wanted to notice his structure: but it is also because the structure has been mutely erased.

Conventionally, because of the way it was edited by Kafka's

executor and best friend, Max Brod, *The Trial* is read as a novel with a continuous plot. But I am not so sure that this is true. Instead, the form of this novel is much more musical, and much more unique.

In this new form, events constellate; the chapters both continue and sit alongside other chapters. They overlap.

The Trial tells the story of a man called Joseph K, who is wrongfully arrested. He then spends the rest of the novel trying to find out the nature of the charges against him, and therefore the nature of his presumed guilt, first through conversations with his landlady, Frau Grubach, and then a girl who is staying in the same house, Fräulein Bürstner. He is summoned to court, where he undergoes an unsatisfactory hearing; then returns later to the empty courtroom, where he flirts with the wife of the court usher, and is vanquished by a law student. This constitutes the first three or four chapters (depending on how they are divided) of the novel: these chapters form a linear narrative unit.

But then something unusual happens to this unusual plot.

First, Joseph K witnesses some kind of sado-masochistic moment between two men in a box room at his offices. Then his uncle comes to town to help him clear the business up, which institutes another narrative cycle, involving his uncle's lawyer – a man who lives in bed – and his nurse and housemaid called Leni. Joseph K then tries to befriend a painter, who is said to have powerful connections in the court. Finally, K decides to dismiss his lawyer. There is then a penultimate episode in Prague Cathedral, where he is lectured to from the pulpit. And then, at the end, Joseph K's life also ends. The guards come to take him away, and kill him in a quarry.

This novel seems like a novel, with a plot, but I am not so sure.

We cannot quite be sure that Kafka wanted to publish his book in the order in which it was published, because he never finished it. His executor, Max Brod, decided both to disobey Kafka's wishes, in publishing the novel after his death, and also to presume to judge how Kafka might have wanted to present the material. But there is another way of reading Kafka's stories about Joseph K in Prague – which makes these stories closer to Chekhovian chapters: variations on a theme.

The chapter called 'The Flogger', for instance, featuring the sadomasochistic couple in the box room, must happen after the chapter called 'Initial Inquiry', but that is all. At the moment, it is the fifth chapter. But it could occur later. There are no other plot markers to anchor it into position. In the same way, the chapter called 'In the Cathedral' does not necessarily need to occur as the penultimate episode. Positioning it there is not neutral: it helps Max Brod's thesis, that Kafka is a religious novelist; that the meaning of this novel consists in its allegorical status. According to Max Brod, this book is about the search for belief. Necessarily, therefore, it must converge on Joseph K's visit to a cathedral, prior to his death.

But if this episode occurred earlier, it might then lose some of its seriousness – it might seem more comic, more dense with interconnected themes. Kafka's form was more experimental than it looked. The structure of this book was more like a spiral – progressive and digressive, at the same time – not a straight line. It was bemused, refractory, comic.

But no: at this point, I need to talk about this problem of meaning. Towards the end, *The Delighted States* must, for a moment, become a theocracy.

Chapter xi
Prague, 1921: Moses

Kafka took two features of Flaubert's style – his way of talking in his characters' language while pretending not to, and his dense orchestrated detail – and reused them, in his version of Prague German, to deliver new effects. This combination, however, of a dream-like impersonality and a minute density of particulars, has made Kafka's fictions difficult to interpret. The new things he did with Flaubert's techniques created a form which made it unclear what was metaphorical and what was literal.

In one of his notebooks, Kafka made up a two-sentence character: 'He felt it at his temple, as the wall feels the point of the nail that is about to be driven into it. Hence he did not feel it.' This anonymous character feels nothing in the second sentence, because the first sentence has turned him into a wall. And this was a central technique for Kafka – to turn metaphor inside out: to state a metaphor, and then make it literal.

This happened on a larger scale as well, in the longer fictions: his refusal to describe them explictly as a dream – an extension of his technique of the missing word – created a style which hinted at the metaphorical, but confirmed nothing.

The strangeness of Kafka's prose is his obtrusive literality. Everything is on the same plane: so that a bank clerk may seem like a scapegoat, but on the other hand Kafka could just as well have imagined a story where a scapegoat is imagined as a bank clerk.

On 19 October 1921, writing in his diary, Kafka began by imagining what the meaning might be of the Biblical 'path through the desert'. The central figure of this story was a person, wrote Kafka, who 'has had Canaan in his nostrils his whole life long; that he should not see this land until just before his death is difficult to believe. This final prospect can only have the meaning of showing what an imperfect moment human life is, imperfect because this kind of life could go on endlessly and yet at the same time would not produce anything more than a moment.' And so this, asserted Kafka, is the narrative's meaning: it is an allegory of the inevitable failure that is a human life: the narrative equates life with failure. 'Not because his life was too short does Moses fail to reach Canaan, but rather because it was a human life.' But then Kafka ended the entry with an afterthought: 'This end of the five books of Moses has a similarity with the final scene of the *Éducation Sentimentale*.'

The final scene of Flaubert's novel *L'Éducation Sentimentale* (*Sentimental Education*) was a conversation between the novel's melancholy hero, Frédéric Moreau, and his best friend, Deslauriers. They recalled their botched visit, as teenagers, to a brothel – where they arrived bearing bouquets. But the young Frédéric had been too embarrassed to speak. So he stood there, with his bouquet. 'The girls all burst out laughing, amused by his embarrassment; thinking they were making fun of him, he fled, and as Frédéric had the money, Deslauriers had no choice but to follow him.' Many years later, the two of them tell each other the story, helping each other with the details.

'That was the happiest time we ever had,' said Frédéric.

'Yes, perhaps you're right. That was the happiest time we ever had,' said Deslauriers.

It has taken them all their lives to realise this. But these are the novel's last lines. Everything has failed.

With his new style, whose roots were in Flaubert, Kafka came up with a new way of reading Flaubert (and all realistic fiction). Instead of the usual intuitive distinction between a story which was terrestrial and domestic, and a story which was theological and allegorical, Kafka's new style allowed him to equate the two. So that the story of Moses becomes oddly literal, and the story of Frédéric becomes oddly allegorical.

The two can have the same form. They have the same romantic theme, subjected to the same ironic structure.

One evening in Flaubert's Paris flat, in the Rue Murillo, his friend Henry Céard expressed the admiration he felt for *Sentimental Education*. Moved, Flaubert answered: 'So you like it, do you? All the same, the book is doomed to failure, because it doesn't do this.' He put his hands together in the shape of a pyramid. 'The public,' he explained, 'wants works which exalt its illusions, whereas

Sentimental Education . . .' And he turned his hands upside down and opened them, as if to empty them.

The opened pyramid: this is the shape of Flaubert's story, and the story of Moses, and the story of Joseph K. And it is a similarity which is more minutely visible in the innovations of Kafka's style, inherited from Flaubert's style in French. Which Flaubert invented, after all, on top of and inside the Great Pyramid of Cheops.

This is not, obviously, the only way Kafka has been read.

In 1936, the Polish writer Bruno Schulz published a translation, from German into Polish, of Franz Kafka's novel *The Trial*. This may have been his own translation or it may have been by his fiancée, Józefina Szelínska. But Schulz definitely wrote his own essay on Kafka, which was published with the translation, and in which Schulz explained what Kafka meant to him. According to Schulz, the crucial thing about Kafka was not the style, it was not the playfulness, but was instead the 'supreme religious value by which he measured his work'. For Schulz, Kafka was a religious writer, a man who recorded spiritual visions. As such, he was not a writer with a developed and patient style, but instead was part of an anonymous community of mystics. Kafka's work, therefore, was notable for its creation of 'a parallel reality, a double, a supplementary world which, to tell the truth, has no predecessor.'

Even if you are a clever writer, like Bruno Schulz, misreading is always a hazard. Reading is a talent. Poor Kafka had his precursors (and his followers). It is just that they were literary, not mystical.

Kafka extended fiction's range – into the area of flirtation, of teasing. Details were no longer split, as they were before, into a binary hierarchy of important narrative detail, and irrelevant atmospheric filler. Instead, everything could be both, or neither, at once. It is therefore possible to read in his stories a tone of worry, of anxiousness and menace and religious allegory. But it is also possible to relax; and then his stories can be read in a different way – as intricate, stylish, poetic manifestations of flippancy, of fun.

Like this true story.

One day, in the spa town of Marienbad, Kafka was taking the waters. He observed a famous rabbi, accompanied by his acolytes, setting out to take the medicinal waters, parading in his hands an open, empty and expectant bottle. But the spa had closed for the day, and it was raining, and so as the rabbi and his acolytes schlepped round town, trying to find a spring that was open, the bottle gradually began to fill up anyway, with rainwater. And Kafka's final comment was on one of the rabbi's students, who 'tries to find or thinks he finds a deeper meaning in all this: I think the deeper meaning is that there is none, and in my opinion that is enough.'

Chapter xii
Warsaw, 1933: A Short Description of Originality

When Witold Gombrowicz, many years after Bruno Schulz was dead, considered the likelihood of Schulz's success in a recent French translation, his ambiguous thoughts on Schulz were the result of Schulz's ambiguous relation to Kafka: 'His relation to Kafka can as much open the way for him as bar it. If they present him as another one of Kafka's multiple cousins, he's lost. On the other hand, if they perceive his specific sparkle, that particular light with which he glows like a phosphorescent insect, he'll be able to penetrate quickly into imaginations already formed by Kafka and his lineage . . . and the delight of his fans will propel him to the top.'

On the one hand, therefore, Schulz could be read as unoriginal, since his style was similar to Franz Kafka's. On the other hand, his style could be read as original, since his style was not the same as Franz Kafka's.

In Paul Valéry's 'Letter about Mallarmé', Valéry comments that 'if we look for the source of an achievement we always observe that *what a man does* either repeats *what someone else has done*, or refutes it'. 'We say that an author is *original*,' concluded Valéry, 'when we do not know the hidden transformations that others underwent in his mind.' According to Valéry, there is no such thing as pure originality. Originality is just the name we give to writers who cover their tracks.

But I am not sure I agree with this. This theory of Paul Valéry is too easily academic, too smugly reductive. In many ways, I prefer the grandness of Vladimir Nabokov – answering the charge that his work was too repetitious and saying: 'Derivative writers seem versatile because they imitate many others, past and present. Artistic originality has only its own self to copy.'

On the other hand, there is a correlative to Valéry's theory. It is easy to say, wrongly, that a writer is unoriginal, when it is all too easily obvious what transformations others have undergone in a writer's mind. For instance: the transformations Kafka underwent in the mind of Bruno Schulz. In the same way as Milan Kundera noted how it would be unfair to devalue Diderot's originality, just because he seems to be similar to Laurence Sterne, so it would be unfair to devalue Bruno Schulz's originality, just because he seems so similar to Franz Kafka.

Where Kafka's prose is deliberately denuded of metaphor (because everything, for Kafka, is capable of becoming a metaphor), Schulz's prose is rich with metaphors. It is much happier with the lyrical; whereas Kafka's style is very rarely lyrical.

Schulz's prose is based on nostalgia. That is one aspect of his originality. And it is also why he misread Franz Kafka as a mystic, not an ironist. He elevated his nostalgia to the status of a home-made theology. He came up with a style which was hyperbolic, sometimes cloying, sometimes funny – where everything happens cartoonishly, allegro, not adagio.

The styles of both Kafka and Schulz are based on subjecting real life to small tweaks, small inconsistencies. They are both experiments with the everyday. This is one reason why Schulz, understanding the importance to Kafka's style that the extraordinary version of real life it describes should seem ordinary, and unremarkable, decided to translate Joseph K's name.

In his Polish version of *The Trial*, Schulz transformed Joseph K into a Polish counterpart, a double: Joseph became Jurek K. So that the Polish reader could not receive the consolation of the foreign.

BOOK 14

Ferdydurke

The history of the novel is a history of waste. But this is not always the novelists' fault.

By 19 November 1942, Bruno Schulz – who was Polish, and Jewish, but more importantly to me was a novelist and short-story writer, as well as being the art teacher at the local school – had managed to get together the necessary false papers and false passport which would allow him that day to leave his town of Drohobycz, in Poland, and escape from the occupying Nazis.

But at around eleven in the morning, shooting broke out in the town's ghetto. In response, the Gestapo embarked on what they called a 'wild action'. They shot randomly at people in the streets. Two hundred and thirty people were killed. One of them was Bruno Schulz, who was out trying to buy some bread. He was shot twice in the head by SS-Scharführer Karl Günther. According to some versions of this true story, Günther used to boast about his murder of Schulz – since Schulz had been the personal protégé of Felix Landau, another Gestapo officer, who had taken an interest in Schulz's art. One of Schulz's commissions, in 1941, was to paint the walls of Landau's son's bedroom with scenes from fairy tales. And Günther hated Landau, because Landau had recently shot a Drohobycz dentist called Löw – whom Günther, for his part, rather liked.

Or, more happily, there is another true story which is part of the history of waste – about the Polish but not Jewish novelist Witold Gombrowicz. One day, in 1939, he was in a Warsaw café, having an after-work drink. A friend of his, who was a journalist, came in

with a proposition. He had to cover the maiden voyage of the transatlantic liner, the *Chrobry*. Would Witold like to come along? Witold thought he might. He had nothing better to do. So he rushed to the shipping line's office, reaching it just before it closed, and seduced the receptionist into giving him a pass.

Gombrowicz arrived in Buenos Aires on 22 August 1939. Not too many days later, the Second World War began. And so Gombrowicz, who thought he was just on the way to Buenos Aires as a joke version of a tourist, became an exile – first from the Nazis, then from the Communists, for the next thirty years.

Chapter ii
Vence, 1961: Witold and Bruno

When he looked back on it – having been an exile in Buenos Aires, then Berlin, and having finally ended up in Vence, in the south of France – the feelings Witold Gombrowicz felt about his friendship with Bruno Schulz, in the Warsaw of the 1930s, were complicated.

These feelings were rueful and proud and tender. In July 1961, for just over a week, from a Friday through to the following Saturday, Gombrowicz examined the question of Bruno.

This account had been prompted by the fact that Gombrowicz had just received the first French translation of some stories by Schulz – a book which came complete with a blurb from the celebrity French writer, Maurice Nadeau: '. . . one must assure him his place among the great writers of our time.' The translation marked Schulz's entrance into world literature. And so Gombrowicz, in Vence, paused.

But I need to pause for a moment, too.

What is the drama of a journal entry? The drama is the attempt to be honest, the resolution not to obey the maturity of good taste. A journal entry can be envious, put out, obstreperous. A journal has the luxury of privacy. But Gombrowicz's journal was slightly different. Rather than being purely private, his journal was written for publication in Jerzy Giedroyc's magazine for Polish émigrés, published in Paris, called *Kultura*. For a long time – especially while he was in Buenos Aires – it was Gombrowicz's only means of communicating with a literary community: it was, therefore, always self-interested; an advert, a manifesto.

The pathos of literary criticism is that no novelist can depend on his or her readers. All novelists also need critics. And in exile, this problem becomes more acute; in exile, a novelist may have to triple up, and do the work not just of the reader, but of the critic as well.

The journal entries which followed were not just about Schulz. They were also Gombrowicz's competitive attempt to define what he thought was the essence of a novelist. His journal was ostentatiously egotistical, self-regarding, immature. The very first four days of Gombrowicz's journal, after all, which began in 1953, had started like this:

Monday.
ME

Tuesday.
ME

Wednesday.
ME

Thursday.
ME

(And so it resembles another publicised, honestly egotistic journal, which belonged to the Goncourt brothers in nineteenth-century Paris: when Edmond de Goncourt's novel *La Fille Élisa* was published, this entry appeared in the journal for Saturday 31 March 1877: 'I have just seen a big bookshop on a new boulevard which has nothing on show except *La Fille Élisa*, displaying in every one of its windows, to the people who stop outside, my name, my name alone.' Which has a charm reminiscent, I think, of Brás Cubas's charm: I can understand where Edmond is coming from.)

In the end, according to Gombrowicz, as he compared himself to Bruno Schulz, a novelist is a person who respects no one but himself. He will not agree to the maturity of good taste: 'I want to begin by emptying my bag of irritating indecencies and bad taste: *Bruno adored me but me – no.*'

The story in Warsaw – as it now appeared to him in Vence – had been like this. Schulz had adored Gombrowicz, but Gombrowicz was more reserved. 'My nature never allowed me to approach him other than with distrust, I doubted him and his art. Did I ever once honestly read, from the beginning to the end, one of his stories? No – they bored me.' It's true that they were often linked as an experimental twosome by Polish critics, but 'if there existed in Polish art someone diametrically opposed to me, it was certainly him.' Every day for a week, therefore, Witold continued his opposition of Bruno and Witold. Continuously, Gombrowicz tried to define their deep opposition. 'While he let himself be dominated by art, me I wanted to be "above". That is what essentially opposed us.' Gombrowicz was an ironist, and Schulz was not: 'I, on the contrary, I wanted to be – to be me – myself, neither an artist, nor an idea, nor my own works – nothing but myself. Above art, above the work, above style, above ideas.'

And yet suddenly, after five days of journal entries, Witold, without seeming to notice it, changed his mind. Rather than being opposites, wrote Gombrowicz, he and Schulz 'were effectively conspirators. We devoted ourselves to experiments with a certain explosive called Form. Not form in its ordinary sense – for us it was about "creating form", "producing" it, and "through this production of form, to create oneself".' 'We were both', he concluded, 'completely alone before Form.'

But then two days later: 'I reread the pages I wrote on Schulz. Is the portrait truly faithful? And mine?'

This story is about immaturity. It is about the immature and admirable refusal to do or say the done thing. Gombrowicz, instead, is tenacious for truth. But the word I want to pause on is this word *Form*.

This penultimate volume, set in Central Europe, in the early twentieth century, is as far as I will go. Its subject is the more way-out experiments with fiction made by Central Europeans like Witold Gombrowicz, Bruno Schulz and – my favourite – Franz Kafka. In Central Europe, these novelists were trying to come up with stories whose subject matter was oddly new, and whose styles were therefore new as well.

But since it is about way-out experiments with fiction in Central Europe, it therefore continues my hunch about another, later Central European experimentalist, Bohumil Hrabal. These experiments with fiction also entail more way-out problems of translation. Not only, obviously, do I speak no Polish, or German or Czech, but it is not always possible to read these novelists in English translations. Sometimes I have to try with a French translation as well.

In this respect, and no other (except maybe the height), I resemble the Russian poet and novelist Alexander Pushkin – who is about to make his late entrance on the scene – who read Laurence Sterne not in Russian, and certainly not in English, but in French.

In 1938, as well as writing his depressed article about James Joyce's *Ulysses*, in French, Gombrowicz wrote an article on Schulz – after the publication of Schulz's second collection of stories (and of Gombrowicz's first novel, *Ferdydurke*).

The essence of his essay was a thought experiment. Gombrowicz invited his reader to imagine that he or she were sitting at a desk, about to write a story. Suddenly, this imaginary novelist is stymied by self-doubt: since, after all, 'to relate imaginary events as if they had really taken place, to breathe into them an appearance of real life while everyone knows that they have just been born in your head is nothing but a form of mystification as false as it is pitiful.' This novelist feels a radical disappointment in fiction. He or she is not impressed by the art of the novel. And the conclusion reached by this imaginary writer – in Poland, in 1938 – is unsettling: 'not only imaginary events, but those which are real, in their flesh and bone, are really nothing but a form of chance, just a mask behind which a chaos watches us, a magma as sombre as it is anonymous.'

It is scary, but then again it is perhaps an understandable theory, in Warsaw in 1938. Chaos, in these circumstances, is plausible.

According to Gombrowicz, the consequence of chaos, of this inability to play the game of fiction, was that Schulz's fictional method was more faithful to real life than other fiction: he would not invent false symmetry, or false plausibility. He would not be bothered by the artificial constraints of realism – 'to construct his universe, Schulz chooses elements as fortuitous as they are arbitrary and, in doing this, he permits us to follow, in a world which is nothing but artifice, the very action itself of the laws and forms which govern the real world . . .'

In Central Europe, in 1938, both Gombrowicz and Schulz were

trying to invent a new style, to describe a new version of real life. They were trying to move beyond psychological realism, and the delicacy of ordinary causes, so that their style could discover something else. They were formalists, bored by traditional forms, who wanted to describe something which no one had described before.

This subject was immaturity.

Chapter v
Warsaw, 1937: A Plot

Gombrowicz's most celebrated novel, *Ferdydurke*, was published at the end of 1937. It was his first novel, but second book – following a collection of stories, *Memoirs from the Time of Immaturity*, in 1933. The first book had not been the success he had hoped: its title, especially, had not charmed in the way he thought it might. And so, rather than retreating, and revising his position, Gombrowicz decided to make things worse. 'Immaturity – what a compromising, disagreeable word! – became my war cry.' And so he wrote *Ferdydurke*.

The first joke was the title, because it was meaningless. It is possible that it is derived from a minor, momentary character in the American novelist Sinclair Lewis's novel *Babbitt* – 'old Freddy Durkee, that used to be a dead or alive shipping clerk in my old place' – but this derivation is only confirmation of the title's point. It is a garble of an irrelevant name. It is flippant.

The title was therefore the first flippancy of *Ferdydurke*; but there were more.

The narrator – who was not called Witold but, obviously, was Witold himself – woke up into a bad morning. He was racked with tricky thoughts. His first book had not been the success he had hoped. He was anguished with regret: 'Why did I, as if thwarting my own purpose, entitle my book *Memoirs from the Time of Immaturity?* In vain my friends advised me against using such a title, saying that I should avoid even the slightest allusion to immaturity . . .' The narrator's argument was that he had decided not 'to dismiss, easily and glibly, the snivelling brat within me, I thought that the truly Adult were sufficiently sharp and clear-sighted to see through this, and that anyone incessantly pursued by the brat within had no business appearing in public without the brat. But perhaps I took the serious-minded too seriously and over-estimated the maturity of the mature.' In bed, depressed, the narrator ran through his embarrassing entrance into the adult world. 'There is too much silence', he concluded, 'about the personal, inner hurts and injuries inflicted by that entrance, the grave consequences of which remain with us forever.'

When Bruno Schulz came to review this book a few months later, he was adept enough to see that this refusal not to be imma-ture was one of Gombrowicz's most endearing innovations. His fiction was content with its dull singularity; it did not try to hide the rubbish of its theme, and so Gombrowicz 'reveals that all the main and "general" motives of our behaviour – all navigation under the flag of ideas and official words – neither express us truly or completely . . .'

Back at the start of his novel, Gombrowicz continued to revel in the lovely shame of his bad morning, refusing to grow up, petu-lant at the fact that 'everyone must be aware of and be judged by everyone else, and the opinions that the ignorant, dull, and slow-witted hold about us are no less important than the opinions of the bright, the enlightened, the refined. This is because man is profoundly dependent on the reflection of himself in another man's soul, be it even the soul of an idiot.' And so he formed a resolu-tion: 'to create my own form! To turn outward! To express myself!' And he began to write again – as the maid brought in his hot coffee and fresh rolls.

But then 'suddenly the bell rings, the maid opens the door, and

T. Pimko appears – a doctor of philosophy, in reality just a school-teacher, a cultured philologue from Kraków, short and slight, skinny, bald, wearing spectacles, pin-striped trousers, a jacket, yellow buckskin shoes, his fingernails large and yellow.

Do you know the Professor?
Have you met the Professor?
Professor?

Stop, stop, stop, stop, stop!'
But nothing stops. Just as this narrator has decided to grow up, he enters a nightmare. Professor Pimko begins to talk to him as if he were a kid. He not only talks to him like a kid, but benignly assumes that in fact he is a kid, and leads him off to school. Yes, he takes a writer in his thirties back to school. And the narrator, for some reason, cannot say no to this calm coercion: he goes back to school, and becomes a kid again.

That is how the plot of *Ferdydurke* begins.

Chapter vi
Drohobycz, 1938: Bruno on Witold

A year later, in another small magazine called *Skamander*, Schulz published his essay on *Ferdydurke*, acknowledging that with this book the reader was in the presence of 'a new and revolutionary novelistic form and method, in sum, of a fundamental discovery: the annexation of a new territory of spiritual phenomena, a domain which up to now had been utterly ignored'. So far, thought Schulz, literature had been hopelessly official and professional. Gombrowicz's novel, however, was founded on the other, unofficial existence – of shame, and wishes, and infantilisation.

According to Schulz, Gombrowicz had escorted the reader out

of the salon, down the elegant corridors, into what Schulz called 'the kitchen of our self'. And Schulz also understood that Gombrowicz's subject was therefore double: his discovery of immaturity led to the twin discovery that everything which seemed natural in human conversations was in fact unnatural; all culture was a system of imposed and adopted forms. 'Man cannot bear his nudity. He only communicates with himself and with those around him through the intermediary of forms, of styles, of masks.'

But Schulz ended his piece on a note of worry, of caution; a note of self-criticism: 'wrenched from an organism as alive as *Ferdydurke*,' he said, 'how decrepit and skeletal does this thematics seem!'

Throughout his piece, Schulz had been entirely silent about the organism that was as alive as *Ferdydurke*. He praised Gombrowicz's new form and method, and then went on to concentrate only on the subject matter. But Gombrowicz's true strangeness was just as much in the form as in the content. And Schulz ignored this form.

Maybe Gombrowicz was right in 1961. Maybe in the end these two novelists were not good friends at all.

But I am a better friend to Gombrowicz.

Rather than letting his novel continue along its (admittedly weird) plot, Gombrowicz interrupted the narrative twice, with two short stories – one of them unusually called 'The Child Runs Deep in Filidor', and the other unusually called 'The Child Runs Deep in Filibert'. That was one innovation. The second innovation was that the Polish reader had seen these stories before, since they were reprinted from Gombrowicz's 1933 collection *Memoirs from the Time of Immaturity*. The third innovation was that each short story was preceded by a preface.

In his preface to the first story, 'The Child Runs Deep in Filidor', Gombrowicz told the reader, perhaps perplexed at the intrusion of a random short story (and a random preface) into the narrative, that 'one should not look for an exact connection between the two parts of the said whole; and whoever thinks that by including this story, "The Child Runs Deep in Filidor," I wasn't just trying to fill space on paper and slightly reduce the enormous number of white pages before me, is sorely mistaken.' It was filler, a ragbag. And yet, the preface continued, 'I will prove that my construction is in no way inferior, as far as precision and logic are concerned, to even the most precise and logical constructions.'

The theme of this preface, and of Gombrowicz's novel as a whole, was the coercive power of external forms – the way in which people happily and often unconsciously borrow second-hand forms – just as Madame Bovary wants to be a romantic heroine rather than Madame Bovary, or Don Quixote wants to be a knight errant and not Alonso Quixano. And so, consistently, Gombrowicz's preface boasted of the novel's ramshackle structure, its egotistical imperfection and repetition, its refusal to adhere to normal ideas of literary form. Instead of the harmonious interlinking of a whole, Gombrowicz's novel was built 'on a foundation of individual parts – treating the work itself as a particle of the work, man as a union of parts, and mankind as a composite of parts and pieces.' It was bric-a-brac. And to the reader who might object that such a concept was no concept at all, that Gombrowicz was just mocking literary forms, and conventions, Gombrowicz concluded: 'yes, yes indeed, these and none other are my intentions.'

Gombrowicz was an experimentalist: his intention was to make up an entirely individual literary form, an entirely personal one, in opposition to forms that had been inherited, forms that were second-hand. And naturally the first principle of such a form will be flippancy; it will be undeterred by contradiction.

It will be amateur.

Gombrowicz discovered a new area of subject matter, a queasy area of childhood and immaturity. But he also came up with a new form. That is what Bruno Schulz failed to say. This new form was immature too, it was deliberately malformed and sarcastic, like some kind of infantile graffiti, a grand rebuke to potty-training.

Chapter vii
London, 2007: A Tradition

I am not sure what to make of him, this odd writer, Witold Gombrowicz – whom I want to like, and cannot quite. I am convinced by the idea that his experiments were original, were advances in the art of the novel, and yet at the same time I am less convinced by the idea that they were fully successful. I am not sure if these experiments quite worked.

And this worries me. This conclusion seems to represent a contradiction to the argument of this book. It seems to imply that some writers are not fully translatable. Their styles are elsewhere.

But there is another solution.

My problem is not, perhaps, a problem of translation. Really, it is a problem of literary history. It is the problem of tradition. Unfortunately for Gombrowicz, no one followed him. And therefore no one made it possible to understand precisely what Gombrowicz was up to. No one continued to explore the implications of the queasiness and formlessness which Gombrowicz made the centre of his style. No one has explored the potential for immaturity.

Except, perhaps, Bruno Schulz. But Schulz is part of the history of waste, as well.

Chapter viii
Drohobycz, 1934: On Style

In Schulz's preface for a projected German translation of his first book, *Cinnamon Shops*, a collection of short stories, he tried to be clear about his fictional method. His book, he wrote, 'undertakes the attempt to describe the story of a family – of a house – in the provinces'. This, then, was his first innovation: although the book

358

was a collection of stories, it was also a novel. The stories were linked by a continuous narrative. But Schulz's next innovation was in the prose itself: he did not want to use 'external description' or 'psychological analysis': 'The ultimate givens of a human life are situated,' he thought, 'in a completely different dimension of the spirit; not in the category of facts, but in that of their spiritual meaning.' And that is why his novel – which was also a collection of short stories, and was a biography of a family – 'touches on myth'. Only in this way could Schulz be accurate to 'this atmosphere which is sombre and full of presentiments, this aura which condenses around all family history'.

Schulz's preface was an attempt to explain his own prose style – a style which magnified the little things, which exaggerated and intensified. It was accurate not to the facts, but to impressions of facts.

In Schulz's story 'The Book' a boy tries to rediscover a book which once, when he was much younger, seemed to him to be so magical, an expression of the world's spiritual meaning. But he could not. Finally, one day, he discovered the servant girl tearing out pages from a scraggy volume, which she told him they'd been using to wrap up food. And this, it turned out, was the Book he had been searching for. And yet it was almost demolished. Only the adverts at the back, the classifieds, the humdrum, were left – the adverts for 'a woman called Magda Wang', whose 'speciality was to break the strongest characters'. Reading this advert, recorded Schulz, the reader felt 'overcome by a strange vertigo, one felt that moral definitions had curiously been displaced, that one was in another climate, where the compass functioned upside down.'

The essence of this perfect book from his childhood was an S&M specialist, who solicited through the small ads.

Schulz knew all about the grand emotions, like shame and lust and pride: he knew their sources were located in the smallest, most everyday things, like almanacs and adverts. In a letter to his friend

S. I. Witkiewicz, Schulz explained that '*Cinnamon Shops* gives a certain recipe for reality, positing a particular type of substance. The substance of this reality is in a perpetual state of fermentation, it is characterised by its continual shifting, by the secret life which inhabits it.' This was what was behind his style: 'A particular principle manifests itself in the habits and manners of this reality: the principle of universal masquerade.' Both Gombrowicz and Schulz recognised in the other a common perception of masks: so that Gombrowicz saw in Schulz a reality which was 'nothing but a form of chance, just a mask behind which a chaos watches us, a magma as sombre as it is anonymous.' And Schulz commented on *Ferdydurke*: 'Man cannot bear his nudity. He only communicates with himself and with those around him through the intermediary of forms, of styles, of masks.' But in each case, the mask is different, particular. Gombrowicz's masks are social: they are existential, inauthentic. Whereas Schulz's mask is more spiritual: it is an expression of mysticism.

And Schulz's mystical principle of universal masquerade, of the idea that only the visionary was real, caused a prose style with a penchant for a particular technique: the universal masquerade was expressed through hyperbolic metaphor, and relentless personification.

Chapter ix
Drohobycz, 1934: Metaphor

I said that, very rarely – in the height, and in the linguistic problems – I resemble Alexander Pushkin. Like Pushkin, I sometimes find it more useful to triangulate, and read a translation into a second language. So that in the French translation, translated back into English by me, Bruno Schulz's second published paragraph sounds something like this:

Shopping

On luminous mornings, Adela, as Pomona, would return from the fire and the burned-out day and would empty her basket of all the coloured beauties of the sun. First there would be shining cherries, swollen with water beneath their fine transparent skin, mysterious black morellos, whose taste would not fulfil all the promises of their smell, apricots in the gilded pulp which they slept in through long overheated afternoons; after the pure poetry of fruit would come the enormous cuts of meat, powerful and nutritious, with the musical keyboard of flanks of veal; vegetables like sea plants, dead octopi or squid – all the raw material of the meal with a taste not yet determined and inert, the vegetal and earthly ingredients of a future lunch from which drifted a wild and rustic smell.

'And if the poetic manner of his prose doesn't bore people,' wrote Gombrowicz, 'it'll dazzle them'.

But poetry is difficult. In these sentences by Schulz, poetry means that everything is written under the sign of hyperbole. So that a housemaid – Adela – is classically shadowed by Pomona, the goddess of the morning, a morning which is not cloudy, or blustery, but fiercely sunlit, and flaming. The fruit – the cherries, the morellos, the apricots – are all described as latent with something, they are pregnant with ulterior meaning. At this point, more conventional poetic techniques take over – so that there is the precise simile of ribs to a keyboard, and then vegetables which are no longer kitchen-like but slumped like seaweed, alive with tentacles. Poetry, here, means sentences repetitive with exaggeration, where the banal and the everyday are elongated.

This is the Schulzian, and it is visible in French or English, in Franglais or Englench. 'A particular principle manifests itself in the habits and manners of this reality: the principle of universal masquerade.'

Chapter x
Buenos Aires, 1957: Exile

A style is not linguistic.

That is why I disagree with Isaac Bashevis Singer, who was not an elegant stylist, whose style was visible in translation, and yet who believed that style was also inherently linguistic.

Talking to Philip Roth about Schulz's decision to write in Polish, not Yiddish, Singer said – factually, and neutrally – that the 'Jews had a number of important writers who wrote in Polish, and all of them were born more or less at this time, in the 1890s': 'the truth is, they had no choice and we had no choice. They didn't know Yiddish, we didn't know Polish.' Schulz knew no Yiddish – that is the unremarkable reason why his stories are written in Polish. But soon Singer's resigned acceptance of the necessity for Schulz of writing in Polish – the fact that it was Schulz's first language – disappeared. Singer compared Schulz to Kafka: 'I think that Schulz had enough power to write real serious novels but instead often wrote a kind of parody. And I think basically he developed this style because he was not really at home, neither at home among the Poles nor at home among the Jews. It's a style that's somewhat characteristic also of Kafka, because Kafka also felt that he had no roots.' And Singer's conclusion was that 'from my point of view, I would rather have liked to have seen him as a Yiddish writer. He wouldn't have had all the time to be as negative and mocking as he was.'

This is one way of not being as universal as Witold Gombrowicz.

In the 1950s, Gombrowicz – living in Buenos Aires – was asked to reply to an article by the Romanian writer E. M. Cioran, an émigré living in Paris, on the advantages and disadvantages of exile. In his journal, Gombrowicz recorded his thoughts: prosaically, he thought about this poetic thing called exile.

A map of Buenos Aires. © Librairie Larousse, 1959

He began by listing the inconveniences which exile caused a novelist: the annoyance of being deprived of readers; the disagreeable problem of not being able to publish books; the depressing fact that no one knows who you are, that the publicity machine which organises other people's celebrity will not do the same for you. Exile is a problem of vanity. And vanity is not the same as art. 'Art is charged and nourished by elements of solitude and perfect autonomy', so that there is no need to lament the loss of a country, since 'every eminent man, by the simple fact of his eminence, is a foreigner, even in his own home.' And as for readers, any novelist in love with art has 'never written *for* readers, always *against* them.'

And his conclusion was majestic and simple: 'To lose one's country will only disrupt the harmony of those whose country is not the universe.'

Chapter xi
Drohobycz, 1937: Immaturity

The introduction to Schulz's story 'The Age of Genius' developed a new theory of time. According to Schulz, there was a usual concept of time, in which facts 'are arranged within time, strung along its length as on a thread.' This was the normal basis of a narrative. But then Schulz asked the question: 'what is to be done with events that have no place of their own in time; events that have occurred too late, after the whole of time has been distributed, divided, and allotted; events that have been left in the cold, unregistered, hanging in the air, homeless, and errant?' In Schulz's idea, time is too narrow for all events. Instead, for Schulz, time was like a railway, with diverging parallel lines: after all, argues Schulz, 'there are such branch lines of time, somewhat illegal and suspect, but when, like us, one is burdened with a stashed-away suitcase of supernumerary events that cannot be registered, one cannot be too fussy.'

These lines should be compared with two sentences from a letter Schulz wrote as he was writing his unfinished novel, *Messiah*: 'My ideal is to "mature" to childhood. That would be real maturity at last.' An inverted attitude to time was behind all of Schulz's fiction, and his experiments with metaphor, and his fractured novels made up of individual stories. Truth is fleeting, and fragmentary. It is stashed away, in a valise or a trunk. It is something which can only be recovered through upending normal values.

Schulz's subject, like Gombrowicz's, was immaturity.

And in the same way as Schulz believed in branch lines of time, I believe that there are therefore also branch lines of literature. Some people are way ahead. Yet at any given moment, in general, literature may be going backwards. It may be relying on techniques which have been already superseded.

This means that something sad is also true: that the literature which is going forwards may not be known about at all.

Cervantes gave a portrait of the romantic as a misreader. Flaubert's romantics were characters whose ideas were banal *idées reçues*. And Gombrowicz and Schulz discovered a new form of romance, a new form of comic subject matter which they could play around with, and ironise: the immature.

This area, like all other new areas of subject matter, at first seems nebulous and without form. All new subject matter seems at first to have no form: then the novelist finds the form that copes with it.

СОЧИНЕНІЯ

А. С. ПУШКИНА

ПОЛНОЕ СОБРАНІЕ

въ

ОДНОМЪ ТОМѢ

Со статьей **А. Скабичевскаго:** «Александръ Сергѣевичъ Пушкинъ» (бı
фическій очеркъ) и портретомъ автора, гравированнымъ **В. Матэ.**

Встань — и міру вновь явись!

Второе изданіе

дополненное двумя политипажами (портретомъ Н. Н. Пушкиной и сценой дуэли поэта), вновь
найденными стихотвореніями и **500 письмами Пушкина.**

ЦѢНА ОДНОТОМНАГО ИЗДАНІЯ:		
Безъ иллю-страцій	на обыкнов. бумагѣ 1 р. 50 к.	
	» лучшей » 2 » — »	
Съ 44 иллю-страціями	на обыкнов. бумагѣ 2 » 50 »	
	» лучшей » 3 » — »	

VOLUME V

BOOK 15

The Fluke

This, the fifth and final volume, is sadder. Its subject is two perplexing trains of thought: one of them about history, and the other about the history of style. And its heroes are two cosmopolitan Russian writers: Alexander Pushkin and Vladimir Nabokov.

Throughout the book, there has been a tension – between an idea that the history of an art form is in some way ideal, and the knowledge that this ideal art form is always only approximate. Everything is subjected to the tyranny of mistakes.

In this final volume, these two ideas are pushed as far as I can go.

The first French translation of Laurence Sterne's novel *The Life and Opinions of Tristram Shandy, Gentleman* – up to the end of the fourth volume – came out in 1776, made by a man called Joseph Pierre Frénais. The rest of the novel was then taken up simultaneously by Griffet de la Beaume and the Marquis de Bonnay. De la Beaume's translation, though slightly better than de Bonnay's, was for some reason not reissued; so the standard reprinted translation became an amalgam of Frénais and de Bonnay.

Unsurprisingly, it was not a perfect translation. It had its mistakes. There were the mistakes which I mentioned in Volume II, involving the omission of Sterne's loopy lines and diagrams; but, more important, Frénais seems to have found Sterne's sense of humour a little unsettling and unlikeable.

The main problem Frénais had with the text he was translating was Sterne's obscenity. In French polite society, obscenity was not the done – or at least not the said – thing. In his 'Advertisement' at the start of the book, he therefore told the reader that 'Monsieur Sterne's jokes have not always seemed to me to be very good. I have left them where I have found them, & substituted others in their place.' This led to Frénais tampering with Sterne's structure of innuendo, so that his trademark technique of missing out words, or pretending to miss out words, was truncated back into normality again.

Two sentences in English by Laurence Sterne

My sister, I dare say, added he, does not care to let a man come so near her * * * *. I will not say whether my uncle Toby had completed the sentence or not . . .'

One sentence in French by Joseph Pierre Frénais

Ma soeur ne veut apparemment pas qu'un homme l'approche de si près . . . [Apparently my sister doesn't want a man to approach her so closely . . .]

Frénais's three dots of an ellipsis after a perfectly finished sentence, and his cutting of Tristam's extra nod to the reader, are a tame substitution for Sterne's winking asterisks.

But Frénais did not just tamper with the obscenity; he restructured paragraphs, omitted lines which seemed to bore him, and added in things of his own. Unlike Samuel Johnson, he did not tell the reader that this was what he was doing. Frénais had a particular problem with Sterne's typographical and bookish tricks – like his blank page, or black page. Where Sterne had inserted a marbled page ('motley emblem of my work!'), Frénais did not. And yet where Sterne had Tristram's father lamenting the mishaps of Tristram's birth in perfectly sequential prose, Frénais decided that it would be better, in order to represent the ascending and descending tone of Walter's lament, to add in a line of *hélas* – 'alas' – going upwards:

hélas

hélas

hélas

hélas

hélas

and then to add in a line of *hélas* going in the opposite direction.

My problem is this: what were the French-speakers really reading, if they were reading Sterne in this translation? And this seems especially important because it was the translation read by two of the main characters in this book – by Machado de Assis, in Rio de Janeiro, and by a new character: Alexander Pushkin, in St Petersburg.

Unlike with Machado de Assis, I know for sure that Pushkin read Sterne in Frénais's translation because after his death a catalogue was made of his library. Thanks to the catalogue, it is possible to know that Pushkin read the 1818 *Oeuvres Complètes* edition of Laurence Sterne. He also owned a dual French and English edition of *Sentimental Journey* – '*Voyage sentimental, suivi des Lettres d'Yorick à Éliza, par Laurent Sterne, en anglais et en français*. Paris. 1799.'

My baffled conclusion is that the version of Sterne they were reading was an entirely plausible one; it was still useful. In the end, translations can be scrappier than most people, perhaps, would like. However uneasy this makes me, it is obvious that in Rio de Janeiro, or St Petersburg, reading this approximation to a rough translation, it was still possible to see what Sterne was up to and develop his techniques.

There is one final addition to this theme of the mistake.

In trying to think up an equivalent to Sterne's English word *hobby-horse*, Frénais invented the French word *dada* – and three hundred years later this word would be picked at random from a French dictionary by Richard Huelsenbeck, Hugo Ball and Tristan Tzara as they tried to christen their polyglot, international movement obsessed with bad reproductions, with playfulness and flaws.

Yes, every theory of literature has to incorporate a theory of the fluke. But it also has to cope with the persistent conspiracy of themes signalling to each other, with no regard for time or place – just like the conspiracy of words Vladimir Nabokov noticed in Pushkin's novel *Eugene Onegin*, winking behind the backs of the innocent reader.

Chapter ii
St Petersburg, 1833: Boy Rejects Girl Who Rejects Boy

Alexander Pushkin's variation on *Tristram Shandy* is his novel *Eugene Onegin*. And Pushkin's variation is a particularly original variation, from the start, because it is a novel in verse. Its plot is told through a series of fourteen-line stanzas with an intricate rhyme scheme.

The plot of *Eugene Onegin*, however, is very simple: Tatiana loves Eugene, but Eugene does not love Tatiana. So Eugene rejects Tatiana. By the time he realises that he loves her, Tatiana is now married to another man. And so she, in her turn, rejects Eugene.

It is possible, I suppose, to read this as a noble tragedy, a story of lovers fated to remain apart. And some romantic (and Russian) readers have read it in this way. But it is also possible to see Pushkin's story as something tinged with comedy – a tragic form of irony, involving emotional complication.

The novel ends with Tatiana's rejection of Eugene. But it is a complicated kind of rejection, in a complicated kind of novel.

Tatiana rejects Eugene, in Vladimir Nabokov's English

Yet happiness had been so possible,
so near! . . . But my fate is already
settled. Imprudently,
perhaps, I acted.
My mother with tears of conjurement
beseeched me. For poor Tanya
all lots were equal.
I married. You must,
I pray you, leave me;
I know: in your heart are
both pride and genuine honor.
I love you (why dissimulate?);
but to another I belong:
to him I shall be faithful all my life.

Tatiana rejects Onegin: and she also admits that she loves him. Her romantic statement of duty is also tinged with regret.

According to Tolstoy, who got it from Princess Meshchersky, Pushkin lamented: 'Imagine what happened to my Tatiana? She up and rejected Onegin . . . I never expected it of her!' But this is a joke, obviously. It is a joke at the expense of less interesting novels. The freedom to upend convention which Tatiana exhibits is directly related to the way in which she is so delicately and unconventionally displayed by Pushkin himself.

And the way she is displayed is through a variety of techniques which Pushkin happened on in the imperfect French translation of *Tristram Shandy*. The first great Russian novel was a rewrite of a French travesty of an English avant-garde novel.

Chapter iii
Buenos Aires, 1931: Argentina

A few years before Witold Gombrowicz arrived in Buenos Aires, Jorge Luis Borges gave a lecture on 'The Argentine Writer and Tradition'. Like Gombrowicz, Jorge Luis Borges argued against nationalism in literature. He was true to Buenos Aires.

There was no need for a writer, argued Borges, if they were Brazilian, or Russian, or whatever, to be a Brazilian or Russian writer – or whatever: 'the idea that a literature must define itself in terms of its national traits is a relatively new concept; also new and arbitrary is the idea that writers must seek themes from their own countries.' Just as Gustave Flaubert, in Croisset, had noted his axioms about literature – that poetry is purely subjective, and that you can therefore write well about absolutely anything at all. And Borges added, cheekily, talking of his own country, that the 'Argentine cult of local colour is a recent European cult which the nationalists ought to reject as foreign.'

Borges was playing with an important paradox – that the more Western a book is, the more Argentinian it is too, and vice versa: 'What is our Argentine tradition? I believe we can answer this question easily and that there is no problem here. I believe our tradition is all of Western culture . . .'

In the world of novels, there is no such thing as a large or small country. Everywhere can be everywhere. But this everywhere takes work.

So that Witold Gombrowicz, in Argentina, could argue with the Cuban novelist Virgilio Pinera, who complained that Europeans look down on Americans, of both the North and South variety, unable to accept that literature was possible in Buenos Aires, or Havana, too. 'Virgilio, I said,' wrote Gombrowicz, in his journal, 'don't be a child. All these divisions into continents and nationalities, this is really just a lousy schema imposed on art. Why, everything you write leads

Witold Gombrowicz's flat in Buenos Aires. Archives: Rita Gombrowicz.

me to believe that you don't know the word "we", only "I". Why the division then into "We, Americans" and "You, Europeans"?'

The problem of living in Brazil, or Cuba, or Russia, and wanting to write a novel, is the same problem as living in France, or Britain, and wanting to write a novel. The problem is universal: it is about finding a way of describing real life. And real life is infinite; real life is, from an artistic point of view, often unacceptable.

This is one of the lessons taught by Buenos Aires; and it is a lesson which Gombrowicz would write down in his journal, twenty years later, in 1954: 'What is Argentina? Batter that has not yet become cake, or something that is simply unshaped . . .' And in this way, concluded Gombrowicz, 'a genuine and creative protest against Europe could arise' – a protest against pride, against the vanity of the European tradition, if only 'softness found a way to make itself hard or if the indistinctness could become a program, a definition': which, of course, happily, it cannot.

Yes, this everywhere takes work.

When he met Borges, at dinner one evening in Buenos Aires, Gombrowicz did not take to him. 'Bypassing technical difficulties, my unruly Spanish and Borges's faulty pronunciation – he spoke quickly and incomprehensibly . . .', there was a more important problem. Gombrowicz was not convinced by Borges's love of Europe. He did not understand why he was not more fascinated by Argentina. Because Gombrowicz was in love with Argentina. 'I was enthralled by the darkness of the Retiro, they, by the lights of Paris.' Without quite noting the sad symmetry of their mutual positions, the diners ended their meal argumentatively, with Gombrowicz cataloguing 'this international, sophisticated Borges' as 'something extraneous, pasted on'.

As with every value, there is a flipside, a shadow, a secret twin, to this value called cosmopolitanism. The opposite of cosmopolitanism is provincialism. And provincialism is emptiness. It is an absence of subject matter; a lack of local ephemera.

Chapter iv
St Petersburg, 1824: Freedom (I)

In 1837, in the eighth issue of the magazine which Pushkin had helped to found, called the *Contemporary*, the editors published – posthumously – a selection of Pushkin's 'table-talk'. Apparently, Pushkin was given to chatting about the technical problem which bothered him in Tatiana – how to create a character who is not fixed by a plan, a character who possesses a realistic indeterminacy. His example was Shakespeare, who could create characters who are 'living beings, compacted of many passions and many vices'. Unlike the French playwright Molière, Shakespeare was true to the multiple perspectives of real life. 'Molière's Miser is miserly – and that is all; Shakespeare's Shylock is miserly, resourceful, vindictive, a fond father, witty.'

Pushkin's theory was that as soon as a character has more than one character, as soon as they can change their mind, they become realistic. The unexpected consequence was that, as soon as they can change their mind, a character can also get free of a plot, and the plot's narrator. That is what happened in the final scene of *Eugene Onegin*. Tatiana did not act in the way a romantic heroine was supposed to act.

But Pushkin was not content with this. He was more experimental.

In November 1824, Pushkin wrote to his brother, Lev. The first canto of *Eugene Onegin* was to be published three months later, on 18 February 1825. In his letter, Pushkin included a drawing, saying that he absolutely needed it to be published with the novel. The drawing, of the embankment on the River Neva in St Petersburg, depicted Pushkin, who was trendy and handsome; Onegin, who was slightly less dashing, without Pushkin's romantic curls; a sailing boat; and the Peter and Paul fortress.

The illustration was, however, never made for the 1825 edition.

Alexander Pushkin with his friend Eugene Onegin (by Alexander Pushkin)

It eventually appeared, redrawn, by the artist Alexander Notbek, in a series of *Onegin* illustrations published in January 1829, in the *Nevski Almanac*. In it, Pushkin was no longer good-looking. He seemed tense, and strained – as if, he pointed out, he were fighting a difficult case of diarrhoea.

The point, however, is not the drawing's execution, but the joke behind it. The joke is why he needed it to be published with the novel. The drawing showed an author who was a friend of one of his characters. And this parity is the secret of the fictional games in *Eugene Onegin*. 'The hero of my novel, / without preambles, forth-with, / I'd like to have you meet: / Onegin, a good pal of mine . . .' Everyone is on the same plane. 'At a dull aunt's having met Tanya, / once V sat down beside her / and managed to engage her soul . . .' 'V' is Pushkin's friend, Prince Viyazemsky. And I like this a lot, this trick of having Tatiana be a peripheral part of Pushkin's social circle.

The reason for this trope, that the characters are acquaintances of the author, is that it gives Pushkin another way of inventing the idea that characters have freedom. He invents the idea of the fictional fluke. His *Eugene Onegin*, therefore, like Diderot's novel *Jacques the Fatalist and His Master*, and his story which isn't a story, is a joke which is also a variation on Sterne's theme.

Any freedom that a character has in fiction is an illusion. They are only made up. But everything is made up. Having accepted that, then there are more and less precise ways of pretending. One of the better ways is to let the character contradict him or herself – not do the predicted thing, or not fit the thematics of the story.

But there is another way, where the novelist turns up in the story. Because this creates an ambiguity, a complication.

The characters' lack of freedom in a novel is based on the fact that the author is real, while the characters are not. But once Pushkin is in the story, and is therefore fictional, then the fictional characters gain a new appearance of freedom. Freedom in Pushkin is developed through freedom from the omniscient narrator. Since they are on the same level, then Pushkin and his characters are not on the level. Pushkin can pretend not to know everything about them. 'Now let us eavesdrop furtively / upon our heroes' conversation . . .' The characters are always fugitive – they even, quite literally, run away, so that Pushkin can make jokes about how, distracted by his description of a ball, he has lagged behind and must rush off to overtake Onegin on his drive home.

The relation between author and character which Pushkin developed was the affectionate but necessarily separate relationship between friends. So, after Onegin has killed Lenski in the duel, Pushkin the narrator can say: 'but now I am not in the mood for him'. Or he can talk affectionately, as if he is snugly ensconced in the world of his characters: 'Tatiana's letter is before me; / religiously I keep it; / I read it with a secret heartache / and cannot get my fill of reading it.'

This technique allows, however, not just one freedom but two. Although this is my idea, not Pushkin's. As well as allowing the freedom of a character from its narrator, it also allows a freedom for the narrator from his or her character. And this is something that Pushkin does not quite exploit. It would be left to more audacious narrators, like Tolstoy, to leap around the characters, happily, with his essayistic digressions, his theories of history and of war.

The history of the novel's form is not perfect, or linear; it abandons some possibilities and favours others. The novel, this international mongrel, is patchy at best.

Chapter v
St Petersburg, 1837: The Fluke

On 27 January 1837, Pushkin fought a duel with a Frenchman, Georges D'Anthès. Pushkin was shot through the abdominal cavity.

The bullet shattered the sacrum, and remained there. Two days later, on 29 January, aged thirty-seven, Pushkin died.

This duel took place because of a letter which Pushkin received at nine in the morning on 4 November 1836, a Wednesday.

In French – since that was the first language of the St Petersburg court, that was the language of gossip – the anonymous author of the letter accused Pushkin of being a cuckold. He was therefore welcomed, through a unanimous vote, into the Order of Cuckolds.

The letter was signed with a flourish, rather like Corporal Trim's flourish with a stick in the air.

Pushkin's letter in French on a Wednesday morning

Les Grands-Croix Commandeurs et Chevaliers du Sérénissime Ordre des *Cocus* réunis en grand chapitre sous la présidence du vénérable grand-Maître de l'Ordre, S.E.D.L. Narychkine, *ont nommé à l'unanimité Mr Alexandre Pouchkine coadjateur du grand Maître de l'Ordre des Cocus et historiographe de l'Ordre. Le Sécrétaire pérpétuel: Cte I. Borch*

And this moment was the beginning of the end of Pushkin's life. His death was determined by a chain of unexpected causes, by the unintended consequences of backchat. It was a fluke.

Chapter vi
St Petersburg, 1822: What Is Poetry and What Is Prose?

Eugene Onegin is subtitled by Pushkin 'A Novel in Verse'. And while this is a joke, a deliberate oxymoron, it is also not a joke. Because there is no real disjunction between a novel and poetry.

In a draft article from 1822, with the title 'On Prose', Pushkin was grouchy at Russian and romantic writers, who 'deeming it too low to write plainly of ordinary things, think to liven up their childish prose with embellishments and faded metaphors! These people will never say "friendship" without adding "that holy sentiment, of which the noble flame, etc." They want to say "early in the morning", and they write "hardly had the first rays of the rising sun irradiated the eastern edge of the azure sky". How new and fresh all this is! Is it better simply for being longer?'

Pushkin's conclusion, when he was only twenty-two, was the sensible one that the two virtues of prose are not length, but 'precision and brevity'. Because prose 'demands matter and more matter – without it brilliant expressions serve no purpose. In this it differs from poetry. (But actually it would not harm our poets to have a considerably larger stock of ideas than it is usual to find among them. Our literature will not go far on memories of departed youth.)' It seems there is an essential difference between poetry and prose – the need prose has for subject matter. But, in the end, this is not such a major difference. Poetry needs subject matter, too. And prose needs the precision of poetry.

One of the things Pushkin was doing in *Eugene Onegin*, by writing a novel in verse, was showing how much more subject matter could be got into poetry. And how much brevity could be got into the novel.

The only duty, for a novelist, or a poet, or a novelistpoet, is to be interesting.

'Is it not simpler to follow the Romantic school,' notes Pushkin, three years later, 'which is marked by the absence of all Rules but not by the absence of art? Interest is All.'

And I like this. It brings Pushkin close to another of my characters, Denis Diderot. Since Pushkin owned a copy of Diderot's *Oeuvres*, published in Paris in 1821, as well as an 1821 copy of the *Oeuvres inédites*, he could have read Diderot's 'Eulogy' of the English novelist Samuel Richardson, where Diderot centres the art of prose on being 'interesting', on the mass of detail. 'You can think whatever you like about these details; but they'll be interesting to me if they're true, if they bring out the emotions, if they display the characters.' Like Saul Bellow in Chicago, in St Petersburg Pushkin needed to include as much of real life as he could. He needed to be interesting. He needed detail. The art of the novel is the same as the art of conversation: 'A novel demands *chat*; everything must be expressed . . . ,' wrote Pushkin, to one of his friends.

Like conversation, a novel only works if it is prickly and malicious with specifics.

In Nabokov's edition of Pushkin's *Eugene Onegin*, there is this exemplary note to a passage in which Pushkin notes the lamps' 'rainbows on the snow', noted by Eugene as he passes in his carriage: 'My own fifty-year-old remembrance is not so much of prismatic colors cast upon snowdrifts by the two lateral lanterns of a brougham as of iridescent spicules around blurry street lights coming though its frost-foliated windows and breaking along the rim of the glass.'

This improvised, assured, unforgettable extra rainbow is the centre of the art of prose.

And in *Eugene Onegin* there are similar delicate moments, minuscule precisions: 'frostdust silvers / his beaver collar'. Or the theatre, where 'still at the carriage porch the weary footmen / on the pelisses are asleep'. Or the blood 'steaming' from a wound. Or the description of Eugene's dressing room, with its texture of the minute, the useful: 'perfumes in crystal cut with facets; combs, little files of steel, / straight scissors, curved ones, and brushes / of thirty kinds . . .' Onegin, as Nabokov said, is 'a man with a wardrobe'. And this is unusual for a character – to have a wardrobe. So many previous characters in fiction seemed to have magically got along without one, dressing themselves out of nowhere. Onegin's wardrobe full of clothes is a welcome innovation.

It's no longer a character lamenting his memories of departed youth.

But I can still be worried by how international *Eugene Onegin* really is. There are the poetic aspects of prose style, true, but the poetic aspects of prose style do not mean that a novel is suddenly a *poem*. Whereas *Eugene Onegin*, unfortunately, is a poem just as much as it is a novel.

A poem! How can a poem be translated, style for style?

In America, Nabokov took on a series of teaching jobs in the 1940s and 1950s which culminated in his stay at Cornell University, leading a course on masterpieces of European literature. Quickly, Nabokov became tetchy at the translations he had to use. The versions of Pushkin depressed him. So he decided to do his own version of *Eugene Onegin*. In 1964, he published his four volume edition: an introduction; a literal translation; and two volumes of commentary – together with an index, and a facsimile of the Russian text.

And he caused the biggest argument in the twentieth century about translation.

In Nabokov's 'Foreword' to his translation he asked a simple question: 'Can Pushkin's poem, or any other poem with a definite rhyme scheme, be really translated?' He answered this by saying that the answer would follow from a true definition of translation. And so he defined three ways in which it was possible to render a poem in another language. The first was 'Paraphrastic': a free version of the original. The second was 'Lexical (or constructional)': the basic meaning of the words, in their original order. And the third was 'Literal: rendering, as closely as the associative and syntactical capacities of another language allow, the exact contextual meaning of the original. Only this is true translation.'

Now, argued Nabokov, we are 'in a position to word our question more accurately: can a rhymed poem like *Eugene Onegin* be truly translated with the retention of its rhymes? The answer, of course, is no. To reproduce the rhymes and yet translate the poem entire is mathematically impossible.' And yet: 'in losing its rhyme the poem loses its bloom, which neither marginal description nor the alchemy of a scholium can replace.'

Nabokov, obviously, was right. The rhymes are not an optional extra. They are not a side of fries. They are part of the Big Mac, the Royale, itself.

Pushkin's novel was partly about the love affair between Eugene and Tatiana, but it was also about the game it was playing with the novel as a form. The intricate, comic, delicate rhymes were part of this parodic dissection of the novel's forms – removing it from the world of prosaic seriousness. (Which is why, perhaps, Pushkin played fewer overt structural games than his English source, Laurence Sterne: the Russian rhymes were already playful enough.)

If the rhymes disappear, then a large part of the poem's implied subject disappears as well. But it is not so easy to preserve the rhymes in English: for a start, rhyme in English often has different cultural connotations from rhyme in Russian; and, more importantly, rhyme is such a constraint that inevitably some precision in meaning will have to be lost.

Two alternatives therefore present themselves to a translator of Pushkin's novel, argued Nabokov: to render the subject matter exactly, and forget the form; or to imitate the novel's form, while trying to include as much of the subject matter as possible. The danger of this second alternative is the danger of prettification. Apparently condoned by the honest desire to replicate form, not content, the translator can therefore ignore whichever passages seem too odd, too unfashionable in the original poem. Or, to perhaps put it more pragmatically than Nabokov, the problem with the second alternative was talent – the massive difficulty of combining formal mimicry with the total inclusion of content.

Quite rightly, one of the things Nabokov most hated in a translation was the cliché of the smooth translation. We know what he thought about bad translations of Lermontov. A few years later, in his preface to Pushkin, he was still saying the same thing: 'I have been always amused by the stereotyped compliment that a reviewer pays the author of a "new translation." He says: "It reads smoothly." In other words, the hack who has never read the original, and does not know its language, praises an imitation as readable because easy platitudes have replaced in it the intricacies of which he is unaware.' And so Nabokov comes to a famous conclusion, that 'it is when the translator sets out to render the "spirit," and not the mere sense of the text, that he begins to traduce his author.' The best translations, on this theory, are not embarrassed to sound like translations: they give up on the style, and explicate the content.

This, argued Nabokov, was a literal translation; and only this method was acceptable: 'to my ideal of literalism I sacrificed everything (elegance, euphony, clarity, good taste, modern usage, and even grammar) that the dainty mimic prizes higher than truth. Pushkin has likened translators to horses changed at the posthouses of civilization. The greatest reward I can think of is that students may use my work as a pony.' It was hardly a translation at all: rather than fulfilling the traditional function of replacing the original, it was now only useful as a crib, a prompt to the original, instead.

But Nabokov's boast, his pony's bray, was followed immediately, in the next paragraph, by something more troubling. 'Perfect interlinear correspondence, however,' admitted Nabokov, 'has not been achieved. In some cases, for the translation to make sense, certain requirements of construction had to be taken into consideration, calling for changes in the cut and position of the English sentence.' It is a small slip, but it is also an important one. Even Nabokov could not be as happily literal as he would like; and once this is admitted, then everything else can follow. As soon as degrees of literal translation can be identified, as soon as it is obvious that no translation is purely literal, then the advocates of all the haywire ideas – of imitation, adaptation, variation – can start to disagree with Nabokov's pony.

My small contribution to this impertinence would be the title. Евгений Онегин, transliterated out of the Cyrillic script, is something like Yevgéniy Onyégin. It so happens that in English there exists a name Eugene – which now, to me, sounds oddly rare, and from a different era. It is from the American 1920s. So it is just about allowable, as a substitution for the more normal name, in Russian, Yevgeniy. But there never has been, and never will be, a surname in English called Onegin, let alone Onyégin. Nabokov's *Eugene Onegin* is therefore oddly transatlantic, straddling two continents, and two different theories of verbal transformation: it is an imitation and a transliteration at the same time.

In the same way as with Akaky Akakievich Bashmachkin, or Joseph K, there is a problem with literal translations.

Chapter viii
Washington, 1941, & Berlin, 1923: Literal Translation (III)

Another person who disagreed with Nabokov was Nabokov.

Twenty years earlier, in 1941, having lived in America for two years, Nabokov wrote an article for an American magazine, the *New Republic*, on the subject of literal translation. This was partly because translation was on his mind, having just translated nineteenth-century Russian poems into English. But it was also because translation was necessarily at the centre of Nabokov's thoughts on style.

Every theory of style will also, at some point, have a corresponding theory of translation.

Nabokov offered the American reader the 'opening line of one of Pushkin's most prodigious poems', which he transliterated as 'Yah pom-new chewed-no-yay mg-no-vain-yay'. And although 'their mimetic disguise makes them look rather ugly', Nabokov argues that these words are taut and musical with association. But, continued Nabokov, sadly, 'if you take a dictionary and look up those four words you will obtain the following foolish, flat and familiar statement: "I remember a wonderful moment."'

Nabokov's conclusion was that 'the expression "a literal translation" is more or less nonsense.'

A literal translation of the line is no translation at all, since it abandons the most important things – the connotations and phonetics of the words, a central aspect of poetic style. If there is no way for all the connotations of sound and meaning to be transferred from one language into another, then what Nabokov would later define as 'the exact contextual meaning of the original' is impossible: '"Yah pom-new" is a deeper and smoother plunge into the past than "I remember," which falls flat on its belly like an inexperienced diver; "chewed-no-yay" has a lovely Russian "monster" in it, and a whispered "listen," and the dative ending of a "sunbeam," and many other fair relations among Russian words.' No translation can reproduce all the effects. No one, not even Nabokov, can re-create in English the dative ending of a sunbeam.

Nabokov's position in 1941 – that literal translation is an oxymoron – was consistent with all his translations up to that point. In 1923, in Berlin, the émigré Russian publishing house Gamaiun produced Nabokov's translation into Russian of Lewis Carroll's *Alice in Wonderland*.

In this translation, Nabokov naturalised everything.

Since the ordinary Russian transliteration of Alice – Alisa – sounds oddly foreign in Russian, he changed her name to Anya, the Russian diminutive of Anna. Her friends Ada and Mabel became the more Russian Ada and Asya. The French-speaking mouse no longer came across with William the Conqueror, but was now left behind by Napoleon on his retreat from Moscow. The history lesson recited by the Mouse just before the Caucus race became a quotation from a nineteenth-century history book about Vladimir Monomakh's successors to the Kievan throne.

Carroll's *Alice in Wonderland* describes a dream, but it is also a small library of parodies. Parody is the way in which Carroll's dream-like sense of humour works. It is a display of small unsettling adjustments.

Parody, like poetry, is a quilting of form and content: its subject is also its style.

And so, correctly, I think, having changed Carroll's English historical references, Nabokov changed all Carroll's parodic literary references, as well. 'You are old, Father William' became a distorted version of Lermontov's poem 'Borodino'; 'Speak roughly to your little boy' became a travesty of Lermontov's 'The Cossack Lullaby'. While the first line of ''Tis the voice of the Lobster' found itself transformed into the first line of Pushkin's poem 'The Song of the Vatic Oleg'.

Nabokov's *Anya* was not a conventional literal translation of Lewis Carroll's *Alice*: it respected the form but not the content. It was true to Carroll's parodic style. It preserves the content by being true to its intended effect. And more and more, I am quite convinced by this translation; more and more I prefer the younger Nabokov's theory over the older Nabokov's theory. His *Anya* seems the most accurate translation, after all.

Chapter ix
St Petersburg, 1833: Departed Youth

In *Eugene Onegin*, there is another young love interest – as well as Eugene – called Lenski. Like the real life Pushkin, the fictional Lenski dies in a duel.

Lenski dies in a duel

Softly he lays his hand upon his breast
and falls. His misty gaze
expresses death, not pain.
Thus, slowly, down the slope of hills,
shining with sparkles in the sun,
a lump of snow descends.
Deluged with instant cold,
Onegin hastens to the youth,
looks, calls him . . . vainly:
he is no more. The young bard has
found an untimely end!
The storm has blown; the beauteous bloom
has withered at sunrise; the fire
upon the altar has gone out! . . .

The first six lines are by Pushkin. The last five are by Lenski. We know they are by Lenski because they are stodgy with conventional poetic imagery. Yes, Lenski, as well as being the young love interest, is also a poet. His own style, as he dies, is leaking into Pushkin's less poetic, more ironic one.

Pushkin's summary of Lenski's poetry

He sang parting and sadness,
and a vague something, and the dim
remoteness, and romantic roses.
He sang those distant lands
where long into the bosom of the stillness
flowed his live tears.
He sang life's faded bloom
at not quite eighteen years of age.

'Our literature will not go far', wrote Pushkin, 'on memories of departed youth.' It will therefore not go far with Lenski. But luckily Lenski will not go far, either. He will die prematurely.

The theme, as so often – in London, or Buenos Aires – is immaturity. Even Lenski's death secretes its own comedy; it is not allowed the luxury of sentimentality. He sang life's faded bloom, and now his life resolves in the tinkling, perfect cadence of Pushkin's parody, as the beauteous bloom of his life fades at sunrise, exactly as Lenski would have described it, if he could.

'There is a conspiracy of words signaling to one another, throughout the novel, from one part to another', writes Nabokov in his commentary. The perception of these conspiratorial patterns is the new task of reading invented by *Eugene Onegin* – as the reader amuses himself or herself tracking a cast of romantic selves, each with their personal, repetitive style. Just as in a fugue, themes become parodies of each other.

This is one reason why the eighteenth century is still contemporary.

Just for a moment, I want, unusually for me, to think about Denis Diderot in his role as a *philosophe*, not a novelist.

When Diderot was compiling his famous *Encyclopédie*, he invented a system of *renvois*, of cross-references. These cross-references, argued Diderot, 'will oppose notions; they will state principles; they will attack, amaze, secretly overturn ridiculous opinions which one would never dare to insult openly. If the author is impartial, they will always have the double function of confirming and refuting, of troubling and reconciling ...' In the *Encyclopédie*'s entry on God, therefore, Bayle, who argued against the proof for the existence of God according to the idea that his existence is universally agreed on, is dismissively refuted. But the *renvoi*, the cross-reference, sends the reader to the entry for Atheism – which explains that many people do not believe in God, which thus supports Bayle, silently, secretly. It dares to be more radical than it might normally be safe to be. And this new way of organising information in a work is something which Diderot would then use in his experiments with the novel – where meaning has to be inferred, where moral judgement is suspended.

And which Pushkin could also invent, with his themes which parody each other.

The style of Pushkin's novel is based on mimicry: it is an encyclopaedia of parody, in the form of *style indirect libre*. Pushkin develops parody as a mode of characterisation. And this is a technical advance, in Russia, in the 1820s and 30s. It is a technical advance anywhere. It is a rejection of romanticism.

I was wrong, at the start of this book, to say that Flaubert had invented this way of reading. Really, it was Pushkin. But no one quite knew about Pushkin, in the rest of Europe. He was on a branch line, out of sight.

Chapter x
London, 2007: Literal Translation (IV)

This, in my last chapter on translation, is my quick list of things which cannot always be translated literally: names, clothes, objects, brand names, clichés, puns, colloquial speech, bad syntax, elaborate syntax, alliteration, assonance, rhythm. What resists translation, therefore, is the most ordinary, unnoticed content, and the most unusual, ostentatious form.

But form is part of content, and content is part of form.

For instance, take Pushkin's parodies: if a translator translates a parody literally, it will, most of the time, no longer be a parody. If a translator instead replaces that parody with another parody, it is no longer a literal translation. But is this really true? What, in the end, does this word *literal* really mean? It normally means that the translator translates word for word. But the man who my hero Valery Larbaud considered to be the patron saint of translators, Saint Jerome, famously said that when he translated the Bible from Greek and Hebrew into Latin, he translated not word for word, but sense for sense.

Jerome, however, is not really helpful either, since Jerome could have been meaning two things here. The first is a low-key thing – that a word's meaning is not a purely lexical matter; it is often defined and made precise by context. Therefore a word-for-word translation may not be a literal translation at all. But he was also saying, possibly, something more radical: that it is not so important to be literally accurate – what is important is to get the general meaning across. Once someone gets into this definition of translation, then ideas like imitation, paraphrase, adaptation, variation – and all the other problems – come in.

But I am not quite sure how these haywire ideas can ever be fully kept out.

If a formal property of a novel, like a parody, is part of the novel's intended effect, then it becomes part of the intended content of a novel as well – and therefore, in an accurate translation, needs to be reproduced. But then even this, which seems roughly logical, becomes a little more dizzying: there can be problems with the translation of an effect – caused by chronology. Translating a parodic effect in a text which a hundred and fifty years ago seemed radical to the reader, may well not be noticed as an effect now, since that effect could well have been assimilated into the history of the novel, and therefore now seems usual, even humdrum, to the reader.

There seems no way, to me, of successfully historicising a translation.

But the problems can be contemporary, too. An effect which is normal in one language, say, may still seem revolutionary in another. Languages, and literatures, are often in different time zones.

My last chapter on translation is unfortunately not a conclusion. It is more hesitant than that. But some things are always true.

Underneath all theories of translation is the idea of the synonym: the benign and eighteenth-century idea that there is a reality external to words; that words represent this reality to a more or less precise extent; and that some words are similar in meaning to others, in another language. They represent roughly the same thing. Translation has a very down-to-earth linguistics. It is, inherently, sceptical of the idea and ideal that form and content are inextricable. Which is why André Gide became suddenly so het-up about translation, as he thought about it in his journal: in translating, he wrote, 'one becomes convinced that there are twenty ways of saying anything whatever and that one of them is preferable to all the others. One gets into that bad habit of dissociating form from content, the emotion and the expression of the emotion from the thought, which ought to remain inseparable.'

General rules about translation are not possible: there are so many ambiguities. The theory of translation may well be different for a poem than for a novel. All theories of translation depend on a genre. A theory which may fit the translation of a poem may not fit the translation of a novel at all. Or, even more minutely, a theory which fits one novel may not fit another one.

Sometimes, for instance, I think that the argument about the translation of this novel in verse called *Eugene Onegin* was an argument caused by the fact that it was such an odd object. That is why most of the arguments which everyone came up with were slightly skewed, too related as they were to a unique work of art.

Chapter xi
Ravenna, 1821: The Fluke (II)

In the notes to his edition of *Eugene Onegin*, Nabokov pointed out that there was fun to be had if the patient reader correlated the diary of Lord Byron – the most romantic of romantics, whom Gustave Flaubert would translate in Croisset with his niece's governess, Miss Juliet Herbert – with the events which Pushkin described from the life of Eugene Onegin.

Lord Byron's diary

On Jan. 12, 1821, Old Style (Jan. 24, New Style), while Lenski in northwestern Russia went to his last ball, Byron in Ravenna, Italy, noted in his diary: '. . . met some masques in the Corso . . . they dance and sing and make merry, "for tomorrow they may die."'

Next evening, Jan. 13 (Jan. 25 N.S.), while Lenski was writing his last elegy, Byron noted: 'One day more is over . . . but "which is best, life or death, the gods only know," as Socrates said to his judges . . .'

And Jan. 14 (Jan. 26, N.S.), the day Lenski and Onegin were having their duel, Byron jotted down: 'Rode – fired pistols – good shooting.'

This will probably remain, added Nabokov, 'the classical case of life's playing up to art.'

And it seems right to end here, before the final Book, which is all about Nabokov. Because it was Nabokov who most rigorously and most sadly tried to refuse the idea of the fluke: tried to make real life into something identical to the machinations and deliberations of art, by reversing the normal order of things. By making life a version of art, rather than art a version of life.

BOOK 16

Sirin

Early in 1937, in exile in Paris, long before he thought about translating *Eugene Onegin*, Vladimir Nabokov delivered a lecture on his
beloved writer, the Russian poet, short-story writer and novelist
Alexander Pushkin. The lecture's title was 'Pushkin, or the Real
and the Plausible'.

As I said before, in Volume I, Nabokov was not the first choice
for this lecture.

At the last moment, he had replaced a bestselling Hungarian
writer, who was suddenly taken ill. And yet, although Nabokov's
friends had tried to fill the hall with sympathetic listeners, the
message had not quite got through to the Hungarian writer's fans.
And so, as Nabokov began his lecture, he looked out on the conso-
latory sight of 'Joyce sitting, arms folded and glasses glinting, in
the midst of the Hungarian football team'.

Obviously, this makes me happy – that James Joyce, not quite
knowing who Nabokov was, sat there listening to Nabokov lecture
about Pushkin, in French. It is good to see history still coming up
with its own thematic links, without my help. It is good that history
was trying to behave Nabokovianly.

Nabokov's lecture had two main themes: the impossibility of
imagining the reality about Pushkin's past; and the impossibility of
a real translation of Pushkin. Only a plausible version of each, not
a real one, was possible – a point which Nabokov then demonstrated with three virtuosic but arguably inadequate translations of
Pushkin's poems. 'I nurture no illusions about the quality of these

Vladimir and Dmitri Nabokov, courtesy of the Estate of Vladimir Nabokov

translations', said Nabokov. 'It is reasonably plausible Pushkin, nothing more: the true Pushkin is elsewhere. Yet,' he continued, and immediately contradicted himself, in a contradiction I find very moving, because it is not quite rational and yet seems also true, 'if we follow the riverbank of this poem as it unfolds, we do note, in the bends I have managed to comply with here and there, something truthful flowing melodiously past, and that is the sole truth I can find down here – the truth of art.' Somehow, although translation was necessarily imperfect, something survives translation: this is Nabokov's theory, in Paris, in 1937.

Even in French, lecturing to an Irishman and a football team, Nabokov identified something which was residually and inescapably Pushkin's style – which has nothing to do with time, or history, or politics, or language. It has nothing to do with passports or suitcases, this thing called style.

And as a coda, Nabokov finished the lecture with his own development of this idea, that the truth of art survived the imperfections of the world. He pointed out that sometimes, mystically, one could glimpse improvised examples of offhand art in the apparent mess of real life: 'I have watched comedies staged by some invisible genius, such as the day when, at a very early hour, I saw a massive Berlin postman dozing on a bench, and two other postmen tiptoeing with grotesque roguishness from behind a thicket of jasmine to stick some tobacco up his nose.'

Life – this was Nabokov's final point, in exile, in Paris – life, this succession of failures and mistakes, at certain visionary moments was structured with the deft formal properties of art.

Chapter ii
Paris, 1937: A Life of Vladimir Nabokov Whose Theme
Is Translation

In 1937, when he gave this lecture, Nabokov was thirty-eight. He had been born in St Petersburg, and had grown up speaking English, Russian and French. His name, at this point, was Владимир Владимиривич Набоков – Vladimir Vladimirovich Nabokov. In 1917, following the revolution in Russia, he fled with his family to Berlin. He never learned to speak good German.

Between 1926 and 1938, Nabokov published nine novels in Russian, all under the pseudonym Sirin; in 1939 he moved to America; between 1941 and 1974 he published eight more novels, in English, initially as Vladimir Nabokoff, and finally as Vladimir Nabokov.

'The very term "émigré author"', wrote Nabokov in 1940, in a Russian émigré journal published in New York, 'sounds somewhat tautological. Any genuine writer emigrates into his art and abides there.' And twenty-five years later, in 1966, he would develop this position of non-alignment: 'I have always maintained, even as a schoolboy in Russia, that the nationality of a worthwhile writer is of secondary importance. The writer's art is his real passport. His identity should be immediately recognized by a special pattern or unique coloration. His habitat may confirm the correctness of the determination but should not lead to it. Locality labels are known to have been faked by unscrupulous insect dealers.' Only style counts. The country, and the language, is irrelevant.

And I agree with him, obviously. But this theory still needs the complicating weight of facts.

Between 1936 and 1971 Nabokov translated – mostly in collaboration with other people – all nine of his Russian novels into English. A volume of memoirs, *Conclusive Evidence*, was published in 1951 in English. Nabokov translated these memoirs into Russian with the title *Drugie berega* (*Other Shores*) in 1954. He then re-Englished this translation, with many additions and revisions, to become *Speak, Memory*, published in 1966. And one of the chapters for this memoir, 'Mademoiselle O', had been originally written in French, before its subsequent versions in both English and Russian.

Nabokov also made translations of other people's work: he published *Nikolka Persik*, a Russian version of Romain Rolland's French novel *Colas Breugnon*, in 1922; and made his Russian version of Lewis Carroll's *Alice in Wonderland* in 1923. He translated French poems by Alfred de Musset and Rimbaud into Russian; Russian poems by Pushkin into French; and in 1944 he published translations into English of Russian poems by Pushkin, Lermontov and Tyutchev. His English translation of Lermontov's novel *A Hero of Our Time* was published in 1958; his English translation of the Russian twelfth-century epic *The Song of Igor's Campaign* came out in 1960. And his edition of Pushkin's novel in verse, *Eugene Onegin*, came out in 1964.

The history of Nabokov's translations therefore has three layers: translations of his Russian novels into English (and one English novel, *Lolita*, into Russian); translations of other Russian writers into English; and the translation of his memoir from French to English to Russian and back to English. In terms of technique, however, these layers of translations morphed through two modes: his early translations of other Russians were free, formal translations; he then moved to a theory and practice of strict literalism, in his translations of novels by Lermontov and, most famously, Pushkin. But, at the same time, his later translations of his own works were marked by precisely the non-literal, formal equivalence which he attacked in the translations of other people (although, obviously, this is a special ethical case: a novelist, after all, can be allowed to take liberties with his own work in a way inadmissible to another person, since the work is his own property).

Only the style matters, argued Nabokov: but this style had to survive a variety of complicated manoeuvres. It had to live in three separate time-zones.

Chapter iii
Paris, 1936: A Short Story About Exile

In 1936, in the second issue of Adrienne Monnier's latest magazine, *Mesures*, Nabokov published a text called 'Mademoiselle O', written in French, about his French governess. Nabokov had written the piece in two weeks, and had read it to the PEN Club in Brussels, then the Russian Jewish Club, and finally, on 25 February 1936, at a reading in Paris, after which the French writer Jean Paulhan asked the young and unknown Russian novelist if he might grant permission to have the piece published in *Mesures*, which Paulhan helped to edit.

It opens with Nabokov explaining to his audience a phenomenon he has often noticed – as soon as he lends a snippet of his past to a character in one of his novels, that snippet from then on belongs to the character, no longer to Nabokov. And this is happening once more, he asserts, in the case of his French governess, a portrait of whom he had recently lent to Luzhin, the hero of his novel *Zashchita Luzhina* (*The Luzhin Defence*).

In opposition to voracious fiction, Nabokov wants to write a true memoir, to save his governess from leaving him altogether.

But this immediately raises a paradox: in order to save his Mademoiselle O from fiction, Nabokov intends to write about her one last time. He is not content with preserving her in his own memory – and perhaps this might have made the audience in the PEN club in Brussels, or at the Russian Jewish Club, or in a salon in Paris, pause on this paradox, and consider what might have been happening. Perhaps it was stranger than it looked.

Nabokov soon reaches a moment in his memoir which is not,

in fact, his own memory of Mademoiselle O, but instead his account of what she might have thought as she arrived at the local village train station in Russia: 'I strive now to imagine what she saw and felt as she came, this old demoiselle on her first long journey and whose entire Russian vocabulary consisted of one single word which ten years later she would take back with her to Switzerland: the word 'gdye' which means 'where is it?', but which, leaving her mouth like the raucous cry of a lost bird, developed such a force of interrogation that it satisfied all Mademoiselle's needs'.

This effort of imagination might have led Nabokov's various audiences to another thought, that perhaps this is not just a memoir with an artistic design, but is tinged with fiction, as well. And if Mademoiselle O is not quite real, is more like fiction than Nabokov is admitting, then could there be reasons other than the precision of memory for her only word of Russian to be *gdye*, the word for *where*? It might not be so much true, as artistically true: it might be a theme.

This memoir is also a story: it is an account of exile, in a language which is not Nabokov's first language. In it, there are various motifs on the theme of exile: Mademoiselle O, born of French parents outside France, in Switzerland; her soul, in exile in the fatness of her body; the French language, in exile in Russia. And there is also Vladimir Nabokov, now exiled from Russia, talking in French about the woman, in Russia, who taught him French. This story is about not being in the right language. Its central motif is the repeated word, *gdye*.

Nabokov explains that his theme is nothing so small as political exile: it is something much more comprehensive and universal: 'The anguish that I feel now when I remember the beautiful house where I lived as a child has nothing to do with those political events which, to use a journalistic cliché, have overturned my country. I find nothing but amusement in these political events. It is on a whole other level and according to a turn of mind which is not concerned with the accidents of history that my memory moves and rests. No, I do not sigh the sigh of an exile, unless the life of a mature man may be a type of exile in relation to his first fervour.' It is not about anything so parochial as being an émigré from the Bolsheviks, from the Communists. It is about the universal problem of preserving the things one values. Everything disappears, always. Therefore everyone is an émigré, an amateur émigré. No one is in possession of their past.

Early on in his memoir or story, Nabokov asserts that O was his Mademoiselle's full name: it is not an abbreviation. But this odd name is a prompt, a deliberate giveaway. It is there to show that this memoir is fiction, itself. In the shape of this O resolve the story's images of the moon, of emptiness, of absence, of the lake by which Mademoiselle O grew up and which Nabokov will come back to many years later. O is a motif, both visually and also phonetically – because its sound is the French word for water, *eau*, which itself is heard inside the French word for beauty, *beauté*.

And it is also not her real name. It is only a hint of her name, only a fiction, a third of its sound. The real name of Mademoiselle O, her original, was Cécile Miauton.

Chapter iv
New York, 1943: An Ending in Three Languages

The borderland between fiction and fact is the location of Nabokov's style. His style, and theory of style, is based on an inversion of the conventionally accepted order of things: rather than art being inferior to life, life is inferior to art. For art is permanent, and life is not.

This belief is at the centre of 'Mademoiselle O', and it also shapes the text's various translations into English, then Russian, and then English again – in which Nabokov continued to shift and slide, trying to make more precise this idea of stories and their less real histories: each different ending, in a different language, pronounced the problem differently.

The first French version ends with Nabokov's account of going to visit Mademoiselle in Lausanne, long after she had left the family, and Nabokov was now in exile. Since by now she was almost entirely deaf, Nabokov bought her an ear trumpet – for which she thanked him profusely, politely and, Nabokov adds, deceitfully. She still cannot hear a thing. But then follows a coda, where Nabokov describes how he left her and went for a walk, where he saw on the lake an old swan, trying and failing to haul itself into a boat. It was this swan, writes Nabokov, 'which I immediately remembered when I learned, several years later, that Mademoiselle was no more.' And then he moves into an astonishing conclusion: 'I thought it would console me to talk about her, and now that it is done I have the strange sensation of having invented her in every particular, as entirely as the other characters who pass through my books. Did she truly live? No, now that I think about it hard – she never lived. But from now on she is real, since I have created her, and this existence I give her would be a very candid sign of gratitude, if she had ever truly existed.'

And this is delicate, I think. It is much more unusual than it may at first look. Nabokov is not suddenly revealing, with a flourish of fabric, that everything has been a trick, a sleight of hand. His ending is full of a much more grandiose form of chutzpah entirely. He is saying that everything, always, in life just as much as art, is precarious – since it is mutable: everything is a disappearing act. Things only survive if given an artistic form.

Art is therefore, in a way, more real than life. It is only art which is not mutable, which does not disappear: everything else is transient. Only art, with its passion for form, makes up a permanent version from the made-up things of this world.

But I'm overtaking myself.

Translated into English by a woman called Miss Hilda Ward, and revised by Nabokov, 'Mademoiselle O' was published in America, without any hint as to fiction or fact, in the January 1943 issue of the *Atlantic Monthly*. In English, the piece now ended differently:

My enormous and morose Mademoiselle O is all right on earth but impossible in eternity. Have I really salvaged her from fiction?

Just before the rhythm I hear falters and fades, I catch myself wondering whether, during the years I knew her, I had not kept utterly missing something in her that was far more she than her name or her chins or her ways or even her French – something perhaps akin to that last glimpse of her, to the radiant deceit she used in order to have me pleased with my own kindness, or to that swan whose agony was so much more real than a drooping dancer's white arms; something in short which I could appreciate only after the things and beings that I had most loved in the security of my childhood had been turned to ashes or shot through the heart.

Rather than being a literal translation, this was an entirely new addendum. But it was still obsessed with the same problem: it was trying to find something permanent, beyond the transience of reality. It is there in the 'radiant deceit' which is a particular aspect of Mademoiselle O, made all the more poignant by the real pain she feels – figured in the dying swan: a pain which is far more painful than its conventional representation in the conventional art of the ballerina. According to Nabokov's theory, there must be some way to create something which would not be subject to death and change, which would correspond to his Mademoiselle – a meaning only revealed to Nabokov when he has finally learned that everything is transient, that the most loved people and objects will still be lost.

An altered version of this version then appeared as chapter five of Nabokov's autobiography, *Conclusive Evidence*, published in America in 1951. This was translated – and, in the process, revised

– for Nabokov's Russian version of *Conclusive Evidence*, which was given its new title, *Drugie berega* (*Other Shores*), and published in 1954. The Russian version was different again. It was much more laconic: Nabokov simply described his walk round the lake, his glimpse of the swan, and concluded with his admission that when, two years later, he found out about her death, 'the first thing which occurred to me was not her chins, and not her stoutness, and not even the music of her French speech, but precisely that poor, late, triple form: boat, swan, wave.'

The discussion of fiction has gone. It has been replaced with a triple chord, a form, which has also replaced Mademoiselle O herself.

Finally, still trying to make his meaning more precise, for *Speak, Memory*, in 1966, Nabokov retranslated and revised the Russian version: 'Mademoiselle O' was published as chapter five – where Nabokov in fact returned, essentially, to the 1951 English version, with a few revisions. But the ending, again, was different: following the final lines of the 1951 version, Nabokov added an extra final paragraph, which was a paragraph of pure fact, detailing 'certain amazing survivals' of other governesses: 'Sixty-five years later, in Geneva, my sister Elena discovered Mme Conrad, now in her tenth decade. The ancient lady, skipping one generation, naïvely mistook Elena for our mother, then a girl of eighteen, who used to drive up with Mlle Golay from Vyro to Batavo, in those distant times whose long light finds so many ingenious ways to reach me.'

The theme was still the same. Although the past was obliterated, something still survived. In its final language, this piece was still about the search for another world, a new world, out of time.

Chapter v
New York, 1967: Ustin, Justin

In *Speak, Memory*, a minor character, Ustin, recurs at occasional moments, a servant who is also a spy: he is a character just on the edge of the narrative's frame. And this makes me wonder whether Ustin was a real name, since it is very similar to the (differently pronounced, it's true) name Justin – a character in *Madame Bovary* who is also just outside the frame, and the artistry of whose arrangement by Flaubert was praised by Nabokov in his lecture on the novel.

For Nabokov, pattern conferred permanence on art: just as it was the perception of pattern in real life which hinted at an invisible, mystical stage manager. For him, the orchestrations of motifs were not a sleek embellishment to a form, but form's essential structure. Whereas most novelists use a pattern of themes for emphasis, to point a meaning, Nabokov uses pattern for its own sake: in order to point to meaning abstractly, to the underlying formal play of the world, unmotivated by utility. It was the fact that pattern could also be perceived in the stray details of everyday life which meant that his forms could often be so odd – so blurred between memoir and fiction – allowing him to describe 'the anonymous roller that pressed upon my life a certain intricate watermark whose unique design becomes visible when the lamp of art is made to shine through life's foolscap.' And it is also why the difference between autobiography and fiction becomes more and more unsure. The blur was part of his style.

'The memoir', said Nabokov, 'became the meeting point of an impersonal art form and a very personal life story.' 'It is', he continued, 'a literary approach to my own past. There is some precedent for it in the novel, in Proust say, but not in the memoir.' And so there also exists an unpublished sixteenth chapter of *Speak,*

Memory, where a fictional reviewer analyses the book's artistically arranged themes – a role which in the end was taken over by the book's index, an index which catalogues themes and fondles the text's details, like Nabokov's ideal reader.

In her bibliography of Nabokov's writings, Nabokov's wife, Véra, classified 'Mademoiselle O' as a story, a *nouvelle écrite en français*. But it was a memoir as well. With Nabokov, the distinction starts to become untenable. In his note to a 1958 collection of stories, *Nabokov's Dozen*, containing the story 'Mademoiselle O', Nabokov made an extravagant statement: 'I am no more guilty of imitating "real life" than "real life" is responsible for plagiarizing me.'

It is important not to make Nabokov's paradoxes less tense than they are. He is not artistic, and stylish, in order to boast of the flimsiness of art. That is what some writers use their style to do, but it is not Nabokov's intention. Instead his style shows that since art is more permanent than reality, it exists as a separate reality.

Once you have admitted the possible existence of one extra world, the world of art, then – it followed, for Nabokov – you had to admit the possibility of another extra world, a world that was out of this world. And so in the same way as a reader gradually notices the thematic patterns in Nabokov's fictions, the folds in his magic carpets – in which something is seen but not at first understood, and yet when once seen cannot be unseen – so a human gradually notices thematic patterns, evidence of a style, in the world itself. This perception of pattern is more usually called mystical experience.

'I have watched comedies staged by some invisible genius,' that is what Nabokov told his audience, in French, lecturing them on a Russian stylist. 'Not a day goes by that this force, this itinerant inspiration, does not create here or there some instantaneous performance.'

It is not wrong to believe in an other world, or an unknown stage manager. That is one of the truths on which Nabokov's style, his vision, is dependent. 'That human life is but a first instalment of the serial soul and that one's individual secret is not lost in the process of earthly dissolution, becomes something more than an optimistic conjecture, and even more than a matter of religious faith, when we remember that only commonsense rules immortality out,' Nabokov once told his students. 'A creative writer, creative in the particular sense I am attempting to convey, cannot help feeling that in his rejecting the world of the matter-of-fact, in his taking sides with the irrational, the illogical, the inexplicable, and the fundamentally good, he is performing something similar in a rudimentary way to what the spirit may be expected to perform, when the time comes, on a vaster and more satisfactory scale, under the cloudy skies of gray Venus.' Nabokov believed that the soul could travel; the soul could venture, in the end, into outer space.

I am not sure I believe this. It seems unlikely. I feel more like Anton Chekhov, with his worry that Tolstoy's version of immortality 'appears to me to be a shapeless mass of jelly'. But this is not my style I am describing. All styles are singularities; and Nabokov, rightly, believed that he was right.

Ustin's resemblance to Flaubert's Justin could be, after all, a coincidence – a proof of life on earth hastening, too late, to live up to the elegance of art, under the cloudy skies of grey Venus.

Chapter vi
Venus, — : The Misprint

Defending Charles Dickens's novel *Bleak House* against the charge of sentimentality, Nabokov deftly asked his students to distinguish between sentiment and sentimentality. 'I want to submit that people who denounce the sentimental are generally unaware of what sentiment is.' And this is a crucial distinction for Nabokov. It is a crucial distinction for anyone, but it is especially an important distinction for Nabokov – whose style, with its harsh elegance, its fierce nostalgia, is based on an often overwhelming sensitivity to pain. It is based on sentiment. That is why, simultaneously, it denounces the sentimental. (Just as the Argentinian novelist Roger Pla, in a memoir, described Gombrowicz as fighting against himself: 'At bottom, I'm sure he was a man of feeling who never allowed himself a relapse into sentimentality.') It replaces the sentimental with the pathos of eternal and comic mistakes.

Nabokov once noted in his diary a chance news item:

Axel Abrahamson, a moody B+ student, yesterday committed suicide by taking a fatal dose of potassium cyanide in an Evanston, Ill. apartment (which he shared with his mother), after taking a French exam at Northwestern. In answering the last question on the exam he wrote in French 'I am going to God. Life does not offer me much.'

With his next paragraph, Nabokov then took over as a novelist. He wanted to make this news item into a story: and the first change he noted was to add in a spelling mistake. 'Adopt him. I see the story so clearly. Combine him with notes of Jan. 26 . . . Make him make some pathetic mistake in that last sentence.'

This may be troubling for the gentler reader. The gentler reader may well be flummoxed, when remembering that it was Nabokov who found the humour in *Don Quixote*, with its jokes at the expense of its well-meaning hero, too cruel, too barbaric. And this addition may therefore, in comparison, seem mildly hypocritical. It may seem cruel and barbaric as well.

But Nabokov believed in other worlds, in the transience of this world: because of this, some elements of his style are explicable not in terms of cruelty, but pathos.

Spelling mistakes, for instance, are a minor theme for Nabokov. They are not just a theme for James Joyce, and his hero L Boom. In Nabokov's novel *Pnin*, Pnin, a Russian émigré, sits down, having been told that he is due to be replaced at the university, and decides to write a letter: '"Dear Hagen," he wrote in his clear firm hand, "permit me to recaputilate (crossed out) recapitulate the conversation we had tonight . . ."' And this crossing out relates the spelling mistake to another moment in Nabokov, in *Lolita*, where Lolita writes home from her holiday camp to Humbert and Charlotte Humbert, *née* Haze: 'Hope you are fine. Thank you very much for the candy. I [crossed out and re-written again] I lost my new sweater in the woods.'

The point of these mistakes is not that Nabokov wants to be cruel to his characters; instead, he wants to be true to his sad but accurate perception that at no point is the human animal allowed seriousness, unblemished by irony.

The cosmic is always misspelled as comic.

'I remember a cartoon,' he reminisced, fondly, 'depicting a chimney sweep falling from the roof of a tall building and noticing on the way that a sign-board had one word spelled wrong, and wondering in his headlong flight why nobody had thought of correcting it.' And I can see why Nabokov loved this cartoon: it combines two of his style's motifs – the spelling mistake, and the sudden aside – as well as being a neat description of real life, where people have expertise and professional pride. 'This capacity to wonder at trifles – no matter the imminent peril –', finished Nabokov, 'these asides of the spirit, these footnotes in the volume of life are the highest form of consciousness, and it is in this childishly speculative state of mind, so different from commonsense and its logic, that we know the world to be good.'

Even a description of a death is still gorgeous, if it is described with art. Nothing is purely grandiose. Instead, the novel is an art of miniaturisation and complication, of restoring objects to their true and small size. And this is an entertaining project. For all art is delighted.

Chapter vii
London, 2007: Either/Or

At this point, I think I need to contradict myself, ever so slightly.

As soon as the aesthetic is taken as seriously as Nabokov took it, then something odd occurs. The aesthetic becomes something else as well: it becomes its opposite. As soon as the aesthetic is taken seriously, then it becomes an ethics, also.

It is not, perhaps, a question of either/or. It is both at once.

The effects of an absolute aesthetics – a concern for detail, for ironic particularity, for the suspension of immediate or conventional moral judgement, for the restoration to objects of their correct and small size – are ethical. They constitute a small, amateur but sincere ethical system – which teaches respect for the minor, the overlooked, the unsure.

Throughout this book, I have been arguing for a separation of ethics and aesthetics. But I am not sure how easy this is to maintain. Unfortunately, irrevocably, the two turn into each other. The desire for an absolute aesthetic – which is a desire felt not just by me, but by much more important people, like Witold Gombrowicz or Gustave Flaubert – is itself a form of romanticism. It is absolute as well. It is a wish not to acknowledge the imperfect, haphazard truth about real life.

Chapter viii
Venus, – : The Galley Slaves

Nabokov believed in other worlds, the other world of Venus, the other world of art. This belief was the central element of his style. Because style is not linguistic; style is not just sentences. It is spelling mistakes, as well.

Style is everywhere.

When Pushkin wrote his novel *Eugene Onegin*, he wanted to create the illusion that a character was free to think as he or – especially – she might like. It was a joke at the expense of clichéd plot, part of his playful style. But there is a different version of this effect, which I do not – and Vladimir Nabokov did not – admire. This is the cliché that if a character is imagined enough, if the novelist enters the mind of the character fully, then the novelist somehow cedes his or her authority: the character takes over. According to this version, the effect which Pushkin created so patiently is not an effect at all, but is real instead.

And this is sentimental.

When Nabokov was interviewed in the small American magazine, the *Paris Review*, its editor sent Nabokov some questions, of which one was this: 'E. M. Forster speaks of his major characters sometimes taking over and dictating the course of his novels. Has this ever been a problem for you, or are you in complete command?' But according to the principles of Nabokov's style, the question was meaningless. According to the strict rules of Nabokov's style, no character is believable, to the extent that the writer, or reader, might forget that they are fictional. Fiction is always and only a game.

Nabokov was a connoisseur of belief.

So his reply was haughty: 'My knowledge of Mr Forster's works is limited to one novel which I dislike; and anyway it was not he who fathered that trite little whimsy about characters getting out of hand; it is as old as the quills, although of course one sympathizes with *his* people if they try to wriggle out of that trip to India or wherever he takes them. My characters are galley slaves.'

A year later, another interviewer asked Nabokov if his characters had ever taken over. Patiently (and, I think, incontrovertibly), Nabokov explained himself again: 'I have never experienced this. What a preposterous experience! Writers who have had it must be

SIRIN

very minor or insane. No, the design of my novel is fixed in my imagination and every character follows the course I imagine for him. I am the perfect dictator in that private world insofar as I alone am responsible for its stability and truth.'

A character can have no genuine freedom, since a character is not real: a character is invented by its author, and any orthodox theologian, or literary critic, knows that a creation is always subject to its creator.

Nabokov's style was based on perfection of design, on a system of motif and echo. It created separate worlds. This meant that his fictions are both more frivolous than other novelists' fictions and, seen from another angle, more serious. They take this world less seriously, because they take art more seriously.

That is one thing, but not the only thing, which is lovable about Nabokov. He is never embarrassed by the dictatorial fun to be had by the infantile novelist.

Chapter ix
Venus, – : A Magic Carpet

In its final version, in *Speak, Memory*, as he imagined Mademoiselle O leaving the local village station in Russia, Nabokov paused, and stopped: 'Very lovely, very lonesome. But what am I doing in the stereoscopic dreamland? How did I get here? Somehow, the two sleighs have slipped away, leaving behind a passportless spy standing on the blue-white road in his New England snowboots and storm-coat. The vibration in my ears is no longer their receding bells, but only my old blood singing. All is still, spellbound, enthralled by the moon, fancy's rear-view mirror. The snow is real, though, and as I bend to it and scoop up a handful, sixty years crumble to glittering frost-dust between my fingers.'

For me, this is one of the most moving paragraphs in Nabokov's writing – as he bends down to pick up some real and remembered snow – predicated as it is on the poignancy of memory. But it is also emblematic of his style. In whichever language he was writing, Nabokov enjoyed the fact that, in a sentence, the writer controls all the information. This means that it is very easy to be deceptive, to momentarily shift the reader into a suddenly irrational, inexplicable landscape.

(Just as Laurence Sterne boasted that 'my reader has never yet been able to guess at any thing . . . if I thought you was able to form the least judgement or probable conjecture to yourself, of what was to come in the next page, – I would tear it out of my book.')

In 'Mademoiselle O', Nabokov was explicit about this technique. But he was not always so helpful.

In July 1910, for instance, the young Vladimir Nabokov went out butterfly-hunting in the marshland beyond the Oredezh:

Vladimir Nabokov goes butterfly-hunting

Through the smells of the bog, I caught the subtle perfume of butterfly wings on my fingers, a perfume which varies with the species – vanilla, or lemon, or musk, or a musty, sweetish odor difficult to define. Still unsated, I pressed forward. At last I saw I had come to the end of the marsh. The rising ground beyond was a paradise of lupines, columbines, and pentstemons. Mariposa lilies bloomed under Ponderosa pines. In the distance, fleeing cloud shadows dappled the dull green of slopes above timber line, and the gray and white of Longs Peak.

I confess I do not believe in time. I like to fold my magic carpet, after use, in such a way as to superimpose one part of the pattern upon another. Let visitors trip . . .

The connection between the first paragraph and the second is this. There are no Ponderosa pines near the Oredezh; these pines are only American. Nabokov has emerged from a Russian forest, in 1910, into America, some time in the 1940s and 1950s, under the cloudy skies of gray Venus.

That is why he emerged on the magic carpet of a paragraph break.

Maybe I should pause on this word: *magic*. Depending on the nature of the viewer, the nature of the believer, there can be two definitions of magic. According to a believer, magic is a miracle – where something occurs miraculously, without a rational explanation. But there is a more terrestrial version of the otherworldly thing called magic, where something happens which seems to be miraculous, but which has a simple rational and human explanation. It is just that the magician has been able to hide the mechanics. Magic, on this terrestrial definition, is an effect whose cause remains hidden.

Each definition is a parody of the other. It is impossible to believe in both versions at once. And yet Nabokov's prose style is based on ambiguous moments, where the terrestrial explanation seems to be, in fact, impossible, and only the believers' version will do.

Nabokov's technique, from the smallest level of the sentence to the larger level of plot, is always the same: it is deception through concealment. And he tells us this himself, in his description, in *Speak, Memory*, of the émigré Russian novelist Sirin's 'clear, but weirdly misleading sentences'. Consistently, he fails to tell the reader that this writer called Sirin was the pseudonym of Vladimir Nabokov, who has therefore just written yet another clear but misleading sentence.

Everything Nabokov writes is intent on exploiting the possibilities which language offers to do more than one thing at once. This medium called literature is the perfect medium for turning a person into a medium, a person to whom time does not exist. And so Nabokov's definition of poetry, in his book on Nikolai Gogol, is a definition of his own style too: 'the mysteries of the irrational as perceived through rational words'. With his magic carpet, his clear misleading sentences, Nabokov shows how two moments separated in time can be made congruent, how they can be folded on top of each other, neatly, and mystically.

And, less mystically, I can do this too.

Nabokov's magic carpet itself is a translation from one of his Russian poems, written in 1943, in Massachusetts, called 'The Paris Poem'. His prose is a disguised poem. And this poem, itself, is all about pattern. It is all about the permanence of art.

Nabokov's Paris poem

In this life, rich in patterns (a life
unrepeatable, since with a different
cast, in a different manner,
in a new theater it will be given),

no better joy would I choose than to fold
its magnificent carpet in such a fashion
as to make the design of today coincide
with the past, with a former pattern,

in order to visit again – oh, not
commonplaces of those inclinations,
not the map of Russia, and not a lot
of nostalgic equivalences –

but, by finding congruences with the remote,
to revisit my fountainhead,
to bend and discover in my own childhood
the end of the tangled-up thread.

And, carefully then to unravel myself
as a gift, as a marvel unfurled,
and become once again the middle point
of the many-pathed, loud-throated world.

And by the bright din of the birds
by the jubilant window-framed lindens
by their extravagant greenery,
by the sunlight upon me and in me,

by the white colossi that rush through the blue
straight at me – as I narrow my eyes –
by all that sparkle and all that power
my present moment to recognize.

Cambridge, Massachusetts, 1943

In the prose version, Nabokov folded the carpet one last time. He reworked his Russian poem, written in America, into his memoir of his Russian childhood, written in America as well. He asserted the primacy of the art of language over the various languages in which this art takes form.

Chapter x
America, 1951: A Short Story About Exile

But I should not be too lyrical.

In a 1962 interview Nabokov mentioned his 'private tragedy' – that he had to abandon his natural language, his natural idiom, his 'rich, infinitely rich and docile Russian tongue, for a second-rate brand of English.' He was never convinced by the tricks of his inherited English. In exile, he nurtured a belief in the perfect

Russian which he now could no longer use. But when, five years later, Nabokov finished his translation of *Lolita* into Russian, he wrote a sad, honest postscript: 'I am only troubled now by the jangling of my rusty Russian strings. The history of this translation is a history of disillusion. Alas, that "marvellous Russian" which, I always thought, constantly awaited me somewhere, blooming like true spring behind hermetically sealed gates to which I kept the key for so many years – that Russian turns out to be non-existent. And behind the gates there is nothing, except charred stumps and a hopeless autumn vista; the key in my hand is more like a lock-pick.'

I cannot help remembering this sudden admission, when thinking about Nabokov's assertion that any genuine writer emigrates into his art and abides there. Or remembering this halting, painfully exposed poem which the novelist Nina Berberova quoted in her memoir of Nabokov, dating it to 1951:

When I saw in the fog

That which I preserved
For so long . . .
I imagine now the twittering

and the railroad station,

And further on
All the details . . .

I feel like going home,
I am longing to go home.

I have had enough . . . May I go home?

Or remembering how in 1975 Nabokov gave an interview on French television, where he simply asserted that he was in exile always; exile was for him a permanent state, a job: *'Je suis dépaysé partout et toujours. C'est mon état. C'est mon emploi. C'est ma vie'* ('I am adrift everywhere and always. It's my state. It's my job. It's my life'). And then he paused. And added, simply, *'Voilà.'*

All these move me very much. All these show how Nabokov's artistic position of non-alignment – which is so admirable, and true – was also one which was precarious with hurt.

But I should not be too lyrical.

Nabokov's story about exile involved a character called Pnin. (And this name, again, is not international: it needs a translation. In Russia, in the nineteenth century, convention allowed a nobleman who had spawned an illegitimate child to give it the last half of his name, in quasi-recognition of its status. The descendants of Prince Repnin's illegitimate children were therefore allowed to take the name of Pnin.) Pnin was a Russian professor in America, an émigré from the Russian Revolution – complete with mispronounced English, an inability to be on the right train, seriousness, tearfulness, a 'passionate intrigue' with the washing machine. He was clumsy, a comic figure. And each episode, or chapter, of *Pnin* described a humiliation, a let down, a sadness. Its structure was cartoonish: its structure was Tom and Jerry. Pnin's failures were funny. So *Pnin* – the novel of Pnin – seemed like a farce. In fact, the reader was told that this novel was a farce, by the narrator, who is not Nabokov. The narrator's theory of literature was this: 'Harm is the norm. Doom should not jam.'

But *Pnin* was not a farce. It was not an exaggerated comedy, written by the narrator. It was a subtle comedy, written by Nabokov.

My favourite moment in *Pnin* is when Pnin is washing up after a party. Lovingly, he places an aquamarine bowl in the water. This bowl is a gift from his young son. It is Pnin's most precious object.

From the sink, he hears the sound of breaking glass.

At first, you nearly find this funny. Another goof from Pnin! But you know it is not funny. Pnin is not only goofy. He is lovable and noble too.

Then something wonderful happens: 'with a moan of anguished anticipation, he went back to the sink and, bracing himself, dipped his hand deep into the foam. A jagger of glass stung him. Gently he removed a broken goblet. The beautiful bowl was intact. He took a fresh dish towel and went on with his household work.'

Nabokov is on my side. He signals this by rejecting the farcical pattern, and refusing to let Pnin break his beloved bowl. Nabokov understood that, to be genuine, comedy cannot be untrue. It must be complicated and subtle. It must allow the game to end in a tie.

But the comedy is still there.

All new novels discover new content as well. And, since they are truthful about this comic thing called real life, all new novels discover new versions of the comic as well. The most radical novels find comedy in places which people do not want to see as comic at all – like sex, or concentration camps. And Nabokov found comedy in the tragic condition of exile.

At the end of this novel, Pnin drives away, having lost everything. And the narrator, who has taken Pnin's job at the university, watches him leave: 'a great truck carrying beer rumbled up the street, immediately followed by a small pale blue sedan with the white head of a dog looking out, after which came another great truck, exactly similar to the first. The humble sedan was crammed with bundles and suitcases; its driver was Pnin.' Pnin is just a bracket, he is squashed between two parentheses of beer. But he emerges and escapes: 'the little sedan boldly swung past the front truck and, free at last, spurted up the shining road, which one could make out narrowing to a thread of gold in the soft mist where hill after hill made beauty of distance, and where there was simply no saying what miracle might happen.'

The paragon is just a parody – since this is the narrator speaking, and the narrator is not to be trusted: the soft mist, the thread of gold, the unexpected miracle are clichés; they are myths about the future, not truths. It is Nabokov's final, comic, refusal to allow himself or his character the luxury of romance – because romance is always a luxury.

No, I should not be too lyrical.

Where are they gone? lamented Bohumil Hrabal, in 1990, still in Prague, in the Golden Tiger pub. Where has everybody gone? 'Kundera's an émigré, that playboy who knew how to write and to talk, and when he walked down Národní třída, all the girls turned their heads, but so did everyone that appreciated Czech literature'. And where is Eduard Goldstücker, '"der schöne Edó", as they called him? that admirer of Franz Kafka, who wore Budapest and Viennese fashion and whose curly hair shone with brilliantine'; and who, asks Hrabal, 'will take the blame for forcing the poet Jiří Kolář to move his chair and table to Paris from the Café Slavia?' – 'that founding member of the Bohemians Fan Club, who always stood at Slavia football matches behind the goal beneath the clock in his casual gear?'

Exile is a version of real life. Its sadness is not abstract: it is poignant with particulars. And it is also poignant with irony. This is one thing Hrabal discovered, and one thing which Nabokov gave form to in his comic and unhappy novel *Pnin*.

Sentiment is not the same as sentimentality.

Chapter xi
Elsewhere, – : Elsewhere

In his commentary to *Eugene Onegin*, Nabokov wrote that 'To the artist whom practice within the limits of one language, his own, has convinced that matter and manner are one, it comes as a shock to discover that a work of art can present itself to the would-be

translator as split into form and content, and that the question of rendering one but not the other may arise at all. Actually what happens is still a monist's delight: shorn of its primary verbal existence, the original text will not be able to soar and to sing; but it can be very nicely dissected and mounted, and scientifically studied in all its organic details.'

Nabokov, in the end, is saying something similar to me. He is saying that the style of Pushkin's novel is a larger thing than the simple matter of rhyme schemes. Its style can therefore still be mounted, in another language.

But there is something scandalous about this. It does not seem right.

All through this book, I have been arguing that style is the most important thing, and survives its mutilating translations – that although the history of translation is always a history of disillusion, somehow something survives. Yet this still shocks me, with my aesthetic prejudices, and preferences.

I therefore have a theory of why Nabokov changed his mind about translation in the 1950s and became so stern.

Nabokov began as a novelist for whom form and content, manner and matter, were one. One of the saddest things of Nabokov's exile in various languages was his discovery that style translated, that the form was more durable, and therefore less specific, than he thought. It was not quite inextricable from content.

Nabokov's dream of total accuracy on the part of the reader and translator is the obverse of his dream of control on the part of the novelist, who creates a novel as formally unique and unrepeatable as a poem by, say, Mallarmé. But even Mallarmé could be translated.

No novelist has everything under control. Even novelists whom Nabokov loved, like Sterne and Proust, knew this: 'a true feeler always brings half the entertainment along with him,' wrote Sterne. 'His own ideas are only call'd forth by what he reads . . . 'tis like reading *himself*, and not the *book*.' And Proust repeated the same idea, a hundred and fifty years later: 'In reality, every reader, while he reads, is the reader of himself. The writer's work is only a kind of optical instrument which he offers to the reader so that he might allow him to make out what, without this book, he might perhaps not have seen in himself.'

Like a style, the finished book, for Proust, was optical. The paradox is that the more styled a novel is, the more it turns into an optical instrument which is personal to the reader as well.

A style creates multiple, universal singularities.

Exile proved to Nabokov a philistine, necessary truth. This truth was one which Albert Camus (who is an entirely new theme, a surprise, at the end of this series – a ragged baroque extra) also knew about. 'People imagine – wrongly – that novels do not require style,' wrote Camus. 'They do, in fact, demand style of the most difficult kind, the one which takes second place.' That, I think, is why Nabokov is so lacerating in the notes to his edition of Pushkin: to refuse this implacable and irrefutable philistinism as much as he could.

And so, in homage to Nabokov, I have written an appendix in the form of a translation of 'Mademoiselle O', with its French original patiently alongside. It is my attempt to be faithful; to be Miss Herbert.

The very first draft of 'Mademoiselle O', after all, which is now lost, was written in English, while he was living in London. In another world, in another version of this planet, Nabokov could have become an English novelist.

But he went to the United States instead.

But his form is neither Russian nor American. Nor is it Swiss. No, the true Nabokov is elsewhere – in the homeland, the utopia, of his art; with Mrs Shandy, he is bending eternally at a keyhole, unless someone remembers to find him; in London; in the Golden Tiger pub; in Europiccola; in the Delighted States. He is sunbathing. And Miss Herbert, another governess, is there, almost invisible – in the background beside him.

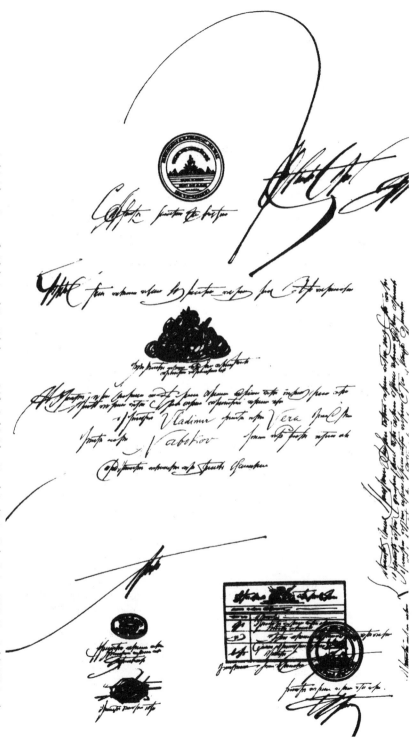

I have attempted to track down all references and debts, but some, due to the haphazard effects of my reading, have proved untraceable. The reader should not be surprised to discover different editions of the same novel being referred to at one time or another; nor be shocked by references to paperback editions, bad translations, and even my own attempts at translation.

Volume I

5   'I've imagined a style': Gustave Flaubert to Louise Colet, 24 April 1852, reprinted in *Oeuvres Complètes*, vol. 13, *Correspondance 1850–1859*, Paris, 1974, p. 186.

5   'You say that I pay too much': Gustave Flaubert to Mademoiselle Leroyer de Chantepie, 12 December 1857, reprinted in ibid., p. 617.

5   'Once prose makes such a claim': Milan Kundera, *Žert*, Prague, 1967, translated by Michael Henry Heim, *The Joke*, London, 'Author's Preface', p. xi.

8   'It is annoying': Witold Gombrowicz, 'James Joyce: *Ulysse*', *Kurier Poranny*, no. 16, 1937, translated by Allan Kosko, translated by AT, *Varia 1*, Paris, 1978, pp. 51–2.

9   'It was an experimental translation': Humberto Rodríguez Tomeu to Rita Gombrowicz, Buenos Aires, 1978, translated by AT, in Rita Gombrowicz, *Gombrowicz en Argentine 1939–1963*, Paris, 1984, p. 82.

11   'What clashes here': James Joyce, *Finnegans Wake*, Paris, 1939, reprinted Harmondsworth, 1992, p. 4.

13   'Can't hear with the waters': ibid, pp. 215–16.

13   'N'entend pas': quoted in Richard Ellmann, *James Joyce*, Oxford, 1982, reprinted 1983, p. 633.

14   'His writing is not *about* something': Samuel Beckett, 'Dante . . . Bruno.

Vico ... Joyce', in *Our Exagmination Round His Factification for Incamination of Work in Progress*, Paris, 1929, p. 11.

15 'poeticise it': Adolf Hoffmeister, 'The Game of Evenings', *Rozpravy Aventina*, Prague, 1930–31, translated by Michelle Woods, *Granta*, Spring 2005, pp. 239–54, p. 248.

15 'Create a language': ibid., pp. 239–54, p. 251.

16 If these lists: quoted in Boris Eikhenbaum, 'How Gogol's "Overcoat" Is Made', in *Gogol's 'Overcoat': An Anthology of Critical Essays*, edited by Elizabeth Trahan, 1982, p. 26.

17 'Vishel na ulitsu': Nikolai Gogol, 'Shinel', St Petersburg, 1842, reprinted in *Povesti. Mertvie Dushi*, Moscow, 2004, p. 383.

18 'When he got into the street': Nikolai Gogol, 'Shinel', St Petersburg, 1842, 'The Overcoat', in *The Complete Tales of Nikolai Gogol*, translated by Constance Garnett, edited by Leonard J. Kent, 2 vols., Chicago, 1985, vol. II, p. 314.

19 'the dazzling combinations': Vladimir Nabokov, *Nikolai Gogol*, New York, 1971, p. 56.

19 'May I die like a dog': Gustave Flaubert to Maxime du Camp, 26 June 1852, translated by Geoffrey Wall in Gustave Flaubert, *Selected Letters*, Harmondsworth, 1997, p. 181.

19 'almost back': Gustave Flaubert to Mademoiselle Leroyer de Chantepie, 14 January 1857, translated by Geoffrey Wall in ibid., 1997, p. 242, revised by AT.

20 'I can't stop myself': quoted by Roland Barthes in 'Flaubert and the Sentence', in *A Roland Barthes Reader*, edited by Susan Sontag, London, 1993, p. 302.

20 'I'd like to be working': Gustave Flaubert, *Selected Letters*, translated by Geoffrey Wall, Harmondsworth, 1997, p. 217.

20 'has nothing to do with embellishment': Marcel Proust, interview with Élie-Joseph Bois, *Le Temps*, 13 November 1913.

21 'Just as the pearl': Gustave Flaubert, *Correspondance*, Paris, 1973–, edited by Jean Bruneau, vol. III, p. 431.

21 'Womb? Weary?': James Joyce, *Ulysses*, Paris, 1922, reprinted London, 1992, p. 996.

24 'appears as a positive value': René Wellek, *The Literary Theory and Aesthetics of the Prague School*, Ann Arbor, 1969, p. 16.

24   'A living work of art': Jan Mukařovský, *Aesthetic Function, Norm and Value
      as Social Facts*, Prague, 1936, translated by Mark E. Suino, Ann Arbor,
      1970, p. 36.

24   'every struggle': ibid., p. 69.

24   'the most popular authors': René Wellek, *The Literary Theory and
      Aesthetics of the Prague School*, Ann Arbor, 1969, p. 22.

25   'Dear Sirs': quoted in Richard Ellmann, *James Joyce*, Oxford, 1982,
      reprinted 1983, p. 630.

26   'There can be no question': Vladimir Nabokov, *Strong Opinions*, New
      York, 1973, reprinted 1990, p. 33.

26   'I am writing a novel': Anton Chekhov to Alexei Suvorin, 11 March 1889,
      in *Letters of Anton Chekhov*, translated by Michael Henry Heim, in collab-
      oration with Simon Karlinsky, New York, 1973, p. 135.

28   'What seems to explain': Anton Chekhov, 'O Lyubve', Moscow, 1898,
      'Concerning Love', in *The Russian Master and Other Stories*, Oxford, 1975,
      translated by Ronald Hingley, p. 136.

28   'And they imagined': ibid., p. 143.

28   'One of the functions': Vladimir Nabokov, *Strong Opinions*, New York,
      1973, reprinted 1990, p. 115.

29   'What an exciting experience': Vladimir Nabokov, 'Pouchkine, ou le
      Vrai et le Vraisemblable', Paris, *Nouvelle Revue Française*, 1 March 1937,
      translated by Dmitri Nabokov, 'Pushkin, or the Real and the Plausible',
      New York Review of Books, 31 March 1988, pp. 38–42.

29   'at table': Gustave Flaubert, *Oeuvres complètes*, Paris, 1971–75, xiii, 497,
      no. 597.

29   'I hold myself back': ibid., 535, no. 638.

30   'English translation': Gustave Flaubert, *Lettres inédites de Gustave Flaubert
      à son éditeur Michel Lévy*, edited by Jacques Suffel, Paris, 1965, pp. 36–8.

30   'I had one of Bovary': Gustave Flaubert, *Oeuvres complètes*, Paris, 1971–75,
      xiv. 111, no. 986.

31   'The very term': Vladimir Nabokov, 'Opredeleniia', New York, c. 1940,
      quoted by Alexander Dolinin in 'Nabokov as a Russian Writer', *The
      Cambridge Companion to Vladimir Nabokov*, edited by Julian W. Connolly,
      Cambridge, 2005, pp. 49–64, p. 57.

31   'Ze "Spokojeneych"': Bohumil Hrabal, 'Public Suicide', Prague, 1990,
      reprinted in *Total Fears*, translated by James Naughton, Prague, 1998, p. 25.

33   'Because I wouldn't swap': Bohumil Hrabal, 'A Few Sentences', Prague, 1990, reprinted in *Total Fears*, translated by James Naughton, Prague, 1998, p. 68.

37   'Oh, I adore the sea': Gustave Flaubert, *Madame Bovary*, Paris, 1857, translated by Geoffrey Wall, Harmondsworth, 1992, p. 65.

37   'I detest common heroes': ibid., p. 66.

38   'So lovely': ibid.

40   'Where have you acquired': Gustave Flaubert, *Correspondance*, Paris, 1973–, edited by Jean Bruneau, vol. II, pp. 654–5.

40   'Some novels are written': Gustave Flaubert, *Dictionnaire des idées reçues, The Dictionary of Received Ideas*, translated by Geoffrey Wall, London, 1994, p. 47.

40   'I am in the act': quoted by Vladimir Nabokov, *Lectures on Literature*, New York, 1980, edited by Fredson Bowers, p. 149.

41   'You melt into the characters': Gustave Flaubert, *Madame Bovary*, Paris, 1857, translated by Geoffrey Wall, Harmondsworth, 1992, p. 66.

41   'Allow only the indispensable: André Gide, *The Journals of André Gide*, vol. 3, 1928–1939, translated by Justin O'Brien, 1949, quoted in Miriam Allott, *Novelists on the Novel*, London, 1959, reprinted 1980, p. 237.

43   he received a parcel: cited in Geoffrey Wall, *Flaubert: A Life*, London, 2001, p. 230.

43   'cities with domes of gold': Gustave Flaubert, *Flaubert in Egypt*, translated and edited with an introduction by Francis Steegmuller, Penguin, 1996, p. 48.

45   'an immense, delightful expanse': ibid., pp. 52–3.

45   'On the side of the Pyramid': ibid.

45   'As we emerge': ibid.

45   Sometimes I like to think: but it isn't just characters who are eternal. Good ideas, unfortunately for me, are eternal too. The same combination of Humberts occurred to the narrator of Julian Barnes's novel *Flaubert's Parrot*, as well.

46   it was not her real name: pointed out to me by my polyglot friend Noel Malcolm.

46   'She falls asleep': Gustave Flaubert, *Flaubert in Egypt*, translated and edited with an introduction by Francis Steegmuller, Penguin, 1996, p. 118.

46   'To shield herself': ibid., p. 119.

47   'You tell me that': ibid., p. 220.

47   'irony does not impair': quoted by Vladimir Nabokov, *Lectures on Literature*, New York, 1980, edited by Fredson Bowers, p. 149.

47   'Oh, to be bending forward': Gustave Flaubert, *Flaubert in Egypt*, translated and edited with an introduction by Francis Steegmuller, Penguin, 1996, p. 178.

47   'Here and there': ibid., p. 181.

49   'as rhythmical as verse': Gustave Flaubert to Louise Colet, 24 April 1852, reprinted in *Oeuvres Complètes*, vol. 13, *Correspondance 1850–1859*, Paris, 1974, p. 186.

50   'What I'd like to do': Gustave Flaubert, *Correspondance*, Paris, 1973–, edited by Jean Bruneau, vol. II, p. 31.

50   On other occasions: ibid., vol. IV, p. 310.

51   'The next day, for Emma': Gustave Flaubert, *Madame Bovary*, Paris, 1857, translated by Geoffrey Wall, Harmondsworth, 1992, p. 98.

52   'this book will have one great defect': Gustave Flaubert, *Selected Letters*, translated by Geoffrey Wall, Harmondsworth, 1997, p. 216.

52   'I already have 200 pages': ibid.

53   'finally, on the upper platform': Gustave Flaubert, *Madame Bovary*, Paris, 1857, translated by Geoffrey Wall, Harmondsworth, 1992, p. 22.

53   'a white house': ibid., p. 56.

53   But when Emma comes to beg: ibid., p. 245.

53   'On the clock': ibid., p. 216.

53   'with artificial dew-drops': p. 38.

54   'What a piece of machinery': Gustave Flaubert to Louise Colet, 6 April 1853, translated by Geoffrey Wall in Gustave Flaubert, *Selected Letters*, Harmondsworth, 1997, p. 209.

54   'He has arranged': Henry James, 'Guy de Maupassant', 1888, reprinted in *The Critical Muse: Selected Literary Criticism*, edited by Roger Gard, Harmondsworth, 1987, p. 251.

54   'especially to be recommended': ibid., p. 252.

57   'went through the wood': Guy de Maupassant, *Une Vie*, Paris, 1883, *A Life*, translated by Roger Pearson, Oxford, 1999, p. 90.

58   'And Jeanne suddenly': ibid., p. 156.

58   'On they would go': ibid., p. 14.

58   'Two armchairs still stood': ibid., p. 236.

59   'She often spoke ... First he proposed': Gustave Flaubert, *Madame Bovary*, Paris, 1857, translated by Geoffrey Wall, Harmondsworth, 1992, pp. 137, 187, 282.

60   'Form (structure and style)': Vladimir Nabokov, *Lectures on Literature*, New York, 1980, edited by Fredson Bowers, p. 113.

61   'And all at once': Guy de Maupassant, *Une Vie*, Paris, 1883, *A Life*, translated by Roger Pearson, Oxford, 1999, p. 55.

61   'As Jeanne slept on the right': ibid., p. 72.

62   'a man who by the entirely new': Marcel Proust, 'A propos du "style" de Flaubert', Paris, 1920, reprinted in *Flaubert savait-il écrire?: Une querelle grammaticale (1919–1921)*, edited by Gilles Philippe, Grenoble, 2002, p. 83.

62   'eternal imperfect': ibid., p. 86.

62   'it seems to me': Gustave Flaubert, *Selected Letters*, translated by Geoffrey Wall, Harmondsworth, 1997, p. 217.

62   'using the least speech-marks': Marcel Proust, 'A propos du "style" de Flaubert', Paris, 1920, reprinted in *Flaubert savait-il écrire?: Une querelle grammaticale (1919–1921)*, edited by Gilles Philippe, Grenoble, 2002, p. 86.

63   'The conjunction "and"': ibid., p. 87.

67   'Life meanwhile': Leo Tolstoy, *Voina i Mir*, Moscow, 1865–69, *War and Peace*, translated by Louise and Aylmer Maude, Oxford, 1998, p. 443.

68   'What's really going on': Georges Perec, 'Approches de quoi?', *Cause commune*, Paris, February 1973, pp. 3–4, reprinted in *L'Infra-ordinaire*, Paris, 1989, translated by John Sturrock as 'Approaches to What?', in Georges Perec, *Species of Spaces and Other Pieces*, Harmondsworth, 1997, pp. 205–7.

68   'lusty country-fellow': Miguel de Cervantes Saavedra, *Don Quixote*, Madrid, 1605 and 1615, *The Life and Exploits of the Ingenious Gentleman Don Quixote de la Mancha*, translated by Charles Jarvis, London, 1742, reprinted Oxford, 1999, p. 45.

69   '"The mischief is"': ibid., p. 46.

70   '"for had you gone on your way"': ibid., p. 320.

72   'with such simple, such natural': Denis Diderot, 'Les Deux Amis de Bourbonne', Zurich, 1773, reprinted in Denis Diderot, *Oeuvres*, edited by André Billy, Paris, 1951, p. 757, translated by AT.

72   'A painter depicts': Denis Diderot, 'Les Deux Amis de Bourbonne',

Zurich, 1773, reprinted in Denis Diderot, *Contes et Romans*, edited by Michel Delon, Paris, 2004, p. 449, translated by AT.

75 'Pasha felt that on this lady': Anton Chekhov, 'The Chorus Girl', Moscow, 1892, translated by Constance Garnett, reprinted in *My Life and Other Stories*, London, 1992, p. 258.

76 'perhaps one and the same': Gustave Flaubert, *Flaubert in Egypt*, translated and edited with an introduction by Francis Steegmuller, Penguin, 1996, pp. 216–17.

76 'What pleases me': Vladimir Nabokov, *Speak, Memory*, London, 1967, reprinted Harmondsworth, 1969, p. 23.

76 'used to say that': V. Annenkov, 'N V Gogol' v Rime letom 1841 goda', *Literaturnye vospominaniia*, Moscow, 1960, p. 77.

77 '3 or 4 Families': Jane Austen, *Jane Austen's Letters*, edited by R. W. Chapman, Oxford, 1962, p. 401.

77 'in Gogol's books': Vladimir Nabokov, *Nikolai Gogol*, New York, 1971, p. 152.

77 'I will have established': Gustave Flaubert, *Selected Letters*, translated by Geoffrey Wall, Harmondsworth, 1997, p. 217.

78 'must be subjoined': Samuel Johnson, 'London', London, 1738, reprinted in *The Yale Edition of the Works of Samuel Johnson*, vol. 6, *Poems*, edited by E. L. McAdam, Jr, with George Milne, New Haven and London, 1964, reprinted 1975, p. 46.

78 'between Roman images': Samuel Johnson, 'Life of Alexander Pope', in *Lives of the English Poets*, London, 1779–81, reprinted 1946, 2 vols., edited by Ernest Rhys, vol. 2, p. 228.

79 'We must try its effect': quoted in James Boswell, *Life of Johnson*, London, 1791, reprinted 1992, p. 809.

79 'the ninth and thirty-eighth chapters': Jorge Luis Borges, 'Pierre Menard, autor del Quijote', *Sur* 56, May 1939, reprinted in *Labyrinths*, edited and translated by Donald A. Yates and James E. Irby, preface by André Maurois, Harmondsworth, 1970, p. 65.

79 'He did not want': ibid., pp. 65–6.

81 'The archaic style of Menard': ibid., p. 69.

82 'has enriched': ibid., p. 71.

83 as Nicholson Baker notes: Nicholas Baker, *U and I: A True Story*, London, 1991, p. 11.

84   'Emma se penchait': Gustave Flaubert, *Madame Bovary*, Paris, 1857, reprinted 1986, edited by Bernard Ajac, p. 293.

84   'Emma leant forward': Gustave Flaubert, *Madame Bovary*, Paris, 1857, London, translated by Eleanor Marx-Aveling, second impression, 1934, p. 209.

85   'the intellectual creations': Karl Marx and Friedrich Engels, *The Communist Manifesto*, London, 1848, reprinted Harmondsworth, 2004, p. 8.

86   *'What is home without'*: James Joyce, *Ulysses*, Paris, 1922, reprinted Oxford 1993, p. 72.

88   Her effects were worth: quoted in Hermia Oliver, *Flaubert and an English Governess: The Quest for Juliet Herbert*, Oxford, 1980, p. 146.

88   'make a voluntary pastiche': Marcel Proust, 'A propos du "style" de Flaubert', Paris, 1920, reprinted in *Flaubert savait-il écrire?: Une querelle grammaticale (1919–1921)*, edited by Gilles Philippe, Grenoble, 2002, p. 91.

89   'At these words a deathly paleness': Denis Diderot, 'Ceci n'est pas un conte', Paris, 1798, reprinted in Denis Diderot, *Oeuvres*, edited by André Billy, p. 796, translated by AT.

93   '"I am just taking the names"': James Joyce, *Ulysses*, 1922, reprinted London, 1992, p. 161.

93   'L Boom': ibid., p. 857.

93   'Just let the artist': Denis Diderot, 'Les Deux Amis de Bourbonne', Zurich, 1773, reprinted in Denis Diderot, *Contes et Romans*, edited by Michel Delon, Paris, 2004, p. 449, translated by AT.

94   '–Nother dying come home': James Joyce, *Ulysses: A Critical and Synoptic Edition*, prepared by Hans Walter Gabler with Wolfhard Steppe and Claus Melchior, New York and London, 1984, 3 vols., pp. 84–5.

94   'little writing blocks': Frank Budgen, *James Joyce and the Making of* Ulysses, London, 1934, second edition 1937, pp. 176–7.

94   'I have seen him collect': ibid., p. 176.

95   'globetrotters': James Joyce, *Joyce's* Ulysses *Notesheets in the British Museum*, edited by Phillip. F Herring, Charlottesville, 1972, p. 369.

95   Of these, only 'turning money away': ibid., p. 369.

96   'all adorned with': Sylvia Beach, *Shakespeare and Company*, London, 1959, p. 68.

98   'what we all want': quoted in Béatrice Mousli, *Valery Larbaud*, Paris, 1998, p. 389.

98   'prospector for foreign literatures': quoted in ibid., p. 375.

98   'Dear Sylvia': Valery Larbaud to Sylvia Beach, 22 February 1921, in Valery
        Larbaud, *Lettres à Adrienne Monnier et à Sylvia Beach 1919–1933*, edited by
        Maurice Saillet, IMEC, Épinal, 1991, p. 40.

99   'ULYSSES suppressed': reproduced in Lawrence Rainey, *Institutions of
        Modernism*, London, 1998, pp. 52–3.

101   'uncorrected semifinal form': James Joyce, *Letters*, vol. I, edited by Stuart
        Gilbert, New York, 1957, reprinted 1966; vols. II and III edited by Richard
        Ellmann, New York, 1966; III, 57.

101   '*We do warn the public*': reproduced in Richard Ellmann, *James Joyce*,
        Oxford, 1983, illustration XXXIV, between pp. 482–3.

102   'we begin with him': Valery Larbaud, 'The "Ulysses" of James Joyce',
        in *The Criterion: A Quarterly Review*, vol. I, no. 1, October 1922, London,
        pp. 94–103, p. 95.

102   'in this book': ibid., p. 96.

104   'Fingering still the letter': James Joyce, *Ulysses*, Paris, 1922, reprinted
        London 1992, pp. 109–11.

104   'We begin to discover': Valery Larbaud, 'The "Ulysses" of James Joyce',
        in *The Criterion: A Quarterly Review*, vol. I, no. 1, October 1922, London,
        pp. 94–103, p. 97.

105   'It is a genuine example': ibid., p. 97.

106   'Still I got to know': Michael Groden, Ulysses *in Progress*, Princeton,
        1977, p. 198.

106   'This book is a new world': Vladimir Nabokov, *Lectures on Literature*,
        edited by Fredson Bowers, New York, 1980, p. 363.

107   'voilà tout': Ezra Pound, 'James Joyce et Pecuchet', *Mercure de France*,
        Paris, 1 June 1922, reprinted in *Pound/Joyce: The Letters of Ezra Pound to
        James Joyce, with Pound's Essays on Joyce*, edited and with a commentary
        by Forrest Read, London, 1968, p. 206.

107   'I am quite content': James Joyce, *Letters*, vol. I edited by Stuart Gilbert,
        New York, 1957, reprinted 1966; vols II and III edited by Richard Ellmann,
        New York, 1966; I, 297.

108   'What limitations': James Joyce, *Ulysses*, Paris, 1922, reprinted London
        1992, pp. 994–5.

109   'Pillowed on my coat': ibid, pp. 255–6.

110   'the sun shines': ibid., p. 1068.

111 'They shot the six': Ernest Hemingway, *in our time*, Paris, 1924, reprinted in *The Collected Stories*, edited by James Fenton, London, 1995, p. 20.

112 '9 rooms where the floor': Georges Perec, *Espèces d'espaces*, Paris, 1974, translated by John Sturrock, 'The Apartment Building', in Georges Perec, *Species of Spaces and Other Pieces*, Harmondsworth, 1997, pp. 42–3.

114 'Examine the drawing': ibid., pp. 43–4.

114 'The woman doing nothing very much': ibid., p. 44.

114 'Indeed, as you say': quoted in Laure Murat, *Passage de l'Odéon*, Paris, 2003, reprinted 2005, pp. 172–3.

115 he read his fiction in translation: cited in ibid., p. 146.

120 'Had they nothing else': Gustave Flaubert, *Madame Bovary*, Paris, 1857, translated by Geoffrey Wall, Harmondsworth, 1992, pp. 75–6.

120 'Whether I shall turn out': Charles Dickens, *David Copperfield*, London, 1849–50, reprinted Harmondsworth, 1996, p. 11.

121 'What's that waiter up to?': Edouard Dujardin, *Les Lauriers sont coupés*, Paris, 1887, *We'll to the Woods No More*, translated by Stuart Gilbert, New York, 1938, p. 24.

121 'I shall always regret': Dujardin, 'Le Monologue intérieur', Paris, 1931, translated by Anthony Suter, 'Interior Monologue', in *The Bays Are Sere and Interior Monologue*, London, 1991, p. 89.

121 'life, immediate, dear': Stéphane Mallarmé, *Oeuvres Complètes*, Paris, 1945, p. 718.

122 'I can see you have': Dujardin, 'Le Monologue intérieur', Paris, 1931, translated by Anthony Suter, 'Interior Monologue', in *The Bays Are Sere and Interior Monologue*, London, 1991, p. 89.

123 The poem's form is an analogue: Graham Robb, *Unlocking Mallarmé*, New Haven and London, 1996, p. 24.

123 'Even though we have come to doubt': Witold Gombrowicz, *Diary*, vol. 1, translated by Lillian Vallee, New York, 1988, p. 215.

124 'We should never lose sight': ibid., p. 217.

124 'My art . . . has shaped itself': ibid.

125 'And that's the end': Edouard Dujardin, *Les Lauriers sont coupés*, Paris, 1887, *We'll to the Woods No More*, translated by Stuart Gilbert, New York, 1938, p. 71.

125 'A woman in front': ibid., p. 13.

125 'Now why is the stair carpet': ibid., pp. 6 and 50.

125   'rose and kissed Vera's hand': Leo Tolstoy, *War and Peace*, translated by Louise and Aylmer Maude, Oxford, 1998, p. 497.

126   'must be nearly six hours': Edouard Dujardin, *Les Lauriers sont coupés*, Paris, 1887, *We'll to the Woods No More*, translated by Stuart Gilbert, New York, 1938, pp. 132–3.

126   'That's enough of it': ibid., p. 135.

129   'Gertrude Stein always speaks': Gertrude Stein, *The Autobiography of Alice B. Toklas*, London, 1933, reprinted Harmondsworth, 1966, pp. 86–7.

129   'and his heart': James Joyce, *Ulysses*, Paris, 1922, reprinted London, 1992, p. 1069.

129   'Again; no, imposs.': Edouard Dujardin, *Les Lauriers sont coupés*, Paris, 1887, *We'll to the Woods No More*, translated by Stuart Gilbert, New York, 1938, p. 27.

131   'Lovely name you have': James Joyce, *Ulysses*, Paris, 1922, reprinted London, 1992, p. 403.

Volume II

138   'Now the king of Bohemia': Laurence Sterne, *The Life and Opinions of Tristram Shandy, Gentleman*, London, 1759–67, reprinted Harmondsworth, 1985, pp. 541–2.

138   'Jacques. My captain': Denis Diderot, *Jacques le fataliste et son maître*, Paris, 1796, translated by David Coward, *Jacques the Fatalist*, Oxford, 1999, p. 3.

138   'if it had not been': Laurence Sterne, *The Life and Opinions of Tristram Shandy, Gentleman*, London, 1759–67, reprinted Harmondsworth, 1985, p. 542.

140   'Jacques. For instance': Denis Diderot, *Jacques le fataliste et son maître*, Paris, 1796, translated by David Coward, *Jacques the Fatalist*, Oxford, 1999, pp. 3–4.

141   'was responsive to this invitation': Milan Kundera, 'Introduction to a Variation', in *Jacques et son maître*, Paris, 1981, translated by Simon Callow, *Jacques and His Master*, London, 1986, pp. 11–12.

141   'endless melody': Friedrich Nietzsche, *Menschliches, Allzumenschliches*, 1878–80, *Human, All Too Human: A Book for Free Spirits*, translated by R. J. Hollingdale, Cambridge 1996, reprinted 2003, pp. 238–9.

143 The two letters: Laurence Sterne, *Letters of Laurence Sterne*, edited by Lewis Perry Curtis, Oxford, 1935, p. 162.

143 'the 6 Vols. of Shandy': quoted in Ian Campbell Ross, *Laurence Sterne: A Life*, Oxford, 2001, p. 285.

143 'the maddest, the wisest': quoted in ibid.

145 '*Pray, my dear*, quoth my mother': Laurence Sterne, *The Life and Opinions of Tristram Shandy, Gentleman*, London, 1759–67, reprinted Harmondsworth, 1985, pp. 35–6.

146 'the essence of Sterne's novel': cf. A. D. Nuttall, *Openings: Narrative Beginnings From the Epic to the Novel*, Oxford, 1992, p. 159.

147 'holding in her breath': ibid., pp. 352–3.

147 'I am a Turk': ibid., pp. 361.

147 'a cow broke in': ibid., p. 240.

148 'by resorting to published memoirs': Denis Diderot, *Jacques le fataliste et son maître*, Paris, 1796, translated by David Coward, *Jacques the Fatalist*, Oxford, 1999, p. 237.

149 'unless, that is, the conversations': ibid., p. 238.

149 '– And then thou clapped'st it': Laurence Sterne, *The Life and Opinions of Tristram Shandy, Gentleman*, London, 1759–67, reprinted Harmondsworth, 1985, p. 549.

150 'Who's saying different?': Denis Diderot, *Jacques le fataliste et son maître*, Paris, 1796, translated by David Coward, *Jacques the Fatalist*, Oxford, 1999, p. 239.

150 'that ornamental figure': Laurence Sterne, *The Life and Opinions of Tristram Shandy, Gentleman*, London, 1759–67, reprinted Harmondsworth, 1985, p. 120.

150 'now and then, though never': ibid., p. 217.

150 'My sister, I dare say': ibid., p. 119.

151 'for that is how it is written': Denis Diderot, *Jacques le fataliste et son maître*, Paris, 1796, reprinted in Denis Diderot, *Contes et Romans*, edited by Michel Delon, Paris, 2004, p. 885, translated by AT.

152 'cross-reckonings and sorrowful *items*': Laurence Sterne, *The Life and Opinions of Tristram Shandy, Gentleman*, London, 1759–67, reprinted Harmondsworth, 1985, p. 279.

152 'What a chapter of chances': ibid., p. 281.

152 'What a lucky chapter': ibid.

153   'Is it not a shame': ibid., p. 282.

153   'let that be as it will': ibid.

154   'my chapter upon chapters': ibid.

155   'I will chide no breather': quoted by Helen Caldwell in *Machado de Assis: The Brazilian Master and his Novels*, Berkeley, 1970, pp. 94–5.

155   'Now, as I write this': Joaquim Maria Machado de Assis, *Memórias póstumas de Brás Cubas*, 1881, Rio de Janeiro, *The Posthumous Memoirs of Brás Cubas*, translated by Gregory Rabassa, Oxford, 1997, p. 121.

155   'Inside I blessed the tragedy': ibid., p. 146.

156   'an antihypochondriacal poultice' . . . 'to drive the *gall*': ibid., p. 9. Laurence Sterne, *The Life and Opinions of Tristram Shandy, Gentleman*, London, 1759–67, reprinted Harmondsworth, 1985, p. 299.

156   'Perhaps I'm startling': Joaquim Maria Machado de Assis, *Memórias póstumas de Brás Cubas*, 1881, Rio de Janeiro, *The Posthumous Memoirs of Brás Cubas*, translated by Gregory Rabassa, Oxford, 1997, p. 52.

156   'slackness of will': ibid., p. 27.

157   'And now watch the skill': ibid., p. 22.

157   'for a sad and banal chapter': ibid., pp. 77–8.

158   'Brás Cubas/ . . .': ibid., 90–91.

159   'I'm sure it's crazy': André Gide, *Journal des faux-monnayeurs*, Paris, 1927, pp. 11–12, translated by AT.

160   '"is something like the art of fugue writing"': André Gide, *Les Faux-Monnayeurs*, Paris, 1925, translated by Dorothy Bussy, *The Counterfeiters*, London, 1931, reprinted Harmondsworth, 1966, p. 171.

161   'I called myself prodigal': Joaquim Maria Machado de Assis, *Memórias póstumas de Brás Cubas*, 1881, Rio de Janeiro, *The Posthumous Memoirs of Brás Cubas*, translated by Gregory Rabassa, Oxford, 1997, p. 48.

162   an anthology was made: cited in Roberto Schwarz, *A Master on the Periphery of Capitalism: Machado de Assis*, Rio de Janeiro, translated by John Gledson, Durham, NC, 2001, p. 116.

167   'I am now beginning to get fairly': Laurence Sterne, *The Life and Opinions of Tristram Shandy, Gentleman*, London, 1759–67, reprinted Harmondsworth, 1985, pp. 453–4.

168   'In a word': ibid., p. 95.

169   'His digressions are at the same time': Friedrich Nietzsche, *Menschliches, Allzumenschliches*, 1878–80, *Human, All Too Human: A Book for Free Spirits*,

translated by R. J. Hollingdale, Cambridge 1996, reprinted 2003, pp. 238–9.

171   *The Beauties of Sterne Including All*: W H, *The Beauties of Sterne*, London, 1782, p. i.

171   '*his Sentimental Journey*': ibid., p. v.

171   'Hail ye small sweet courtesies': ibid., p. 23.

173   'The poor man blush'd': ibid., p. 118.

173   'a certain generosity': ibid., p. 121.

174   '"It isn't race"': Sergio Solmi, 'Ricordo di Svevo', *Solaria*, no. 3–4, Florence, 1929, p. 71, quoted in P. N. Furbank, *Italo Svevo: The Man and the Writer*, London, 1966, p. 99.

174   'What do I have in common': quoted in Jeremy Adler, *Franz Kafka*, New York, 2004, p. 18.

175   'descriptive lust': cited in Richard Ellmann, *James Joyce*, Oxford, 1982, reprinted 1983, p. 342.

175   '"in such a way that I shan't"': Guy de Maupassant, 'Le Roman', Preface to *Pierre et Jean*, Paris, 1888, reprinted in *Novelists on the Novel*, edited by Miriam Allott, London, 1959, reprinted 1975, pp. 130–31.

175   'When I see him walking': quoted in P. N. Furbank, *Italo Svevo: The Man and the Writer*, London, 1966, p. 85.

179   'a coloured picture': cited in Richard Ellmann, *James Joyce*, Oxford, 1982, reprinted 1983, p. 636.

179   'Two pairs of short socks': Italo Svevo, *La Coscienza di Zeno*, Trieste, 1923, translated by William Weaver, *Zeno's Conscience*, New York, 2001, p. 10.

179   'her portrait, or rather certain details': Vladimir Nabokov, 'Mademoiselle O', *Mesures*, Paris, no. 2, 1936, pp. 147–72, p. 148, translated by AT.

180   'If I had stopped smoking': Italo Svevo, *La Coscienza di Zeno*, Trieste, 1923, translated by William Weaver, *Zeno's Conscience*, New York, 2001, p. 12.

180   'a fortune teller': Bohumil Hrabal, *Tanecní hodiny pro starsí a pokrocilé*, Prague, 1964, *Dancing Lessons for the Advanced in Age*, translated by Michael Henry Heim, London, 1998, p. 58.

181   'Was he seeing right?': Italo Svevo, *Corto Viaggio Sentimentale*, Milan 1957, reprinted Rome, 2002, translated by AT.

185   'la grrrrrande Comédie Humaine': quoted in Graham Robb, *Balzac*, London, 1994, p. 342.

186   'I have undertaken and completed': Xavier de Maistre, *Voyage autour de ma chambre*, 1795, *A Journey Around My Room*, translated by Andrew Brown, London, 2004, p. 3.

187   'it's a carnival flower': ibid., p. 49.

187   'Once you've left my armchair': ibid., p. 8.

191   the curvy Line of Beauty [drawing]: William Hogarth, *The Analysis of Beauty*, London, 1753, reprinted New Haven, 1997, edited with an introduction and notes by Ronald Paulson, title page.

192   'Imagine to yourself': Laurence Sterne, *The Life and Opinions of Tristram Shandy, Gentleman*, London, 1759–67, reprinted Harmondsworth, 1985, pp. 125–6.

193   'The *Woman Eating Sea Urchins*': Françoise Gilot, *Living With Picasso*, New York, 1964, reprinted London, 1990, pp. 129–30.

193   'the urgent cry of the future': Vladimir Mayakovsky, 'The Two Chekhovs', Moscow, 1914, quoted in *Letters of Anton Chekhov*, translated by Michael Henry Heim, in collaboration with Simon Karlinsky, New York, 1973, p. 31.

194   'Whilst a man is free': Laurence Sterne, *The Life and Opinions of Tristram Shandy, Gentleman*, London, 1759–67, reprinted Harmondsworth, 1985, p. 576.

195   'The *papier collé*': Françoise Gilot, *Living With Picasso*, New York, 1964, reprinted London, 1990, p. 70.

196   'once sat at the window': quoted in Neil Stewart, 'From Imperial Court to Peasant's Cot: Sterne in Russia', in *The Reception of Laurence Sterne in Europe*, edited by Peter de Voogd and John Neubauer, London, 2004, pp. 127–53, p. 143.

197   'There was not the least sense': Leo Tolstoy, *Voina i Mir*, Moscow, 1865–9, *War and Peace*, translated by Louise and Aylmer Maude, Oxford, 1998, p. 807.

197   'A rough outline': ibid., p. 810.

198   [drawing by Tolstoy]: Leo Tolstoy, *Voina i Mir*, Moscow, 1865–69, reprinted in 2 vols., Moscow, 2005, vol. 2, p. 210.

199   'Bauhausy philosophy': quoted in *Saul Steinberg: Illuminations*, edited by Joel Smith, New Haven, 2006, p. 82.

199   'as a form of writing': quoted in ibid., p. 168.

199   'My idea of the artist': quoted in ibid., p. 212.

201   'An active line on a walk': Paul Klee, *Pädagogisches Skizzenbuch*, Dessau, 1925, translated by Sibyl Moholy-Nagy, *Pedagogical Sketchbook*, London, 1953, reprinted 1981, p. 16.

201   'The same line': ibid., p. 17.

205   'comic Epic-Poem': Henry Fielding, 'Preface' to *Joseph Andrews*, London, 1742, reprinted Oxford, 1999, p. 3.

206   'The plot thickens': Vladimir Nabokov, *Lectures on Russian Literature*, edited and with an introduction by Fredson Bowers, New York, 1981, p. 9.

207   'Olga was silent': Antonov, *The Big Heart*, 1957, quoted in Vladimir Nabokov, *Lectures on Russian Literature*, edited and with an introduction by Fredson Bowers, New York, 1981, p. 10.

207   'a realist with an adjective': Josef Škvorecký, 'Introduction', in Bohumil Hrabal, *The Little Town Where Time Stood Still*, translated by James Naughton, London, 1993, p. xvi.

208   'my defence against politics': Bohumil Hrabal, 'Public Suicide', *Total Fears*, Prague, 1990–91, translated by James Naughton, Prague, 1998, p. 40.

208   'Just like I come here': Bohumil Hrabal, *Tanecní hodiny pro starsí a pokrocilé*, Prague, 1964, *Dancing Lessons for the Advanced in Age*, translated by Michael Henry Heim, London, 1998, pp. 3–4.

211   'path of destructive experimentalism': quoted by Bohuslav Mánek, 'The Czech and Slovak Reception of James Joyce', in *The Reception of James Joyce in Europe*, 2 vols, edited by Geert Lernout and Wim Van Mierlo, London, 2004, vol. 1, pp. 187–97, p. 192.

211   'hit smashes over the nets': Bohumil Hrabal, 'Jeu de la vérité', in *A bâtons rompus avec Bohumil Hrabal*, interviews with Christian Salmon, Paris, 1991, p. 66.

211   'you should have seen': Bohumil Hrabal, *Tanecní hodiny pro starsí a pokrocilé*, Prague, 1964, *Dancing Lessons for the Advanced in Age*, translated by Michael Henry Heim, London, 1998, pp. 87–8.

212   'capable of attaining the point': James Joyce, *Ulysses*, Paris, 1922, reprinted London, 1992, p. 942.

213   'I was walking along the river': Bohumil Hrabal, *Tanecní hodiny pro starsí a pokrocilé*, Prague, 1964, *Dancing Lessons for the Advanced in Age*, translated by Michael Henry Heim, London, 1998, pp. 72–3.

213   'he never can explain': James Joyce, *Ulysses*, Paris, 1922, reprinted London, 1992, pp. 1022–3.

214   'My *femme de ménage*': Valery Larbaud to Adrienne Monnier, in Valery Larbaud, *Lettres à Adrienne Monnier et à Sylvia Beach 1919–1933*, edited by Maurice Saillet, IMEC, Épinal, 1991, p. 163.

215   'LB have I offended': James Joyce, *Joyce's* Ulysses Notesheets *in the British Museum*, edited by Phillip F. Herring, Charlottesville, 1972, p. 503.

217   'When I was in Sofia': Bohumil Hrabal, 'Meshuge Stunde', *Total Fears*, Prague, 1990–1, translated by James Naughton, Prague, 1998, p. 116.

219   'In Kladno': Bohumil Hrabal, *A bâtons rompus avec Bohumil Hrabal*, interviews with Christian Salmon, Paris, 1991, p. 17, translated by AT.

220   'just as in a musical fugue': Vladimir Nabokov, *Lectures on Literature*, New York, 1980, edited by Fredson Bowers, p. 89.

220   'As for me, I follow': Bohumil Hrabal, *Jarmilka*, Prague, 1991, translated by Benoît Meunier with Jean-Gaspard Páleníček, Paris, 2004, p. 15, translated by AT.

221   'I take a pair of scissors': Bohumil Hrabal, *A bâtons rompus avec Bohumil Hrabal*, interviews with Christian Salmon, Paris, 1991, p. 33, translated by AT.

221   'We leave the shadows': Bohumil Hrabal, *Jarmilka*, Prague, 1991, translated by Benoît Meunier with Jean-Gaspard Páleníček, Paris, 2004, pp. 27–8, translated by AT.

223   Machado de Assis owned: Jean-Michel Massa, 'La Bibliothèque de Machado de Assis', *Revista do Livro*, no. 21–2, Março-Junho, 1961, Rio de Janeiro.

225   'attached to it by organic links': Witold Gombrowicz, 'James Joyce: Ulysse', *Kurier Poranny*, no. 16, 1937, translated by Allan Kosko, translated by AT, *Varia 1*, Paris, 1978, p. 47.

225   'would be able to inject': ibid., p. 49.

Volume III

233   'My art . . . has shaped itself': Witold Gombrowicz, *Diary*, vol. 1, translated by Lillian Vallee, New York, 1988, p. 217.

235   'What has led to the significant': Count Lyof N. Tolstoï, *The Physiology of War*, translated by Huntington Smith, London, 1889, p. vii.

235   '"Oh, Natasha!" she cried': Leo Tolstoy, *Voina i Mir*, Moscow, 1865–9, *War and Peace*, translated by Louise and Aylmer Maude, Oxford, 1998, pp. 567–8.

236   '"I saw him lying"': ibid., pp. 1023–4.

238   'Tolstoy is a magnificent writer': James Joyce to Stanislaus Joyce, 18 September 1905, reprinted in *Selected Letters of James Joyce*, edited by Richard Ellmann, London, 1975, reprinted 1992, p. 73.

238   'an author who': quoted in Kjell Espmark, *The Nobel Prize in Literature: A Study of the Criteria Behind the Choices*, Boston, 1991, p. 17.

238   'The aim of an artist': letter to P. D. Boborykin, July/August 1865, not sent, Leo Tolstoy, *Tolstoy's Letters*, two vols., selected, edited and translated by R. F. Christian, London, 1978, vol. I, p. 197.

242   'Andrey Yefimitch understood': Anton Chekhov, *The Essential Tales of Chekhov*, edited by Richard Ford, translated by Constance Garnett, London, 1999, p. 182.

242   'began to count': Leo Tolstoy, 'Sevastopol v mae 1855', Moscow, 1855, reprinted London, 1994, edited by M. Pursglove, p. 49, translated by AT.

244   'I started with Turgenev': Ernest Hemingway, *A Moveable Feast*, London, 1936, reprinted 2000, pp. 31–2.

244   'is clearer and more free': quoted in Richard Garnett, *Constance Garnett: A Heroic Life*, London, 1991, p. 205.

245   'creative repetition': Vladimir Nabokov, *Lectures on Russian Literature*, edited by Fredson Bowers, New York, 1981, p. 238.

245   'The thought came to him': Ann Pasternak Slater, 'Translator's Note', in *The Death of Ivan Ilyich* and *Master and Man*, New York, 2003, p. xxxi.

246   'the easiest author going': quoted in Richard Garnett, *Constance Garnett: A Heroic Life*, London, 1991, p. 205.

246   'In the first place': Vladimir Nabokov, 'Foreword', Mikhail Lermontov, *A Hero of Our Time*, translated by Vladimir Nabokov in collaboration with Dmitri Nabokov, New York, 1958, reprinted Oxford, 1992, p. xiii.

247   'his similes and metaphors': ibid.

248   'hampered by traditions': quoted in R. F. Christian, *Tolstoy's* War and Peace: *A Study*, Oxford, 1962, p. 16.

248   'Russians generally speaking': quoted in ibid., p. 21.

249   'Historical science': Leo Tolstoy, *Voina i Mir*, Moscow, 1865–69, *War and Peace*, translated by Louise and Aylmer Maude, Oxford, 1998, p. 880.

249   'In terms of artistic structure': Vladimir Nabokov, *Strong Opinions*, New York, 1973, reprinted 1990, p. 148.

250   'The sergeant came over': Stendhal, *La Chartreuse de Parme*, Paris, 1839, *The Charterhouse of Parma*, translated by Richard Howard, London, 2002, p. 47.

250   'I owe it to him': Paul Boyer, 'Chez Tolstoi', 1901, in *Leo Tolstoy, A Critical Anthology*, edited by Henry Gifford, Harmondsworth, 1971, pp. 112–13.

251   'The defect of so many novels': Giuseppe Tomasi di Lampedusa, *Lezioni su Stendhal*, Palermo, 1977, in *The Siren and Selected Writings*, translated by Archibald Colquhoun, David Gilmour and Guido Waldman, London, 1995, pp. 175–6.

251   'Young girl murdered': Stendhal, *Journal*, 1834, p. 191, translated by AT.

251   'The wounded crept together': Leo Tolstoy, *Voina i Mir*, Moscow, 1865–69, *War and Peace*, translated by Louise and Aylmer Maude, Oxford, 1998, p. 300.

252   'large loose baggy monsters': in Henry James, 'Preface' to *The Tragic Muse*, New York, 1908, reprinted Harmondsworth, 1995, p. 4.

252   '"I am grateful"': Ivan Turgenev to Leo Tolstoy, 24 January 1880, in *Polnoe sobranie sochineniy i pisem*, 1960–68, in *Leo Tolstoy, A Critical Anthology*, edited by Henry Gifford, Harmondsworth, 1971, pp. 54–5.

253   'In everything': quoted in Richard Pevear, 'Introduction', Leo Tolstoy, *Anna Karenina*, translated by Richard Pevear and Larissa Volokhonsky, Harmondsworth, 2000, pp. xv–xvi.

253   'The most important thing': A. B. Goldenweiser, *Vblizi Tolstogo*, Moscow-Leningrad, 1959, p. 68.

254   'To say nothing': Leo Tolstoy, *Voina i Mir*, Moscow, 1865–69, *War and Peace*, translated by Louise and Aylmer Maude, Oxford, 1998, p. 93.

254   '"What an appalling disaster"': Vladimir Nabokov, *Lectures on Literature*, edited by Fredson Bowers, New York, 1980, p. 156.

255   'all these descriptions': Leo Tolstoy, *Jubilee Edition*, VIII. 312, quoted in R. F. Christian, *Tolstoy's* War and Peace: *A Study*, Oxford, 1962, p. 138.

255   'Turgenev's opinion': Leo Tolstoy, *Tolstoy's Letters*, two vols., selected edited and translated by R. F. Christian, London, 1978, vol. 1, p. 205.

255   '"May I ask you"': Leo Tolstoy, *Voina i Mir*, Moscow, 1865–69, *War and Peace*, translated by Louise and Aylmer Maude, Oxford, 1998, p. 815.

259   'An old Rolls Royce': quoted in Jane Grayson, *Nabokov Translated*, Oxford, 1977, p. 184.

259   'This great conversation': 'Introduction' to *The Syntopicon: Great Books of the Western World*, edited by Mortimer J. Adler, Chicago, 1952, reprinted 1990, p. xiii.

260   '1 pedal bin': Georges Perec, *Espèces d'espaces*, Paris, 1974, translated by John Sturrock, 'The Apartment Building', in Georges Perec, *Species of Spaces and Other Pieces*, Harmondsworth, 1997, pp. 42–3.

260   'The ideas are': André Gide, *Dostoevsky*, Paris, 1923, translated by Arnold Bennett, London, 1925, p. 101, amended by AT.

260   'Certainly, psychological': ibid., p. 92, amended by AT.

263   'Eventually I learned': Saul Bellow, *Dangling Man*, New York, 1947, reprinted in Saul Bellow, *Novels 1944–53*, New York, 2003, p. 70.

263   'Long live regimentation': ibid., p. 140.

263   'And what is it we sometimes': Fyodor Dostoevsky, *Zapiski iz podpolya*, St Petersburg, 1864, *Notes from Underground*, translated by Jessie Coulson, Harmondsworth, 1972, p. 122.

264   'Now since I've mentioned': Saul Bellow, 'A Sermon by Doctor Pep', *Partisan Review*, May 1949.

265   'It was a big Jowett's *Plato*': Saul Bellow, *The Adventures of Augie March*, New York, 1953, reprinted in Saul Bellow, *Novels 1944–53*, New York, 2003, p. 603.

265   'This is a chapter': Saul Bellow, 'The Trip to Galena', *Partisan Review*, November–December 1950.

266   'I am an American': Saul Bellow, *The Adventures of Augie March*, New York, 1953, reprinted in Saul Bellow, *Novels 1944–53*, New York, 2003, p. 383.

266   'I am an American': Saul Bellow, 'From the Life of Augie March', *Partisan Review*, November 1949.

268   'you seek for nothing more': George Sand to Gustave Flaubert, 10–14 March 1876, in *Flaubert–Sand: The Correspondence of Gustave Flaubert and George Sand*, translated by Francis Steegmuller and Barbara Bray, London, 1993, reprinted 1999, p. 393.

268   'By inclination and intent': Vladimir Nabokov, *Strong Opinions*, New York, 1973, reprinted 1990, p. 147.

269   'the forty episodes': Vladimir Nabokov, *Lectures on Don Quixote*, edited by Fredson Bowers, New York, 1983, p. 89.

269   'Let us now follow': ibid., p. 93.

269   'So the final score': ibid., p. 110.

270   'When we met': Saul Bellow, *The Adventures of Augie March*, New York, 1953, reprinted in Saul Bellow, *Novels 1944–53*, New York, 2003, p. 980.

271   'She was strong, brave, German': quoted in Eric Auerbach, *Mimesis*, Berne, 1946, translated by Willard R. Trask, Princeton, 1953, p. 419.

272   'With the holder in her dark': Saul Bellow, *The Adventures of Augie March*, New York, 1953, reprinted in Saul Bellow, *Novels 1944–53*, New York, 2003, p. 387.

272   'Literature has neglected': quoted in *Isaac Bashevis Singer: An Album*, edited by Ilan Stavans, New York, 2004, pp. 29–30.

273   'If there wouldn't be': quoted in ibid., p. 61.

273   'I am Gimpel': Isaac Bashevis Singer, 'Gimpl tam', New York, 1945, 'Gimpel the Fool', translated by Saul Bellow, *Partisan Review*, New York, 1953, reprinted in *Collected Stories*, 3 vols., edited by Ilan Stavans, New York, 2005, I, p. 5.

273   'Ikh bin gimpl': Isaac Bashevis Singer, 'Gimpl Tam', New York, 1945, reprinted 1963, p. 5.

274   'I certainly looked like': Saul Bellow, *The Adventures of Augie March*, New York, 1953, reprinted in Saul Bellow, *Novels 1944–53*, New York, 2003

275   'Doesn't want to be': quoted in James Atlas, *Bellow: A Biography*, London, 2000, p. 188.

275   'But what did people seem': Saul Bellow, *The Adventures of Augie March*, New York, 1953, reprinted in Saul Bellow, *Novels 1944–53*, New York, 2003, p. 841.

275   In Balzac's opinion: Honoré de Balzac, 'Etudes sur Beyle', *Revue Parisienne*, Paris, 25 September 1840, reprinted in *Oeuvres Complètes*, vol. 28, Paris, 1963, pp. 234–5.

275   'We will admit that': Stendhal, *La Chartreuse de Parme*, Paris, 1839, *The Charterhouse of Parma*, translated by Richard Howard, London, 2002, p. 10.

276   But Balzac: Charles Baudelaire, 'Théophile Gautier', *L'Artiste*, Paris, 13 March 1859, reprinted in *Oeuvres Complètes*, two vols., edited by Claude Pichois, vol. 2, p. 120, translated by AT.

276   'Fuss / Adjust': reprinted in *Isaac Bashevis Singer: An Album*, edited by Ilan Stavans, New York, 2004, p. 31.

277 'Yiddish literature': quoted by Michael André Bernstein, 'Yes, I Pray God', *Times Literary Supplement*, London, 24 September 2004, p. 19.

277 'I dictate to them': quoted in Joseph Sherman, 'Translating *Shotns Baym Hudson*', in *Isaac Bashevis Singer: His Work and His World*, edited by Hugh Denman, Leiden, 2002, pp. 49–80.

277 'The English translation': Isaac Bashevis Singer, 'Author's Note', *The Image and Other Stories*, New York, 1985, reprinted in *Collected Stories*, 3 vols., edited by Ilan Stavans, New York, 2005, III, p. 292.

278 '"You weren't going to shoot"': Saul Bellow, *The Adventures of Augie March*, New York, 1953, reprinted in Saul Bellow, *Novels 1944–53*, New York, 2003, p. 569.

278 'all was rich': ibid., p. 664.

278 'I still had the dysentery': ibid., p. 799.

278 'straight, heavy squirt': ibid, p. 766.

278 '"What I guess about you"': ibid., p. 879.

280 'Pretty soon': quoted in James Atlas, *Bellow: A Biography*, London, 2000, p. 260.

285 'Every cloud': Anton Chekhov, *A Life in Letters*, edited by Rosamund Bartlett, translated by Rosamund Bartlett and Anthony Phillips, Harmondsworth, 2004, pp. 369–70.

285 'Tolstoi as usual': A. B. Goldenveizer, *Talks with Tolstoi*, translated by S. S. Koteliansky and Virginia Woolf, London, 1923, p. 41.

287 'In the first place': Anton Chekhov, *A Life in Letters*, edited by Rosamund Bartlett, translated by Rosamund Bartlett and Anthony Phillips, Harmondsworth, 2004, p. 434.

288 'it might be spring': Anton Chekhov, 'In the Cart', in *The Oxford Chekhov*, vol. VIII, translated and edited by Ronald Hingley, London, 1965, p. 251.

288 'All she had left': ibid., p. 251.

288 'that if she was his wife': ibid., p. 254.

288 'They kept turning back': ibid., p. 255.

289 'Marya's galoshes': ibid., p. 257.

289 'the school with its green roof': ibid., p. 257.

289 'On the small platform': ibid., pp. 257–8.

289 'Suddenly, it all vanished': ibid., p. 258.

290 'capable of distinguishing': Anton Chekhov to Alexei Suvorin, 30 May

1888, in *Letters of Anton Chekhov*, translated by Michael Henry Heim, in collaboration with Simon Karlinsky, New York, 1973, p. 104.

290 'мама': Anton Chekhov, *Polnoe sobranie sochinenii i pisem v tritsati tomakh*, Moscow, 1977, vol. 9, p. 342.

291 'that life consists': Samuel Johnson, *A Journey to the Western Islands of Scotland*, London, 1775, reprinted Edinburgh, 1996, pp. 18–19.

292 'You are right to demand': Anton Chekhov to Alexei Suvorin, 27 October 1888, in *Letters of Anton Chekhov*, translated by Michael Henry Heim, in collaboration with Simon Karlinsky, New York, 1973, p. 117.

293 'A psychologist should not': Anton Chekhov to Ivan Shcheglov, 9 June 1888, in ibid., p. 106.

293 'that finale': Ivan Shcheglov to Anton Chekhov, 29 May 1888, in ibid., p. 106.

293 'Turgenev's opinion': Leo Tolstoy, *Tolstoy's Letters*, two vols, selected edited and translated by R. F. Christian, London, 1978, vol. 1, p. 205.

294 'Your first chapter': Anton Chekhov to Alexander Kuprin, 1 November 1902, in *Letters of Anton Chekhov*, translated by Michael Henry Heim, in collaboration with Simon Karlinsky, New York, 1973, p. 432.

296 'Catherine was delighted': Jane Austen, *Northanger Abbey*, London, 1818, reprinted Harmondsworth, 2003, p. 32.

296 '"Had I the command"': ibid., p. 114.

296 '"C'est grand"': Leo Tolstoy, *War and Peace*, translated by Louise and Aylmer Maude, Oxford, 1998, pp. 1143–4.

298 '"I thank you"': Jane Austen, *Emma*, London, 1815, reprinted Oxford, 2003, p. 89.

298 'It is about an hour and a half's': Laurence Sterne, *The Life and Opinions of Tristram Shandy, Gentleman*, London, 1759–67, reprinted Harmondsworth, 1985, p. 122.

299 'When one has written': Ivan A. Bunin, 'A P. Tchekhov', in *Anton Tchekhov: Literary and Theatrical Reminiscences*, translated and edited by S. S. Koteliansky, London, 1927, p. 86.

299 'Try to tear up': quoted in Y. Sobolev, 'Tchekhov's Creative Method', in ibid., p. 23.

299 'new theory': Ernest Hemingway, *A Moveable Feast*, London, 1936, reprinted 2000, p. 63.

299   '"Otherwise he will reduce"': Y. Sobolev, 'Tchekhov's Creative Method', in *Anton Tchekhov: Literary and Theatrical Reminiscences*, translated and edited by S. S. Koteliansky, London, 1927, p. 21.

299   'To the question': ibid., p. 22.

300   'In Act IV': 'Reminiscences by K S Stanislavsky', in ibid, pp. 160–61.

300   'used this expression': James Boswell, *Life of Johnson*, London, 1791, reprinted 1992, p. 346.

301   '"Characters of manners"': ibid., p. 346.

301   'When I stopped writing': Ernest Hemingway, *A Moveable Feast*, London, 1936, reprinted 2000, p. 64.

302   'all I can make out': Vladimir Nabokov, *Strong Opinions*, New York, 1973, reprinted 1990, p. 286.

303   'A count, a countess': Anton Chekhov, 'Chto chashche vsego vstrechaetsya v romanakh, povestyakh i t p', Moscow, 1880, translated by Harvey Pitcher, 'What You Nearly Always Find in Novels, Stories, etc', in *Chekhov: The Comic Stories*, London, 1998, reprinted 2004, pp. 87–8, p. 87.

304   'The biter bit': Anton Chekhov, 'Two tales from the Russian of Anton Tschehow. The biter bit. Sorrow.' *Temple Bar; a London magazine*, 1897, vol. III, pp. 104–13, anonymous translator.

304   'a hefty great peasant': Anton Chekhov, 'Peresolil', Moscow, 1885, translated by Harvey Pitcher, 'Overdoing It', in *Chekhov: The Comic Stories*, London, 1998, reprinted 2004, pp. 74–7, p. 74.

304   'It was dusk': ibid., p. 75.

305   '"God forgive you"': ibid., p. 77.

306   'the sure presence': quoted in William Weaver, 'Translator's Introduction', in Italo Svevo, *Zeno's Conscience*, translated by William Weaver, New York, 2001, pp. xxii–xxiii.

306   'which is bound to lose': Eugenio Montale, 'Svevo', in *Svevo–Montale Lettere*, Milan, translated by G. Singh, in Eugenio Montale, *Selected Essays*, Manchester, 1978, p. 44.

308   'The perfect page': Jorge Luis Borges, 'La supersticiosa ética del lector', Buenos Aires, 1931, reprinted in *Discusión*, Buenos Aires, 1932, 'The Superstitious Ethics of the Reader', in *The Total Library: Non-Fiction 1922–1986*, edited by Eliot Weinberger, translated by Esther Allen, Suzanne Jill Levine and Eliot Weinberger, New York, 1999, reprinted Harmondsworth, 2001, p. 54.

315   'The strange thing is': Franz Kafka, *Der Prozess*, Berlin, 1925, edited by Malcolm Pasley, in *Kritische Ausgabe*, 1990, Frankfurt, app. 168.

315   'if you can manage': ibid., app. 168.

317   'We call that': Marcel Proust, *A la recherche du temps perdu*, Paris, 1913–1927, *Remembrance of Things Past*, translated by C. K. Scott Moncrieff, revised by Terence Kilmartin, further revised by D. J. Enright, London, 1992, vol. III, pp. 93–4, quoted in Malcolm Bowie, *Proust Among the Stars*, London, 1998, pp. 3–4.

319   'He realized': Franz Kafka, *Der Prozess*, Berlin, 1925, *The Trial*, translated by Breon Mitchell, New York, 1998, pp. 62–4.

323   Small magazine *Areté*: Craig Raine, 'Special K', *Areté*, no. 2.

324   'like everything that is spiritually': Franz Kafka, *Das Schloss*, edited by Malcolm Pasley, in *Kritische Ausgabe*, Frankfurt, 1982, p. 13, quoted by Roberto Calasso, *K*, Milan, 2002, translated by Geoffrey Brock, London, 2005, p. 60.

324   'and if they believed': Franz Kafka, *Das Schloss*, edited by Malcolm Pasley, in *Kritische Ausgabe*, Frankfurt, 1982, pp. 12–13, quoted by Roberto Calasso, *K*, Milan, 2002, translated by Geoffrey Brock, London, 2005, p. 60.

325   'How could she ensnare': Franz Kafka, *Der Prozess*, Berlin, 1925, *The Trial*, translated by Breon Mitchell, New York, 1998, pp. 61–2.

325   'What's truly comic': Franz Kafka, *The Castle*, Bürgel variant, SA 424.

327   'I was walking aimlessly': Robert Walser, 'Zwei kleine Sachen', II, May 1914, *Deutsche Monatshefte 'Die Rheinlande'*, translated by Nicole Taubes as 'Deux petites choses', in Robert Walser, *Petits textes poétiques*, Paris, 2005, pp. 149–50, translated by AT.

327   'experimenting in the linguistic field': quoted in the translator's preface to Robert Walser, *Masquerade and Other Stories*, translated by Susan Bernofsky, London, 1993, p. xxi.

329   'If I think about it': Franz Kafka, *Tagebücher*, 17, 9–10, quoted in Roberto Calasso, *K*, Milan, 2002, translated by Geoffrey Brock, London, 2005, p. 144.

329   'This reproach': Franz Kafka, *Tagebücher*, 18, 3–12, 21–6; 19, 1–10, quoted in Roberto Calasso, *K*, Milan, 2002, translated by Geoffrey Brock, London, 2005, p. 146.

330 'I've had to, you understand': Witold Gombrowicz, *Cosmos*, Paris, 1971, pp. 165–8, translated by AT.

331 'The tradesmen': Gertrude Stein, *Three Lives*, New York, 1909, reprinted Harmondsworth 1990, p. 3.

331 'For fifty years': Gustave Flaubert, 'Un Coeur Simple', *Trois Contes*, Paris, 1877, reprinted 1988, p. 157, translated by AT.

331 Gertrude's parrot: Gertrude Stein, *Three Lives*, New York, 1909, reprinted Harmondsworth, 1990, pp. 17–18.

332 'Cézanne conceived': quoted by Ann Charters, 'Introduction' to ibid., p. xiv.

332 'real black negress': ibid., p. 59.

332 'Love is like': Stendhal, *De l'amour*, Paris, 1822, *Love*, translated by Gilbert and Suzanne Sale, London, 1957, reprinted Harmondsworth, 1975, p. 28.

333 'Jeff never': Gertrude Stein, *Three Lives*, New York, 1909, reprinted Harmondsworth 1990, p. 110.

336 'He felt it at his temple': Franz Kafka, *The Blue Octavo Notebooks*, edited by Max Brod, translated by Ernst Kaiser and Eithne Wilkins, Cambridge, MA, 1991, p. 52.

336 'path through the desert ... *Éducation Sentimentale*': Franz Kafka, *The Diaries of Franz Kafka*, edited by Max Brod, translated by Martin Greenberg with the cooperation of Hannah Arendt, New York, 1949, reprinted London, 1999, pp. 393–4.

337 '"That was the happiest time"': Gustave Flaubert, *L'Éducation sentimentale*, Paris, 1869, *Sentimental Education*, translated by Robert Baldick, 1964, p. 419.

337 'So you like it': quoted in 'Introduction' to ibid., p. 13.

338 'supreme religious value': Bruno Schulz, 'Postface' to Franz Kafka, *The Trial*, Warsaw, 1936, reprinted in *Oeuvres Complètes*, traduit du polonais par Suzanne Arlet, Thérèse Douchy, Christophe Jezewski, François Lallier, Allan Kosko, Georges Lisowski, Georges Sidre, Dominique Sila-Khan, Paris, 2004, p. 382, translated by AT.

338 'a parallel reality': ibid., p. 385, translated by AT.

340 'tries to find': quoted in J. P. Stern's introduction to *The World of Franz Kafka*, as reported by R. J. Hollingdale in the *Times Literary Supplement*,

6 March 1981, reprinted in *The Modern Movement*, edited by John Gross, London, 1992, pp. 198–9.

340   'His relation to Kafka': Witold Gombrowicz, *Journal Tome II 1959–1969*, traduit par Dominique Autrand, Christophe Jezewski et Allan Kosko, Paris, 1995, p. 205, translated by AT.

340   'if we look for the source': Paul Valéry, 'Lettre sur Mallarmé', *La Revue de Paris*, 1 April 1927, Paris, reprinted in *Oeuvres*, edited by Jean Hytier, Paris, 1957, p. 635.

341   'Derivative writers': Vladimir Nabokov, *Strong Opinions*, New York, 1973, reprinted 1990, p. 95.

345   'But at around eleven in the morning': details from Jerzy Ficowski, *Regions of the Great Heresy: Bruno Schulz, A Biographical Portrait*, New York, 2003, pp. 135–6.

349   'Monday / ME': Witold Gombrowicz, *Journal Tome I 1953–1958*, traduit par Dominique Autrand, Christophe Jezewski et Allan Kosko, Paris, 1995, p. 17, translated by AT.

350   'I have just seen': Edmond and Jules de Goncourt, *Journal des Goncourt*, Paris, 1887–96, in *Pages from the Goncourt Journal*, edited, translated and introduced by Robert Baldick, Oxford, 1962, reprinted London, 1980, p. 251.

350   'I want to begin': Witold Gombrowicz, *Journal Tome II 1959–1969*, traduit par Dominique Autrand, Christophe Jezewski et Allan Kosko, Paris, 1995, p. 206, translated by AT.

350   'My nature never allowed me': ibid., p. 209, translated by AT.

350   'if there existed': ibid., p. 210, translated by AT.

350   'While he let himself': ibid., p. 214, translated by AT.

350   'I, on the contrary': ibid., pp. 215–16, translated by AT.

350   'were effectively conspirators': ibid., pp. 217–18, translated by AT.

351   'I reread the pages': ibid., p. 220, translated by AT.

352   'to relate imaginary events': Witold Gombrowicz, 'The Work of Bruno Schulz', *Kurier Poranny*, 112, 1938, in Witold Gombrowicz, *Varia I*, Paris, 1978, p. 93, traduit par Allan Kosko, translated by AT.

352   'not only imaginary events': ibid., p. 93, translated by AT.

352   'to construct his universe': ibid., p. 95, translated by AT.

353   'Immaturity': quoted by Susan Sontag in her 'Foreword' to Witold

Gombrowicz, *Ferdydurke*, translated by Danuta Borchardt, New Haven, 2000, p. viii.

353 'Why did I, as if thwarting': Witold Gombrowicz, *Ferdydurke*, translated by Danuta Borchardt, New Haven, 2000, pp. 4–5.

354 'reveals that all the main': Bruno Schulz, 'Ferdydurke', *Skamander*, July–September 1938, XCVI–XCVIII, Warsaw, 1938, in Bruno Schulz, *Oeuvres Complètes*, traduit du polonais par Suzanne Arlet, Thérèse Douchy, Christophe Jezewski, François Lallier, Allan Kosko, Georges Lisowski, Georges Sidre, Dominique Sila-Khan, Paris, 2004, pp. 442–52, p. 448, translated by AT.

354 'everyone must be aware': Witold Gombrowicz, *Ferdydurke*, Warsaw, 1937, translated by Danuta Borchardt, New Haven, 2000, pp. 5–6.

354 'suddenly the bell rings': ibid., p. 14.

355 'a new and revolutionary novelistic form': Bruno Schulz, 'Ferdydurke', *Skamander*, July–September 1938, XCVI–XCVIII, Warsaw, 1938, in Bruno Schulz, *Oeuvres Complètes*, traduit du polonais par Suzanne Arlet, Thérèse Douchy, Christophe Jezewski, François Lallier, Allan Kosko, Georges Lisowski, Georges Sidre, Dominique Sila-Khan, Paris, 2004, pp. 442–52, p. 442, translated by AT.

356 'the kitchen of our self': ibid., p. 446, translated by AT.

356 'Man cannot bear': ibid., p. 447, translated by AT.

356 'wrenched from an organism': ibid., pp. 449–50, translated by AT.

356 'one should not look for': Witold Gombrowicz, *Ferdydurke*, Warsaw, 1937, translated by Danuta Borchardt, New Haven, 2000, p. 69.

357 'I will prove that my construction': Witold Gombrowicz, *Ferdydurke*, Warsaw, 1937, translated by Danuta Borchardt, New Haven, 2000, p. 69.

357 'on a foundation': Witold Gombrowicz, *Ferdydurke*, Warsaw, 1937, translated by Danuta Borchardt, New Haven, 2000, p. 74.

358 'undertakes the attempt ... all family history': Bruno Schulz, *Oeuvres Complètes*, traduit du polonais par Suzanne Arlet, Thérèse Douchy, Christophe Jezewski, François Lallier, Allan Kosko, Georges Lisowski, Georges Sidre, Dominique Sila-Khan, Paris, 2004, p. 379, translated by AT.

359 'overcome by a strange vertigo': Bruno Schulz, *Sanatorium pod klepsydra*, Warsaw, 1937, reprinted in ibid., pp. 125–38, p. 134, translated by AT.

360 '*Cinnamon Shops* gives a certain': ibid., p. 658, translated by AT.

360 'Man cannot bear': Bruno Schulz, 'Ferdydurke', *Skamander*, July—September 1938, XCVI–XCVIII, Warsaw, 1938, in ibid., pp. 442–52, p. 447, translated by AT.

361 'On luminous mornings': Bruno Schulz, 'Août', in ibid., p. 19, translated by AT.

361 'A particular principle': Bruno Schulz, *Oeuvres Complètes*, traduit du polonais par Suzanne Arlet, Thérèse Douchy, Christophe Jezewski, François Lallier, Allan Kosko, Georges Lisowski, Georges Sidre, Dominique Sila-Khan, Paris, 2004, p. 658, translated by AT.

362 'Jews had a number of important': Philip Roth, *Shop Talk*, London, 2001, pp. 80–82.

362 'from my point of view': ibid., pp. 84–5.

364 'Art is charged': Witold Gombrowicz, *Journal*, Paris, 1957, Tome 1, 1953–1958, translated by Dominique Autrand, Christophe Jezewski and Allan Kosko, Paris, 1995, p. 93, translated by AT.

364 'To lose one's country': ibid., p. 96, translated by AT.

364 'what is to be done': Bruno Schulz, 'The Age of Genius', *Sanatorium pod klepsydra*, Warsaw, 1937, reprinted in Bruno Schulz, *The Street of Crocodiles & Sanatorium Under the Sign of the Hourglass*, London, 1988, p. 140.

365 'My ideal is to "mature"': quoted in Jerzy Ficowski, *Regions of the Great Heresy: Bruno Schulz, A Biographical Portrait*, New York, 2003, p. 157.

Volume V

372 'Monsieur Stern's jokes': quoted in Anne Bandry, 'The First French Translation of *Tristram Shandy*', *The Shandean*, vol. 6, November 1994, pp. 67–85, p. 68, translated by AT.

372 'My sister, I dare say': Laurence Sterne, *The Life and Opinions of Tristram Shandy, Gentleman*, London, 1759–67, reprinted Harmondsworth, 1985, p. 119.

372 'Ma soeur ne veut': quoted in Anne Bandry, 'The First French Translation of *Tristram Shandy*', *The Shandean*, vol. 6, November 1994, pp. 67–85, p. 73, translated by AT.

372 'motley emblem': Laurence Sterne, *The Life and Opinions of Tristram Shandy, Gentleman*, London, 1759–67, reprinted Harmondsworth, 1985, pp. 232–3.

373   'hélas / hélas': quoted in Anne Bandry, 'The First French Translation of
      Tristram Shandy', The Shandean, vol. 6, November 1994, pp. 67–85, p. 76.

375   'Voyage sentimental': bibliography in Alexander Pushkin, Pushkin on Liter-
      ature, edited and translated by Tatiana Wolff, London, 1986, pp. 485–522.

375   'Yet happiness had been': Alexander Pushkin, Eugene Onegin, St Peters-
      burg, 1833, translated by Vladimir Nabokov, New York, 1964, 4 vols.,
      vol. I, p. 317.

375   'Imagine what happened': quoted by Richard Pevear, 'Introduction', Leo
      Tolstoy, Anna Karenina, Moscow, 1873–77, translated by Richard Pevear
      and Larissa Volokhonsky, Harmondsworth, 2000, p. x

376   that poetry is purely subjective: Gustave Flaubert, Selected Letters, trans-
      lated by Geoffrey Wall, Harmondsworth, 1997, p. 217.

376   Argentine cult: Jorge Luis Borges, The Total Library: Non-Fiction 1922–1986,
      edited by Eliot Weinberger, translated by Esther Allen, Suzanne Jill
      Levine and Eliot Weinberger, Harmondsworth, 1999, p. 423.

376   'What is our Argentine': ibid., pp. 425–6.

376   'Virgilio, I said': Witold Gombrowicz, Diary, vol. 1, translated by Lillian
      Vallee, New York, 1988, p. 70.

378   'What is Argentina?': Witold Gombrowicz, Journal, Paris, translated by
      Lillian Vallee as Diary, edited by Jan Kott, vol. I, Chicago, 1988, reprinted
      in The Argentina Reader, edited by Gabriela Nouzeilles and Graciela
      Montaldo, Durham and London, 2002, pp. 319–23, p. 323.

378   'a genuine and creative protest': ibid.

378   'I was enthralled by': Witold Gombrowicz, Diary, vol. 1, translated by
      Lillian Vallee, New York, 1988, pp. 134–5.

378   'this international, sophisticated': ibid., pp. 135.

379   'living beings . . . a fond father, witty': quoted in Alexander Pushkin,
      Pushkin on Literature, edited and translated by Tatiana Wolff, London,
      1986, pp. 464–5.

381   'The hero of my novel': Alexander Pushkin, Eugene Onegin, St Peters-
      burg, 1833, translated by Vladimir Nabokov, New York, 1964, 4 vols., vol.
      I, p. 96.

381   'At a dull aunt's': ibid., p. 285.

382   'Now let us eavesdrop': ibid., p. 155.

382   'but now I am not in the mood': ibid., p. 256.

382   'Tatiana's letter': ibid, p. 168.

383 'Les Grands-Croix Commandeurs': quoted in Serena Vitale, *Il bottone di Pushkin*, Milan, 1995, translated by Ann Goldstein and Jon Rothschild, *Pushkin's Button*, London, 1999, p. 128.

383 'deeming it too low': Alexander Pushkin, 'On Prose', 1822, in *Pushkin on Literature*, selected, translated and edited by Tatiana Wolff, London, 1986, p. 43.

384 'demands matter and more': ibid., p. 43.

384 'Is it not simpler': Alexander Pushkin, 'Draft Notes on Tragedy', 1825, in *Pushkin on Literature*, selected, translated and edited by Tatiana Wolff, London, 1986, p. 130.

384 'You can think whatever': Denis Diderot, 'Eloge de Richardson', *Journal étranger*, 1761, reprinted in *Oeuvres*, edited by André Billy, 1951, p. 1094, translated by AT.

385 'My own fifty-year-old': Vladimir Nabokov, 'Commentary', Aleksandr Pushkin, *Eugene Onegin*, St Petersburg, 1833, translated by Vladimir Nabokov, 4 vols., New York, 1964, vol. II, p. 110.

386 'Can Pushkin's poem . . . true of translation': Vladimir Nabokov, 'Foreword' to ibid., vol. 1, pp. vii–viii.

387 'in losing its rhyme': ibid., p. ix.

388 'it is when the translator sets out': ibid.

388 'to my ideal of literalism': ibid., p. x.

388 'Perfect interlinear correspondence': ibid.

390 'the expression "a literal translation"': Vladimir Nabokov, 'The Art of Translation', *New Republic*, 4 August 1941.

390 Nabokov changed all Carroll's parodic: all this is taken from Simon Karlinsky, 'Anya in Wonderland: Nabokov's Russified Lewis Carroll', in *Nabokov: Criticism, reminiscences, translations and tributes*, edited by Alfred Appel, Jr, and Charles Newman, London, 1971, pp. 310–15, pp. 312–13.

392 'Softly he lays': Aleksandr Pushkin, *Eugene Onegin*, St Petersburg, 1833, translated by Vladimir Nabokov, 4 vols., New York, 1964, vol. 1, p. 250.

393 'He sang parting': ibid., p. 134.

393 'will oppose notions': quoted in Daniel Brewer, *The Discourse of Enlightenment in Eighteenth-Century France*, Cambridge, 1993, pp. 48–9.

395 said that when he translated the Bible: Jerome, 'Letter to Pammachius', 395, translated by Kathleen Davis, reprinted in *The Translation Studies Reader*, edited by Lawrence Venuti, New York and London, 2004, p. 24.

396   'one becomes convinced': André Gide, *The Journals of André Gide*, vol. 3, 1928–1939, translated by Justin O'Brien, 1949, quoted in Miriam Allott, *Novelists on the Novel*, London, 1959, reprinted 1980, p. 322.

397   'the classical case': Vladimir Nabokov, 'Commentary' to Aleksandr Pushkin, *Eugene Onegin*, St Petersburg, 1833, translated by Vladimir Nabokov, 4 vols., New York, 1964, vol. 2, p. 546.

401   'Joyce sitting': Vladimir Nabokov, *Strong Opinions*, New York, 1973, reprinted 1990, p. 86.

401   'I nurture no illusions': Vladimir Nabokov, 'Pouchkine, ou le Vrai et le Vraisemblable', Paris, *Nouvelle Revue Française*, 1 March 1937, translated by Dmitri Nabokov, 'Pushkin, or the Real and the Plausible', New York, *New York Review of Books*, 31 March 1988, pp. 38–42, p. 42.

403   'I have watched comedies': ibid.

404   'The very term': Vladimir Nabokov, 'Opredeleniia', New York, *c*. 1940, quoted by Alexander Dolinin in 'Nabokov as a Russian Writer', *The Cambridge Companion to Vladimir Nabokov*, edited by Julian W. Connolly, Cambridge, 2005, pp. 49–64, p. 57.

404   'I have always maintained': interview with Alfred Appel, Jr, Wisconsin, 1967, reprinted in *Strong Opinions*, New York, 1973, reprinted 1990, p. 63.

406   'In 1936, in the second issue': many of the facts and dates in this chapter are taken from Brian Boyd, *Vladimir Nabokov: The Russian Years*, Princeton, 1990.

407   'I strive now to imagine': Vladimir Nabokov, 'Mademoiselle O', *Mesures*, no. 2, 1936, pp. 147–72, p. 151, translated by AT.

407   'The anguish that I feel': ibid., pp. 153–4, translated by AT.

409   'I thought I might console myself': ibid., pp. 170–72, translated by AT.

410   'My enormous and morose': Vladimir Nabokov, 'Mademoiselle O', *The Atlantic Monthly*, January 1943, pp. 66–73, p. 73.

411   'the first thing which occurred': Vladimir Nabokov, *Drugie Berega*, New York, 1954, reprinted in *Sobranie sochinenii russkovo perioda v pyati tomakh*, St Petersburg, 2003, vol. 5, edited by M. V. Kozikova, p. 219, translated by AT.

411   'Sixty-five years later': Vladimir Nabokov, *Speak, Memory: An Autobiography Revisited*, London, 1967, reprinted Harmondsworth, 1969, pp. 91–3.

412   'the anonymous roller': ibid., p. 22.

412   'The memoir . . . became': Vladimir Nabokov, quoted in Harvey Breit,
        'Talk with Mr Nabokov', *New York Times Book Review*, 1 July 1951.

413   In her bibliography: *L'Arc*, Paris Issue 24, p. 88.

413   'I am no more guilty': Vladimir Nabokov, note to *Nabokov's Dozen*, 1958,
        reprinted in *Collected Stories*, edited with a preface and translated by
        Dmitri Nabokov, New York, 1995, reprinted Harmondsworth, 2001,
        p. 662.

413   'I have watched comedies': Vladimir Nabokov, 'Pouchkine, ou le Vrai
        et le Vraisemblable', Paris, *Nouvelle Revue Française*, 1 March 1937, trans-
        lated by Dmitri Nabokov, 'Pushkin, or the Real and the Plausible', New
        York, *New York Review of Books*, 31 March 1988, pp. 38–42, p. 42.

413   'That human life is': quoted and collated by Vladimir E. Alexandrov,
        Nabokov's Otherworld, Princeton, 1991, p. 57.

414   'I want to submit': Vladimir Nabokov, *Lectures on Literature*, New York,
        1980, edited by Fredson Bowers, p. 86.

415   'At bottom, I'm sure': Roger Pla to Rita Gombrowicz, November 1978, in
        Rita Gombrowicz, *Gombrowicz en Argentine 1939–1963*, Paris, 1984, p. 47.

415   'Axel Abrahamson': quoted in Brian Boyd, *Vladimir Nabokov: The Amer-
        ican Years*, London, 1991, p. 190.

416   '"Dear Hagen"': Vladimir Nabokov, *Pnin*, reprinted Harmondsworth,
        2000, p. 145.

416   '"Hope you are fine"': Vladimir Nabokov, *Lolita*, reprinted Har-
        mondsworth, 2000, p. 81.

416   'I remember a cartoon': Vladimir Nabokov, *Lectures on Literature*, edited
        by Fredson Bowers, New York, 1980, pp. 373–4.

418   'My knowledge of Mr Forster's works': Vladimir Nabokov, *Strong Opin-
        ions*, New York, 1973, reprinted 1990, p. 95.

418   'I have never experienced': ibid., p. 69.

419   'Very lovely, very lonesome': Vladimir Nabokov, *Speak, Memory*, London,
        1967, reprinted Harmondsworth, 1969, p. 78.

420   'my reader has never yet': Laurence Sterne, *The Life and Opinions of Tris-
        tram Shandy, Gentleman*, London, 1759–67, reprinted Harmondsworth,
        1985, p. 101.

420   'Through the smells of the bog': Vladimir Nabokov, *Speak, Memory: An Auto-
        biography Revisited*, London, 1967, reprinted Harmondsworth, 1969, p. 109.

421   'clear, but weirdly misleading': ibid., p. 221.

421   'the mysteries of the irrational': Vladimir Nabokov, *Nikolai Gogol*, New York, 1959, reprinted 1971, p. 55.

422   'In this life': Vladimir Nabokov, 'Parizhskaya Poema', Cambridge, MA, 1943, translated by Vladimir Nabokov, 'The Paris Poem', in *Poems and Problems*, London, 1972, pp. 114–25, pp. 123–5.

423   'rich, infinitely rich': Vladimir Nabokov, *Strong Opinions*, New York, 1973, reprinted 1990, p. 15.

424   'I am only troubled now': Vladimir Nabokov, postscript to *Lolita*, translated into Russian by the author, New York, 1967, cited and translated by Irwin Weil, in 'Odyssey of a Translator', in *Nabokov: Criticism, reminiscences, translations and tributes*, edited by Alfred Appel, Jr, and Charles Newman, London, 1971, pp. 266–83, p. 282.

424   'When I saw in the fog': quoted by Nina Berberova in 'Nabokov in the Thirties', in ibid., pp. 220–33, p. 230.

425   *Je suis dépaysé*: Vladimir Nabokov, interview with Bernard Pivot, *Antenne 2*, 30 May 1975.

425   'passionate intrigue': Vladimir Nabokov, *Pnin*, New York, 1957, reprinted Harmondsworth, 2000, p. 33.

425   'Harm is the norm': ibid., p. 22.

426   'with a moan': ibid., pp. 144–5.

426   'a great truck': ibid., pp. 159–60.

426   'the little sedan': ibid.

427   'Kundera's an émigré': Bohumil Hrabal, 'Public Suicide', Prague, 1990, reprinted in *Total Fears*, translated by James Naughton, Prague, 1998, pp. 35–6.

429   'a true feeler': Laurence Sterne, *The Letters of Laurence Sterne*, edited by Lewis Perry Curtis, Oxford, 1935, p. 411.

429   'In reality, every reader': Marcel Proust, *À la Recherche du Temps Perdu*, 3 vols, edited by P. Clarac and A. Ferré, Paris, 1954, vol. 3, p. 911.

430   'People imagine': Albert Camus, 'Problèmes du roman', *Confluences*, July 1943, translated as 'Intelligence and the Scaffold' by Philip Thody in *Albert Camus, Selected Essays and Notebooks*, Harmondsworth, 1970, reprinted 1979, p. 185.

ACKNOWLEDGEMENTS

The Delighted States is in many ways the product of my friendship with the poet, critic, editor – and my former tutor – Craig Raine. And so he is inevitably one of the characters – advising, disagreeing, exasperated. This book is part of a very long conversation. His ideas and examples are everywhere: I have acknowledged specific debts where I can, but I am sure some have escaped me. And some are too integral to be given specific form. In particular, I want to acknowledge how much I owe him for my idea of style; for the transformation – central to this book, and to myself – of style as a system of sentences, into style as a quality of vision.

I am also indebted to Ann Pasternak Slater for encouraging me to learn (unsuccessfully) Russian; for enduring many boring conversations with me in my broken, badly pronounced version of Russian; and for persuading her relatives in Moscow to look after me for six weeks.

Irina Duddell patiently and courageously made the attempt to teach me Russian, for which I am very grateful.

In Moscow, I was cared for with drastic generosity and charm by Petya and Moura Pasternak, Asya Pasternak, Anya Margolis, and especially Dilshat Harman and her sister Zhenya.

I am deeply grateful to the estate of Vladimir Nabokov, for permission to translate 'Mademoiselle O'; and for the detailed corrections and encouragement which Dmitri Nabokov lavished on the draft translation.

Michael Sheringham and Gully Cragg provided help with my translations from French, and corrected many mistakes; Malcolm Bowie and Noel Malcolm both read this book in typescript, and made many valuable suggestions. Sadly, Malcolm Bowie died while this book was in press – as did another much loved teacher of mine, A. D. Nuttall, who had been my tutor at New College, Oxford.

This book could not have been completed without the generosity of two unique institutions. I am very grateful to the Fellows of All Souls College, Oxford – and in particular to its Warden, John Davis – for electing me to a

Prize Fellowship. The Baronessa Beatrice Monti von Rezzori, at the Santa Maddelena Foundation in Donnini, provided a crucial month in which to concentrate on this book, and also her own delicate, unforgettable advice on style.

Without the help of the librarians at the Bodleian Library, Taylorian Library, Slavonic Library, English Faculty Library and Codrington Library, all in Oxford, as well as the British Library in London, I could not have written this book.

Some sentences and paragraphs of this book formerly appeared, variously disguised, in *Areté*, the *Guardian*, the *Jewish Chronicle*, *Modern Painters* and *Le Monde*; and in an introduction to Willa and Edwin Muir's translation into English of Franz Kafka's *Metamorphosis and Other Stories*, published by Vintage.

Some chapters of this book were also prompted by invitations to speak on three occasions – to celebrate the centenary of Isaac Bashevis Singer at the 2005 London Jewish Book Week; at a conference in honour of Malcolm Bowie, organised by the Cambridge Research Centre for Arts, Social Sciences and Humanities; and at the Victoria and Albert Museum, in a talk on modernism with Benjamin Markovits.

At my agency, Rogers, Coleridge and White, I have been constantly – often daily – supported by Laurence Laluyaux, Stephen Edwards, Lisa Baker, Susannah Gowers, Rowan Routh and Jenny Hewson.

Peter Straus's erudition, good humour, scowls and affection were a constant and necessary condition for the writing of this project.

I am extremely grateful to my editor at Jonathan Cape – Dan Franklin – for his benign and informed enthusiasm for this quixotic project; and to Courtney Hodell, my editor at Farrar, Straus and Giroux, for her meticulous and incisive reading of the typescript. Alex Bowler calmly and thoroughly solved every editorial problem which occurred during the book's production; Andrew Armitage provided the rich and various indexes.

Suzanne Dean worked generously and tirelessly on the design of the book, making it a far more beautiful and elegant object than it deserves to be. Lily Richards patiently searched for pictures, which I almost always remembered in the wrong locations – and came up with her own rarer, more unusual and more evocative images.

Devastatingly, and politely, Julian Barnes forced me to rethink the provenance of several Flaubertian images, for which I am very grateful.

468

Above all, I would like to thank my family: my parents, John and Angela Thirlwell, who have been my first, most patient and most altruistic readers; my sister, Zoë Thirlwell; and my grandfather Alfred Goldman.

The author is grateful for permission to reproduce text and images from the following: Valery Larbaud's letters, translated by permission of IMEC, Paris. *Chekhov: Comic Stories*, translated by Harvey Pitcher (Andre Deutsch, 2004), reproduced by permission of Andre Deutsch. 'Ward Number Six' by Anton Chekhov, translated by Constance Garnett, reproduced by permission of Granta Books. *The Adventures of Augie March* by Saul Bellow © 1953, Saul Bellow, reprinted by permission of The Wylie Agency (UK) Ltd, 17 Bedford Square, London, WC1B 3JA. *The Autobiography of Alice B. Toklas* by Gertrude Stein (Penguin), reprinted by permission of David Higham Associates, 5–8 Lower John Street, Golden Square, London, W1F 9HA. *The Bays Are Sere* by Edouard Dujardin, translated by Anthony Suter (Libris, 1991), reproduced by permission of Libris Ltd, 26 Lady Margaret Road, London, NW5 2XL. *The Charterhouse of Parma* by Stendhal, translation © 1999, Richard Howard. First published 1999 by the Modern Library, an imprint of Random House Inc., New York. *Don Quixote* by Cervantes (translated by Charles Jarvis, 1999 edition), *Jacques le Fataliste* by Diderot (1999 edition), *War and Peace* by Tolstoy (translated by A. & L. Maude), 'On the Cart' by Chekhov (translated by Ronald Hingley), *A Life* by Maupassant (translated by Roger Pearson, 1999 edition): all reproduced by permission of Oxford University Press. *A Sentimental Journey* by Laurence Sterne (1963 edition) and *Posthumous Memoirs of Brás Cubas* by Machado de Assis (translated by Gregory Rabassa, 1998 edition). Both reproduced by permission of Oxford University Press, Inc. *Three Lives* by Gertrude Stein reprinted by permission of Peter Owen Ltd., London. *Flaubert in Egypt: A Sensibility on Tour* by Gustave Flaubert, translated and edited by Francis Steegmuller, copyright © Francis Steegmuller, 1972, reprinted with permission of McIntosh & Otis, Inc. *Dangling Man* by Saul Bellow (Penguin Books, 1997), copyright © Saul Bellow, 1944, reprinted by permission of Penguin Books Ltd. *Madame Bovary* by Gustave Flaubert, translated by Geoffrey Wall (Penguin Books, 1993), copyright in this translation © Geoffrey Wall, 1993, reprinted by permission of Penguin Books Ltd. *Species of Spaces and Other Pieces* by George Perec, translated by John Sturrock (Penguin, 1997), copyright © John Sturrock, 1997, reprinted by permission of Penguin Books Ltd.

ACKNOWLEDGEMENTS

Short Sentimental Journey by Italo Svevo, translation © Secker & Warburg, reprinted by permission of The Random House Group Ltd. *A Moveable Feast* by Ernest Hemingway, published by Scribner, reprinted by permission of Simon and Schuster, Inc. *in our time* by Ernest Hemingway, published by Scribner, reprinted by permission of Simon and Schuster, Inc. *Dancing Lessons for the Advanced in Age* by Bohumil Hrabal, published by Harcourt, reprinted by permission of Harcourt, Inc. *The Trial* by Franz Kafka, published by Schocken Books, reprinted by permission of Random House, Inc. *Total Fears: Letters to Dubenka* by Bohumil Hrabal, translated by James Naughton, reprinted by permission of Twisted Spoon Press, Prague. 'The Overcoat' by Nikolai Gogol, translated by Constance Garnett, reproduced by permission of A. P. Watt Ltd on behalf of the Executors of the Estate of Constance Garnett. *Pedagogical Sketchbook* by Paul Klee, translated by Sibyl Moholy-Nagy (Faber and Faber, 1953), first published by the Bauhaus in 1925. Reprinted by permission of the Klee Estate, Zentrum Paul Klee, Bern. Vladimir Nabokov's French version of 'Mademoiselle O', together with Adam Thirlwell's English-language translation of the text and excerpts from the works of Vladimir Nabokov, appear here by arrangement with the Estate of Vladimir Nabokov. All rights reserved.

DE

GUY DE MAUPASSANT

MONT-ORIOL

DESSINS DE F. BAC

Graves sur bois par G. *LEMOINE*

PARIS

SOCIÉTÉ D'ÉDITIONS LITTÉRAIRES ET ARTISTIQUES

Librairie Paul Ollendorff

50, CHAUSSÉE D'ANTIN, 50

1901

Второе изданіе

і (портретомъ Н. Н. Пушкиной и сценой дуэли по
стихотвореніями и **500 письмами** Пушкина.

ОДНОТОМНАГО ИЗДАНІЯ:

$\Big\{$ на обыкнов. бумагѣ **1** р. **50** к.
$\phantom{\Big\{}$ » лучшей » **2** „ — „

$\Big\{$ на обыкнов. бумагѣ **2** „ **50** „
$\phantom{\Big\{}$ » лучшей › **3** „ — „

---

40 коп.; за роскошный каленкоровый съ золотомъ—1
ію—за 3 фунта. Переплетъ увеличиваетъ вѣсъ на 1

THE

R K S

OF

CE STERNE:

'R VOLUMES:

NTAINING

AND OPINIONS

M SHANDY, GENT.;

ENTAL JOURNEY

ANCE AND ITALY;

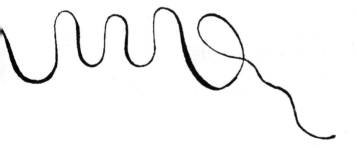

504

 pp. ix, x, xiv, 189, 193, 195, 197, 199, 201
by Paul Klee from his *Pedagogical Sketchbook*, 1925
© DACS, London 2008

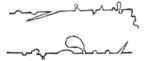 p. 201 by Paul Klee from his *Pedagogical Sketchbook*, 1925 © DACS, London 2007

 p. 167 from *Tristram Shandy* by Laurence Sterne

 p. 167 from *Tristram Shandy* by Laurence Sterne

 p. 167 from *Tristram Shandy* by Laurence Sterne

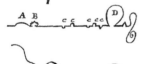 p. 168 from *Tristram Shandy* by Laurence Sterne

 p. 168 from *Tristram Shandy* by Laurence Sterne

 pp. v, xiii, 169, 194
Trim's flourish from *Tristram Shandy*

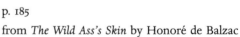 p. 185
from *The Wild Ass's Skin* by Honoré de Balzac

pp. xv, 191
'The Line of Beauty' from *The Analysis of Beauty*, 1753, by William Hogarth

Недугъ, котораго причину
Давно бы отыскать пора,
Подобный Англійскому *сплину*,
Короче: Русская *хандра*
Имъ овладѣла по немногу;
Онъ застрѣлиться, слава Богу,
Попробовать не захотѣлъ:
Но къ жизни вовсе охладѣлъ.
Какъ *Child-Horald*, угрюмый, томный
Въ гостиныхъ появлялся онъ;
Ни сплетни свѣта, ни бостонъ,
Ни милый взглядъ, ни вздохъ нескромный,
Ничто не трогало его,
Не замѣчалъ онъ ничего.

XXXIX. XL. XLI.

. . . .
. . . .
. . . .

JOYCE

YSSES

EL INGENIOSO HIDALGO

N QUIXOT

E LA MANCHA

COMPUESTA POR

uèl DE CERVANTI
SAAVEDRA.

*uy bellas Eſtampas, gravadas ſo
Dibujos de Coypel, primer Pinto
de el Rey de Françia.*

N QUATRO TOMOS.

MO PRIMERO

COLLECTION MICHEL LÉVY

— **1 franc le volume** —

1 franc 25 centimes à l'étranger

GUSTAVE FLAUBERT

MADAME
BOVARY

— MŒURS DE PROVINCE —

I

PARIS

MICHEL LÉVY FRÈRES, LIBRAIRES-ÉDITEURS

RUE VIVIENNE, 2 BIS

—

1857

Rouen, coédition
Alinéa, éd. Point de vues, Libr. Élisabeth Brunet

Mademoiselle O

Mademoiselle O

Vladimir Nabokov

With a translation by Adam Thirlwell

FARRAR, STRAUS AND GIROUX

NEW YORK

In a book, I lent my hero's childhood the governess to whom I owe the pleasure of understanding French. I say 'I lent', but it would be more accurate to say: 'My hero took her.' For it is truly distressing to see how these dull characters, issuing from the dark moonlight of the inkwell, abuse the beautiful things and dear faces which one provides for them, to the point of, little by little, depopulating one's own past. In the same way a doting forbear – perhaps from a kind of laziness and to sidestep the labour of keeping alive an entire past – might give his grand-nephew, on his wedding day, some object replete with memories, one of those objects which no longer has any beauty, or meaning, apart from the fact that they have existed, a fact which no longer means anything to the person who receives the humble and useless thing, which is placed in a corner and immediately forgotten. I have often observed this singular phenomenon of sentimental disproportion when, making a present to my fictitious characters not of great swathes of my past – I am too miserly for that, – but of some image which I believed I could easily do without, I have observed, I say, that the beautiful thing I gave perished in the atmosphere of the imagination in which I abruptly placed it. Nevertheless it persisted in my memory as if it had become foreign to me. What's more, from then on it had more of an affinity with the novel in which I had imprisoned it than with that warm and live past in which it had been so well sheltered from my literary art. On the other hand, as I have just remarked, the character to whom I made the gift of a tree beneath which I had

played, a path down which I had run, a play of light which celebrated like a firework some unforgettable event in my childhood
festivities, seemed not to attach any value to it or even took on the
discomforted air of a person who does not know what to do with
the old-fashioned ornament he is offered. It is in this way that the
portrait of my old French teacher – she made it her little point of
honour to be called a teacher and not governess, – a word which
made one think, she would say, of some old maid full of austere
puritan instincts who might run the household of a difficult bachelor, – it is in this way then that her portrait, or rather certain
details of her portrait, seem to me to be lost forever, bound up as
they are with the description of a childhood which to me is totally
foreign. So, the idea came to me of saving what remains of this
image, particularly since I have always had the desire to revive for
my own pleasure, and also as a sign of posthumous gratitude, the
exact inflection which the French language gave to my life in Russia.

Since I have hardly ever lived in a country where this language
might be spoken, I have lost the habit of it, so that it is an unheard-
of task, an exhausting labour simply to seize hold of the moder-
ately precise words which clamour to clothe my thought. I feel a
very painful sense of suffocation, accompanied by the fear of
spoiling things, in other words of contenting myself with terms
which I have the luck to meet with on my way – instead of searching
with love for the radiant word which is dying from its wait behind
the mist, the vague, the not-quite in which my thought hesitates.
I wonder, moreover, what Mademoiselle O would think of these
lines if she were still alive and could read me – she who regarded
with such horror my spelling mistakes, and my unheard-of turns
of phrase.

I have just called her by her real name, for 'Mademoiselle O' is
by no means the abbreviation of a name beginning with O. This
O, exposed to all the winds of a hiatus, is not the capital of Olivier
nor Orose nor even Oudinet, but is the name itself; a round and

naked name which, written down, seems to be off balance without a full stop to prop it up; a wheel that has come off and which remains upright, about to crash; an open mouth; a world; an apple; a lake. She had in fact spent half her life beside a lake, for it was in Switzerland that Mademoiselle O was born, incidentally, of French parentage; and with this Lake Leman as a backdrop, her name took on all the allures of a *chanson de geste* or a novel, made one think of Lancelot of the Lake or Oberon, but without shaking off, alas, that easy mockery which the eye and ear of a child were quick to discover. For soon, once she had given my brother and me the power to speak her language, – a weapon which was turned against her – it became a way of enraging her horribly; we derived everything we could from this distressed name: we made it bounce like a ball, invented puns, imagined Mademoiselle's father arriving at some watering place, which – preceded by an exclamation – gave the stupid formula of four Os following each other in a row. The worst was that in the pink squat volume which was her bedside book – I mean *Larousse* – the first name which came under the letter O was that of François, marquis d'O, born and died in Paris, Finance Minister, whom we made into Mademoiselle's entirely legendary ancestor (which annoyed her because she would have liked to believe it herself).

Very stout, completely round like her name, Mademoiselle O arrived among us when I was entering my sixth year. Her bosom, her thick black eyebrows which made each other's acquaintance, the quivering of her jowls when she sat herself down – letting her monstrous backside descend little by little, then at the last moment commending her soul to God and sitting down for good with a terrifying crackling (when it was one of those woven wicker chairs of which our country house was full); what's more, a reddish complexion which in great moments of repressed anger attained a purple around the region of her second and third chins which extended regally over the blouse which she wore on Sundays; a

hint of moustache, steel-grey eyes behind one of those old pince-nez whose lenses, largely and darkly inserted, could not hide their genetic similarity to the spectacles from which they were still not differentiated; and then still there was a forehead with three wrinkles swallowed up by the curve of an abundant black hairdo which was becoming grey in an atmosphere of supreme mystery, – all this gave Mademoiselle O a severe, even rebarbative appearance.

As if destiny, wanting to do things properly, correct down to the last detail, had wanted to present a Russia as Russian as possible to the foreign visitor, it so happened that it was the single winter of my childhood that I spent in the country and not the city, a particularly ungracious winter, which enveloped the arrival of Mademoiselle in that abundance of snow which she had probably imagined to herself the day before her distant and dangerous journey. In the arrival of these foreigners to Muscovy there still remained a little of that frisson of adventure which in the olden days accompanied the deluge of French, Germans and Italians of every profession, beginning with the architect who breathed a little of the bronzed air of Rome into the dome of an orthodox temple, continuing with the naturalist, the enlightened merchant, the young tutor (disciple of Jean-Jacques), down to the motley and shivering crowd of hairdressers, hatmakers and courtesans. Several of these travellers have left their mark: Cagliostro who arrives, drawn by the empire of the North; Diderot who, in his audience with Catherine, strikes distractedly the imperial knee with his chubby little hairy hand, the better to emphasise the idea he is suggesting; Marat's brother who teaches French to Russian schoolchildren. But there is also an enormous influx of anonymous nurses, for during the nineteenth century there probably did not exist a single noble family throughout Russia which did not have its French governess, its fräulein or its Miss Jones. Each of these women stayed with the same family for many years, sometimes a lifetime; she became part of it, even while remaining in a slightly false position: always rele-

gated to the end of the table, with the poor relation and the estate manager she detested; never marrying; never learning Russian; living therefore an unreal life, full of a traditional nostalgia which was a support to her more than a cause of suffering, and with a certain feeling of contempt for the people who had welcomed her not as a live person, but rather as a necessary and thousand times repeated detail of their everyday existence – like the furniture which no one notices before the day when it is carried off to the hayloft.

So, it is in a winter twilight that Mademoiselle gets off at the small station from which there are still ten kilometres to cover in a sledge before arriving at our house. I strive now to imagine what she saw and felt as she came, this old demoiselle on her first long journey and whose entire Russian vocabulary consisted of one single word which ten years later she would take back with her to Switzerland: the word 'gdye' which means 'where is it?', but which, leaving her mouth like the raucous cry of a lost bird, developed such a force of interrogation that it satisfied all Mademoiselle's needs: 'Gdye? gdye?' she would repeat, not only to know the place where she was or the direction to follow, but in that way giving you to understand an entire world of suffering: that she was foreign, shipwrecked, without resources, and that she was searching for the Eldorado where at last she would be comprehended.

I imagine her getting off on her own at the little frozen station in the grey twilight; a few rare lights stain with an oily yellow the darkness which does not seem to descend from the sky, but to rise from behind the vaguely blueish clouds. It was, I think, very cold, a classic Russian cold whose measure was taken by the enormous Réaumur thermometer which each station owned . . . The door of the waiting room opened, giving out the long screak of our great icy nights – and a puff of hot air came out, as thick as the steam from the train with its conical chimney and fan-shaped snow plough. I see our coachman who is waiting for Mademoiselle, a coarse brown man with a red belt, his gloves fit for a giant emerge

from the belt into which he has stuffed them, and I hear the snow which creaks beneath his arctic boots. With anguish Mademoiselle mounts the sledge, clinging to the man with a terrible fear of feeling the sledge move off before her ample and weak forms might be fixed properly in place, panting, groaning and at last, with an 'ouf!' which creates a small cloud in the frozen mist, installing herself, finally in her seat, her two hands buried in her nasty little fur muff; and then executing the jolt backwards which every traveller in a sledge makes at the abrupt moment when the horses, with an effort of the knees, withdraw from the snow this still weighty object which moans and then immediately, as if entering a new atmosphere, slips silently over a road which it hardly seems to touch.

All at once, and only for an instant, I see Mademoiselle in the sledge, accompanied by an enormous shadow which – clinging to its own muff – passes in silhouette, stretches itself out, curves on the snow where a lantern follows it with a look, and then loses itself, leaving Mademoiselle to sink on her own into what she will happily call 'the steppe'. From time to time she turns round with difficulty to see if – at a distance which always stays the same, as if in some optical illusion – the vague form of another sledge, bearer of her trunk and hatbox, is following her. Then her glance which searches the snowy shadows believes it has seen the shining eyes of wolves light up here and there but which in truth are only the village lights – which some accident of snow and darkness makes appear for a tiny instant. Without doubt there is a moon there – it also belongs to our wintry ardours, – very large, very clear and completely round, the ideal aspect of Mademoiselle O's name, who contemplates it through eyelashes prismatic with frost; it slips, this moon like a great round velvet-backed mirror, among a pied crowd of small identical clouds which catch the reflection of a lost rainbow in the place where it skims past, illuminating them . . .

Mademoiselle is cold despite her cloak, – she is sad as well,

'spent', she will say later, 'frozen to the very marrow of my bones'. It is as if she has been travelling like this 'for centuries' (hyperbole comes easily to her), that her trunk is no longer in the sledge which is following her, that finally the coachman is a brigand in disguise who, in the blackness of this pine forest, where the horse races along with a muffled jingling of sleigh bells, is going to rob her, even cut her throat, 'what do I know!'; but the wood has now been crossed and once more the plain unfolds with telegraph poles, all along the road, which seem of different heights according to the depth of snow which envelops their base. Then, they are passing a village, a sombre whiteness, cunningly blanketed, without fires, or sounds of life; and the snow on the roofs is one with the snow bordering the road, which the moon, now risen higher, begins to glaze, in such a way that soon the tracks of the sledge shine, while each irregularity, each little lump of snow is marked by an amplification of limitless shadow.

This world opened up to us by our memory is admirable for the perfectly pure and healthy things to be found in it. What we remember, while intensely affecting our senses, does not harm them. The icy wind which once was the cause of pneumonia reaches us now in all its intensity, but is absolutely inoffensive: a vague promise perhaps of the future state of our soul, where the universe will appear in a sort of abstract beatitude. It is in this way that with complete impunity and without harming my old and fearful body, I can make my memory slip into the depths of a snowy night to remember as well – leaving this icy gulf with a beat of my wing – the warmth, the well-being which reigns in this house – Mademoiselle used to call it a *chateau* – towards which the sledge is bringing her with the pronounced and acute ringing of its bells. The anguish that I feel now when I remember the beautiful house where I lived as a child has nothing to do with those political events which, to use a journalistic cliché, have overturned my country. I find nothing but amusement in these political events. It is on a

whole other level and according to a turn of mind which is not concerned with the accidents of history that my memory moves and rests. No, I do not sigh the sigh of an exile, unless the life of a mature man may be a type of exile in relation to his first fervour. If even today I were the peaceable citizen of a Russia which allowed me to follow my vocation in complete liberty, with the same anguish I would remember the first form, the true image of the things and beings growing old around me. For this truth which I am looking for, I only knew in my childhood and the small amount of good which is found in my books is nothing but its reflection. It is the old lamp which, in the gloaming, is brought in; its reflection returned by the window which in a moment will hide itself away for the night behind its wooden shutters; then the pink lampshade descending over the lamp which immediately animates the little marquises who decorate, in their silk medallions, its vermilion fringes. The oval mirror hung on the wall at an angle which makes the furniture and the yellow parquet it reflects seem to slide from its arms and fall eternally into an abyss of light; the delicate clicking of the chandelier's crystals, when someone moves something in the room upstairs; the unforgettable engravings on the walls, – the same which I happened to come across once more in some hotel room or waiting room, as if I wanted to collect them again so that I might decorate a house to which I would one day return; the marble Diana who, in her corner, seems to look obliquely at my miniature tricycle. Helterskelter I remember all these things as if my past had just woken up with a start, with burning cheeks, dishevelled hair, slightly mad eyes – but when I want to restore some order to my memory, its colour and its sparkle escape me.

On the evening I'm speaking about, we were probably sitting round that table covered with its wax cloth, in which my finger would always enlarge with its nail a small stain to make it rapidly into a hole. By we, I mean my brother and I, and then Miss Jones who, with an ironic displeasure, occasionally looks at her watch,

because the unknown woman, the Frenchwoman, the one who is going to replace her in the family, is late in her arrival from the station, – simple professional displeasure, whose ironic point is due to her perfect knowledge of all the hardship attendant on the responsibility which awaits Mademoiselle O. The clock makes a loud tick-tock and its bronze disc, passing and repassing in its glass prison, shines, goes out, and shines once more. We are, I suppose, midway through drawing in some large notebooks. How I used to love those coloured pencils! The green which creates, as it whirls, a dishevelled tree, the blue of which a single horizontal line forms a maritime horizon. Above all I loved the little purple gentleman who had become so short from overuse that I could hardly hold him between my fingers; on the other hand, the white pencil, white crow, thin albino, had remained very long – until the moment, however, when I understood that, far from being devoid of existence, as it seemed to me when it left no trace on the white paper, it was truly the ideal pencil, for I could imagine to myself everything I wanted as I scribbled lines on the page, which were obviously invisible, but they were there, since the point became shorter and shorter.

Those pencils, I shared those out as well among the characters who appear in my books, so that now I no longer try to remember their first form. Somewhere I have stored away this hanging mirror and the smoking lamp. I have few things left. I have squandered most of them. Completely round, his white muzzle buried in the fold of his thigh, the old basset sleeps on a cushion embroidered with roses, and a loud sigh occasionally makes an appearance to inflate his flanks. He is so old and his sleep is so muffled by layers of dreams that he only reacts when at last from outside comes the sound of horseshoes, then a door which opens with a clank, at last here is the unknown woman, Mademoiselle.

A child is generally a conservative. I could not bear the idea that Mademoiselle was going to change any of my habits. The

chronological order, the mechanism of the day seemed to me to be immutable, since I was used to them. For example there was the glass of milk which Mademoiselle, in her language which was a little larger than life, used to call, when she saw me swallow it in great haste on a hot afternoon: 'this big bowl of iced fat'; perhaps also played a part that disgust which the obese person, who is not a cannibal, feels for a food which recalls his own flesh. So, I could not countenance the softened temperature which Mademoiselle wanted to give my drink by rewarming the glass between her palms. What's more, I disliked her hands immediately. At that age we intimately know the hands of adults thanks to our small height and because these hands flutter constantly at our childhood's level, descending from the superior clouds where faces reside. That is why I knew very fast what there was to learn about Mademoiselle's hands: they were quite small, with ugly skin, liver-spotted, a little shiny as well and cold to the touch, with swollen wrists and white patches on her nails. No one had ever stroked my face, whereas from the start Mademoiselle used to perform that unaccustomed gesture, which threw me into a melancholy stupor, of dabbing my cheek solicitously with her clumsy hand. Later there also came what she called, according to the degree of force used, a tap, slap or blow; this last, executed at high speed, resembled what tennis players call a backhand smash, and generally reached the ear. My brother received more than I did. Nevertheless, he also loved Mademoiselle more than I did; as a punishment, she often made him copy out fifty times the phrase 'the person who loves well, punishes well', which she had first written out in her pretty round handwriting with its slightly infantile grace, which singularly contrasted with Mademoiselle's heavy and gauche gait (while she always asserted in spite of everything that all slightly stout women waltz better than skinny ones). All her gestures come back to me as soon as I think of her hands: her way of sharpening a pencil, holding the point towards her immense bust enveloped in emerald

wool, towards her monstrous and infertile breast, which would rise with the pronounced movement peculiar to those for whom breathing is a privilege, since the poor woman was asthmatic and suffered from terrible attacks; then, that way she had of twiddling her little finger very fast in her ear, her elbow cocked. And then the unforgettable ritual which took place every time she gave me a new exercise book for dictation: I can clearly see her take out this black waxy notebook, – always panting a little, her mouth always slightly open and making a little sound like 'peuh . . . peuh . . . peuh . . .'; she would open this notebook to make a margin, that is to say she would trace a vertical line with her nail, then fold back the external edge of the page, which she would press down hard in this position letting the palm of her hand slide over it, then return this page to its liberty, smoothing it with a small final gesture and making the open notebook somersault in such a way that it placed itself ready for anything in front of me. She also had a special rite for each new pen, which she would moisten with saliva, accompanied by an indrawn whistle before it was given its baptism of ink. With great care and entirely delighting in an orgy of calligraphy, all the more excitedly since the preceding notebook always finished in hideous scribble, with exquisite care I traced the word 'dictation' while Mademoiselle searched in a book of 'choice pieces' for the substance of what she would call 'a good dictation'.

Meanwhile the décor has changed: no longer, outdoors, is there this dazzlement of snow beneath a sky almost violet in its effort to be blue; no longer are there these trees whose every minuscule branch is sketched by frost, making each tree an embroidered ghost; no, it is no longer a winter landscape, but a beautiful shining summer's day, with the tender green of the buds emerging against the pines' blackness, for my memory has made short work of transporting Mademoiselle from one day to another. And no longer are we writing out a dictation, my brother and I; 'a full stop, that's it', Mademoiselle had said, closing her Martin and Feuillet, – now it is

reading, this daily reading, traditional, repeated eternally by my memory; reading, during which Mademoiselle blossoms.

What an immense number of volumes she read to us on those afternoons spotted with sun, on the veranda! Her fine voice unspooled, unspooled through all these books, without ever weakening, without the slightest pause or stutter, an admirable reading machine, which seemed entirely distinct from Mademoiselle's sick lungs. The entire *bibliothèque rose* and then Jules Verne, Victor Hugo, Dumas *père*, – endless novels from which perhaps she derived as keen a pleasure as we did, however impassive she seemed; one of her chins, the smallest, but the true one, was, apart from her lips, the only moving point in her ample and immobile whole. The black pincers of her formidable pince-nez accomplished their task with such diligence that you believed you could feel them embed themselves on either side of her upturned nose in order to meet again inside, like two teams of labourers digging from opposing sides the Saint-Gothard tunnel, this tunnel which was one of the seven wonders of Mademoiselle's world. Sometimes, without troubling in any way the pure and composed voice, her little finger would quickly hide itself away in her ear in order to vibrate there briefly, or a fly would inspect the severe forehead whose wrinkles immediately began to move, without anything changing the expression of this face which so often I tried to draw, – the jowls tempted my sly pencil in an irresistible way.

'Ah, we loved each other so much!' said Mademoiselle several years later, when she would evoke her arrival among us and the beginning of our life together, – 'when you were little, dirty little pigs, but we loved each other so much!' And she would remember all the obstacles I had leaped over in order to arrive faster at these readings on the veranda, she remembered these early times, illuminating them and tying them up with a neat bow. 'You remember,' she would say, 'that time when you left the house, both of you, just so high (her hand demonstrated the height of a

log or a boot), just you and the guard dog.' And she would describe all the details of that day, one of the first she had ever spent with us, her mad despair, the panicked fear she felt that she would never find us again, in all this heaped-up snow, in an unknown country. 'And your parents in town, and me who didn't know what to do, who cried, who screamed, who ran bareheaded into the snow and the night.' 'Gdye! Gdye!' she repeated loudly. 'Ah, what a spanking . . .' she would finally say, her eyes to heaven, and pass on to other memories:

'That first fable we learned together, yes? Or when we stopped in the middle of the countryside, all three of us, to sing *Marlborough s'en va t'en guerre* at the top of our voices?', and this tiddly-om-pom-pom, she hummed it now, which made the past come alive again much more clearly and in a completely different manner than the snore of a sentence.

Once more I see that country house with its lightning conductor which seems to slip between the great white clouds; the verdigris roof, the sculpted wood ornaments; and above all the little rhomboidal and multicoloured windows on the veranda. The garden, seen through this coloured glass, would become singularly immobile and silent, as if it were occupied in admiring itself, plunged into an enchanted crystal: if you looked through the blue glass, all at once it was an underwater landscape; then you passed to the red – and the green above the pink sand took on a wine-dregs tint; the yellow, finally, increased a hundredfold the sun's flame; and so I tasted, while Mademoiselle read, small joys in the margin of her reading; sometimes a butterfly, some Red Admiral or Mourning Cloak, would place itself on the pitted step, and would open to the sun its velvet wings.

For me, Mademoiselle's room was always a foreign place; full of the heavy atmosphere of a hot greenhouse, where some fat plant blessed with a curious odour would have sprouted, this room had become so different from all the others that it seemed foreign to

our house with its well-aired and smiling rooms. In Mademoiselle's room, it smelled of imprisonment, of the chamber pot, of rotting apple skin, and the air itself was in some way sombre and thick. In the midst of this heavy darkness which the lit lamp did not manage to dissipate, the writing table remotely rocked – but by stretching myself on tiptoe, I could examine at leisure objects which were as peculiar to Mademoiselle as her embonpoint and her asthma. On the table there was a pearl penholder with a very small hole at its tip, in which, bringing your eye so close that the eyelashes brushed it, you could admire the chateau of Chillon beneath an azure and pink sky, entirely and miraculously contained in this tiny space. There was also that lacquered box which enclosed a thimble, a watch which no longer ticked or tocked and those liquorice pastilles which Mademoiselle indulged in so liberally; with her pretty pocket knife she pared the little black angles of the sticks she gave us in the hollow of her hand, while advising us to keep the liquorice under our tongue – 'I go to sleep with it in,' she used to say, 'and in the morning when I wake up it is still there.' Finally there were photographs of Mademoiselle's nephews and nieces, in frames studded with little false stones, which seemed to me – garnets, rubies, dark sapphires – to be priceless jewels; and among all these photographs the one which, superseding all the others, presented a young svelte girl, in a sort of Scottish dress which clung to her figure, a three-quarter face, bright eyes, the *chignon* descending very low on a gracious neck – 'Ah, a plait as thick as your arm,' Mademoiselle used to say, 'which went down as far as my toes.' For it was definitely her, this miraculous being, whom I searched for in vain as I interrogated Mademoiselle's face, as if I were trying to prise out the exquisite creature she had swallowed up.

What the adults never knew, since during the day they only saw a Mademoiselle laced tight and covered with decorous veils, what no one knew about her, we, the children, knew well, this

trembling mass of fleshes which flowed in a coarsely embroidered shirt underneath the crimson wool dressing gown with gold epaulettes. In this way – her hair undone, a candle in her hand – she would suddenly come to us, prised from her bed by the cry of a child's nightmare.

I have slept badly all my life; every evening, every night, I have always been afraid of sleep, an intense fear which increased in proportion to my tiredness. Sleep has always seemed a masked torturer, cloaked and hooded, who seizes me by his butcher's fist, – it is a scaffold which I mount every night, where every night I struggle with hideous Morpheus who overcomes me at last and binds me to the scales. I have now broken with this terror at last and almost go whistling to the scaffold, but in my childhood I had no weapon against this death each night, apart from a thin ray of light left behind by the half-open door of the adjoining bedroom.

Now my memory, leaving the country, takes up residence for the winter in our Petersburg house – our *hôtel*, Mademoiselle used to say, – so that this night must definitely be a winter's night, – the milky globes of the gaslights, invisible, can be made out behind the windows' blue and opaque blinds. I do not sleep and madly envy my brother who has been snoring for hours, sheltered by a screen on the other side of the room. Everything is black in there, only the crack in the door throws a ray of light over the shadows in which I feel myself drown. I cling to this luminous bar, without which my eye would be without solace, and my head would turn in a black abyss. Over there, in the empty and illuminated adjoining room, is Mademoiselle's bed, while her room is situated at the end of a long corridor, in another part of the house. I know that at a certain time in the night she will come to bed, directing her heavy tread (which makes a small porcelain object tinkle somewhere) down this corridor and that she will go into the neighbouring room. I would still have a moment of respite, as long as she reads in bed, but afterwards, it will be the end.

So I wait, knowing that I must go to sleep before she comes, that I must go to sleep at once, to spare myself the abominable suffering of no longer having the thin ray of light to support me; but I am afraid of sleep which, moreover, seems to take delight in being late. No sound comes from the street where the snow makes the rare passing of a sledge silent. I try not to look in a certain corner of the immense room where the shadow takes on sinister aspects – nocturnal metamorphoses of the wardrobe or chest, terrifying contours which draw me in despite myself. The clock deletes the seconds with dry chops, with a sort of ill exhalation in the middle, for it is very old. I force myself to think about amusing things, surprises, promises of toys, but everything is spoiled by the horror of staying awake. Finally, the familiar step, inexorable, comes along the corridor, disturbing some little object which has stayed awake like me. I hear Mademoiselle enter the room next door. She lights the candle in her nightlight, turns off the ceiling light (so that she does not have to get up when she has finished reading) and already there is a diminishment of brightness which paves the way for total night; the crack is still there, but paler, dull, and troubling itself strangely when a crackling tells me that Mademoiselle has made some movement in her bed, which makes the flame flutter. For I continue to listen to her, all my senses are acute to a prodigious degree. I hear her paperknife cut the pages of the *Revue des Deux Mondes* – in which Paul Bourget, I think, used to give her exquisite pleasure. I hear her breathing. But I am dying of distress, imploring destiny to prolong indefinitely Mademoiselle's reading, so that the light might stay there for me, I imagine paradise as an endless book which she would read without ever tiring, by the light of an eternal candle. Then the inevitable happens; I hear the book being shut, a pince-nez taken off chimes on the marble bedside table and then Mademoiselle blows at her candle. Her first attempt fails, the dying light makes a desperate somersault, so the second 'blow' comes, more violent, and it is black. No, for a second floats

before my eyes the ghost of the band of light which I have coveted so long with my eyes. Finally, in total darkness, I feel myself weaken, my bed drifts away slowly, until the moment when my eyes, getting used to the blackness, end up distinguishing the colourless folds of the blinds, pale stains which float slowly until finally settling here and there. And with this last consolation I fall asleep on a pillow wet with tears.

By contrast, how charming the mornings were, when the beautiful blond light of the frosted lamps marked out on the parquet its dazzling geometry of crosses and the logs crackled, impregnating the ceramic heater with such heat that it could not be touched with one's hand. And then there was what we used to call 'going on an outing', – a drive in a carriage with Mademoiselle, – my brother next to her, me opposite them, – with immense tricoloured banners (for I always seem to be present at some great festival on the days when my memory returns) hung above the streets and swelling in the wind. The shiny wing of an exotic bird in Mademoiselle's hat, the broad back of the coachman, swathed in padding in the Russian fashion, the rapid clouds, the gilded dome of the cathedral, the seagulls beating above the blue Neva, – all this forms an image of a surprising distinctness which I love contemplating, as I would a precious miniature.

Two or three times it happened that the coachman had got drunk and I hear Mademoiselle, immediately on her return from the drive, telling my mother: 'Imagine my horror, Madame, when I saw the man swaying on his seat, I was frozen with terror, I held the children close to me, against my poor panting body, – what more could I do, Madame?' This slightly extravagant manner of expressing herself had soon become a free entertainment for us, the children, for within us was a refined and joyful cruelty which would turn abruptly to a ferocious compassion, when the ravages caused by us were manifest. I think the main characteristic of Mademoiselle O was her capacity to be wounded. Her extraordinary name – so

round, so rolypoly – seemed to be a target for any joker's arrows; when she was introduced to someone new, she had to endure either a plea for indulgence on behalf of this abnormal name, without a paw to stand on, or an embarrassed or knowing surprise, depending on whether the newcomer regarded the little monster with disgust or amusement. Mademoiselle's absolute immunity to the Russian language luckily allowed her not to know everything that the house-hold staff – the 'starrf' as we said in our house – the servants and the maids, made of her name, when they did not simply call her 'Mamzelle'. Her fearful obesity was another reason why she should be always on her guard, defending her corpulence as if she had found herself in a country of anthropophagi obsessed with eyeing her avidly. She maintained bravely that, whilst being a little stout, as she said, she possessed physically all the attributes of grace and distinction which were not available to 'skeletons'. She overflowed with candied fruit, sweets, chocolates, and asserted that nothing was healthier than marrons glacés. We had a relative, also obese, but less fat than Mademoiselle – who would nevertheless scoff: 'But come on, I am a nymph beside your aunt.' In the Petersburg house, in preference to the marble staircase, she chose the little old-fashioned hydraulic lift which the concierge used to set off with a lever fixed to the wall of the hallway. 'Quick march!' he would invariably say as he closed the two doors on Mademoiselle, who collapsed slowly onto the bench. And the heavy lift, wheezing and creaking, rose incredibly slowly up the length of the fat cable covered in velvet, while on the peeling wall which was visible through the glass slowly descended dark stains reminiscent of an atlas: stains of damp and old age, in which one could recognise the contours of the Black Sea or Australia which clouds and stains borrow at every oppor-tunity. As for me, who had remained below, I would hear the machine climb painfully and would always maliciously hope that it would stop half way. Sometimes that would happen. The noise would stop. All that could be heard was the fall of some plaster

crumbling somewhere. Then, from a mysterious space between the walls arrived the 'gdye, gdye', so well known, the cry of Mademoiselle in distress. So the Swiss chap down below would push the lever with an effort, then would open the door in the blackness and would look up to see if it was working. Finally, the lift set off, and a short while later Mademoiselle would be found in tears in her room, – sure that the concierge did it deliberately, that she did not weigh as much as that, after all. 'Ah, the torments I suffered up there, suspended alone in the void!' Throughout her life, things seemed to be there only to mock her obesity – and when one day she sat down on a glass-covered case containing rare and carefully dried and mounted butterflies, her look was filled with a terrible suspicion, at the very moment when the glass cracked beneath her, as if she believed that the case had been placed expressly there, to prove to her by the destruction which followed that the weight of her body was really formidable.

As if nature had not wanted to spare her anything which makes a person vulnerable, she had bad hearing, and this weakness, which got worse with age, added to her physical shame. All this made her a difficult person, sensitive and suspicious, taking offence at every remark. Sometimes, at the table, you would suddenly notice that two chubby tears were slowly descending the length of Mademoiselle's large cheeks, Mademoiselle, who was saying in a fluting voice: 'Ah, it's nothing', and continuing to eat without wiping away the tears which obscured her vision; then, with a desolate sob, she would get up and leave the dining room under the sarcastic eye of the staff. 'No, leave me, I'm just a poor little thing, all tatters,' she would say when people tried to understand what could have upset her; little by little the truth was discovered that she was always irrational; for example, someone at the table had spoken about the navy – I had an uncle who was an admiral – and Mademoiselle had persuaded herself that it had been done on purpose, because Switzerland possessed no fleet. Or it was

simply because it seemed to her that, although people spoke French at the table, she was prevented from directing the conversation, – for she believed that she knew all the intricacies of the 'French art of conversation', as she used to say. But she was in such a hurry to seize the thread of the conversation before it escaped her and fell into the abysses of Russian jargon, that it was always with clumsiness that she practised her art. Certain reflections she offered remained in our family, – amusing curiosities we recalled with love. 'One day, I heard silence,' she would say, then paused and repeated in a low voice: 'I heard silence. It was in a deserted valley in the Alps.' There was also the miracle of the mushrooms: 'One morning,' said Mademoiselle, 'as I was picking flowers, I saw a mushroom sprout, – it left the earth very softly, with small almost imperceptible thrusts.' Quips of this sort never developed into the brilliant, sparkling, witty conversation of which Mademoiselle dreamed. On the contrary, people fell silent as soon as she had said her piece, then talked about something else, at the risk of hearing Mademoiselle complain a little later that she had been rudely interrupted. The most annoying of all was that sometimes she wrongly thought that someone had been talking to her, for her deafness encumbered her more and more, and with a little flick of the head she threw out a distinct 'sorry?' to the inoffensive guest who had said nothing.

I should note that, despite her pompous language and the naïveté of her ideas, Mademoiselle's French was divine. For, if I throw a retrospective glance on this former Russia, – now entered into an era of naïve barbarism and whose name now sounds in our time like 'Greece' or 'Rome' – in this Russia there was not only the French taught by teachers like Mademoiselle, but still a sort of French tradition, an ordinary French, which was passed directly from father to son. It formed part of our civilisation. First of all there were numerous French words and phrases inserted into Russian conversation, passing from one language to another with

surprising facility, and it must have amused a Gallic ear to be present at the intrusion, in a quite pure torrent of French, of a Russian word which exhibited itself there with perfect assurance, even preceded by an elision. In extreme cases syntax was entirely based on Russian; phrases were translated literally, which made them incomprehensible to someone who did not know our language. If, on the one hand, this French degenerated into a kitchen version of French, there was also, on the other hand, a version which rose to a very pretty degree of album French, maiden French, with an entire poetry which was a little old-fashioned, a little bit rosewater, as if our Slavic lyres would have made too coarse a sound for young girls' ears. 'The Broken Vase' by Sully Prudhomme – the vase in which this verbena languishes . . . – and the *Nights* of Alfred de Musset with their sobbing and reckless lyricism are typical examples of what this type of Russian reader liked in French poetry. On the other hand, in the milieu where I grew up, the literary tendency was of another order, and it was not Coppée or Lamartine, but Verlaine and Mallarmé who took care of my adolescence. So, the role of the French nurse more concerned the form than the substance itself, grammar rather than Literature, that is to say it remained removed from this Franco-Russian tradition of which I have just spoken, as if this tradition had formed some picturesque dialect, but overly provincial, overly parochial for her taste. Taste, good taste – in the sense which it was given in the seventeenth century – formed, I believe, the essential part of Mademoiselle O's education. From that there resulted a purity of language, a severe sonority, a sort of cold and sparkling flow, – all qualities which I only appreciated much later.

Thus, it is with sadness that now I make out the cruel suffering which Mademoiselle must have felt hearing this voice of a nightingale lost in vain as it left her elephantine body. I do not remember precisely the esteem in which she held the three poets who were the idols of Russian readers just before the war: Rostand, whose

inept *Chantecler* had just created a new fashion in women's hats;
Maeterlinck, whose *Blue Bird* was brilliantly played by our best
theatre – which was moreover at that time the best theatre in the
world; and finally Verhaeren whose robust muse had an enormous
influence on the development of the so-called urban branch of our
poetry. No, I do not remember what Mademoiselle thought of these
three poets, who for her were young, were 'moderns'. But what I
remember with total clarity is the exceptional cult she made of
Corneille and Racine.

I, a barbarian, the friend of Rabelais and Shakespeare, have always
had a problem with Corneille and Racine, for their perfect, ideal
banality – for this sublimation of the commonplace into a masterpiece of falsity. Their best alexandrines fill my mouth like mouth-
wash and make no appeal to my imagination. I hate their
redundancies, the poverty of their style, the servility of the adjective, the indigence of rhyme, – everything, in fact, – and I would
not give one sonnet by Ronsard for all their drama.

So, there in the schoolroom was Mademoiselle who had chosen
the role of Chimène or Athalie, while we shared the male roles, –
with me always trying to take the part of the confidant since there
was less to read. I can still hear her, this slightly simpering Chimène,
whom I tried to imagine, seduced by her chimerical name, while
looking at Mademoiselle who accentuated the sweet falls of the
alexandrines by making little *moues* – her mouth pursed in the shape
of a heart or a pout; I can hear Athalie, terrified but chatty, telling
her dream, – and Mademoiselle, her eyebrows raised and the entire
series of her chins in motion, gave herself a little tap on her breast
like an Italian tenor. Poor Mademoiselle! But now I must reach the
critical point of her life among us, of this strange and terrible novel
which finishes so sadly. For it was an upside-down novel, a sort
of negative plate, where open tenderness would be replaced by a
mute struggle, exhausting, without let-up, whose assaults ended for
Mademoiselle in swoonings and palpitations of the heart.

Several years had gone by since her entrance into our house, when a stranger arrived. He was a man we called a 'répétiteur' rather than, more accurately, a 'tutor' – a young Russian student whose job in winter was to help us prepare our lessons for school and whose duty, in summer, involved taking part in our games and our equestrian strolls (although he rode very badly, as it happens). From the very first moment, Mademoiselle thought she could scent an enemy in this young man with a goatee, with myopic eyes, badly cut hair, dressed in the green and blue trousers of the university and a Russian smock. Of simple origin, and therefore of an almost unhealthy pride, what's more very radical in his politics, poor, doing the job of a children's tutor not out of any pedagogical vocation, but because it was a way of earning his living which was permitted by his principles, Petrov had never learned French, which moreover he considered to be an antidemocratic luxury. A charming being, nevertheless, as honest as bread and wonderfully gifted at mathematics, – but in no way formed to live side by side with a jealous and tyrannical Mademoiselle, especially one who assumed that Petrov, as soon as he arrived, had a single aim, which was to get her to leave. Our souls were therefore at stake, or at least that was Mademoiselle's opinion, for in reality, derisive and carefree, we used to follow the course of this struggle without according much importance to its result, nor to the secret sufferings it caused.

We used to serve each guest after the meal a bowl containing a beaker filled with a lightly perfumed water which we used to rinse our mouths and then deposited it back into the bowl; then, we left the table – a hygienic end to a meal, and even gracious, at least in Mademoiselle's case, who cared for pretty gestures. But after the first dinner at which he was present, Petrov placidly drank, and even savoured, what he had taken for a new liqueur, while Mademoiselle, beside him, giggled or pretended to giggle into her serviette, and that, I think, was when hostilities broke out, for

Petrov, completely prepared as he was to accord her supremacy, never forgave this implacable laugh.

For her part, Mademoiselle imagined that if Petrov never spoke to her, and responded to her provoking questions with unintelligible monosyllables, it was not because he did not understand French, but because he wanted to insult her with impunity in front of everybody. I can still see her requesting in her golden voice, but with a certain crease to the lips which augured no good, 'to please be so kind, Monsieur, as to pass me the sugar bowl'; Petrov paid no attention to her words which were repeated several times, until the moment when Mademoiselle, with a demonstrative gesture and an 'excuse me' which stung like a whip, passed her arm across Petrov's plate to reach the sugar bowl which she then brought towards her, tossing to the young man a murmured, soft, 'thank you, Monsieur', saccharine and rumbling with irony so that Petrov's velvety ears took on a violent red. 'A peasant, an illiterate, a terrible person!' she would then say, sobbing in her bedroom. She would go on to say that he had jostled her as they passed on the stairs: 'He pushed me,' she would say, 'he struck me . . . I have bruises everywhere.' More and more often she would leave the table in the middle of dinner because Petrov, who loved telling stories filled with details, was speaking at length, and the general conversation he unleashed was fatally entering Russian labyrinths. From her distant room, she wrote to my parents, who lived on the ground floor, letters sixteen pages long. My mother would go up in haste, finding Mademoiselle packing her trunk. Then there was a week of respite, a consoled Mademoiselle pretended to be ignorant of Petrov's presence. One day, finally, came the total debacle.

I think the last event in this saga was the cataclysm, the noisy explosion, the cry, 'You are a thief, Monsieur!' that was heard the day when, searching for my brother who had hidden himself away, Petrov had the unfortunate idea of crossing the threshold of Mademoiselle's room, whose door was half open. Just at the

moment when Petrov paused in the middle of this forbidden room, Mademoiselle came out of the bathroom, bearing an azalea, which she had just been watering. I remember this detail in the same way one remembers some insignificant thing encountered in the course of a catastrophe, – for it was truly an irreparable catastrophe between Mademoiselle, mordant and terrible, and Petrov, suddenly emerging from his muteness to register the slanderous term which, by an unhappy miracle, he had suddenly just understood.

And then, Mademoiselle left. It was in 1914, and the official pretext for her departure was, I remember, the fear of being definitively cut off from her homeland by political events. All that I still possess of our goodbyes is a flood of tears and her two arms held wide open. For a year or two, she wrote to us quite regularly, – pages and pages covered in her small fine handwriting without any mistake. Then came the revolution. Ten years later, through one of the flukes of exile, I found myself one day in Switzerland and there I was entering Mademoiselle's room.

Stouter than ever, her hair grey, and almost totally deaf, she received me with an outburst of tenderness. She talked of her life in Russia so warmly that one might have believed she had lost her own homeland. In contrast, she accused Switzerland of having become unrecognisable, and there were endless complaints. Our revolution, abolishing the use of French in Russia, had exiled as casually as true Russians several thousand old women who now stayed together, met each other and stuck together, forming an island in a country which had become foreign to them. They had invented another country, – the past, – and it was truly upsetting, this poor posthumous love for Russia which they hardly knew.

Since our interview had been made terribly difficult by the deafness of Mademoiselle, the next day I brought her one of those gadgets which promise the deaf more than they can perform. When she had installed the tube, she thanked me with a dazzled look and swore that she could hear the slightest whisper. She was lying, she

could hear nothing at all, and was lying to give me pleasure, and this naïve, delicate, adorable lie is the last memory I possess of Mademoiselle.

Before leaving, I went quite pointlessly to walk in the cold and misty night by the lake. The water clopped a little, but nothing shone in the nocturnal fog, except a pale street-lamp. A movement, a vague whiteness, drew my attention. In the water, a swan, very fat, very old and very clumsy, was making ridiculous efforts to drag itself into a moored boat. It could not. I heard the heavy shock of its wings and the sound of the rocked boat; with the logic of the subconscious, it was this passing vision which I immediately remembered when I learned, several years later, that Mademoiselle was no more. She had spent her life in being unhappy, and unhappiness was for her a natural element, whose changes in depth gave her the sensation of movement, of doing something, of living, finally. I feel great remorse when I think about certain small moments when the idea came to me of giving her some small pleasure and I immediately replied to myself that it was not worth the effort. I thought it would console me to talk about her, and now that it is done I have the strange sensation of having invented her in every particular, as entirely as the other characters who pass through my books. Did she truly live? No, now that I think about it hard – she never lived. But from now on she is real, since I have created her, and this existence I give her would be a very candid sign of gratitude, if she had ever truly existed.

Dans un livre, j'ai prêté à l'enfance de mon héros l'institutrice à qui je dois le plaisir d'entendre le français. Je dis 'j'ai prêté', mais il serait plus juste de dire: 'Mon héros me l'a prise. 'Car c'est vraiment pitoyable de voir comme ces personnages falots sortis du noir clair de lune de l'encrier abusent des belles choses et des chers visages qu'on leur fournit, jusqu'à dépeupler peu à peu notre propre passé. C'est comme un tendre aïeul qui – peut-être par une sorte de paresse et pour échapper au travail d'y tenir en éveil tout un passé – donnerait à son petit-neveu, au jour de ses noces, quelque objet farci de souvenirs, un de ces objets qui n'ont plus de beauté, ni de sens, sinon qu'ils ont été, ce qui n'est plus une raison pour qui reçoit la chose humble et inutile qu'on met dans un coin et qu'on oublie aussitôt. J'ai souvent observé ce singulier phénomène de disproportion sentimentale lorsque, faisant présent à mes personnages factices non de grands pans de mon passé – j'en suis trop avare pour cela, – mais de quelque image dont je croyais pouvoir me défaire sans détriment, j'ai observé, dis-je, que la belle chose que je donnais dépérissait dans le milieu d'imagination où je la mettais brusquement. Cependant elle subsistait dans ma mémoire comme si elle me fût devenue étrangère. Bien plus, elle possédait désormais plus d'affinité avec le roman où je l'avais emprisonnée qu'avec ce passé chaud et vivant où elle avait été si bien à l'abri de mon art littéraire. Par contre, comme je viens de le noter, le personnage à qui je faisais don d'un arbre sous lequel j'avais joué, d'un sentier que j'avais parcouru, d'un effet de lumière

qui célébrait comme un feu d'artifice quelque événement inoubliable de ma jeunesse en fête, semblait n'y attacher aucun prix ou même prenait l'air gêné de celui qui ne sait que faire de la parure désuète qu'on lui offre. C'est ainsi que le portrait de ma vieille institutrice française – elle mettait son petit point d'honneur à s'appeler institutrice et non gouvernante, – ce dernier mot faisait penser, disait-elle, à quelque vieille fille pleine de pudeurs austères qui conduirait le ménage d'un célibataire grognon, – c'est ainsi donc que son portrait, ou plutôt certains détails de son portrait, me semblent perdus pour jamais, enlisés qu'ils sont dans la description d'une enfance qui m'est totalement étrangère. Or, l'idée m'est venue de sauver ce qui reste de cette image, d'autant plus que j'ai toujours eu le désir de raviver pour mon propre agrément, et aussi comme signe d'une gratitude posthume, l'exacte nuance que la langue française donnait à ma vie de Russe.

Comme il ne m'est presque jamais arrivé de séjourner dans un pays où cette langue soit parlée, j'en ai perdu l'habitude, de sorte que c'est une tâche inouïe, un labeur éreintant que de saisir les mots médiocrement justes qui voudront bien venir vêtir ma pensée. J'en ressens un essoufflement fort pénible, accompagné de la peur de bâcler les choses, c'est-à-dire de me contenter des termes que j'ai la chance de happer au passage – au lieu de rechercher avec amour le vocable radieux qui se meurt d'attente derrière la brume, le vague, l'à-peu-près où ma pensée oscille. Je me demande, du reste, ce que Mademoiselle O penserait de ces lignes-ci si elle était encore en vie et pouvait me lire – elle qui voyait avec un tel effroi les écarts de mon orthographe, et mes tournures insolites.

Je viens de l'appeler par son vrai nom, car 'Mademoiselle O' n'est nullement l'abréviation d'un nom en O. Cet O, ouvert à tous les vents de l'hiatus, n'est pas la majuscule d'Olivier ni d'Orose ou encore d'Oudinet, mais bien le nom intégral; un nom rond et nu qui, écrit, semble en déséquilibre sans un point pour le soutenir; une roue qui s'est détachée et qui reste toute seule debout, prête

à chavirer; une bouche en rond; un monde; une pomme; un lac. Elle avait justement passé la moitié de sa vie près d'un lac, car c'est en Suisse que Mademoiselle O naquit, de parents purement français, du reste; et avec ce Lac Léman pour décor de fond, son nom prenait des allures de chanson de geste ou de roman, faisait penser à Lancelot du Lac ou à Obéron, mais sans perdre, hélas, ce ridicule facile que l'œil et l'ouïe d'un enfant furent prompts à découvrir. Car ce fut bientôt, dès qu'elle nous eut donné à mon frère et à moi le pouvoir de parler sa langue, – arme qui se retourna contre elle – un moyen de la faire enrager horriblement; on tirait tout ce qu'on pouvait de ce nom en détresse: on le faisait bondir comme une balle, on inventait des calembours, on imaginait le père de Mademoiselle arrivant dans une ville d'eaux, ce qui – précédé d'une exclamation – donnait la formule idiote de quatre 'o' se suivant à la queue-leu-leu. Le pire était que dans le gros volume rose et trapu, qui était son livre de chevet – je veux dire le Larousse – le premier nom qui figurât à la lettre O était celui de François marquis d'O, né et mort à Paris, Surintendant des finances dont nous faisions l'ancêtre tout à fait légendaire de Mademoiselle (que cela agaçait parce qu'elle eût voulu y croire elle même).

Très forte, toute ronde comme son nom, Mademoiselle O arriva chez nous comme j'entrais dans ma sixième année. Son embonpoint, ses gros sourcils noirs qui se rejoignaient, le tremblotement de ses bajoues lorsqu'elle s'asseyait – laissant peu à peu descendre sa croupe monstrueuse, puis au dernier moment se donnant à Dieu et s'asseyant pour de bon avec un craquement effroyable (lorsque c'était une de ces chaises de paille bariolées dont notre maison de campagne était pleine); de plus, un teint couperosé qui dans les grands moments de colère contenue passait au pourpre dans la région des second et troisième mentons qui s'étalaient royalement sur la blouse à jabot qu'elle portait les dimanches; un rien de moustache, des yeux d'un gris d'acier derrière un de ces pince-nez anciens qui retenaient dans la forme des verres largement et sombrement

enchâssés la marque de leur parenté avec les lunettes dont ils ne s'étaient pas encore différenciés; puis encore un front à trois rides mangé par la courbe d'une abondante chevelure noire qui grisonnait en grand mystère, – tout ceci donnait à Mademoiselle O un aspect sévère, voire rébarbatif.

Comme si le destin, en voulant bien faire les choses et les poussant jusqu'au poncif, avait désiré présenter à l'étrangère une Russie aussi russe que possible, il arriva que ce fut justement l'unique hiver de mon enfance que je passai à la campagne et non en ville, un hiver particulièrement rude, qui entoura la venue de Mademoiselle de cette abondance de neige qu'elle s'était probablement figurée à la veille de son lointain et dangereux voyage. Il subsistait dans ces arrivées d'étrangers en Moscovie un peu de ce frisson d'aventure qui accompagnait au vieux temps la ruée chez nous des Français, des Allemands, des Italiens de toutes professions en commençant par l'architecte qui soufflait un peu de l'air bronzé de Rome dans le dôme d'un temple orthodoxe, en passant par le naturaliste, le marchand éclairé, le jeune gouverneur d'enfants, disciple de Jean-Jacques, jusqu'à la foule bigarrée et frileuse de coiffeurs, de chapeliers et de lorettes. Plusieurs de ces voyageurs ont laissé une trace: c'est Cagliostro qui arrive, attiré par l'empire du Nord; c'est Diderot qui, dans un entretien avec Catherine frappe distraitement le genou impérial de sa petite main potelée et velue, pour mieux accentuer l'idée qu'il soutient; c'est le frère de Marat qui enseigne le français aux lycéens russes. Mais c'est aussi un énorme afflux d'institutrices anonymes, car au cours du dix-neuvième siècle il n'existait probablement pas une seule famille noble dans la Russie entière qui n'eût sa gouvernante française, sa fräulein ou sa miss Jones. Chacune d'elles restait dans la même famille pendant de longues années, parfois toute une vie; elle en faisait partie, tout en restant dans une position un peu fausse: toujours reléguée au bout de la table, avec la parente pauvre et le gérant qu'elle détestait; ne se mariant jamais; n'apprenant jamais le russe; vivant ainsi une vie

irréelle, pleine d'une nostalgie traditionnelle qui lui était plutôt un soutien qu'une souffrance, et d'un certain sentiment de dépit à l'égard du peuple qui l'avait accueillie non pas comme une personne vivante, mais plutôt comme un détail nécessaire et mille fois répété de son existence quotidienne, – pareille à ces meubles qu'on ne remarque pas avant le jour où on les emporte au grenier.

Donc, c'est par un crépuscule d'hiver que Mademoiselle descend à la petite gare d'où il y a encore une dizaine de kilomètres à faire en traîneau avant d'arriver chez nous. Je m'évertue maintenant à imaginer ce qu'elle voyait et éprouvait en venant, celle vieille demoiselle dont c'était là le premier grand voyage et dont tout le vocabulaire russe consistait en un mot unique que dix ans plus tard elle devait remporter avec elle en Suisse: le mot 'gdié' qui veut dire 'où cela?', mais qui, sortant de sa bouche comme le cri rauque d'un oiseau perdu, développait une telle force interrogative qu'il subvenait à tous les besoins de Mademoiselle: 'Gdié? gdié?' répétait-elle non seulement pour connaître le lieu où elle était ou la direction à suivre, mais encore donnant à entendre par là tout un monde de souffrance: qu'elle était étrangère, naufragée, à bout de ressource, et qu'elle cherchait l'Eldorado où enfin elle serait comprise.

Je me la représente descendant seule à la petite gare figée dans le crépuscule gris; quelques rares lumières tachent d'un jaune huileux l'obscurité qui ne semble pas descendre du ciel, mais bien monter de derrière les neiges vaguement bleuâtres. Il faisait, je pense, très froid, c'était ce froid russe classique dont tenait compte l'énorme thermomètre Réaumur que possédait chaque gare . . . La porte de la salle d'attente s'ouvrait en poussant le long grincement de nos grandes nuits de gel – et une bouffée d'air chaud en sortait, aussi profuse que la vapeur de la locomotive à cheminée en entonnoir et à chasse-neige en éventail. Je vois notre cocher qui attend Mademoiselle, c'est un rude homme brun ceinturé de rouge, ses gants de géant sortent de la ceinture où il les a fourrés, et j'entends la neige qui craque sous ses bottes arctiques. C'est avec angoisse

que Mademoiselle monte en traîneau tout en se cramponnant à l'homme avec une peur atroce de sentir le traîneau démarrer avant que ses formes amples et veules ne soient bien fixées à leur place, soufflant, geignant et enfin, avec un 'ouf!' qui fait dans la brume glacée un petit nuage, s'incrustant, assise enfin, les deux mains enfoncées dans son mauvais petit manchon de peluche; et puis, exécutant ce haut-le-corps en arrière que fait tout voyageur en traîneau au moment brusque où les chevaux, avec un effort de jarrets, retirent des neiges cette chose encore lourde qui gémit et tout de suite, comme entrant dans une ambiance nouvelle, glisse silencieusement sur une route qu'elle semble à peine toucher.

Tout à coup, et pour un instant seulement, je vois Mademoiselle en traîneau, accompagnée d'une ombre énorme qui – tenant comme elle un manchon – passe en silhouette, s'allonge, se courbe sur la neige où une lanterne la suit du regard, et puis se perd, laissant Mademoiselle s'engouffrer toute seule dans ce qu'elle appellera volontiers 'la steppe'. De temps en temps elle se retourne péniblement pour voir si – à une distance qui reste toujours la même, comme dans quelque illusion d'optique – la forme vague d'un autre traîneau, porteur de sa malle et de son carton à chapeaux, la suit. Puis son regard qui fouille les ténèbres neigeux croit y voir s'allumer de ci de là des yeux brillants de loup qui ne sont en vérité que les lumières des villages que quelque accident de neige et d'ombre fait apparaître pour un bref instant. Sans doute y a-t-il là une lune – elle aussi appartient à nos ardeurs hivernales, – très grande, très claire et toute ronde, aspect idéal du nom de Mademoiselle O, qui la contemple à travers ses cils irisés de givre; elle glisse, cette lune pareille à un grand miroir rond à dos de velours, parmi une foule pommelée de petits nuages tous pareils qui prennent un reflet d'arc-en-ciel manqué à la place où elle les effleure . . .

Mademoiselle a froid malgré sa pelisse, – elle est triste aussi, 'fourbue', dira-t-elle plus tard, 'transie jusqu'aux moelles'. Il lui

semble qu'elle voyage ainsi 'depuis des siècles' (car elle a l'hyper-bole facile), que sa malle n'est plus dans le traîneau qui la suit, qu'enfin le cocher est un brigand déguisé qui, dans le noir de cette sapinière, où le cheval fonce avec un tintement assourdi de ses grelots, va la dévaliser, l'égorger même, 'que sais-je!'; mais voici le bois dépassé et de nouveau la plaine se déroule avec, tout le long de la route, des poteaux télégraphiques qui semblent de différente grandeur suivant la hauteur de la neige qui enveloppe leur pied. Puis, c'est un village qu'on passe, d'un blanc sombre, sournoise-ment tapi, sans feux, ni bruits de vie; et la neige des toits s'unit à la neige bordant la route, que la lune, montée plus haut, commence à vernir, de sorte que bientôt les traces des traîneaux luisent, tandis que chaque inégalité, chaque petite motte de neige est soulignée par une enflure d'ombre démesurée.

Ce monde que nous ouvre notre mémoire est admirable par ce qui s'en dégage de parfaitement pur et sain. Ce que nous nous rappelons, tout en affectant vivement nos sens, ne les endommage pas. Le vent glacé qui fut jadis cause d'une pneumonie nous parvient maintenant dans toute son intensité, mais absolument inof-fensif: vague promesse peut-être de la vie future de notre âme, où l'univers lui apparaîtra dans une sorte de béatitude abstraite. C'est ainsi qu'avec une complète impunité et sans dommage pour mon corps vieilli et peureux, je puis faire glisser mon souvenir au fond d'une nuit de neige pour rappeler aussitôt – quittant ce gouffre glacé d'un coup d'aile – la chaleur, le bien-être qui règne dans cette maison – Mademoiselle l'appelait château – vers laquelle le traîneau l'emmène au tintement soutenu et grêle de ses clochettes. L'an-goisse que je ressens à présent lorsque je me rappelle la belle maison où je vivais enfant n'a rien à voir avec ces événements politiques qui, pour employer un cliché de journaliste, bouleversèrent ma patrie. Je m'en moque, de ces événements politiques. C'est dans un plan tout autre et dans un ordre d'idées qui n'a pas souci des accidents de l'histoire que se meut et se repose mon souvenir. Non,

ce n'est pas un soupir de banni que je pousse, à moins que la vie de l'homme mûr ne soit un genre de bannissement par rapport à sa ferveur première. Si j'étais même aujourd'hui le citoyen paisible d'une Russie qui me laisserait poursuivre ma vocation en toute liberté, ce serait avec la même angoisse que je rappellerais la forme première, l'image vraie des choses et des êtres qui vieilliraient autour de moi. Car cette vérité que je cherche, je ne l'ai connue que dans mon enfance et tout le peu de bien qui se trouve dans mes livres n'en est que le reflet. C'est la vieille lampe qu'on apporte entre chien et loup; son reflet renvoyé par la fenêtre qui dans un moment se cachera pour la nuit derrière ses volets de bois; puis l'abat-jour rose descendant sur la lampe qui tout de suite anime les petites marquises qui ornent, dans des médaillons de soie, ses volants vermeils. Le miroir ovale suspendu au mur suivant un angle tel que les meubles et le parquet jaune qu'il reflète semblent lui glisser des bras et tomber éternellement dans un abîme de lumière; le cliquetis délicat des cristaux du lustre, lorsqu'on remue quelque chose dans une chambre en haut; les gravures inoubliables sur les murs, – les mêmes qu'il m'arrive de rencontrer encore dans quelque chambre d'hôtel ou quelque salle d'attente, comme si je les voulais collectionner à nouveau pour en orner une demeure où je reviendrais un jour; la Diane en marbre qui, de son coin, semble regarder de biais mon tricycle d'enfant. Je me rappelle pêle-mêle toutes ces choses comme si mon passé venait de se réveiller en sursaut, les joues brûlantes, les cheveux mêlés, les yeux un peu fous, – mais quand je veux mettre un peu d'ordre dans mon souvenir, sa couleur et son éclat m'échappent.

Le soir dont je parle, nous étions probablement assis près de cette table couverte d'une toile cirée, où chaque fois mon doigt agrandissait de l'ongle une petite tache pour en faire bientôt un trou. Nous, c'est-à-dire mon frère et moi, et puis miss Jones qui, avec une rancune ironique, regarde parfois sa montre, parce que l'inconnue, la Française, celle qui va la remplacer dans la famille,

tarde à arriver de la gare, – simple rancune professionnelle, dont la pointe ironique est due à la connaissance parfaite de toute la dureté de la charge qui attend Mademoiselle O. L'horloge fait un gros tic-tac et son disque de cuivre, qui passe et repasse dans sa prison de verre, brille, s'éteint et brille à nouveau. Nous sommes, je suppose, en train de dessiner dans de larges cahiers. Comme j'aimais ces crayons de couleur! Le vert qui crée, en tourbillonnant, un arbre ébouriffé, le bleu dont une seule ligne horizontale forme un lointain maritime. J'aimais entre tous le petit bonhomme pourpre devenu si court à l'usage que je pouvais à peine le tenir entre mes doigts; au contraire, le crayon blanc, corbeau blanc, albinos maigre, était resté très long, – jusqu'au moment, du reste, où je compris que, loin d'être privé d'existence, comme il me le semblait quand il ne laissait aucune trace sur le papier blanc, il était vraiment le crayon idéal, car je pouvais m'imaginer tout ce que je voulais en griffonnant sur la page des lignes, invisibles sans doute, mais qui étaient bien là, puisque la pointe devenait de plus en plus courte.

Ces crayons, je les ai partagés aussi entre les personnages qui paraissent dans mes livres, de sorte que ce n'est plus leur forme première que je tâte du souvenir en ce moment. J'ai fourré quelque part cette glace penchée et la lampe qui fume. Peu de choses me restent. J'en ai gaspillé la plupart. Tout rond, son museau blanc enfoncé dans le pli de sa cuisse, le vieux basset dort sur un coussin brodé de roses, et un gros soupir vient quelquefois lui soulever les côtes. Il est si vieux et son sommeil est si bien capitonné de couches de songes qu'il ne bronche pas lorsque enfin du dehors vient le son des grelots, puis c'est une porte qui s'ouvre avec un bruit de ferraille, enfin voici l'inconnue, Mademoiselle.

Un enfant est généralement conservateur. Je ne supportais pas la pensée que Mademoiselle allait changer quelque chose à mes habitudes. L'ordre du temps, le mécanisme de la journée me semblaient immuables, puisque j'y étais accoutumé. Il y avait par

exemple le verre de lait que Mademoiselle, dans son langage un peu plus gros que nature, appelait, quand elle me voyait l'avaler en toute hâte par une brûlante après-midi: 'ce grand bol de graisse glacée'; peut-être aussi y entrait-il de ce dégoût que l'obèse, lorsqu'il n'est pas cannibale, ressent pour une nourriture qui lui rappelle sa propre chair. Donc, je ne pus admettre la température adoucie que Mademoiselle voulait donner à ma boisson en réchauffant le verre entre ses paumes. Du reste, ses mains me déplurent tout de suite. A cet âge nous connaissons à fond les mains des grandes personnes grâce à notre petite taille et parce que ces mains voltigent constamment au niveau de notre enfance, descendant des nuages supérieurs où demeurent les visages. C'est pourquoi je sus très vite ce qu'il y avait à apprendre sur les mains de Mademoiselle: elles étaient assez petites, laides de peau, tachées de son, un peu reluisantes aussi et froides au toucher, avec des poignets gonflés et des paillettes blanches sur les ongles. Personne jamais ne m'avait effleuré le visage, tandis que Mademoiselle eut dès l'abord ce geste inusité, et qui me jeta dans une morne stupeur, de me tapoter câlinement la joue de sa main maladroite. Plus tard vint aussi ce qu'elle appelait, selon le degré de force, tape, soufflet ou camouflet; ce dernier, exécuté à toute volée, ressemblait à ce que les joueurs de tennis appellent un revers smash, et atteignait généralement l'oreille. Mon frère en recevait plus que moi. D'ailleurs, il aimait aussi Mademoiselle plus que moi; comme pensum, elle lui donnait souvent à recopier une cinquantaine de fois la phrase 'qui aime bien, châtie bien' qu'elle écrivait d'abord de sa jolie écriture ronde à la grâce un peu mièvre, et qui contrastait singulièrement avec la démarche lourde et gauche de Mademoiselle (qui prétendait malgré tout que les femmes un peu fortes valsent mieux que les maigrelettes). Tous ses gestes me reviennent dès que je pense à ses mains: sa manière de tailler un crayon, en tenant la pointe vers son buste immense enveloppé de laine émeraude, vers son sein monstrueux et infé-cond, qui se soulevait avec le mouvement prononcé, propre à ceux

pour qui la respiration est un luxe, car la pauvre dame était asthmatique et souffrait d'étouffements atroces; puis, cette façon qu'elle avait de faire jouer très rapidement son petit doigt en le fourrant dans son oreille, le coude levé. Puis encore le rituel inoubliable qui avait lieu chaque fois qu'elle me donnait un nouveau cahier pour la dictée: je la vois clairement sortir ce cahier noir ciré, – toujours soufflant un peu, la bouche toujours un peu entr'ouverte et rendant un petit son comme 'peuh ... peuh ... peuh ...'; elle ouvrait ce cahier pour faire la marge, c'est-à-dire qu'elle traçait de son ongle une ligne verticale, puis recourbait le bord extérieur de la page, qu'elle pressait fortement dans cette position en laissant glisser la paume de sa main, puis rendait la liberté à cette page, la lissant d'un petit geste final et faisant virevolter le cahier ouvert en sorte qu'il vînt se placer tout prêt devant moi. Elle avait aussi un rite spécial pour chaque nouvelle plume, qu'elle humectait de salive avec un sifflement à rebours avant de lui donner son baptême d'encre. Avec grand soin et tout en me réjouissant d'une orgie calligraphique, d'autant plus vivement que le cahier précédent finissait toujours par un hideux barbouillage, avec un soin exquis je traçais le mot 'dictée', pendant que Mademoiselle cherchait dans un livre de 'morceaux choisis' la substance de ce qu'elle nommait 'une bonne dictée'.

Entre temps le décor a changé: ce n'est plus, au dehors, cet éblouissement de neige sous un ciel presque violet à force d'être bleu; ce ne sont plus ces arbres dont chaque branche minuscule était dessinée en givre, ce qui faisait de l'arbre comme un spectre brodé; non, ce n'est plus un paysage d'hiver, mais une belle journée d'été qui rayonne, avec le tendre vert des bouleaux ressortant sur le noir des sapins, car ma mémoire a vite fait de transporter Mademoiselle d'une journée à l'autre. Et ce n'est plus une dictée que nous écrivons, mon frère et moi; 'un point, c'est tout', avait dit Mademoiselle, en refermant son Martin et Feuillet, – et c'est maintenant la lecture, cette lecture journalière, traditionnelle,

éternellement répétée par mon souvenir; cette lecture, pendant laquelle Mademoiselle s'épanouit.

Quel nombre immense de volumes nous a-t-elle lus par ces après-midi tachetées de soleil, sur la véranda! Sa voix fine filait, filait à travers tous ces livres, sans jamais faiblir, sans la moindre saccade ou le moindre bégaiement, admirable machine à lecture, qui semblait toute distincte des bronches malades de Mademoiselle. Toute la bibliothèque rose puis Jules Verne, Victor Hugo, Dumas père, – romans interminables auxquels peut-être elle prenait un plaisir aussi vif que nous, quoique impassible en apparence; un de ses mentons, le plus petit, mais le vrai, était, ses lèvres mises à part, le seul point mouvant de tout son ensemble ample et immobile. Les pinces noires du pince-nez formidable accomplissaient leur devoir avec une telle diligence qu'on croyait les sentir s'enfoncer des deux côtés de son nez charnu pour se rejoindre enfin au dedans, comme deux équipes de travailleurs entamant des deux côtés opposés le tunnel du Saint-Gothard, ce tunnel qui était une des sept merveilles du monde de Mademoiselle. Quelquefois, sans troubler aucunement la voix pure et posée, le petit doigt venait vite se fourrer dans l'oreille pour y vibrer brièvement, ou bien une mouche visitait le front sévère dont les rides entraient tout-à-coup en mouvement, sans que rien changeât dans l'expression de ce visage que si souvent j'ai essayé de dessiner, – les bajoues tentaient mon crayon sournois d'une façon irrésistible.

'Ah, l'on s'aimait bien!' disait Mademoiselle quelques années plus tard, quand elle évoquait sa venue chez nous et le commencement de notre vie commune, – 'au temps que vous étiez petits, et de sales petits cochons, mais on s'aimait bien, allez!' Et elle se souvenait de tous les obstacles que j'avais enjambés pour en venir plus vite à ces lectures sur la véranda, elle se souvenait de ces tout premiers temps, en les illuminant et les enrubannant. 'Vous rappelez-vous, disait-elle, cette fois où vous vous êtes enfuis de la maison, vous deux, grands comme ça (sa main montrait la hauteur

d'une bûche ou d'une botte), tout seuls vous deux et le chien de garde.' Et elle racontait alors tous les détails de cette journée, une des premières qu'elle avait passées chez nous, son désespoir fou, la peur panique qu'elle avait de ne jamais nous retrouver, parmi tout cet amoncellement de neige, dans une contrée inconnue. 'Et vos parents qui étaient justement en ville, et moi qui ne savais que faire, qui criais, qui hurlais, qui courais tête nue dans la neige et la nuit. 'Gdié! Gdié!' répétait-elle avec force. 'Ah, quelle fessée . . .' disait-elle à la fin, les yeux au ciel, et elle passait à d'autres souvenirs: 'Cette première fable qu'on avait apprise ensemble, hein? Ou bien, lorsqu'on s'arrêtait en pleine campagne pour chanter tous trois à tue-tête *Marlborough*', et ce mironton-ton-ton mirontaine, elle le fredonnait maintenant, ce qui faisait revivre le passé bien plus claire-ment et d'une tout autre manière qu'une phrase ronflante.

Je revois cette maison de campagne avec son paratonnerre qui semble glisser à travers les grands nuages blancs; le toit vert-de-grisé, les ornements de bois sculpté; et surtout les petites fenêtres rhomboïdales et multicolores de la véranda. Le jardin, vu à travers ces verres colorés, devenait singulièrement immobile et silencieux, comme s'il était occupé à s'admirer lui-même, plongé dans un cristal enchanté: si on le regardait par le verre bleu, c'était aussitôt un paysage sous-marin; puis on passait au rouge et la verdure au dessus du sable rose prenait une teinte lie-de-vin; le jaune, enfin, centu-plait la flamme du soleil; et je goûtais ainsi, pendant que Made-moiselle lisait, de petites joies en marge de sa lecture; parfois un papillon, quelque vulcain ou quelque morio, venait se poser sur la marche lézardée, et ouvrait au soleil ses ailes de velours.

La chambre de Mademoiselle fut toujours pour moi un lieu étrange; pleine d'une atmosphére lourde de serre chaude, où aurait poussé quelque plante grasse douée d'une curieuse odeur, cette chambre était devenue à tel point différente de toutes les autres, qu'elle semblait étrangère à notre aimable maison aux pièces bien aérées et riantes. Chez Mademoiselle, cela sentait l'enfermé, le pot

de chambre, la pelure de pomme brunie, et l'air même avait quelque chose de sombre et d'épais. Parmi cette obscurité pesante que la lampe allumée ne parvenait pas à dissiper, la table à écrire voguait vaguement, – mais, en me hissant sur la pointe des pieds, je pouvais examiner à loisir des objets qui étaient aussi particuliers à Mademoiselle que son embonpoint et son asthme. Il y avait sur la table ce porte-plume nacré avec au bout un tout petit trou, par où, en approchant l'œil, si près que les cils crissaient, on pouvait admirer le château de Chillon sous un ciel azuré et rose, le tout miraculeusement contenu dans cet espace infime. Il y avait aussi cette boîte laquée qui renfermait un dé à coudre, une montre qui ne marchait plus et ces réglisses dont Mademoiselle se régalait si volontiers; avec son canif mignon elle rognait les petits angles noirs des batons qu'elle nous donnait dans le creux de sa main, tout en nous recommandant de tenir la réglisse sous notre langue, – 'Je m'endors avec, disait-elle, et quand je me réveille le matin elle est encore là.' Il y avait enfin ces photographies des neveux et des nièces de Mademoiselle, dans des cadres parsemés de petites pierres fausses, qui m'apparaissaient – grenats, rubis, sombres saphirs – comme des bijoux sans prix; et parmi toutes les photographies celle qui, trônant au dessus des autres, présentait une jeune fille svelte, dans une sorte de veste écossaise qui moulait bien sa taille, le visage de trois-quarts, la prunelle humide, le chignon descendant très bas sur une nuque gracieuse, – 'Ah, une tresse grosse comme le bras, disait Mademoiselle, et qui me descendait jusqu'aux orteils.' Car c'était bien elle, cet être miraculeux, que je cherchais vainement en fouillant du regard Mademoiselle, comme si je tâchais de lui arracher la créature exquise qu'elle avait engloutie.

Ce que les grands ne savaient pas, parce qu'ils ne voyaient durant la journée qu'une Mademoiselle fortement lacée et recouverte de voiles pudiques, ce que personne ne connaissait d'elle, nous, enfants, le connaissions bien, cet amas tremblant de chairs qui roulaient dans une chemise grossièrement brodée sous la robe de

chambre de laine écarlate à galons d'or. Telle – les cheveux défaits, une bougie à la main – elle venait soudain à nous, arrachée de son lit par le hurlement d'un cauchemar d'enfant.

Durant toute ma vie j'ai mal dormi; j'ai toujours eu, chaque soir, chaque nuit, la peur du sommeil, peur intense qui augmentait en proportion de ma lassitude. Le sommeil m'est toujours apparu comme un bourreau masqué, en habit et haut-de-forme, qui me saisit de sa poigne de boucher, – c'est un échafaud sur lequel je monte chaque nuit, où chaque nuit je lutte avec le hideux Morphée qui me terrasse enfin et me lie à la bascule. Je suis rompu maintenant à cette terreur et je me livre au supplice en crânant presque, mais dans mon enfance je n'avais contre cette mort de chaque nuit nulle arme, si ce n'est une étroite raie de lumière que laissait la porte entr'ouverte de la chambre d'à côté.

Mon souvenir maintenant, quittant la campagne, s'installe pour l'hiver dans notre maison de Pétersbourg, – notre hôtel, disait Mademoiselle, – en sorte que cette nuit-ci est bien une nuit d'hiver, – les globes laiteux du gaz, invisibles, se devinent derrière les stores bleus et opaques des fenêtres. Je ne dors pas et j'envie follement mon frère qui ronfle, depuis des heures, à l'abri d'un paravent dans l'autre coin de la chambre. Tout y est noir, seule la fente de la porte traverse d'une raie de vie les ténèbres où je me sens sombrer. Je me cramponne à cette barre lumineuse, sans laquelle mon œil serait sans appui, et la tête me tournerait dans un gouffre noir. Là-bas, dans la pièce d'à-côté éclairée et vide, se trouve le lit de Mademoiselle, tandis que sa chambre à elle est située au bout d'un long corridor, dans une autre partie de la maison. Je sais qu'à certaine heure de la nuit elle viendra se coucher, menant sa démarche pesante (qui fait tinter quelque part un petit objet de porcelaine) par ce corridor et qu'elle entrera dans la chambre voisine. J'aurais encore un moment de répit, le temps de sa lecture au lit, mais après, ce sera la fin.

Donc j'attends, sachant qu'il faut m'endormir avant qu'elle ne vienne, qu'il faut m'endormir dès maintenant, pour m'épargner la

souffrance abominable de ne plus avoir pour soutien l'étroite raie de lumière; mais j'ai peur du sommeil qui, d'ailleurs, semble prendre plaisir à tarder. Aucun son ne vient de la rue où la neige rend silencieux le rare passage d'un traîneau. Je tâche de ne point regarder dans un certain coin de l'immense pièce où l'ombre prend des allures suspectes – métamorphoses nocturnes d'armoire ou d'étagère, contours effrayants qui m'attirent malgré moi. L'horloge abat les secondes à coups secs, avec une sorte de soupir rauque au milieu, car elle est très vieille. Je me force à penser à des choses amusantes, à des surprises, à des promesses de jouets, mais tout est gâché par l'horreur de rester éveillé. Enfin, le pas familier, inexorable, vient le long du corridor, ébranlant quelque petit objet resté éveillé comme moi. J'entends Mademoiselle entrer dans la chambre à côté. Elle allume la chandelle sur sa table de nuit, éteint la lampe du plafond (pour ne pas avoir à se lever quand elle aura fini sa lecture) et c'est déjà un déclin de clarté qui prépare la nuit totale; la fente est bien toujours là, mais pâlie, terne et se troublant étrangement lorsqu'un craquement me dit que Mademoiselle a fait quelque mouvement dans son lit, qui affole la flamme. Car je continue à l'entendre, tous mes sens sont aiguisés d'une façon prodigieuse. J'entends son couteau à papier couper les pages de la Revue des Deux Mondes – où Paul Bourget, je crois, faisait ses délices. J'entends sa respiration. Cependant je me meurs de détresse, suppliant le destin de prolonger indéfiniment la lecture de Mademoiselle, pour que la lumière me reste, je m'imagine le paradis comme un livre interminable qu'elle lirait sans se lasser à la lumière d'une bougie éternelle. Puis l'inévitable arrive; j'entends le livre se fermer, un pince-nez que l'on ôte tinte contre le marbre de la table de nuit et puis Mademoiselle souffle sur sa chandelle. Sa première tentative échoue, la lumière moribonde a un sursaut désespéré, alors le second 'coup' vient, plus violent, et c'est le noir. Non, pendant une seconde encore flotte devant mon œil le fantôme de la bande de clarté que j'ai si longtemps couvée du regard. Enfin, dans une obscu-

rité totale, je me sens défaillir, mon lit s'en va lentement à la dérive, jusqu'au moment où mes yeux, en s'habituant au noir, finissent par distinguer les plis blafards des stores, pâles taches qui voguent lentement pour enfin se fixer ici et là. Et c'est dans cette dernière consolation que je m'endors sur un oreiller mouillé de larmes.

Par contre, qu'ils étaient charmants, les matins, lorsque la belle lumière blonde des aurores glacées plaquait sur le parquet la géométrie éblouissante des croisées et que les bûches craquaient en imprégnant d'une telle chaleur la faïence du poêle qu'on ne pouvait y poser la main. Et c'était alors ce qu'on appelait chez nous 'aller en équipage', – la promenade en landau avec Mademoiselle, – mon frère près d'elle, moi en face d'eux, – et d'immenses bannières tricolores (car il me semble toujours assister à quelque grande fête les jours où mon souvenir y revient) accrochées au-dessus des rues et se gonflant au vent. L'aile moirée d'un oiseau exotique au chapeau de Mademoiselle, le large dos du cocher, bourré d'ouate à la mode russe, les nuages rapides, le dôme doré de la cathédrale, les mouettes s'abattant sur la Néva bleue, – tout cela forme une image d'une netteté surprenante que j'aime à contempler comme je ferais une miniature précieuse.

Il arriva deux ou trois fois que le cocher avait bu et j'entends Mademoiselle, sitôt rentrée de la promenade, qui raconte à ma mère: 'Figurez-vous mon horreur, Madame, quand je vis l'homme vaciller sur son siège, j'étais glacée d'effroi, je pressais les enfants contre moi, contre mon pauvre corps pantelant, – que pouvais-je de plus, Madame?' Cette manière un peu extravagante de s'exprimer eut vite fait de devenir un divertissement gratuit pour nous, les enfants, car nous étions d'une cruauté raffinée et allègre qui tournait brusquement à une sorte de compassion féroce, lorsque apparaissaient les ravages que nous avions causés. Je crois que le trait principal de Mademoiselle O était la susceptibilité. Son nom extraordinaire – si rond, si patapon, – semblait être une cible aux flèches des plaisants; quand on la nommait à quelque personne

nouvelle, elle croyait assister, d'une part, à une prière de conde-
scendance pour ce nom anormal, sans pattes, et de l'autre à une
surprise gênée ou égrillarde, selon que le nouveau venu voyait le
petit monstre avec dégoût ou avec gaîté. L'immunité absolue de
Mademoiselle pour ce qui était de la langue russe lui laissait
heureusement ignorer tout ce que les gens de la maison – les 'gensss'
comme on disait chez nous – les laquais et les bonnes, faisaient de
son pauvre nom, quand ils ne l'appelaient pas simplement
'Mamzelle'. Son obésité effroyable était une autre raison pour
qu'elle fût toujours sur ses gardes, défendant sa corpulence comme
si elle s'était trouvée dans un pays d'antropophages tout occupés
à la guetter avidement. Elle soutenait bravement que, tout en étant
un peu forte, comme elle disait, elle possédait physiquement tous
les attraits de grâce et de distinction que n'ont pas les 'squelettes'.
Elle raffolait de friandises, de bonbons, de chocolats, et prétendait
qu'il n'y avait rien d'aussi sain que les marrons glacés. Nous avions
une parente, obèse elle aussi, mais moins grosse que Mademoiselle
– qui s'esclaffait pourtant: 'Mais allons donc, je suis une sylphide
auprès de votre tante'. Dans la maison de Pétersbourg, elle préférait
à l'escalier de marbre le petit ascenseur démodé à propulsion
hydraulique que le concierge mettait en branle au moyen d'une
manivelle fixée au mur du vestibule. 'En route, marche!' disait-il
infailliblement en fermant les deux moitiés de la porte sur Mademoiselle, qui s'écroulait lentement sur la banquette. Et le lourd
ascenseur, soufflant et craquant, montait avec une lenteur incroy-
able le long du gros câble recouvert de velours, tandis qu'avec
lenteur sur le mur écaillé que l'on apercevait par la vitre,
descendaient de sombres taches qui faisaient songer à un atlas
géographique: taches d'humidité et de vétusté, où l'on reconnais-
sait ces contours de mer Noire ou d'Australie que les nuages et les
taches prennent à tout propos. Pour moi, qui étais resté en bas,
j'écoutais grimper péniblement la machine et j'avais toujours
l'espoir mauvais qu'elle s'arrêterait à mi-chemin. Cela arrivait parfois.

Le bruit cessait. On n'entendait que la chute d'un peu de plâtre qui s'effritait quelque part. Puis, d'un espace mystérieux entre les murailles arrivait le 'gdié, gdié', si connu, le cri de Mademoiselle en détresse. Alors le Suisse en bas poussait avec effort la manivelle, puis ouvrait la porte dans le noir et regardait en haut pour voir si cela marchait. Enfin, l'ascenseur s'ébranlait, et quelque temps après on retrouvait Mademoiselle en larmes dans sa chambre, – prétendant que le concierge le faisait exprès, qu'elle ne pesait pas tant que ça, voyons. 'Ah, les affres que j'ai pu souffrir là-haut, suspendue toute seule dans le vide!' Tout le long de sa vie, les choses semblaient n'êtré là que pour se moquer de son obésité, – et lorsqu'un jour elle s'assit sur une boîte à couvercle de verre contenant des papillons rares soigneusement séchés et piqués, que j'avais laissée par mégarde sur une chaise, elle eut un regard chargé d'un soupçon terrible, au moment même où le verre craquait sous elle, comme si elle eût cru que la boîte s'était mise là exprès, pour lui prouver par le dégât qui s'en suivait que le poids de son corps était réellement formidable.

Comme si la nature n'eût rien voulu lui épargner de tout ce qui rend un être susceptible, elle avait l'oreille dure, et ce défaut, s'accentuant avec l'âge, venait s'ajouter à sa honte physique. Tout ceci faisait d'elle une personne difficile, chagrine et soupçonneuse, prenant la mouche à tout propos. Parfois, à table, on remarquait tout-à-coup que deux grosses larmes descendaient lentement le long des larges joues de Mademoiselle qui, d'une voix fluette, disait: 'Ah, ce n'est rien', et continuait à manger sans essuyer les larmes qui l'aveuglaient; puis, avec un hoquet navré, elle se levait et quittait la salle à manger sous le regard narquois des domestiques. 'Non, laissez-moi, je ne suis qu'une pauvre chose de rien, une loque', disait-elle quand on cherchait à comprendre ce qui pouvait bien l'avoir offensée; petit à petit on arrivait à la vérité qui était toujours saugrenue; par exemple on avait parlé à table de la marine – j'avais un oncle amiral – et Mademoiselle s'était persuadée qu'on l'avait fait exprès, parce que la Suisse ne possédait pas de flotte. Ou bien

c'était simplement parce qu'il lui semblait que, bien qu'on parlât français à table, on l'empêchait de diriger la conversation, – car elle croyait savoir toutes les finesses de 'l'art français de la causerie', comme elle disait. Mais elle se dépêchait tant pour saisir le fil de la conversation avant qu'il ne lui échappât pour tomber dans les abîmes du baragouin russe, que c'était toujours maladroitement qu'elle exhibait son art. Certaines réflexions qu'il lui arrivait d'émettre restèrent dans notre famille, – curiosités amusantes que l'on se rappelle avec amour. 'Un jour, j'ai entendu le silence' disait-elle, puis faisait une pause et répétait d'une voix profonde: 'J'ai entendu le silence. C'était dans un vallon perdu des Alpes'. Il y avait aussi le miracle des champignons: 'Un matin, racontait Mademoiselle, comme je cueillais des fleurs, j'ai vu de mes yeux pousser un bolet, – il sortait de terre tout doucement, à petites secousses presque imperceptibles'. Des saillies de cette sorte ne développaient jamais la causerie brillante, gazouillante, spirituelle dont rêvait Mademoiselle. Au contraire, on se taisait tout-à-coup après qu'elle avait dit son mot, puis on parlait d'autre chose, quitte à entendre Mademoiselle se plaindre un peu plus tard qu'on lui eût grossièrement coupé la parole. Le plus gênant était que parfois elle croyait à tort qu'on s'était adressé à elle, car sa surdité l'embarrassait de plus en plus, et avec un petit soubresaut elle lançait un 'plaît-il?' éclatant à travers la table à l'invité inoffensif qui n'avait rien dit.

Il faut bien noter que, malgré l'emphase de son langage et la naïveté de ses idées, le français de Mademoiselle était divin. Or, si je jette un regard rétrospectif sur cette Russie d'antan, – entrée depuis dans une ère de barbarie naïve et dont le nom même sonne de nos jours comme 'Grèce' ou 'Rome' – il y avait dans cette Russie non seulement le français tel que l'enseignaient des institutrices comme Mademoiselle, mais encore une sorte de tradition française, un français usuel, que l'on se passait directement de père en fils. Cela faisait partie de notre civilisation. Il y avait d'abord une quantité de mots et de phrases françaises qui s'inséraient dans la conver-

sation russe, passant d'une langue à l'autre avec une facilité surprenante, et cela devait être une drôle de chose pour une oreille gauloise que d'assister, par exemple, dans un torrent assez pur de français à l'intrusion d'un vocable russe qui se montrait là avec une aisance parfaite, précédé même d'une apostrophe. La syntaxe dans les cas extrêmes était tout bonnement calquée sur le russe; on traduisait littéralement les phrases, ce qui les rendait incompréhensibles pour quelqu'un qui n'eût pas connu notre langue. Si, d'une part, ce français-là dégringolait ainsi jusqu'à un français de cuisine, il y avait, d'autre part, celui qui montait à un très joli degré de français d'album, de français de jeunes filles, avec toute une poésie un peu surannée, un peu à l'eau-de-rose, comme si nos lyres slaves eussent rendu un son trop rude pour des oreilles de demoiselles. 'Le vase brisé' de Sully Prudhomme – le vase où meurt cette verveine . . . – et les Nuits d'Alfred de Musset avec leur lyrisme sanglotant et débraillé sont des exemples typiques de ce que ce genre de lecteur russe aimait en fait de poésie française. Par contre, dans le milieu où j'ai grandi, la tendance littéraire était d'un autre ordre, et ce n'est pas Coppée ou Lamartine, mais Verlaine et Mallarmé qui prirent soin de mon adolescence. Ainsi, le rôle de l'institutrice française concernait plutôt la forme que la substance même, la grammaire plutôt que les Lettres, c'est-à-dire qu'elle restait extérieure à cette tradition franco-russe dont je viens de parler, comme si ç'avait été là quelque dialecte pittoresque, mais trop provincial, trop patois pour son goût. Le goût, le bon goût – au sens qu'on lui prêtait vers le dix-septième siècle – formait, je crois, la partie essentielle de l'éducation de Mademoiselle O. Il en résultait une pureté de langage, une sonorité sévère, une sorte de ruissellement froid et brillant, – toutes qualités que je n'ai appréciées que bien plus tard.

Ainsi, c'est avec tristesse que je devine maintenant la cruelle souffrance que Mademoiselle devait éprouver à voir se perdre en vain cette voix de rossignol qui sortait de son corps d'éléphant. Je

ne me souviens pas au juste, de l'estime où elle tenait les trois poètes qui juste avant la guerre étaient les idoles des lecteurs russes: Rostand, dont l'inepte Chantecler venait de créer une nouvelle mode de chapeaux féminins; Maeterlinck dont l'Oiseau Bleu était merveilleusement interprété par notre meilleur théâtre – qui était d'ailleurs en ce temps-là le meilleur théâtre du monde entier, et enfin Verhaeren dont la muse robuste eut une influence énorme sur le développement de la branche dite urbaine de notre littérature poétique. Non, je ne me rappelle pas ce que Mademoiselle pensait de ces trois poètes, qui pour elle étaient des jeunes, des 'modernes'. Mais ce dont je me souviens en toute netteté, c'est le culte exceptionnel qu'elle vouait à Corneille et à Racine.

Moi, barbare, ami de Rabelais et de Shakespeare, j'ai toujours eu en grippe et Corneille et Racine, pour leur banalité parfaite, idéale – pour cette sublimation du lieu commun d'où résulte un chef-d'oeuvre de fausseté. Leurs meilleurs alexandrins me remplissent la bouche comme un bon gargarisme et ne font point appel à mon imagination. Je déteste leurs chevilles, la pauvreté de leur style, la servilité de l'adjectif, l'indigence de la rime, – tout enfin, – et je ne donnerais pas un seul sonnet de Ronsard pour tout leur théâtre.

Donc, voici dans notre chambre d'études Mademoiselle qui a fait choix du rôle de Chimène ou d'Athalie, tandis que nous nous partageons les rôles masculins, – moi, tâchant toujours d'avoir le rôle du confident parce qu'il y a moins à lire. Je l'entends encore, cette Chimène un peu minaudière, que j'essayais de me représenter, séduit par son nom chimérique, en regardant Mademoiselle qui accentuait les douces chutes des alexandrins en faisant de petites moues – la bouche en cœur ou en cul-de-poule; j'entends Athalie, horrifiée et bavarde, contant son rêve, – et Mademoiselle, les sourcils hérissés et toute la série de ses mentons en branle, se donnait une petite tape sur la poitrine comme un ténor italien. Pauvre Mademoiselle! Mais il me faut arriver maintenant à la partie critique de sa vie chez nous, à ce roman étrange et terrible qui finit si tris-

tement. Car ce fut un roman renversé, une sorte de plaque négative, où la tendresse claire serait remplacée par une lutte sourde; acharnée, sans trêve, dont les assauts finissaient chez Mademoiselle par des palpitations de cœur et des pâmoisons.

Plusieurs années s'étaient écoulées depuis son entrée dans notre maison, et voici qu'un étranger parut. C'était ce que nous nommions 'un répétiteur' plutôt qu'un gouverneur – un jeune étudiant russe chargé de nous aider en hiver à préparer nos leçons pour l'école et dont le devoir, en été, consistait à nous accompagner dans nos jeux et dans nos promenades équestres (il montait très mal, du reste). Dès le premier abord, Mademoiselle crut flairer un ennemi dans ce jeune homme barbichu, aux yeux myopes, aux cheveux mal coupés, vêtu du pantalon vert-bleu universitaire et d'une blouse russe. D'origine simple, et par suite, d'une fierté presque maladive; de plus très radical en politique, pauvre, et faisant le métier de gouverneur d'enfants non par dispositions pédagogiques, mais parce que c'était là un moyen de gagner sa vie que lui permettaient ses principes, Pétrov n'avait jamais appris le français, qu'il considérait d'ailleurs comme un luxe antidémocratique. Un être charmant, du reste, bon comme le pain et merveilleusement doué pour la mathématique, – mais nullement fait pour vivre côte-à-côte avec une Mademoiselle jalouse et tyrannique, et qui supposa que Pétrov, dès son entrée chez nous, ne se proposait que de l'en faire sortir. Ainsi, c'était nos âmes à nous qui étaient en jeu, ou du moins tel était l'avis de Mademoiselle, car dans la réalité, goguenards et libres, nous suivions toutes les péripéties de cette lutte, sans accorder beaucoup d'importance à son résultat, ni aux souffrances secrètes qu'elle entraînait.

On avait l'habitude à table de servir après le repas à chaque convive un bol contenant un gobelet rempli d'une eau légèrement parfumée avec laquelle on se rinçait la bouche et qu'on rejetait ensuite dans le bol; après quoi, on se levait de table – conclusion du repas hygiénique, et même gracieuse, chez Mademoiselle du

moins, qui avait le souci des jolis gestes. Mais voici qu'après le premier dîner auquel il prit part, Pétrov tout tranquillement but, et savoura même, ce qu'il avait pris pour quelque liqueur nouvelle, tandis que Mademoiselle, à côté de lui, pouffait ou faisait mine de pouffer dans sa serviette, et ce fut là, je crois, la déclaration de guerre, car Pétrov, tout prêt qu'il était à lui laisser la suprématie, ne lui pardonna jamais ce rire implacable.

Mademoiselle s'imagina de son côté que si Pétrov ne lui adressait jamais la parole, et répondait par des monosyllabes inintelligibles à ses questions provocantes, ce n'était point parce qu'il ne comprenait pas le français, mais bien parce qu'il voulait l'insulter impunément devant tout le monde. Je la vois encore le priant de sa voix d'or, mais avec un certain plissement des lèvres qui n'augurait rien de bon, 'de bien vouloir me passer, Monsieur, le sucrier'; Pétrov ne prêtait aucune attention à ses paroles plusieurs fois répétées, jusqu'au moment où Mademoiselle, d'un geste démonstratif et avec un 'pardon' cinglant comme un coup de fouet, passait son bras pardessus le couvert de Pétrov pour atteindre le sucrier qu'elle tirait ensuite vers elle, en jetant au jeune homme un 'merci, Monsieur' doucereux et grondant, et tellement chargé d'ironie que les oreilles veloutées de Pétrov devenaient d'un rouge violent. 'Le goujat, le malotru, le grossier personnage!' disait-elle ensuite, en sanglotant dans sa chambre. Elle racontait aussi qu'il l'avait bousculée en passant dans l'escalier: 'Il m'a poussée, disait-elle, il m'a frappée . . . J'ai des bleus partout'. Il arrivait de plus en plus souvent qu'elle quittât la table en plein dîner, parce que Pétrov qui avait la manie de raconter les choses avec force détails parlait longuement, et que la conversation générale qu'il déclenchait entrait fatalement dans les labyrinthes russes. De sa chambre éloignée, elle écrivait alors à mes parents qui habitaient au rez-de-chaussée des lettres de seize pages. Ma mére montait en toute hâte, et trouvait Mademoiselle en train de faire sa malle. Puis l'on avait une semaine de répit, Mademoiselle consolée faisait semblant d'ignorer la présence de Pétrov. Un jour, enfin, ce fut la débâcle complète.

Je crois que le dernier événement de cette épopée fut le grand esclandre, l'explosion bruyante, le cri 'Vous êtes un voleur, Monsieur!' qu'on entendit le jour où, cherchant mon frère qui s'était caché, Pétrov eut l'idée malencontreuse de franchir le seuil de la chambre de Mademoiselle, dont la porte était restée entr'ouverte. Juste au moment où Pétrov s'arrêtait au milieu de cette chambre interdite, Mademoiselle déboucha du cabinet de toilette, portant un azalée, qu'elle venait d'arroser. Je me rappelle ce détail comme on se rappelle quelque petit rien survenu au cours d'une catastrophe, – car ce fut bien la catastrophe irrémédiable entre Mademoiselle, mordante et terrible, et Pétrov sortant soudain de son mutisme pour relever le terme injurieux que, par un malheureux miracle, il venait tout-à-coup de comprendre.

Et puis, Mademoiselle partit. C'était en 1914, et le prétexte officiel de son départ fut, je m'en souviens, la peur d'être définitivement séparée de sa patrie par les événements politiques. Tout ce qui me reste de nos adieux, c'est un déluge de larmes et ses deux bras largement ouverts. Pendant une année ou deux, elle nous écrivit assez régulièrement, – des pages et des pages couvertes de sa petite écriture fine sans une rature. Puis vint la révolution. Une dizaine d'années plus tard, par un hasard de l'exil, je me trouvai un jour en Suisse et me voici entrant dans la chambre de Mademoiselle.

Plus forte que jamais, les cheveux gris et presque totalement sourde, elle me reçut avec un vacarme de tendresse. Elle parla de sa vie en Russie si chaleureusement qu'on eût pu croire qu'elle avait perdu sa patrie. Par contre, elle accusait la Suisse d'être devenue méconnaissable, et c'était des plaintes sans fin. Notre révolution, abolissant l'usage du français en Russie, avait exilé aussi lestement que de vrais Russes quelques milliers de vieilles demoiselles qui maintenant se tenaient, se réunissaient et s'agglutinaient, formant comme un îlot dans le pays qui leur était devenu étranger. Elles s'étaient fait une autre patrie, – le passé, – et c'était vraiment navrant, ce pauvre amour d'outre-tombe pour la Russie, qu'elles ne connaissaient guère.

Comme notre entretien était rendu terriblement difficile par la surdité de Mademoiselle, je lui apportai le lendemain un de ces appareils qui promettent aux sourds plus qu'ils ne peuvent donner. Lorsqu'elle eut fixé le tube, elle me remercia d'un regard ébloui et jura qu'elle entendait le moindre murmure. Elle mentait, elle n'entendait rien du tout, elle mentait pour me faire plaisir, et ce mensonge naïf, délicat, adorable, est le dernier souvenir qui me reste de Mademoiselle.

Avant de partir, j'allai assez sottement me promener par une nuit froide et brumeuse le long du lac. L'eau clapotait un peu, mais rien ne brillait dans le brouillard nocturne, sauf un pâle réverbère. Un remous, une blancheur vague, attira mon regard. Dans l'eau, un cygne, très gros, très vieux et très maladroit faisait des efforts ridicules pour se hisser dans un canot amarré. Il n'y parvenait pas. J'entendais le choc lourd de ses ailes et le bruit du canot ballotté; avec la logique du subconscient, c'est cette vision passagère que je me rappelai tout d'abord lorsque j'appris, quelques années plus tard, que Mademoiselle n'était plus. Elle avait passé sa vie à être malheureuse, et le malheur était pour elle un élément naturel, dont les changements de profondeur lui donnaient la sensation de se mouvoir, de faire quelque chose, de vivre enfin. J'ai de grands remords quand je pense à certains petits instants où l'idée me venait de lui faire quelque menu plaisir et où je me répondais aussitôt que cela n'en valait pas la peine. J'ai cru me soulager en parlant d'elle, et maintenant que c'est fini, j'ai l'étrange sensation de l'avoir inventée de toutes pièces, aussi entièrement que les autres personnages qui passent dans mes livres. A-t-elle vraiment vécu? Non, maintenant que j'y pense bien – elle n'a jamais vécu. Mais désormais elle est réelle, puisque je l'ai créée, et cette existence que je lui donne serait une marque de gratitude très candide, si elle avait vraiment existé.